THE FADE SERIES | BOOK 1

METALLIC HEART

LIAHONA WEST

Editor: Riley at Rosebud Editing
Cover Artist: Danielle Fine of Design by Definition

ISBN 978-1-7368206-1-2 (paperback)
ISBN 978-1-7368206-0-5 (eBook)

Published in the United States of America.

liahonawestauthor.com

*For those who are still here,
despite all you have been through,
this is for you.*

I see you.

You matter.

AUTHOR'S NOTE

This story is about trauma. It is also about the beautiful endurance of those who go through great trauma in their lives and push themselves to heal. Just as with the victims you, dear reader, come across or have in your lives, please remember that the characters you are about to read about are trying to navigate their trauma and what healing means for them. Be patient. Be kind. And most important of all, read to understand.

CHAPTER ONE
ELOISE

Through the grimy window, Eloise watched a magpie preen on a bare branch. The bird, black as night with a white breast and bathed in moonlight, puffed out its feathers, turned its beady eye upon her, and let out a single caw. She clenched the leather-bound hilt of a kukri knife in her fist.

The magpie, now joined by three more, eyed Eloise. She stepped away from the window and placed the kukri on a side table. Six more knives waited there, one for each year since her sister's death. They were her insurance in case something went wrong. Her blood boiled; she knew she couldn't take them with her.

Bali mewed, rubbing her bare skin across Eloise's leg. She picked up the piebald, hairless feline, and a noise of protest escaped Bali's throat. Eloise placed her on the bed, then slid on her leather boot.

Her eyes flicked back to the crows, and her skin crawled. A fourth one sat upon the branch. Even though she wasn't the superstitious type, the history of the birds as ill omens, along with the beady stare of their tiny, round eyes made her stomach churn.

Damn birds.

Before leaving her room, she banged her fist against the tall glass window and the birds, except one, scattered.

Aware of the growing pit in her stomach and sweating palms, Eloise walked down the hallway lined with old classrooms toward a curving staircase.

Once outside, she took in a deep, cleansing breath, then released it. Going back was dangerous, she knew that, but until Seth's health improved, she would never stop. Eloise made a promise at her sister's grave years ago that she would watch over Ada's best friend like he was her own brother.

Eloise waded through the grass that peeked through the hairline cracks on the road leading away from her home, an abandoned high school called the Compound. Stuck between a spit to the north that supplied clams, mussels, and various edible sea life, and a river to the south that offered salmon during their runs with fresh water to use in cooking, bathing, and washing clothes, the Compound was the best location within miles.

She loved her home.

In Eloise's past few visits, Joy had grown hostile and unpredictable, and Eloise chose to ignore it, assuming Joy was simply having a rough day. But now that she looked upon the red brick building from the bottom of the hill, a sense of dread came over her.

This is the last time I'll see the Compound, isn't it?

With a wave of her hand as if to physically push the thought away, Eloise turned and walked toward her final destination: the lab. She only had to get through the abandoned vehicles and forest beyond.

For the next two hours, Eloise maneuvered through the endless graveyard of forgotten cars, rough with rust and covered with blackberry plants and ivy. Even with the moonlight, sight was difficult. More than once, she slammed her knee against car metal until it developed its own heartbeat.

"Damn it." Eloise leaned against the tailgate of a Ford pickup missing its "F" and rubbed at her knees.

I need to be more careful.

Several more minutes of walking, avoiding the extended trailer hitches on some of the cars, brought her to a looming line of trees.

A dark and murky forest swallowed Eloise whole as she entered. The expanse of pine, cedar, and hemlock reached to the stars, their bare branches looming. Since the nuclear war ten years ago, the world had grown colder.

Trees and plants, fooled into believing winter approached, lost their leaves and never attempted to grow new ones. Aside from the plants the Compound grew, Eloise hadn't seen a leaf bud or needle in close to seven years.

She knew what waited for her on the other side of the forest and as she grew closer to the end, her heartbeat amplified, her throat dried out, and she chewed on the inside of her lip. Every three months she completed the same ritual: leave after dusk, walk two hours alone, donate her nanite-laced blood to help Seth, and come home to wait three more months to do it again.

Eloise kicked a rock with a grunt. It clanged against a metal drum lying on its side. *When is he going to get better?*

She wanted, more than anything, for Seth to get better. If he were better, she would never have to see Joy again, never have to be subject to her belittlement. Joy made it clear Eloise was an object, a device for housing nanites for her son. Nothing more.

Seth will get better. He has to. I don't know how much longer I can keep doing this.

The glow from a lone lantern acted as a beacon. She paused. Her hands trembled, and she swallowed hard. Once she walked around the trees and caught sight of her escort, that would be it. She would begin another exhausting cycle of going to Joy then going back home. Except she wasn't sure that this time she'd make it home. Something loomed in the air Eloise couldn't quite pin down, a sense of dread, triggered by the magpies outside her window.

I'm doing this for Seth.

Resolved, Eloise squared her shoulders and walked around the trunk of a tree.

Underneath the lantern light sat a man she called Smith. He refused to share his name, so Eloise had given him one. Smith's blond hair brushed against his shoulders as he glanced up. He wore a green canvas jacket, the high collar folded over to allow a frayed scarf room to wrap around his neck, and a beige tee tucked into whitewashed jeans. His brown, deep-set eyes regarded Eloise, and he walked forward to meet her.

"Hey, kid. Ready?"

"Yeah." Eloise removed her boots, emptied her pockets, and opened up her coat so Smith could pat her down. "I left the knives at home."

"Good. Let's go."

He pulled the lantern off the branch and used it to illuminate their path through the quiet forest. Silver moonlight sliced through the darkness, broken into strands by gnarled branches, to touch the dark earth. Eloise stepped over an exposed root, then used the rocks as natural stairs. Some smaller pieces broke free and tumbled down the hill, cracking echoes bouncing through the forest.

The eerie silence gave Eloise goosebumps. She pulled her jacket close to her body and jogged to catch up to Smith.

"I'm curious," Eloise said. "How come people don't stop Joy? She's done human experiments and literally everyone knows about it, but she's allowed to carry on as if it doesn't matter."

Smith shot her a curious glance. "She has a lot more power than you know." He cleared his throat. "What you know of Joy is a small part of a much bigger and darker picture. Some of those experiments survived and are living in a village far from here. They're safe from Joy, and now that you're working with her, she has no interest in those who survived her torment. But, no one wants a repeat of what happened. When the five clans tried to get people to rise up and fight, they failed. They all remember what she did to their friends and families, how she wipes their memories and promises a reversal if they serve her for however long she wants."

"That's horrible." An angry knot formed in her stomach.

Smith shrugged. "Once in a while, someone is stupid enough to try and stop her again, but they quickly learn how painful it is to come home to a family who doesn't remember them."

The light of the lantern cast shadows across Smith's face. He made a strange noise in his throat and Eloise almost missed the quivering of his lips. "Is that...what happened to you? Did she do something to your family?"

He didn't speak.

The forest opened up to a view of the ocean and a ghost town. Sailboats, forgotten by their owners After the bombs, remained moored and useless against the disintegrating docks. The torn-off rooftops, crumpled buildings that once lined the hillside, and cars laying upside down in a few large trees showed the remnants of a hurricane, unheard of in the entire history of the area.

They hiked down a hill and climbed over the hoods of two cars smashed into each other with a rear-facing infant car seat abandoned in one.

A twinge of sadness hit her stomach and Eloise's gaze found Smith again as she jumped into the grass. "Do they..."

"They don't remember me."

Eloise blinked.

"My family," Smith explained. "I tried to stop Joy several years ago. Her men beat me senseless and tossed me in the river. I think they hoped I would drown. When I found my way home, my wife and two daughters—" Smith's voice broke.

Unsure how to console a man she barely knew, Eloise scratched the inside of her wrist and they continued in silence the remaining hour of their journey to Joy's lab.

Hidden behind a row of shrubbery as long as a football field and overlooking the harbor, with a solitary lighthouse flanking the entrance, sat the facility. One piece of a wrought-iron gate hung by a single hinge, and the opposite side rested on the ground. Beyond it lay a courtyard of concrete tiles, grass, and various weeds pushing through cracks. A collection of twenty solar panels sat atop the roof. As far as Eloise knew, the facility was the only place with them, since they were rare in the Pacific Northwest even Before the war. Joy used them for one thing: powering the machines for nanite extraction.

"So, why go back to the person who destroyed your life?" Eloise picked a tall weed with a tare of seeds at the top and played with it in her hand.

A darkness passed through Smith's eyes. Eloise's throat tightened.

"If I serve her for nine years, she'll restore my family's memories."

Eyes widening, a tingling wave crashed through Eloise. "How could someone be so cruel?"

11

"At her core, she's a mother who is desperately trying to save her dying son. She just took it too far."

"But," Eloise said, scrambling for words, "someone needs to force her to face what she's done."

She jumped at Smith's burst of laughter.

"And who do you suggest?" He asked with a dark tone. "The ones able to stop her won't to protect their families and the ones stupid enough to make it to her facility disappear. Nothing is stopping this woman. Promise me, kid," Smith put his hand on the door handle attached to the glass door, "once you get the opportunity, you will run as far away from here as you can. We're all doomed. No sense for you to get snatched up in all this, too."

Smith held the door open. Eloise paused, her heart sinking as she processed the tragedy he had shared with her, and swallowed despite her tight throat.

"You know where to go," Smith said, his words gruff.

"Smith," she paused at the door. "Why did you wait so long to tell me about your family?"

He scratched at his chin. "You didn't need to know until now. Something's coming and you'll find out my part in it soon." When she opened her mouth, Smith shook his head. "I can't tell you more. Go. Don't keep her waiting."

His expression was one of urgency, so Eloise bit her tongue and jogged down the stairwell into the lower level of the facility. She rubbed her sweaty palms on her thighs.

I need my knives.

Without them, protection turned from sharp objects to fists, kicking, and biting, all inefficient compared to knives. Eloise shuddered and turned a corner.

Joy waited for her by a door halfway down the hallway. She smiled, but it didn't reach her eyes. The woman held her body how Eloise imagined a noble would: head high, shoulders square, and hands clasped in front of her. She wore an emerald, shin-length dress, the sleeves cut off above her elbows, and her hair in a chignon. If it were not for the thick spread of grey hair at the front of her scalp, Eloise would have a hard time believing the woman was older than forty.

A boiling anger bubbled inside Eloise. She looked at the woman, regal and emotionless, and only saw the faceless people Joy had ruined. Families separated. People dead. Eloise's fists shook.

"I trust my guard escorted you without incident?"

Eloise nodded.

"Good." Joy turned and began walking further into the facility. Over her shoulder, she said, "Let's begin nanite extraction."

After years of walking the same path to the same room, following Joy was more ceremonial than necessary. The door creaked open and Eloise's chest constricted. Inside the room was a hospital bed with plastic-coated railings and handlebars and a side table with twelve rubber capped glass vials. They clinked as Joy set them on a metal tray beside a clear, stout machine the size of a coffee maker.

Eloise rubbed her thumb.

Joy motioned to the bed.

For Seth. I'm doing this for Seth.

Joy stroked the vein in Eloise's arm and she gritted her teeth as the nanites, separated from the others, set off small electrical impulses. Her skin stung and itched, and the muscles in her torso, limbs, and face twitched. Biting back embarrassment over the small involuntary movements she made, Eloise focused on the fake skylight with an image of clouds above her.

You can do this.

As a child, a car accident caused a ruptured spleen and when she became ill with a blood infection, her parents took her to Joy, begging the scientist to use the untested nanites to save her life. The tiny robots acted as her immune system, but they were attached to her organs, unable to be removed in large quantities. According to Joy, after the internal bleeding led to the discovery, extracting all of the nanites at once would tear her insides apart and she would die. So, they took only a small number at a time.

Eloise's head grew heavy.

"Done."

Joy pulled the needle from Eloise's arm and transferred the vials of her blood to the centrifuge to separate the blood, plasma, and serum. Eloise's head rocked back and forth as she tried to stay focused but heavy, invisible bricks weighed down her arms. The room tilted. The musky, sterile scent brought bile up her esophagus.

"Take her into recovery," Joy said to a waiting assistant then looked at Eloise. "You can go see Seth now. Come back in three months."

Two metallic *thunks* from the bed's wheel locks sounded. Eloise laid prone on the mattress as the bed moved through the hallways. Residual electrical impulses poked at her body. Her skin hurt, and her bones ached.

She dozed, exhausted from the nanite extraction, and soon fell asleep. When she awoke in a windowless room, she had no way of knowing if it was the next morning or a few hours after the extraction. The irresistible urge to stretch came over her and she put her entire body into it, groaning and adjusting until her bones creaked.

"You're late," a slurred voice said.

Weak, Eloise turned her head to look at Seth. She forced a smile in greeting.

With a bit more meat on his bones, Seth would be the talk of the town. If a town existed. Sparkling grey eyes, curly brown hair that always seemed to fall in front of his eyebrows, and full lips sitting right under a Grecian nose. At seventeen, his sickness stripped the color from his skin, made it hard to breathe, and caused balance issues. The nanites Seth received from Eloise extended his life, but spending it locked up in the facility with no escape and only his mother's mercenaries to talk to, prevented that life from ever blossoming.

Eloise chuckled, and the room spun. "What do you mean?"

Seth pulled a calendar off the wall snuggled among countless pieces of original and detailed architectural designs. He pointed to a red 'X'.

"You're...late."

Eloise nudged him when he came close. "What can I say, I'm a creature of habit."

"Not in...the mood for jokes."

The poor kid was desperate for clean air. She wanted to give him everything a seventeen-year-old deserved, but Joy kept him on a tight leash, allowing him supervised, temporary moments outdoors. As a result, he had grown irritable.

"Sorry," Eloise said. "Your mom seems extra pleasant today."

He rolled his eyes. "Yeah. When is she not? I'm so...tired of being cooped...up here." Seth thought for a moment and then his eyes lit up and he turned to Eloise. "We could sneak...out."

"I don't know."

"Oh, come on. It's not...like you haven't done...anything rebellious in your...life."

"It's not that. Your mom would be furious."

Seth crossed his arms and rolled his eyes.

"I want to stay on her good side."

"Yeah," Seth said, but Eloise knew it was just a placating phrase. He blinked away the moisture in his eyes. "Hungry?"

"I could eat."

The lump in her throat would take time to go away. She hated Joy for keeping him trapped. He was sick, yes, but still a human who needed more interaction than he got, and it affected his mental well-being. He used to be such a happy kid. Now, because of Joy's neglect, he was suffering. Eloise bristled. She clenched her fist.

How could she do this to him?

No one, except Mason and Soora, knew what she did at night every three months, and when people asked, they accepted the simple answer of Eloise being too tired. The entire Compound knew she struggled with trauma, even if they didn't know the details.

As Eloise watched Seth send a nurse for food, her heart dropped a bit lower in her chest. A pang hit her stomach

Without me, you'll die. I don't know if I can lose you, too.

In an attempt to ease the grief, Eloise glanced around the room. Robots made from medical equipment and scrap metal lined the shelves. Posters Seth made himself about how robots worked, robot trivia, and facts littered the walls. Glow in the dark stars peppered his ceiling.

"Do you remember when you used to pester Ada about helping you build with Legos?" Eloise asked.

Seth laughed, a quiet and airy exhale. "I remember. If she didn't...want to, she would ignore...me."

"And you'd spend the whole day begging her to play just for a little bit."

"Then you'd either...get fed up and play or Ada...would give in and...grumble for about five minutes...before she...was into...it."

"Remember the epic Eiffel Tower? It was more like a rectangle than the actual thing?"

"Yeah! She...was so proud of it...too. Her Lego...building skills weren't...pretty."

"No, they were not."

They couldn't hold a long conversation about Ada without the energy in the room dropping to ice-cold levels as they both felt the gravity of her absence. Ada and Seth were always together. Joy would bring Seth over for work nights with Eloise and Ada's parents. The three kids would build blanket forts, have fake campfires, and tell each other ghost stories, and for many wonderful hours, it was just them existing in the world.

Seth chewed on the inside of his lip. "Do you still miss...her?"

"Yes. There's a hole in my heart where she used to be. I don't think that will ever change, but it's more of a dull ache now."

"I know...what you mean." Seth tilted his head back. "I think...what I miss the most...from before I got sick is walking...on the beach. I want to...get better. I hate this chair—I...only sit in it because I get...so tired but I want to do...things, Eloise! I want to run...like actually...run. And see things. Everything. Instead, I'm sick...and I hate it. The nanites are...gross, too. They make me...so sick after."

They'd had the same conversation countless times and every time made Eloise nauseous. Seth was so tired—she could tell from his sullen face—of being sick and cooped up in white walls with a mother who hid him from the world. She knew he resented her for it.

"Tell you what." Eloise reached forward and patted his knee. She ignored the sinking of her stomach when she felt the thin kneecap underneath his pant leg and kept a smile on her face. "When the nanites start helping you, we're going outside and touching the beach. I might throw in some toe wiggling because I'm so generous. Deal?"

Her hands trembled. She hid them in her blanket. Every bit of dread and anxiety Eloise tried to shove away only returned. Vengeful. Seth's smile was infectious, though, and it soothed her sore heart.

"Deal." After a beat, Seth pulled a folded-up paper out from underneath his pillow. He handed it to Eloise, lowered his eyes, and said, "I wrote this for...you."

Eloise smiled and took the paper. "Thank you."

"But don't...open it!" Seth put his hands on hers. "Not yet. I want...you to read it when you get...back home."

"Alright," Eloise chuckled and put it in her pocket.

The sound of a closing door echoed through the room and Eloise's smile faded when she saw Joy holding a syringe filled with a light lavender liquid.

"Hi, Mama."

Joy smiled, something she reserved only for Seth. "Ready?"

The question was more rhetorical than anything. Joy injected the lavender serum into the tube trailing to Seth's arm. He clenched his teeth and groaned.

Eloise scooted off the hospital bed and crouched in front of Seth. "I have to go, okay?"

He nodded.

Eloise walked toward the door.

"I'm not finished." Joy's voice had an edge to it. Eloise paused. After placing a pillow into a more comfortable position for Seth to lay back on, Joy met Eloise at the door. "The nanites aren't enough. I need more."

The color drained from Eloise's face. "What?"

"I ran a few tests before you arrived tonight, and Seth's condition is worse. I thought increasing his dosage of your nanites would be enough, but nothing has changed."

Eloise clenched her fists. Years of late nights meant nothing. The fatal brain disease still steamrolled on its trajectory. Soon—Eloise shuddered—it would take Seth's life and she couldn't do anything to stop it.

"How much more of my blood do you need?" She asked.

"All of it."

"All—" The word came out several octaves higher than expected, and Eloise lowered her voice. "I'll die! If we remove them all, they'll rip my insides to shreds."

"I know."

"And what about the dose he just received tonight?" Eloise snapped. "Why isn't it working?"

Joy stared at Eloise as if she were an infuriating child asking too many questions. She sighed. "We already went over this. These artificially intelligent nanites like your weakened immune system. Seth's body can't keep them alive long enough to self-replicate because his disease is too progressive. At first, I thought every few months would be enough, but now I realize it's not."

"And how do you know giving him all the nanites will even work? Seth could still die."

"Yes. He could still die. I will not rest until I have exhausted every single probability."

Three guards appeared at both ends of the hallway, one beside Joy and two behind Eloise.

Heat rushed down Eloise's arms and legs while the rest of her body grew cold. "After all I've done," Eloise paced in front of Joy, "after everything I've given to your son! You're just going to kill me?"

"You're special to Seth. He loves you, and if he found out I murdered you, he would be destroyed. I won't do that. But I can blame your death on the nanites. They could malfunction and kill you." Joy flicked her wrist.

Eloise rushed forward, ripped off her jacket, and used it to wrench the stun baton out of the female guard's hand. Her jacket still in her hands, Eloise pushed off the wall with her feet, brought her hand back, and made sure the large brass buttons contacted the woman's face.

The guard, a welt underneath her eye, cuffed Eloise's wrist behind her body. She pivoted. The guard swung sideways with the momentum of Eloise's body and smashed against the wall.

Her shoulder burned. Eloise stumbled away, holding her arm. Another guard grabbed at her. With an angry yell, she slammed her knee into the groin of her attacker. He responded with a fist to her cheek. The metallic taste of blood spread throughout her mouth. She gasped, stumbling away. Her face throbbed.

Metal and glass lanterns hung by rings dotted the walls. Before the third guard could grab Eloise, she slid underneath his legs, tore a lantern off the wall, and ran around the corner.

A small trail of blood ran down her lip, and she licked it away. Her breathing ragged and hands shaking, Eloise clicked the opposite end of the handcuffs to the metal ring on top of the lantern and swallowed hard. Joy's furious screams and quick footsteps drew closer. She had seconds. Eloise tested the weight of her makeshift weapon and inhaled.

A red-headed man appeared first. He cried out when Eloise swung as hard as she could, the air carrying a faint whistle, and crashed the lantern into his face. Glass shattered. The guard collapsed, unconscious. She readied for her second victim. Again, she swung. The lantern shattered on contact. Metal and more glass rained onto the floor, but the female guard still stood. Eloise stepped back, and her breathing faltered.

"I'm not going to die for Seth!" Eloise screamed at Joy who she saw turn the corner. "And I'll claw my way out of here if I have to."

Weapon destroyed, Eloise half-crouched, waiting for the two remaining guards to get close enough.

One step.

Two steps.

Three ... Four.

Eloise bent, grabbed the broken lantern, now sharp, and sliced the female guard's arm from her wrist to her elbow, then went after the last guard. She ducked underneath his arm and stabbed his knee. He crumpled.

Joy, blocked by the bodies Eloise left in her wake, watched Eloise with fury contorting her face

A jolt of terror sliced through Eloise and she slipped on the bloody floor as she ran, panting, while the handcuffs jingled at her wrist.

CHAPTER TWO
BANNACK

The locket in Bannack's hand clinked as he lowered it into the hole he had dug, joining the akrafena, a blade with a wide curve at the end and a golden pommel. His agya had spent his life trying to find it, taking Bannack on some of his trips, and now Bannack was returning it to the earth from where it came.

The years alone fighting for shelter and shivering on the cold ground day after day brought him to his knees. Sure, he found the occasional group of people to settle with, but his guilt over destroying countless lives drove him into a life of voluntary solitude. After a few years of bouncing between family groups, he accepted his fate as a wanderer. No one would want him anyway, so he stayed away.

Bannack stroked his maame's face on the photo he held, her arms wrapped around her children. Her forelock of white hair disappeared into her yellow and orange headscarf and her single bright blue eye, many times a fascination for school friends when he was a kid, stood out against her dark skin. He shared the same trait, except he had two blue eyes.

"Forgive me."

The dirt hit the metal of the locket and sword as Bannack covered up the hole. He wouldn't remember anything by the morning. Not who he was, nor his name. He could create a new identity, ignorant of his past, and even his shame over not protecting his family would be fleeting. They were gone, he still lived, and that haunted him for too long.

His cheeks glistening, Bannack began his long walk to Joy.

***

Standing parallel to the facility where Joy had turned him into a monster, Bannack shook, his fists clenched. She had destroyed him, promising a memory wipe and then asking him to do the unthinkable task of kidnapping a young girl. Her command broke him in half. He looked into Joy's heartless, cold eyes all those years ago and knew, right then and there, that he couldn't continue to do what she wanted.

For too long, Bannack stood beside Joy as she experimented on the people he had collected for her. Their screams haunted his days and their faces, begging and terrified, haunted his nights. What he had done he could not atone for, but by forcing Joy to get rid of his memories now, Bannack could fix it all. He would be reborn, no longer weighed down by his sins.

The grass brushed over his thighs as he slunk toward the building.

Whispering voices made the hair on his neck raise, and he slipped behind a bush and watched the source of the whispers, two men, appear. One of them unzipped his pants, relieved himself, and continued his patrol. Bannack waited, counting in his head, and then slunk toward the building.

If Bannack could get to the side, he could slip in through a window. Finding Joy would be the hardest part since she frequented many rooms, and he had no way of knowing how many guards were on the inside.

You're an idiot, Bannack, for thinking this will work.

He rubbed his eyes to rid the thought from his mind. It wasn't helping.

I'm going to do this, even if it kills me.

A space of about three yards stood between him, the guards, and the side door.

Distraction.

Bannack's fingers closed around a rock, and he threw it. The resulting clatter put the guards on edge and they stood, mumbling amongst themselves.

"Come on," one of the guards whispered. Another followed.

Left behind, the youngest guard settled back down on his rock and yawned. Bannack released a quiet grunt. He should have known one would stay.

Hard way it is.

The branches brushed over his back as Bannack slunk behind the young guard, digging a fine cable out of his pocket. Bannack slipped the cording around the man's neck, pulled down hard, and dug his knee into the guard's spine. The neck tried to resist but failed. Bones snapped. Cording sliced into his neck. The guard relaxed.

Bannack lowered the body to the ground and began working on the lock. He had found the lock pick set some years back, and it had saved his ass many times. The first mechanism fell into place, then the second, while Bannack kept his good ear angled toward the front of the building.

Halfway through working with the lock, the guards returned.

They looked at their fallen comrade, shock turned to anger, and they ran toward Bannack. He sighed, grabbed a knife from the fallen guard's thigh, and flicked it into a neck. The third guard paused for just a moment, looked at both of the dead men, then advanced. Bannack ducked, and the last guard's fist crashed into the wall. He whimpered, cradling his injured hand and looked up just as Bannack brought a rock down onto his forehead.

More footsteps sounded while Bannack struggled with the lock. He gritted his teeth and the final mechanism clicked. Bannack threw open the door, used one of the guard's bodies to block the way, pocketed a knife, and ran through the hallway, desperate for any door to hide behind. With each step, the noise from his boots echoed off the blank walls, dull taps ricocheting through his skull.

A guard as tall as he was burst forward. Bannack smashed into the ground. A fist collided with his cheekbone, making him see stars and taste blood.

"You're not going anywhere," one of them said into Bannack's ear.

"The hell I am." Bannack allowed the fury to spread through him like a wildfire, making his skin burn and giving his muscles fuel to twist behind his attacker, aim below the shoulder, and drive the knife he stole from the dead guard into the man's back. Bannack jerked the knife blade up. The man, lying on the floor, made some gurgling noises and died.

Sore, Bannack peered around every corner. Guards were coming. He needed to find refuge. In his frantic run, he discovered many of the hallways were blocked off which he wasn't expecting. Many times, he had to backtrack.

Something is wrong.

Tension rose in his neck and shoulders as he spent the next several minutes searching for a door.

Has she been losing employees?

Bannack remembered Joy's announcement a couple years into his service with her that they would no longer take people from the Compound. It wasn't his place to ask questions, so he accepted the order, but the lack of guards made Bannack consider the possibility that something was changing. A power shift, perhaps?

He saw a door, one he recognized as Joy's office, and tried the doorknob. It opened. Bannack slipped through.

The room was about the size of his bedroom when he was a kid and had a second door at the far end. Her desk sat in the middle of the room, bare except for a baby picture of her son and an open file. She must have been actively reading it because the desk held several stacks of papers. Curious, Bannack pushed them around. He found a title. 'Project Nemosyne' and a photo of a younger Joy surrounded by what appeared to be her colleagues taped below the title. All of them smiled with their arms around each other, dressed in lab coats. Bannack leaned closer to the photo and made out "Artondale Regional Laboratories" engraved into a flat granite slab sitting behind and to the right of the group.

That is just up the hill from here, near the twin bridges.

Bannack looked at each of the people in the photo and his throat closed tight as he recognized Eloise's parents, her dad holding two-year-old Eloise and mom pregnant with Ada. Eloise had been his closest friend from childhood, and her family had lived down the street from him. His memories of the family were some of his most cherished.

Like her mother, Eloise was bold and independent, but she had inherited her father's features of golden freckles and red hair. She stood low to the ground, perfect height for knocking her father off his feet, and possessed the most vibrant golden eyes he had ever seen. Even after ten years, he still remembered those eyes.

Bannack turned the picture upside down and flipped through the documents in the rest of the folder. According to the files, Joy's attempts at developing a brain-healing serum were ruined when she injected it into the body of a six-year-old girl suffering from a blood infection brought on by a compromised immune system. The one reference to this little girl was the name "Donor," her true name redacted in the documents with information on her blood type as a universal donor, the date of a car accident, the hospital's attempt to save her life, and her sickness. But no name.

Joy spoke of the destruction of her lab, losing her research and serum, which left Donor with the only pure version of the nanites inside her body. The girl was missing.

"I've given up my search for Donor. It's a lost cause," Joy explained in the notes. "Seth is too sick. Recreating the serum will take too much time."

A few lines down, dated two years before Bannack's family died, Joy wrote, "Human experiments have begun. My only hope now is to find subjects and pray it works. Seth's life is what matters. Seth's life is what matters."

Several pages followed with profiles of the victims. No faces or names. Just numbers. Bannack shuddered. The top right corner of paper after paper held the words "deceased" or "maimed."

"Nothing is working!" Joy's frantic scrawl covered most of the next page after the victim profiles. "Seth's condition continues to grow worse. What am I missing?"

Joy picked up her journal a few months into Year Six, rejoicing in a new find. "Donor has been found! Work will begin right away on repairing the synapses of Seth's brain."

Bannack's hands threatened to crush the papers. Working for Joy, his job was simple: find victims. To his everlasting shame, Bannack did his job, and he did it well. His training allowed him to use his strength and height as an advantage over the ones who fought back, but everyone fought back. He couldn't blame them.

Then he came across a note, dated yesterday, stuck folded to the top of a paper. It read, "Seth's condition isn't improving despite regular nanite donations. Donor must deliver all serum. No exceptions."

He stared at the slip of paper stuck in the file like an afterthought. *Who is Donor?*

The question spun in his head until he heard a high-pitched scream. Bannack jumped from the chair, its legs scraping against the concrete floor, before crashing to the ground.

Years ago, the screaming wouldn't have affected him as it did in that moment. He had grown soft. The knot in his stomach turned to nausea and his vision tumbled. Bannack gripped the edge of the desk.

Round, dark brown eyes flashed through his head. He saw the silken hair of a little girl, only just twelve years old, brush at her neck when she ran. The girl, Nora, was the job that convinced Bannack he needed to run from Joy, so he met Nora and her family, and together they ran north. Joy's reach was long, but he knew she couldn't reach them there. Bannack stayed long enough to help the family find people to settle with and then left to travel alone.

When his vision cleared, Bannack rushed from the room but stopped short when he came face to face with a guard.

"Hey!" he said and reached for a crossbow slung to his back.

Ignoring the trembling of his limbs, Bannack ran forward and grabbed hold of the guard's arms, twisted his body, then cracked his elbow into the man's face. Bannack's shoulder jerked forward, the collar of his jacket brushing against his cheek, and his shoulder screamed. From behind, damp hands grabbed Bannack's ankle, and he slammed into the ground face first. His body vibrated from the impact. A surge of fear jolted him to his feet and into action. Bannack kicked the crossbow out of the way with one boot and slammed the heel of his palm into his attacker's face. The man stumbled, giving Bannack time to land a final blow to the back of his neck. The man dropped. Still wheezing from hitting the concrete, Bannack coughed, stepped over the unconscious guard and walked down the hallway, trembling.

The hallways all looked similar, so he lost his way more than once until he came to a slightly ajar door nestled in the corner of a hallway. He slipped through.

In the dimly lit room, Bannack leaned against a metal table and inhaled through his nose, his chest expanding, then let it out for a count of seven. He looked at his hands spotted with blood and clenched them.

I can't escape my past, can I?

Despite all his years rejecting the darkness within him, the minute he came back to Joy's accursed facility, the darkness awoke. He felt nothing for the men he killed.

They won't be remembered.

He murdered them without blinking an eye.

The sound of metal clinking made Bannack spin around. He tilted his head, listening for breathing or more noises as his heartbeat quickened, but he heard nothing.

Stop feeling. You'll get killed.

His muscles tightened, winding him up as if he were a spring, and Bannack crouched. Though the room was dark and only one of his ears worked, he scanned the room for movement. A lot of metal surfaces meant reflections, even when the room was dim.

Out of the corner of his eye, someone came at him with a frying pan. Cuffs clinked. With a jolt, Bannack raised his arm, blocked the attack, then used his free hand to hit the pan away. A woman grunted.

She was slight and easy to take down as he slammed his open palm into her chest, sending her tumbling. Bannack slunk toward her, his body prepared for another attack, but she scrambled behind a metal counter. Bannack followed. A knife blade slashed through the air, barely missing his face, and he jumped away, losing his footing. The weapon came down. Bannack rolled away to gather his bearings. He only needed a few seconds.

"Leave me alone!"

What is she talking about? He couldn't give up his position. She attacked him, and he would kill her if need be.

Footsteps came from behind him and a swirl of red hair preceded the burn of a knife across his cheek. Bannack gritted his teeth, silent as he rolled away. The woman, wild-eyed, closed the distance between them. Fast. Her speed caught him off guard. When she slammed her shoulder into his stomach, all the air left him in a single whoosh. They fell together, crashed into the door and tumbled into the hallway.

A vicious scar ran down the entire left side of her face.

She was much stronger than Bannack expected, and he struggled to get her off him. The woman's speed and agility matched his, and they grappled with one another, a flurry of arms and legs.

Finally, Bannack grabbed a hold of her neck. He slammed her back into the wall, tightening his grip. Tears moistened her eyes. Her neck was putty in his hands.

"B...Bannack. St...op."

His shoulders tightened. "How do you know my name?"

The woman wheezed. Her eyes rolled, but when she blinked, they focused again. "I'm...Eloise."

Immediately, Bannack released her, and she landed on the

ground, coughing and holding her neck.

"How?" he asked. His head tumbled. As he stared at her, parts of her mom and dad showed through. She looked at him, pushed against the wall, her eyes wet, and he fell to the ground. Her hair was a bit darker than when she was a kid but still a vibrant red.

When he tried to approach, she gasped and shrunk away from him. His stomach twisted.

"Stay away from me."

"Elle, I—"

"No! Just...no." Her face twisted as she held her neck. "I want you to stay away."

I almost killed her. Bannack looked at his hands with the dried blood over tiny scars from various fights and clenched them. *I almost killed my best friend.*

He hadn't recognized her in his fury but he should have. Damn it, he should have. He cursed his training, which taught him to block everything out, except the target, and the consequence had been near fatal.

Once Eloise disappeared from view, Bannack slammed the heel of his hand into the wall, the noise ricocheting off the walls, spun, and screamed. He shouldn't have cared, not even a little. All Bannack had to do was walk away from the facility and leave his past behind him. Every single memory would be wiped from existence. No memory of his family, Eloise, the bombs, or trauma. He would be clean and able to wander with nothing to pull him down.

That same world would now mean Eloise never existed. He would forever forget her name, their childhood spent together, but then it wouldn't matter after the memory wipe. And she would be dead.

Bannack took a deep, painful breath and closed his eyes. She was in the facility for a reason. He had seen the handcuffs.

Was Eloise's life less important than forgetting his own? No one deserved to be left for dead, but he had spent too long living with the guilt of his mother's and sister's deaths that he didn't know if he had it in him to keep going.

Taking a half-step away, his mother's voice echoed in his head, stopping him cold. "We do not leave those we love behind."

Bannack grimaced. It had been her favorite phrase, and as a child he hated it because whenever he ran off to go play with his friends, his mother would repeat the phrase, and then he'd be stuck with his sister who could barely keep up. Now, her words popped into his head only to poke at his already nauseous stomach.

Swearing to himself, Bannack planted his feet.

"Fine!" Bannack grumbled and began his search for Eloise. "I'll go get her."

He quickly found her trapped by two guards. She stood in a low stance and glared at him when he arrived.

"Until Amee gets back with Joy, we have to keep her here," one man said.

"Well, what do we do with her until then?" The other asked.

The first man shrugged. "She's dangerous. Did you see what she did to Percy? Sliced his face right open."

"Hey!" Bannack yelled, and both men turned.

"What're you doing here?"

He charged the men. They swung at him with their batons, one clocking him under the chin. Bannack's teeth knocked together, and his chin throbbed. This amplified Bannack's fight, and he punched, kicked, and stabbed at the men. With a kick to the gut, a guard fell.

The remaining man grabbed Bannack's torso, pinning his arms to his side. He thrashed, anger rippling through him, but the man held on tight. Something cracked, and the man jerked and fell. Bannack landed on the man, grunting in surprise, and saw an upside-down view of Eloise holding a baton.

She glared at Bannack. "What are you doing here?"

Bannack searched the guards for any usable weapons. "Helping you."

"I don't want your help."

"Look," Bannack, without looking at her, handed Eloise a second stun baton, knife, and cording, "we are better as a team and when we get out, we can talk about what happened. Agreed?"

She stared at him, her jaw muscles working. "Fine."

They wound through the hallways, checking any unlocked doors for a windowed room. They went up a second level before they found one and ran into several guards along the way. Seeing Eloise fight, with her tight and precise attacks, meant someone highly skilled had trained her. And well.

One look at Eloise confused him. No bruises. No cuts. He could have sworn she got injured at one point.

"Come on!" Eloise motioned in a wide arc as she held open a door. "Through here."

Bannack swung his baton toward the ceiling, hitting a woman in the chin, and her body slammed into the wall before she crumpled to the floor.

Joy's scream came from the end of the hallway. Bannack glanced up. He froze. Her face, contorted in anger, brought images of him in rags and huddled on the floor, pleading and screaming.

"Oi!" Eloise's call brought him back to the present, and he ran through the door. While Eloise grabbed a chair to bar the entrance, Bannack ran to open the window. With both exits protected and no time to check them, a window was their only option for escape.

"No one is guarding this one so we—"

The door flung open, sent the chair flying, and Eloise tumbled. Bannack stood by the window with his teeth clenched.

Joy walked in. "You," she said and glared at Bannack. "I should have known."

"You are alone," growled Bannack. "Bad move."

Eloise hit Joy in the back with the chair. A woman appeared around the corner. A single open palmed strike to Eloise's jugular knocked her out. Bannack swore, jumped down from the ledge by the window. The woman swung. Bannack inhaled through his nose when the hit jarred his arm. Lashing out with his hand, he hooked the crook of his elbow around her wrist and twisted. Hard. The woman screamed when her arm snapped.

Wasting no time, Bannack lifted the unconscious Eloise through the window, climbed out, and ran from the facility. Enraged screams took seconds to follow him.

What am I doing? How the hell did I get wrapped up in this?

Of course, he knew, but it hadn't been remotely close to what he wanted to accomplish for the day. Joy would never allow him back. He would never get his memory wipe, and it was all because of his mother and a woman with dark red hair.

The dry grass crunched underneath Bannack's boots and the fresh air rushed past him as the screams grew closer, Joy's voice loudest of them all. He ran in the darkness. Only the moonlight lit his path.

She wailed. "Get her back!"

Almost out of sight of the building, something sliced across Bannack's side. Fire burned across his skin. He stumbled forward, losing his grip on Eloise. To protect her, Bannack rotated as he fell, landing on concrete hidden beneath grass. She knocked the wind out of him when she landed, dead weight, on his stomach. Squirming on the ground while radiating pain flashed across his side, up his torso, and down his legs, Bannack groaned and removed his jacket. He had to move. Now. Or he wouldn't last much longer.

Whirling around in a desperate search for something to hide behind, Bannack saw a shed, part of it hidden by brambles.

It's my only chance.

Groaning in pain and struggling to regain his footing, Bannack pulled Eloise into the shadows. He turned the corner of the shed just as several guards ran past.

What am I going to do now? I need to think. Where can I—

He knew. Somehow, some way, Bannack and Eloise had to get to the twin bridges known as The Narrows.

Only the woman who lived in a plane could help him now.

CHAPTER THREE
BANNACK

"Put me down." Eloise shoved against his chest, and he released her. She glanced at the sunset. "How long was I out?"

"Few minutes."

A sliver of light shone through the trees, and it made the world around them a bit more visible. As they walked, dry twigs and branches splintered underfoot. The sharp scent of pine hung in the air, pushed around by a small breeze. Eloise stepped onto a rusted train track, her arms crossed, and looked at Bannack.

"Are we going to talk about it?"

"Nothing much to say. I broke in, found you, and we escaped."

"Okay. But why? Why were you there in the first place?"

He looked at her, one eyebrow raised, then said in a slow drawl, "Unfinished business."

"That's not a good enough answer."

"Look. You have your reasons, and I have mine. I am not interested in why you were there, please give me the same courtesy."

A stream of water dripped from his hand as he pulled a western skunk cabbage from the ground. His side stung, and he grunted, waiting until the pain subsided to a manageable level. He pulled the balled-up jacket away from his side. Blood covered his shirt and jacket, not enough to be dangerous, but he needed to get patched up.

"You're bleeding," Eloise said.

He looked at her, keeping his gaze neutral.

"Okay, yeah, that was a dumb comment." She walked over to him. "Can I at least help you?"

Human contact had been so scarce in his years alone, Bannack's first reaction was to pull away. The hair on the back of his neck and arms raised. Then he realized he would appreciate the help. He nodded.

Eloise took the jacket and lifted his shirt. She touched his side. Bannack knew she was inspecting his laceration, but the mere experience of touch made his senses flare. He didn't like it. It made his skin crawl.

"Do you know where some broadleaf plantain is?" Eloise asked.

"Up the hill. Be careful. Joy's men may still be around."

She waved her hand over her shoulder. A few minutes later, she returned with the deep green leaves of the plantain and as she began crushing them, Bannack listened for voices or footsteps, anything to signal approaching humans.

Bannack hissed as Eloise spread a poultice of broadleaf plantain and western skunk cabbage onto his cut. It would need stitches. The herbs and strips of his shirt would have to do until he could get to Kendal. The journey would take—Bannack looked skyward—the rest of the day. He groaned internally.

As Eloise wrapped strips of his shirt around his torso, she asked, "What unfinished business?"

She will not let it go, will she?

"It is not a good thing."

"I can handle a bit of unpleasantness."

Bannack looked away as Eloise finished wrapping his torso. "My family died several years back. Joy can wipe memories. I visited the facility, hoping Joy would help."

He didn't expect Eloise to chuckle, but she did. "And what makes you think she would help? She doesn't even know you."

33

Bare tree branches clattered together in the wind, the sound similar to bones being shaken, and the creek gurgled while Bannack stared at Eloise. She blinked, her mouth forming a circle.

"Oh. I get it." She laughed and stood. "So, you not only almost choked me out, but you're a part of Joy's mental plan to save Seth's life, too? Is this some sick joke? Is Joy going to jump out and say "boo" or is that your job? Are you just leading me on, getting me to trust you, only to take me right back to her?"

Her anger put him on edge. He didn't do well with yelling, and even though he did his best to hide his reactions, Bannack couldn't stop the shame from crashing through him. He suffocated under its weight. Eloise continued to rant and with each word, he shrunk further into himself until all that remained was anger. Hot, uncontrollable anger.

"I cannot go back there!" Bannack stood, his fists balled. "I destroyed every chance to forget my family, my sins, and myself when I saved your ass! Five years I've waited! You could be more grateful."

"Excuse me?" Eloise climbed on a rock to stand face to face with him. "I didn't ask you to do that for me. You just assumed I needed help. I had it handled!"

"Does this look like you have things handled?" Bannack grabbed the cuffs still connected to Eloise's wrist and her arm came with it.

Eloise made a loud grunt, her lips pursed, and didn't speak. She watched him, unphased by his outburst. "Fine." She yanked her hand away. "Maybe I needed a bit of help."

They fell into silence, Bannack scrubbing his jacket in the creek with sharp, furious strokes and Eloise tossing rocks upstream. The water turned a rust brown as he cleaned, using rough stones to get the blood out. He watched as Eloise inspected a flat rock, spun it in her fingers, and flicked it toward the water. The stone hopped three times before sinking.

"Eloise," Bannack called out. She turned to face him. "I do not regret saving you."

She smiled and rubbed her wrist. It was red. "You know, I don't need to know every detail of your involvement with her. Just...tell me one thing." She tossed another rock. "Do you regret it?"

His voice caught in his throat. "For as long as I live."

"Okay." She patted down her ass when she stood, and the cuffs jingled as she lifted them in the air. "Know anyone who can get these off?"

"I do."

***

Where the forest ended, a parking lot overgrown with grass began, which then led into the ruins of a strip mall. Perched atop them, with its nose smashed in, sat a plane with vines slithering around the hull. The shorn-off wings lay forgotten somewhere in the landscape. After Kendal converted the plane to a tavern, rapid word-of-mouth spread claiming it as the best watering hole in miles.

Easily seen in the distance, twin suspension bridges, one green and the other grey, spread across the mile-long strait called The Narrows. Through the past decade After the bombs hit, the bridges stood tall and still served as a thoroughfare across the ocean.

Bannack leaned against a boulder, then sat down and tilted his head back, groaning from the pulling of his open wound.

Rapid footsteps through rustling grass caught Bannack's attention and when he stared through the sunlight, Kendal's head blocked the rays.

Kendal Murali was a stout woman with hard eyes. She decorated her locs with silver bands, pulled away from her face in a head wrap. Seeing the fabric wrapped around her head sent nausea into his stomach when he remembered his maame's love for headscarves. He shook his head.

"Why am I not surprised to see you on my doorstep bleeding?" She shrugged the edge of her maroon, tasseled shawl onto her bare shoulders. "And, oh, you brought a stray. What happened this time?"

Her bored eyes turned away from Bannack, scanned through a group of people loitering around the entrance to the plane, lifted her arm, and jerked her head. One of her two bouncers, a large and intimidating man with an eye patch named Jerome, appeared.

"I'm Eloise," Eloise said and extended her hand.

"Kendal Murali. Owner of this establishment and head of the village a few miles from here." Kendal shook Eloise's hand and walked back to the plane, followed by Jerome. Bannack picked himself up off the ground, leaned against a boulder as if it were a cane, then followed Jerome into the plane.

Bannack ducked as he pushed through the canvas tarp acting as a door and surveyed the tavern. A short wave of stale air, alcohol, cooked meat and vegetables smacked into Bannack's nose. Old guns, soldier uniforms, and maps of what used to be the United States lined the perimeter of the plane. A vintage Harley Davidson sat alone at the back with a fake skeleton wearing a gas mask perched atop it because Kendal couldn't resist morbidity. Gone were the rows of cramped airline seats and in their place was a menagerie of house doors, clothing trunks, cart wheels, and a few steel drums slashed in half and placed upside down which all served as tables and chairs.

A split-second hush spread over the plane's occupants as they watched Kendal lead Jerome, Eloise, and Bannack, holding his wet jacket, to the back of the plane. Once the moment passed, everyone turned back to their booze and companions.

Loud laughter came from a group of people while others were more interested in the food, ingesting their drinks and meal without fanfare and giving the side eye to those who made too much noise.

Kendal barked something at the loud groups, weaving around people to get to the front of the plane. On her way, she pushed on several windows, propping them open with a piece of plywood, and waved her hand in front of her face.

"Y'all stink!" Kendal yelled out, and the tavern erupted into laughter and jeering. "Get out of my house and get cozy with a shower!"

Between the open windows and the entrance, fresh air cycled through the interior of the plane.

"Come in here," Kendal said as she walked past Bannack without stopping. "And don't bleed all over my floor."

The fire in the center of the room, contained by a metal drum, projected light a few inches from it before becoming lost in the sunlight. Matches were rare, so if the flames died out, someone had the unfortunate job of laboring over creating a new flame.

She snagged a crude bottle of clear liquid from the bar and ushered Bannack into her private room hidden behind a white shower curtain with blue flowers. Only a few seats from the gutted first-class area were fortunate enough to stay. Old rugs covered the floor. Various skulls, an old cuckoo clock, and animal horns adorned the walls. Bookshelves with tinctures, medicines, a few medical supplies, and a couple rows of novels and scrolls sat against the wall closest to the shower curtain door.

Kendal pointed with a single finger, the other four wrapped around the bottleneck, at a reclined first-class seat. "Sit."

"Have you known Bannack long?" Eloise asked as she inspected a small collection of bottles filled with various liquids and herbs.

Exhaustion overtook Bannack, and he tumbled into a neighboring seat, mildly aware of their conversation.

"Aye. This rugrat has been showing up here for years asking for help with his little escapades."

Kendal hissed at Bannack who was touching a deer skull. He yanked his hand away and faked a pout to which Kendal rolled her eyes. She rifled through her shelves. Bottles clinked. "And you?"

"Well," Eloise released an airy chuckle, "we kinda...bumped...into each other a few hours ago but we knew each other as kids Before."

"Oh!" Kendal waved a bottle of clear liquid in the air as she pulled it from a deep shelf. She jumped down from her step ladder. "Serendipity. Fortunate you found each other again."

I guess that's one way of putting it.

Bannack's side ached something fierce and with each movement, his wound pulled and burned. He had learned how to deal with injuries long ago, but that skill still wasn't enough to stop the pain completely.

"Medaase," said Bannack, reaching for the moonshine Kendal held.

She snatched it away. "Ɛnna ase, Blue Eyes. This ain't for your mouth. Remove the poultice dressing."

Bannack followed her orders. As the liquid seared into his wound, he gritted his teeth and his hands flattened the foam of the seat beneath him. Kendal took a towel then dabbed at the blood drawing lines across his torso. The scratch of the fabric aggravated his skin. His toes curled.

"You could have warned me," Bannack growled.

Kendal took a swig of the last moonshine in the bottle, smiling behind the glass. "Remove your poultice dressing wasn't warning enough?"

"Are you going to stitch me up or what?"

"Of course." Kendal set the bottle down, pulled out a bone needle, and threaded it with dark horse hair. "For this part, you're gonna need to be a bit tipsy. You can hold your liquor, can't ya?"

In response, Bannack downed the drink. It burned his throat, and he set the empty bottle on a fold out tray. His head buzzed, and a warmth spread through his body. He knew the drill.

When he left Joy's command, Bannack had sustained many wounds, a few requiring him to stay for several weeks in Kendal's care. He knew of her because his family had stayed in her village for a time. As he tried to make it out on his own, he returned several other times. She had welcomed him as if they were close friends.

The needle dug into his skin and Bannack grunted, squeezing the armrest. "You're losing your touch, Kendal."

She grunted. "Don't get smart with me, Blue Eyes. I may slip and sew your arm to your side."

A quick glance with her hard eyes at Bannack made him chuckle, the movement of his torso aggravating the sensitive skin and muscle.

She left his side for a moment, gathering a mortar and pestle with a bunch of long, curled, dry leaves. Bannack rubbed a leaf between his fingers.

"Curly dock," she announced and placed the leaves into the

mortar. She grabbed some water from the shelf beside her and poured a bit into it as well. While mixing with the pestle, she explained, "I'm sure you've seen this weed. I keep some on hand, dried, of course, to help with itching, eczema, and skin irritations. But it also helps with healing wounds. Think of it as like...Neosporin. But so much better."

She tapped the pestle against the mortar. The curly dock poultice fell into the stone bowl. Kendal scooped a bit onto her fingertips and spread it over the new stitches. The poultice soothed his skin, allowing him to relax in sweet relief and melt into the cushion of the chair.

"I don't want to see you back here for at least another six months, or longer, ya hear?"

Bannack struggled to nod through the tingling and heaviness.

She grunted and walked to the front of the first-class area, rifling through cabinet doors and pulled out a pair of pliers. She sat beside Eloise.

"Handcuffs are easy to get off if you know how."

"Oh, good." Eloise put her hand in Kendal's. "I thought you were going to saw through them."

Kendal laughed. "Girl, that's barbaric. My way is better."

She pulled a bobby pin out of her hair, took the rubber piece off the straight end, and bent it at a ninety-degree angle. She opened up the pin. Within minutes, the cuffs clicked open.

Eloise rubbed her wrist. "Thanks." She leaned back in her seat and pulled out a folded-up piece of paper. As she read it, her hand went to her mouth and then tears formed.

"What?" Bannack sat up, curious, but Eloise ignored him.

Her brow wrinkled. More tears fell. "Excuse me." She ran from the room, the note fluttering to the ground.

"What was that about?" Kendal asked.

Bannack shrugged his shoulders then picked up the note Eloise dropped. On the back was a drawing of a Victorian-era home surrounded by shrubberies, roses, hanging baskets, and two apple trees so real he could almost smell the fruit growing on them.

He read the letter.

Eloise,
You can't save me. But I can save you.
Please don't come back for me. No matter what.
I'll never forgive you if you do.
Mama is just going to have to deal with it.
I'm glad you escaped because it won't be my fault if you died.
I'm so tired.
I tried to stay strong for Mama and you, but I can feel it.
My body is dying. We did everything we could.
Thank you for not giving up on me.
I know you're crying but you'll be okay.
You must continue on. For me.

P.S. I'll have to take a raincheck on the beach visit. As an
apology, here's my favorite drawing.

CHAPTER FOUR
ELOISE

Her knees hit the ground outside, and she sat back and cried. Snot pooled at the entrance to her nostrils. Unable to care, Eloise swiped her sleeve underneath her nose. The world slowed.

The frigid morning air encouraged birds to begin their morning song. Dew sat on the grass and soaked Eloise's knees.

Footsteps approached her, and she glanced over her fingers. Bannack crouched in front of her. His dark skin caught the morning light. Blue eyes, caused by the condition he was born with, which took the hearing from his left ear, were bright like sunshine through water. Bannack sat in front of her. When he put his hands on his knees, she noticed the small scars on his hands and forearms.

Eloise clenched her fists. "I was going to save him." Bannack listened. Eloise continued. "Now I'm supposed to sit here and let him die?"

"It is what he wants."

"To hell with what he wants! He can't just—"

"Choose for himself?" Bannack interrupted. "He is ready, even if you are not."

Eloise paused with her mouth open, then closed it and turned away from him. A painful hiccup shook her chest. "Do you...know what it's like to be alone? Not alone like you have no one around you but like your heart hurts and your mind is sad and all around you are people, so many people, but you feel nothing. You are visible and loved, but that hurts you to your core and all you feel is ignored.

"And it gets to you. It burns into your mind and rots there, like a carcass, and pushes and pushes and pushes until there is this deep chasm of death and wanting and loneliness. And you start to think 'maybe someone will fix it' but they won't because you can't share what you feel. And that's why you go to help the bad guy, because you are desperate to feel something, anything again! But then you hate yourself for betraying yourself and you hate the world for making you this way and the loneliness only gets worse."

As her words formed, they came out thick and rapid from her mouth, tears dripping off her lips. Her body, cold, made her shiver, yet her face burned. "I'm afraid," she managed to say, "that once Seth leaves, I'll be alone."

"But you have to let him go. He needs your love and support, not your belittlement. Don't focus on his disease, focus on who he is."

When she looked at Bannack, his eyes glistened.

"I do know what it's like to be alone," Bannack whispered and gave her back the letter. His eyes focused on her wrist and he motioned to it. "It's healed already?"

"Huh? Oh." Eloise glanced down at where the handcuffs were minutes ago. Swinging a lantern around had made the cuffs cut into her skin. "Yeah. Watch."

Eloise dipped the edge of her shirt into a small puddle of dew on a leaf and used it to wipe the blood from her wrist.

Bannack leaned in and looked at her arm, devoid of any mark. "Humans do not heal that fast."

"Yeah, well," Eloise dried off her arm. "Not every human has self-replicating nanites in their body, either."

His eyes widened. The comical reaction made Eloise chuckle.

"How is it possible, you ask? I got in a car accident when I was six and the hamster cage I was holding slammed into me, making my spleen rupture. I was fine until I got a blood infection and then started dying. My parents were scientists—you probably remember—and they were working with nanites, trying to program them to target synapses in the brain to heal them. I don't remember anything else about their work. They brought me to their boss, Joy, and she agreed to inject me with the nanites to save me. It worked."

"And you are—were—working with her? Why?"

"Well," Eloise blinked at Bannack, confused at his question. Why did it matter so much? "I was gathering some herbs for Soora—she and Mason adopted me when I was thirteen—and Seth and Joy were outside. They liked to take walks. We got to chatting. I learned about Seth's condition. He was Ada's best friend, so I had to help."

Remembering Seth's letter made her nose sting. She didn't want to admit it, but Bannack was right; she needed to move on and let him choose for himself. It still hurt, though.

"And this?" Bannack touched his cheekbone to signal that he meant her scar. "Her doing as well?"

Eloise rubbed her thumb. He was getting dangerously close to an off-limits conversation. "No. And I'm not saying any more about it."

"Fair enough," Bannack said, then realization spread across his face. "You are Donor."

"What?"

"Uh...In Joy's office, I came across some papers. They mention someone she called Donor. Your story and Donor's match. I cannot believe I did not connect the dots."

"She called me Donor?" Eloise gritted her teeth then spoke under her breath. "She couldn't even respect me enough to use my name."

Bannack laid in the grass and closed his eyes. "Mmm. It is nice to be still," he said.

Eloise tilted her head. "How can you stand it?"

He shrugged. "Practice. I listen for the birds."

"Birds?"

"Shh...Listen."

Quieting, Eloise waited while bouncing her leg. Birdsong built into a chorus of twittering, chattering, and singing in the trees. Red-breasted robins bounced around in the grass. A blue jay flew above them. The wind pushed through the trees, and as the leaves brushed against each other, they rustled and added their own sound to the song of the earth. It never occurred to her to listen.

"Okay. I can see the appeal."

Bannack remained still for so long, Eloise was sure he had fallen asleep. She fiddled with a wide piece of grass and squashed it between her two thumbs, leaving a small gap, then blew hard against her thumbs. The high-pitched whistle filled the air. Once again bored, Eloise moved on to picking tiny daisies, weaving grass together, and fashioned a crown of flowers. She made two. One she offered to Bannack.

"I made you something."

A smile spread across Bannack's face, softening his angular features. It mesmerized her. He went from the terrifying man in the facility to someone who looked like he cuddled puppies for a living.

If the war hadn't happened, his life would have been different. Everyone's would have.

Life had been good Before the war. Then Fade, a splinter group of the United States government focused on restarting society in the United States, kidnapped President Raquel Santos and other delegates, then deployed nuclear bombs. They targeted six major fault lines, causing mass destruction of people's livelihoods with earthquakes, fires, floods, and tsunamis. Hawaii became a crumbled mass in the ocean. Those living in Alaska lost three quarters of their state to fire caused by friction in the Denali Fault. In the first few years After, mobs and raids were common, leading Mason to establish the Compound and others to form clans.

"Eloise?" Bannack asked, and she turned to him. "What happened to Ada?"

She swallowed, her pulse thrumming in her head. "She died."

"There you are!" Kendal called from the bottom of the hill. "I've got warm drinks waiting. Come."

Giving Bannack a mournful smile, Eloise led the way down the hill and back to Kendal's plane. Once there, Eloise settled down adjacent to Bannack, eyeing him curiously, while Kendal disappeared behind the tarp door.

This man is a walking conundrum. He's gentle and quiet, like how I remember him, but he's also terrifying. What happened?

Kendal reappeared. In her hands, she carried two glasses filled with a steaming, golden liquid.

When Eloise accepted one, the warmth thawed her fingers. "What is it?" she asked.

"Hot toddy," Kendal said as she leaned against a crudely cut counter. "My Gran taught me to make them. She swore they were a cure-all for the nastiest of colds. Should help you recover."

"What's in it?"

"Oh, just some water, honey, and lemon I snagged a couple days back from a man traveling up from California." Kendal smiled before closing the curtain to her room. "And a bit of rum." She yawned. "Now...since Blue Eyes woke me before the sun showed its face, I'm going back to bed. Leave. Stay. Don't care."

After Kendal disappeared, Eloise took a sip. The lemon slice slipped to the back rim of the glass and the steaming liquid coated her insides all the way down with a kick at the end.

"Woah." Eloise pulled the glass away and licked her lips.

Bannack nodded as he set down his empty glass. "She gives it to anyone she patches up. She thinks it's liquid duct tape."

Eloise chuckled and took a second sip. "Is it?"

"I would not want to be in the same room as the person who tells her otherwise." Bannack chuckled as he balled up a jacket and leaned back in the plane chair, wincing. "Gotta get some sleep," he said.

"You're sleeping? Now?"

"With the day I've had..." Bannack mumbled something else and opened one eye to look at her. "Just a few hours."

Eloise finished her drink, the lemon slice tapping against her lips while the warmth of the drink soothed her. She hummed in her throat, scooting further down the seat. It didn't take long for her mind to shut off.

Blood dripped down her arms.

In front of her, a crimson puddle formed. Ada lay on the concrete floor. Her dead eyes peered straight at Eloise.

She screamed.

Screamed until she became hoarse.

Until no sound came from her throat.

A deep, terrified gasp escaped Eloise's mouth as she woke. Sweat covered every inch of her body. The blankets, stuck to her skin, came with her as she tumbled out of the seat. The room lurched sideways. Her body hit the floor of the plane, forehead smashing into the metal bottom of a seat.

Someone large came into her field of vision and Eloise cried out, scrambling away. When he backed up, she blinked, trying to calm her body and mind.

His soothing voice echoed in her head. She recognized it. But from where?

She tried to wake up, to cry out, but her shoulders ached, and her mind remained trapped. She couldn't speak, only moan from the pain traveling throughout her body.

Bannack leaned in. He stood at the edge of a long tunnel. She squinted. He spoke something. She didn't register the words, but his smooth tone coated her nerves in warmth. Then he held her, strong and solid, in a cocoon of safety. He set her on the chair, smoothing out the hair stuck to her face.

Kendal appeared and handed a cloth to him. When Bannack spoke, the sound couldn't get past the cotton in her ears. Something about helping her with her head? She couldn't be sure. Then he touched her and she cried out, pulling away.

"It hurts."

Bannack spoke to Kendal in muffled tones. "Something...compressions."

A blanket covered her body along with a wide, thin stone on her chest. The tunnel vision and shoulder pain faded.

"Better?" Bannack asked.

She nodded.

Kendal removed the rock.

"Good. You have a nasty cut on your forehead. I tried to clean it but—"

"I know what happened," she said.

Bannack placed a rag in her palm, his fingers brushing her skin. They were warm to the touch. Calmly, he closed her hand around the cloth and paused before scooting away. The gesture floored her. She watched him, unable to stop herself from staring like an idiot.

He blinked once, then smiled. "Maame struggled with something similar."

With a yawn, Bannack returned to his chair, wrapped his arms around his chest, and grew still. She looked at the brown cloth, fresh blood blotched on the surface. Wincing as the cloth touched her forehead, Eloise found a solid, raised bump. She groaned.

Out the grimy plane window, fog collected on the glass. The sun shining through the window spread a rainbow across her thighs and onto the ground.

People entered and exited the plane, their muffled voices traveling into the first-class area.

What's going to happen to Seth now that I'm not around to save him?

A bug landed low on the glass, flicked its wings, and then took off again. Eloise leaned forward, her mind distracted, and curled her knees into her body. A thump made Eloise jump. Bannack shifted on the reclined seat.

Tears leaked from her eyes. Eloise took a deep breath, her chest heavy.

I'm going to have to learn how to live without him.

***

"What's your plan now?" Eloise asked Bannack.

They stood in front of Kendal's plane, Bannack leaning against vines wrapped around the outside as the afternoon sun beat down on them. A cool breeze carried the scent of fresh water and wet leaves.

"Travel, most likely. Eventually find a home. I have to get the personal possessions I hid before we ran into each other, then I will figure out where to go next."

Saying goodbye was hard. She'd only reconnected with him for a couple days, and with her curiosity piqued, she wanted to know more about him and his past. When Bannack placed the lunch in the travel pack Kendal had loaned him, Eloise saw a stack of adinkra symbols on his arm.

She blinked and forced her eyes upward. He stared at her. Unlike him, with his dark skin that hid all forms of physical embarrassment, Eloise turned pink, and the brief thought that he could see her embarrassment irritated her. "Will I be able to see you again sometime?"

"Maybe." Bannack shrugged.

Her heart fell a little. "Well, if you're ever close to the Compound, feel free to drop in."

"Thanks for the invitation."

Bannack moved to leave but Eloise jumped forward and caught his sleeve. "You're right, you know."

Confused, he watched her. "I am?"

"Yeah." She released his sleeve. "About Seth. If he truly wants me to stop helping, I have to respect that decision."

Bannack smiled. "If it helps, I'm truly sorry you're losing him."

"Thanks."

With a wave, he disappeared into the forest.

Eloise travelled to the Compound. It took her several hours, and on a short water break, she half hoped Bannack would show up. *What am I doing?* She splashed water on her face. *He's got his own life.*

The Compound sat on top of a steep hill, made of red brick and many windows, towels flapping in some, with a sidewalk parallel to the building. The front doors were steel.

"Welcome back, Eloise," Derrick said as she walked up the steep hill. He was one of two Sentinels tasked with greeting any visitor who approached. Eloise wasn't a visitor so their approach was cordial.

"Glad you came back before Mason came to get you," Thomas, the other guard, said. "He was getting ready to find you."

"Where is he?" So much had happened. She needed to debrief him. Joy would come back, and they all needed to prepare for the consequences.

Derrick pointed to the second story. "In his apartment, most likely."

"Thank you, boys."

A few people waved to her as she entered through the loud, creaking doors. Pierre, a young boy in one of Soora's medical classes, gathered his two younger siblings, identical twin boys, onto his lap like a mother hen. He fussed over one and once the barrette secured the toddler's shoulder length hair, Pierre pulled a worn children's book out and read. He glanced up at Eloise, who waved, and gave her a short upward nod.

"Eloise!"

She turned, and a spindly boy carrying Bali plowed into her. She laughed and asked, "What're you doing with my cat, Gavin?"

Gavin bounced on the balls of his feet, his big ears sticking out the side of his head, while Bali wriggled in his hands. "I found her in the hay chasing a poor rabbit."

"She's supposed to do that, silly."

"No. It was so sad. I couldn't let the bunny die." Gavin blinked his big, brown eyes. "Can you keep her in your room? My friends and I are going to find a safe place far away so she can't get it."

"O...okay." Eloise struggled to hold on to Bali as Gavin threw her into her arms. As she watched the boy with his two buddies run off, one carrying a box, she smiled, unable to tell them Bali would most likely find the rabbit again. She lifted Bali in the air. "Why are you scaring the poor kids?"

Bali let out an annoyed mew.

Eloise dropped Bali in her apartment and walked to the end of the hallway. She paused outside Mason and Soora's open door, their conversation leaking into the hallway, and couldn't help but overhear.

"Mason, I know you want life to return to normal, but you need to take a step back and realize that we're doing okay."

"Mookie. I highly doubt Fade is gone."

"But for now, they aren't bothering us. We've built a life here. Let's not go messing it up, okay?"

The conversation died down. Eloise stared at the floor. Fade took down the country by infiltrating the government and turning the people against each other and those who governed over them. Fear-mongering, propaganda, and slow yet deliberate spread of misinformation all culminated in the kidnapping of the President and acquiring of the nuclear launch codes. Hours later, the US people lost everything.

She knocked on the door.

Soora answered. "Come in!"

She was lithe and no more than fifty, but the youthful glimmer in her eyes made her appear younger. On her shaved scalp was a tattoo of a sunflower, her namesake.

Mason gathered Eloise up in his arms, his salt and pepper beard scratching her face. Eloise melted into him.

It's so good to be home.

When Mason pulled away, he blocked the sun coming in from the windows, the rays forming a silhouette around his head and shoulders.

"You came back," Mason whispered.

"Just in time, too, I see. Thomas told me you were planning on mounting an army."

Mason chuckled. "Better to be over prepared than under. So," he pulled her to a pair of chairs, sat, and wrapped his arm around Soora's hip as she settled on the armrest, "what made you late? I was worried."

Eloise puffed out air and leaned back. "So much, Mason."

She relayed the events of the past couple days. As she talked,

Mason grew tense and Soora touched his shoulder, giving her husband a soft look with the bindi mark between her eyebrows wrinkling.

"So," Mason leaned forward, "are you okay?"

At those words, Eloise nearly crumbled. Her hands shook and when she tried to reach up to tuck some hair behind her ear, she couldn't get her fingers around the cartilage. Mason leaned forward, chair creaking, and did it for her.

"Thanks," Eloise said, her smile small. "I failed, Mason."

His brow furrowed. "In what way?"

She produced the letter Seth wrote, wrinkled from being in her pocket, and handed it over to Mason. He read it, mouth formed into a half frown, then gave it back.

"Do you remember when you got sick after the car accident?" Mason asked.

Eloise remembered. The horrid sound of crunching metal as the car rolled over and over still bothered her.

"Yeah. I remember. Why?"

"Who made that decision?"

Eloise blinked at him. "My parents."

"Mmm. And had they not, what would have happened?"

"I would've died—Mason. Where is this going?"

"This scenario is much like that one, all those years ago. Your parents stepped in to save your life, and that's what Seth is doing now."

Eloise scrubbed her palms together and jumped to her feet. She paced. Mason watched her. After a few rounds, Eloise spun toward Mason. "I poured my life into keeping him alive and now I have to live without him."

Mason gathered Eloise in his arms again and whispered, "What you've done for him matters."

"You did everything you could," Soora added.

Suppressed emotions rose out of her with full force. She didn't stop them. They brought Eloise to her knees.

"I don't want it to be over."

Sweat rose into her neck and around her armpits while the room spun. Her body became a pulse, thumping and pounding her insides with a meat tenderizer. Soon, the reeling stopped, and she righted herself.

Soora used the sleeve of her dress to wipe the tears off Eloise's face. "He's not giving up," she said. The expression of sympathy made Eloise smile. "He's moving on."

Tears leapt into Eloise's eyes again. Her shoulders slumped. "What am I going to do?"

Hands wrapped around Eloise's face and she looked at Soora who said, "Live."

Eloise nodded. She held onto Soora's wrists.

"We need to decide what to do about Joy," Mason said. He leaned against the back of a chair and rubbed his beard.

Eloise wiped her eyes. "Do you think she'll come here?"

"I do."

"The contract you have with her prevents her from doing that, doesn't it?" Soora asked.

The contract protected the Compounders from being targeted by Joy. The agreement, written up seven years ago, early in the Compound's life, detailed that if Joy ceased her human experiments, Mason wouldn't go after her with his Sentinels. She also promised to release the people in her employment as soon as they fulfilled their service. Joy didn't have anywhere near the numbers, relying on fear and blackmail to get what she wanted, and Mason's Sentinels were superior in both numbers and training. If an attack happened, Joy would experience swift defeat.

"It does," Mason nodded. "Although, I worry what she'll do when her son is involved." He turned to Eloise, putting emphasis on his words and looking at her with unwavering eyes. "You must be prepared for an angry mother who isn't completely rational. To her, you have endangered her son's life. I'd go as far as to say she could blame you for his death and she will come for you."

Eloise's stomach churned but she squared her shoulders. "Increase the Sentinels on duty. We have the numbers and at the very least we'll know when she comes."

"Alright," Mason nodded. "Mookie, how are your supplies? Do you have enough to support a possible increase in injuries?" Mookie was the last half of her given name, Soorajamukhee, and no one called her Mookie except him.

"I do." Soora gave Mason a kiss. "My nurses can handle things."

"I need to be on duty," Eloise said.

Mason walked around the chair and stood in front of her. "Absolutely not."

"Oh, come on." Eloise's ears heated. "I'm your best knifeman and I can fit into small spaces. You've seen me do it. Joy's going to come after me, or at least send someone, and if I'm holed up in here, you're down one Sentinel."

"As your commander, it would be irresponsible to allow you onto the front lines. You're an easy target out there."

Grumbling, Eloise gave Mason side-eye. "I really hate it when you command me."

"You know I can't play favorites."

Soora put her hand on Mason's chest and smiled. "Honey, you're doing that right now."

"I..." Mason blinked at his wife. He sighed, his fingers pinching the bridge of his nose. "Yes. Fine. Eloise, you can join the Sentinels."

She smiled, on the verge of hugging Mason, but her face fell when he held up a hand.

"But," Mason said, "you must do as I say, and if I make the decision to pull you, I want you to follow orders. Got it?"

"Yes. Understood, sir."

Mason fell into a chair. "Dismissed."

She walked back to her room, a bounce in her step, and laid on her bed. Bali mewed a greeting, rubbed her body up against Eloise's cheek, and settled in the crook of Eloise's arm.

"I've missed you." Eloise snuggled the cat close.

CHAPTER FIVE
JOY

"May I speak freely, ma'am?" Graham asked from behind her.

Her smile faded. She had been watching Seth laugh with one of her employees, who was actively losing his snacks to her son, as they played a card game and Graham's voice reminded her that she couldn't ignore her duties, no matter how much she wanted to.

"Of course," Joy said, still distracted.

"The way you treat Seth, as if he is helpless—"

Joy spun around, eyes narrowed. "Choose your next words carefully. You may be my Head of Command, but I am still your boss."

Graham balked a bit but stayed still. "Do you think he's healthy? Happy?"

"Right now he is."

"No," Graham made a discouraged sigh, "I mean truly happy. People aren't meant to be alone."

She didn't appreciate the direction their conversation was going, so she turned around, fear and dread clenching at her throat. "He's my son. My responsibility. I'd like you to leave now."

"Ma'am. We love him too. We only want what's best for him and if that means letting him experience the world, he needs that."

Frustrated, Joy turned around and walked away. She knew he was right, but she couldn't push past the painful mourning to do anything about it. Besides, he was doing well enough.

Taking a moment to gain composure and uncurl her balled fist, Joy breathed as she stood in front of Seth's door. He needed Mom, not the scientist. She tried so hard to keep them separate, but when he got sick thirteen years ago, the line between mom and scientist blurred. Now, she didn't even know where it existed.

Joy knocked.

"Come in."

As always, her heart clenched when she saw him. Seth was so frail, his breathing getting worse, and she worried even touching him would break him.

When will this nightmare stop? You're supposed to be running, hanging with your friends, and going on adventures. Not this.

She sat by him. He glanced up, smiled, and returned to his drawing of a building. With Seth, the things he drew were from pictures he saw in books or from his own imagination, and Joy always marveled at how he could breathe life into a simple building. His detailed work was breathtaking and intricate, and he always worked various plants and shrubbery into the home as if they were a necessity.

"What do you...think?" Seth asked, tilting his notebook toward her.

She leaned in, amazed at the art déco inspired home with accents of Queen Anne architecture. The curved corners and tall, square windows blended seamlessly with the round towers and lace-like porch brackets.

"Beautiful."

He returned to his work, adding details of shrubbery on the porch. "Are you going...to go after...Eloise?"

Joy leaned away from Seth. "Why would you ask that?"

"I dunno..." Seth shrugged. He paused, sighed, then looked up at her. "...I was...thinking it might...be nice to spend what...time I have left—"

Her heart beat in her head and she stood. "Out of the question. No." Joy knelt in front of Seth, her hand resting on his cheek. "We've worked too hard for this. I'm not going to lose you."

His eyes bored into her and the thought of never seeing them again drove her mad.

"Mama..."

I love it when you call me that. It reminded her of when he was an infant, full of wonder and discovery. She had raised him as a single mother, unable to find someone to start a family with, so she began one through a visit to the sperm bank.

Ever since he started talking, he'd always called her 'Mama' and a bittersweet ache formed in her chest. She blinked the tears from her eyes.

"I can't do it. She's too important. I can start my work over again with Project Nemosyne. Reinstate it."

"Mama. You're not...listening to me."

"Alright," Joy sighed. "I'm listening."

"I don't want this. I want to be...free and I can't live...knowing Eloise is...hurting or dead."

"You will be free soon."

"No." Seth shook his head. "I want to be free. From...my body. Mama, do...you understand?"

She did. Saving Seth had been her life for so long, she didn't know how to let go. A knot formed in her throat, and she struggled to talk past it. "She agreed to this."

"No, she didn't! She agreed...to donate blood, not...dying. Why...can't you understand? I want...this all to stop. I want Eloise...to be alive. I want you to be...my Mama and hold...me when I die. Please! Stop...all of this and just be my...mom!"

Listening to Seth beg ripped her heart to shreds and when she spoke, the rock in her throat only allowed a whisper to pass by. "I don't know how, baby. You're my entire world and I...I don't know how."

"Let go of Eloise...and be here. With me. Don't go...after her.

Stay."

"I..." Joy shook her head. "I can't."

Seth wouldn't look at her. "I don't want...you in my room...anymore."

"Baby," Joy said, doing her best to speak calmly. She hoped he wouldn't notice the shaking of her words. "Okay. I'll leave. But I hope you understand that sometimes a parent has to make the hard decisions for their children."

***

Joy sat in the metal chair, scouring her records, hoping to find anything she missed that might help save Seth's life without the use of the nanites. The folders strewn across her desk had a decade old layer of dust coating them and when she swiped her hand over the surface to clear it, the grey powder rolled up and fell onto the desk.

Once you're healed, I can replicate the leftover nanites and more people will be saved from heartache.

The words echoed around in her head. She closed her eyes. Eloise's nanites were the purest version of her creation. The original. When Amanda and Merrick came to Joy, begging her to help them save Eloise's life, she agreed, not realizing four years later they would destroy everything. The research. The nanites.

At first, she came across recordings she made during Nemosyne's development; the piles of papers devoted to the documentation of their testing phase and the many, many rejection letters. They all noted Nemosyne was 'too dangerous' or 'lacked clarity.'

Joy scoffed. *Why did I keep these?*

She would spend the next eight years after Eloise's parent's death failing to repeat what she had accomplished with Amanda and Merrick. The nanites were never the same. Their impurity caused the mind wipes, not their programming. It seemed Amanda and Merrick knew something she didn't—they had always been smarter than her—and that infuriated her more than anything. She was a

57

brilliant scientist. Her life's work was to heal brain degradation. Seth suffered from a fatal brain disease. The nanites should have worked if she still had the original ones, but they—except for Eloise's nanites—perished in the explosion, and Joy had to settle for half-strength ones from Eloise's body.

Joy couldn't figure out why Eloise's nanites were half strength. None of the tests made any sense. Eloise had the original. So why weren't they healing him? Every single test, after years, said the same thing: Eloise's nanites weren't strong enough. But why?

At the bottom of the stack of documents, Joy found a black, hardbound journal. As she flipped through it, she read about her pregnancy with Seth, him as an infant and young child, his unknown illness, her anger toward the fertility clinic for their oversight in giving her sperm from a donor carrying the disease, and finally his diagnosis. The final entry, dated March 2nd, 3028, was twelve years ago. Seth was five.

A miracle has happened.

Eloise's body, previously immunocompromised due to her blood infection, has accepted the nanites. Is she the key to what we have been looking for? The future of Project Nemosyne is unsure, but I may have just been handed a solution on a silver platter.

Seth is going to be okay!

Joy flicked the book back in the box. She rolled her eyes at her naivety, then turned her attention back to her papers, flipping through the test results of Eloise's past three visits.

The nanites are functioning at full, so what's wrong?

She inhaled, held her breath for four seconds, then exhaled. Her eyes grew heavy.

The door to Joy's office creaked as it opened.

"What is it?" Joy asked. Her office had no window, but she knew the sun was up. She could smell it on Edmund, the guard standing just inside the room. He reeked of it.

"Ma'am. We lost another one."

Joy slammed her open palm on the desk, making the pencil cup rattle, and stood. "Damn those Sentinels!"

"What if we wait until she's off duty and isn't around the Sentinels anymore? We may not lose any more people that way."

"No," Joy said. "We need something else..."

"What about Liam?" Edmund suggested. "He lived in the Compound for about a year but left after he and Mason had a disagreement. He should know how to get past the Sentinels."

Excitement boiled in her stomach. "Get in contact with him and send him my way. Tell him to meet me here tomorrow and I will give him further instruction. In the meantime, I have an appointment."

"Ma'am." Edmund nodded.

CHAPTER SIX
BANNACK

Bannack had resigned himself to a solitary life years ago. He lost his home and entire family in the span of a few years, resorted to kidnapping people for Joy's human trials, and helped her delete the memories of the victim's families who came looking for them, all for the promise that Joy would take away the memories of his family. Bannack allowed Joy to manipulate him into horrible sins. When the time came to hold up her side of the bargain, she gaslighted him, challenging his memory of her promise, and denying she even agreed to wipe his memories.

After five years of being in her service, he left. She didn't seem to care. He devoted his time to finding his father's akrafena sword, his last connection to his family.

He thought back to Eloise as he walked, the newly recovered akrafena attached to his hip and Malikah's locket pressed to his chest. He'd returned to the items' burial site hours earlier and dug them out. Seeing Eloise's face with a scar through it jarred him. In fact, the entire experience had, including when she stood up to him. That hadn't happened for a long time.

I did the right thing by saying goodbye.

What he did, the sins he committed, no one would ever accept him. Better to be alone.

Bannack wandered for most of the day, unable to decide which direction to go. The sun danced through the horizon, painting the heavy cloud cover a brilliant red. Below, the still ocean was a mirror blushing up at the sky.

From the other end of a bridge, Bannack watched the bustle on Raft Island. He perched on a rock, admiring the beauty of the silence. His dark hands fiddled with a small pendant, a pansy engraved on the front, and his thumbprint molded into the back. He'd held onto it more times than he cared to admit, willing it to bring his sister back to him but no matter how he tried, screamed, and threw the damn thing, it always ended up back in his hand and never with his sister.

I miss you most of all.

The day she died in the shooting, along with their mom, haunted him. Sometimes he even dreamed about it. The memory of finding their bodies by the shattered glass front door holding each other, and how he had ignored his maame's warning not to go into the forest because he would get lost, tore into him like a bull goring into his stomach. True trauma came when he buried them. No ceremony. Just him, blinded by tears and pain, forced to listen to the dirt falling on their embraced forms. For seven years, he denied that he was all alone in the world. Anger became his constant companion.

Bannack's eyes drooped as he sat upon the rock, and he shook his head to wake himself up.

Shoving the medallion in his pocket, he stood, trying to remember where the road had been. He ripped plants from the ground, then ran his hand across the cracked asphalt underneath. He squinted. Everything was so different.

Bannack continued down the road and found an abandoned home, shrugged his pack off, and sunk into a seated position on the concrete porch. He rested his forearms on his knees.

People have always been afraid of me. Why would Eloise be any different?

His body shivered as a breeze touched the porch. "I need a fire."

Bannack pried some boards off the house and tossed them into a metal drum he found in the garage.

After an hour or two of attempting to light the wood, the fire finally crackled to life. Bannack piled on kindling. Once the fire grew to a good size, he scooted closer to the warmth and held his hands to the orange glow.

Shadows danced on the bay windows. Bannack threw a thick branch of madrone wood into the fire, sparks floating into the black sky.

As Bannack sat on the cold concrete, his feet resting on the step below him, his mind wandered to the past couple of days. Joy was coming for Eloise. He also knew getting her hands on Eloise was a matter of when, not if.

Sparks sprayed into the air when a log separated from its scorched brethren. Bannack stood, pacing back and forth on the deck with his mother's words, "We do not leave those we love behind," playing over and over in his head.

"There's no escaping you, is there Maame?"

The only answer came from the crackling fire. Crickets chirped in the night. As Bannack surveyed the neighborhood with overgrown hedges, grass, and the occasional flowering rose bush, he worked his jaw.

Eloise is going to be fine. She has the Compound to keep her safe.
We do not leave those we love behind.
Bannack scrubbed his scalp.
Joy's going to have to stop eventually.
She's strong. A fighter. She'll be ok—
We do not leave those we love behind.
Grass flattened under each stomping footstep. The wind whistled, rustling the tree branches and freezing his skin. Bannack growled.

It's fine. Worse comes to worst, she'll find a nice cave to hole up in.
We do not leave those we love behind.

"Fine!"

Nothing made sense anymore. Growling and muttering, Bannack stuffed his belongings into his pack, swung it over his shoulder so violently that the bag hit his side, aggravating his stitches. He cried out, then growled, moving more gingerly than before. The water he had collected in a five-gallon bucket from the nearby pond sizzled loudly, drowning the fire. Steam billowed upward.

He walked away from the neighborhood in angry silence. His lip ached as he gnawed on it. No one was with him to be the voice of reason, so he went straight to the only person he trusted enough to help him.

***

Kendal's tavern sat empty in the late evening. Inside, she cleaned off a table with a large rag, humming quietly. A bucket filled with murky water sat at her feet. Her locs, tied back with a leather string, bounced with the movement of her shoulders.

Bannack cleared his throat.

"Get out of my tavern and go work off your morning imbibing in the sun. Don't bring it 'round here." She then dropped a wet rag into the bucket of water and pulled a dry cloth from her belt.

Bannack cleared his throat again.

"God almighty!" Kendal turned, and her face changed from irritation to a wide smile. "Blue Eyes."

"Hello, Kendal."

"Where's your lady friend?"

"Eloise?" Bannack asked, and at Kendal's nod, he replied. "I came alone."

"Hmm. Well," she tossed a rag at his chest, "talk and work."

After several moments of silence, Bannack relayed every event after leaving. While he spoke, Kendal remained quiet, continuing to clean off tables, toss scraps onto the floor, and switch from her wet rag to her dry one, swapping a new cloth out every time she finished

63

with a table.

"You done?"

"Yes," Bannack lied and fidgeted. Kendal knew of his past, so the only thing he worried about was her disapproval.

"I've known you a long time, Blue Eyes, and I've learned two things." She wiped her hands dry with the last rag. Her eyes bored into him and he willed himself not to look away. "One, you are more honorable than you realize. And two, you shuffle your left foot when you lie."

Blood rushed from his face. Bannack sighed and sat in the closest chair. Kendal did the same, spinning it around to sit backward in it.

"Okay. Yes. I am staying away because of my past. I cannot allow Eloise to find out about it."

"And what are you worried about when she finds out?"

"She will reject me. I know it. It is always the same. I am welcomed and as soon as they learn of my sins, I am banished. Why should this time be any different?"

"Why should it not be different?"

He scrubbed his face. "Because I have never known things to change. Humans are the same."

"Oh, come now." Kendal blinked softly at him and smiled as if amused by his answer. "You know that's not true."

"My experiences have taught me the opposite."

Kendal placed her chin on the back of the chair. "And you believe Eloise will do the same?"

"I only suspect." Bannack stared at his hands. "I need to know what to do. The memory wipe is all I have ever wanted and now that I cannot have it, I am lost."

"And because of your past, you are afraid."

Hanging his head, tears stung his eyes. Bannack nodded.

Kendal stood. "I want to show you something."

"What is it?"

"Ever suspicious. If I reveal too much, it'll give away the surprise." Kendal crossed the room, grabbed a shawl, and smiled. "You know how much I love surprises."

They walked for about an hour and then came to a house with neglected flower beds and a gnarled tree with moss and lichen growing on the bark. Kendal knocked and a man appeared. His black eyes searched Bannack. They narrowed in recognition.

"He's not welcome."

"I understand, Boris," Kendal held up her hands in a placating gesture, "but he is unarmed and harmless."

"Tell that to my wife." Rising anger in Boris' body language made Bannack tense. He took a step back.

"Boris, please. I know how hard it is to let this man into your home, but he's returned to put things right."

"He ain't setting foot inside this house. He does," Boris took a menacing step forward, his eyes dark, "and I'll kill him."

Kendal searched the man's face then peered over his shoulder into the house. A quick, small smile tickled the corner of her mouth. Unable to keep his hands from shaking, Bannack shoved them into his pockets.

A rustle came from the stairs behind Boris, then a woman appeared at the landing. Her dress, shin length and with tight-fitting sleeves, flared outward starting at her waist and complemented her carefully curled hair. Upon seeing her, Bannack's blood ran cold. He knew her. The deaf woman who occasionally appeared in his dreams. She always stood in her garden, carefully tending to the vegetables.

He didn't know what was worse, seeing her in person or knowing he had destroyed her life.

Boris turned to the woman after he noticed Bannack's expression and signed. She shook her head, smiling warmly, and signed back. Boris made no effort to hide his frustration, using a wide, arching gesture as he signed, growling and huffing.

"His wife," Kendal whispered. "She's completely lucid, only she believes it's the Fifties."

Bannack's feet cemented to the porch when Boris turned back around, his wife staying on the stairs. She watched Bannack. His heart beat in his ears so loud he heard nothing except the steady whooshing and thrumming of pulsing blood.

"Kendal," Bannack whispered, unable to remove his gaze from the floor. "I can't be here."

She whispered, "You need to know people are capable of forgiveness."

Palms sweating, Bannack followed Kendal into the house. He recoiled when Tamra stepped close, his eyes flicking to the open door until Boris shut it. Bannack searched for any escape points as his muscles wound tight. Unyielding.

Boris sat opposite them on the tufted couch. His wife sat in the chair to his right, her back straight, ankles crossed, and hands relaxed in her lap.

"My wife has asked me to translate."

Before Boris translated, Bannack asked, "Why did you let us in?"

"Tamra, my wife," Boris grumbled as he glanced briefly at her, "has reminded me of my own past. She also wants to speak with you."

"Why with me?" Bannack couldn't move from where he sat perched on the edge of the couch like a bird on a fence, ready to take flight and escape at a moment's notice. He struggled to focus, as well, and if he looked at either Boris or Tamra for longer than a few moments, his ears would heat and the tremor in his hands would worsen.

Decorated to imitate a typical Fifties home, the house sported blush pink cabinets in the kitchen and floral printed drapes. A console television, set on thin wooden legs, faced the oval coffee table between the blue couch Kendal and Bannack sat on and the mustard yellow chairs Boris and Tamra occupied.

"Only she knows," Boris said and motioned to his wife. "I will translate. Nothing more."

Tamra gestured with her hands and fingers as she communicated through Boris. "Why did you visit?"

"Uh..." Bannack blinked at her. He hadn't expected her to lead with a question. "Kendal asked me to come."

"But why are you here?"

He didn't know why. Kendal brought him so he came, and he wasn't even sure why he joined her. What used to be a simple black and white answer in getting his memory wipe had now morphed into a vast abyss of a gray area he floundered in.

Bannack looked to Tamra. She calmly watched him, so he asked, "Do you know who I am?"

She nodded.

"Then why are you even talking to me?"

Tamra didn't skip a beat. "Everyone deserves a second chance. My Boris says you are here to heal things, and I'm willing to be the first to let you in."

Bannack jumped to his feet. "But I destroyed you."

"You are remorseful."

Her signed words made his mind tumble. A huge knot formed in his throat, pushing and throbbing with each swallow, and Bannack paced. The silence in the room was ear-shattering. *How can anyone give me a second chance?*

"You don't understand," Bannack said as he knelt down in front of her.

Boris surged to his feet, nostrils flaring, but Tamra flicked her hand at him and her husband slowly sat.

"You lost your memory because of me. Horrible things were done to you because of me. It's my fault and there's no way to get that back." He stared at the floor. "I want to apologize, but nothing I say will fix what I did."

Tamra tapped Bannack's shoulder. He looked up at her, eyes glistening. She signed, "Apologies are more than words. I can see your remorse in your body language and your face. Do something. Oppose her, deny her, fight her. Then people will see. Not everyone will accept you, but those who do are the important ones. Keep them close. They are precious." After a slight pause, Tamra continued. "I learned from Dr. Martin Luther King's speech several years ago that we should only be judged on who each person is as a person and looking at you now, I do not believe you are who you think."

Words creaked out of Bannack in barely a whisper. "You do not know me."

Tamra looked to Kendal. "If she is willing to bring you here, you must be a good person. Her presence is why I let you in."

A huge shuddering sigh left Bannack's body and his muscles deflated. No one had ever shown such benevolence to him before; he wasn't sure what to do with it. He sat in front of Tamra, his head in his hands, and shook. After several moments, a hand on Bannack's shoulder made him jump.

When he looked up, Kendal was standing above him. "You were willing to give up everything before and if you had gone through with your plans, you would have ended up lost. Do you still want to walk away? Tell me, Blue Eyes, whatcha gonna do about this?" Kendal placed her hand on Bannack's shoulder. "Few moments happen in a person's life that will define them. This is yours."

Bannack played his memories over and over in his mind. His childhood, when the bombs dropped on the United States, losing his family, saving Nora, wandering homeless, meeting Eloise.

I don't want to be lonely anymore.

He backed away, body shaking and his feet slow to move. Bannack stumbled toward the staircase. The grooves of the wooden planks on the wall bumped the back of Bannack's head as he slid to the floor, shivering and groaning.

This is so hard.

"You're still here?" Kendal asked.

Bannack looked up at her. "Yes." He put his forehead on his knees.

Kendal immediately began laughing. A ping of confused frustration stabbed at his belly as he scowled.

"Oh, don't get your feathers all ruffled. You need some tough love now and then. When you go to the Compound, you gotta make some changes if you want to be a respectable member of society. I love you and all, but you throw some epic pity parties."

"When I go back?"

"Well, yeah. That's the whole point of you sitting here, isn't it? And coming to me. You know what the right choice is but you're throwing..." Kendal let her words fall silent as she gestured at him, waiting for him to finish her sentence.

"A pity party," he grumbled.

"Exactly." Kendal smiled. "Obviously you have a good heart, or you would have done nothing when you met Eloise. You also care about people's opinion of you after finding out about your past, or you wouldn't have come to me. Eloise has been through hell too and I have a hunch she'll understand."

"How do you know?"

"The girl attacked you when you first met. She knows about Joy and the experiments. She has a scar that's connected with the nightmare she had in my plane. I can guarantee you she'll understand. And if she doesn't, my door's always open."

Bannack took a deep breath. He could count on Kendal to be the voice of reason, but his future terrified him. "Can I crash at your place till tomorrow?"

"Sure," Kendal said and stood, offering her hand.

"Hey, Kendal?"

She turned and Bannack smiled. "Medɔ wo. Thank you for being a good friend."

"Awe, shucks, Blue Eyes." Kendal waved him off with her hand. "Love ya, too. You're making me all teary-eyed."

Bannack laughed once. "You? Nah."

They thanked both Tamra and Boris for their hospitality, Boris only shaking Bannack's hand when Tamra encouraged him to, and walked back to the plane. Bannack spent the rest of the day helping out with Kendal's tavern by waiting tables, breaking up a near brawl or two, and keeping the customers entertained. In the evening, they shared a meal of bread, fruit, and salted meat. Then Bannack took a cot on the floor.

By the morning, he rolled up the bedroll, put it away, and penned a thank you note to Kendal.

He didn't know what would happen in the future, but he was willing to try.

CHAPTER SEVEN
ELOISE

Soora burst through Eloise's door, surprising her so much that she had to jump to her feet to avoid the knife she was sharpening slicing through her foot. Eloise turned to Soora, gave a frustrated huff, and picked up the knife.

"I'm sorry but it's important."

"You coulda knocked," Eloise said. She tucked the third throwing knife into her boot and slipped the kukri into its sheath on her thigh. "Sharp things cut."

"Save your mouth and come with me."

The edge to Soora's voice made Eloise's skin prickle. "What's going on?"

Soora turned around and mumbled, "Nothing good."

They walked to Mason's study, voices growing louder as they came closer, and when they came within earshot, Eloise's body froze.

"I want to see her now!"

Eloise's eyes rounded and she looked at Soora who jabbed at the door with her finger. Taking a deep breath, Eloise turned the doorknob.

"How'd you get through our lines?"

Joy stood in front of Mason's desk and spun at Eloise's question, dressed in clothing Eloise had never seen her in. A green jacket with a fur hood, long black leggings torn at the knees, and black hiking boots.

"I'm glad you finally decided to join us," Joy smiled.

Eloise eyed her, screaming inside, and walked to Mason. She leaned over his desk. "What's she doing here?"

"I let her through."

"You...what?" The last word increased the volume of Eloise's voice. She clenched her fists, chest heaving. "Why? We just talked—"

"I know..." he held up a hand. "I know we did. I know she's the enemy." Mason eyed Joy, then his eyes flicked back to Eloise. "She came alone. And before you start asking, yes, we surveyed the area before letting her through. Three klicks in all directions. There's no sign anyone came through or was waiting for us."

"Are you absolutely sure she's alone because someone like her," Eloise pointed at Joy, "doesn't just waltz in here like she owns the place!"

"And that'll be on me!" Mason stood, his fingers splayed out on top of his desk. "We have an agreement that prohibits her from doing anything to us. Now, please, listen to Joy so she can get the hell out of here."

Working her jaw, Eloise turned around and folded her arms. "Well?"

Joy, who had been sitting in a wingback chair with her knees crossed, undid them and stood as if she were the Queen. "Originally, I came to bring you back with me." The room tensed. Joy lowered her eyelids and scanned everyone, her mouth twitching at the corners. "I've come here with an entirely different purpose. Seth is dying, and he's asked me to allow that. I'm inclined to concede my plans to save his life."

"You...you what?" Eloise unfurled her arms and her mouth dropped open. She stared at Joy, and while she did, she saw something so strange, she thought it was a trick of the light. Tears. "Oh, my God. You're actually—"

"No," Joy held up a finger. "You misunderstand. I am inclined to concede, but I'm only backing off. You can have your little party here and the minute Seth takes a turn for the worse, I expect you back."

"So, nothing's changed." Eloise didn't know whether to laugh or cry. "You were going to bleed me dry! What makes you think I will ever go back with you?" Remembering Mason's off-hand comment, she spun around. "And you. What agreement do you have with her?"

Mason opened his mouth, but Joy beat him to it. "If I leave the Compounders alone, he will leave me alone."

"What about the people employed by you?"

Joy rotated her palms to the ceiling. "He let me keep them."

Appalled, Eloise turned to Mason, who said, "She'd already ensnared them, and I couldn't do anything about it, but she agreed to no more."

"How long ago was your agreement?"

"Eight years."

"Okay, so, I'm not going with you. I'll never go back there. Seth has asked me to stay away and I'm going to honor his choice."

"We can do the extractions here."

Once again, everyone in the room tensed.

"I think I understand now." Eloise's anger made her fingers tremor and she flexed them. "You're going to keep this a secret, prolonging the inevitable, to have your son alive? That's messed up on so many levels."

"I never alluded to it being a perfect plan." Joy's shoulders fell just enough for Eloise to see past the elegant façade. Then it faded. "But, considering the circumstances, it's all I have. Eloise," Joy took a few steps forward, "Seth has asked me to leave you alone for him. He's my son. You know I will do anything to make him happy. I can promise to leave you alone, coming here to do extractions so Seth doesn't know."

"No."

Joy blinked rapidly. "No?"

"If you truly love Seth," Eloise narrowed her eyes, "you'll leave me alone completely. No secret blood draws. No lying to that sweet, intelligent boy you are keeping locked up. He deserves better. I hate you so much, but I do believe you love Seth in your own misguided way. Prove to him you love him. Let him experience life. Focus on that and celebrate it. You owe him that."

Expressions of anger, frustration, and remorse flashed across Joy's face. She chewed on the inside of her lips, an audible huffing noise coming from her, then she narrowed her eyes at Eloise and extended her hand.

"Deal."

Eloise took it, gave a shake, and Joy left the room. Eloise, Mason, and Soora stood in silence, not knowing what to do with the strange exit, until Eloise inhaled. "She's not going to leave me alone."

"I agree with you." Mason watched Joy leave with an escort. "We've increased patrols in the area, so that should keep us, and her, busy. And even though we're spread thin as is, I'll order a small team to watch the facility. Any odd behavior will be reported directly to me."

"Let me be on the team. I know the Sentinels as well as you do. I can watch Joy. She'll never expect I'm right next door."

Mason paused for a moment, his hands by his mouth, and slowly nodded. "That's good. Yes. How many do you need?"

"Five. Seven at the most."

"Stay back, Eloise. I know you want to see Joy in your rearview mirror, but don't get carried away, and for God's sake, don't get cocky."

The expression 'see Joy in your rearview mirror' was so odd to Eloise, she spent more time trying to figure it out than she did processing the rest of Mason's sentence. It must've been some phrase from Before.

"Did you hear me?"

Eloise snapped back to the present. "Yes, sir. I mean, no."

"Don't get carried away. Don't get cocky. Do you understand?"

"I do." Eloise rubbed Soora's arm before she turned to Mason. "Is that all?"

"Yes. Make sure your team is assembled and ready to go soon. How long do you need?"

"Just a week."

"Good. Figure it out. Run anyone you aren't sure of by me. We'll be ready."

***

Eloise stood at the edge of a dark store isle, the shelves knocked down or completely bare. She held a candle and a bag of yogurt covered blueberries she snagged before an older lady could get to it, and spun in a circle, trying to find an escape from the nightmare she knew was coming.

"I can't be here."

Blood from her hands dripped onto the smooth concrete.

It wasn't hers.

Someone sat in the center of the isle, shrouded in darkness. Ada's voice croaked out of her, then hissed through the air, the rise and fall of volume chilling Eloise to the bone. "You failed him."

Ada sat in a pool of blood that leaked out of her body and all over her clothes. Her hand rested on the ground. As she lifted it to touch the bullet holes, tendrils of thick, red liquid hung in the air between the floor and her fingers.

As Eloise took slow steps forward, she whispered back to her little sister, "I'm doing what he wants me to do."

"You lie! You're just a liar. All the lies, lies, lies." Ada's yell shot cold into her bones. Her face contorted with rage. "Why all the lying, Eloise? All you do is lie. His death is going to be your fault!"

"I was coming to save him," Eloise said. She collapsed on the ground, the bag of yogurt covered blueberries breaking open and scattering across the floor into the blood, then she gasped for air, clutching her chest. "I was...But he...sent me a letter and—"

"Why didn't you try harder? I can never forgive you for what you did!"

Every word stung deep into her core and made her flinch. She kept her head down, tears creating thick, wet lines down her cheeks.

"You're not real. None of this is real. It's all a dream," Eloise

chanted quietly, trying to focus on her words rather than listen to the nightmare that took Ada's form. Her screams became otherworldly screeches and she stood, head rolling, hands gnarled, and shot through the air at Eloise.

"I hate you!"

She clutched her chest, screaming as Ada passed through her.

Someone lifted Eloise into their arms. Her mind had faded into black and she was alone, an invisible rope burning against her skin.

"Get the door."

Soora.

Eloise wanted to wake up, to cry out, but her shoulders ached, and her mind remained trapped.

Her body touched a bed.

She heard a strange mumbling, as if Soora were speaking to someone, but Eloise's ears were clogged as if underwater so all she heard were deep vibrations from a man's voice.

Soora spoke again, the only voice Eloise could hear clearly. "We'll keep a close eye on her. Eloise, I'll come check on you in an hour, okay?"

An animal nudged Eloise's hand as she laid on the bed. Vague recognition pinged while she scratched the naked animal.

This feels familiar. What is this? She struggled to get her brain to reboot back to the natural world. The darkness opened up to allow a piebald hairless cat into her view. Bali, the only thing she kept of her sister's.

The darkness began to lift as she rubbed the wrinkles on her cat's forehead. She remained in a dreamlike state; aware of water being poured into a large container but unable to distinguish where or why.

A long, warm hand touched her cheek.

Soora again.

Has it really been an hour?

"I've brought you some food and left it beside your bed. It won't spoil, so you can eat it whenever you're able." Eloise turned her head, blinked through the fog, and saw a plate of bread, cheese, salted meat, and huckleberries. "When you can, I've filled the basin with hot water, so it can wait, if you need it to. Take a bath and relax. I will check on you again soon."

The warmth left with the woman.

My head is on fire and my body hates me.

She stayed in a fetal position, blanket over her cold toes, for a long while. Bali curled up against her curved torso. The purring centered her and she was able to focus her eyes to look around the room.

Aside from the food, there were some clothes in a pile, a fraying rug on the floor, and her collection of knives hanging on their hooks against the wall. Tall windows on the north side of the living quarters opened up to a view of the lagoon below the hill. She hated those windows and kept them covered with a mismatched collection of fabric. They blocked out the world.

Sitting between her cot and the door was a large metal trough.

The bath.

Refraining from looking down at her body, Eloise reluctantly undressed. If she didn't look, she wouldn't be reminded of the pain. Embraced by the pressure of the water, Eloise closed her eyes. Muffled noises outside her room echoed distantly in her ears.

Although her body remained still, her brain whipped through every event from the night she met Bannack.

I should have known it was him. Why didn't I?

Flashes of the nightmare bashed into her skull. She shook her head, groaning.

Ada. I miss you so much.

She groaned again, the noise turning into a whimper as she attempted to banish the thoughts to the dark corners of her mind.

Not now. I can't think of this now.

She squeezed her eyes tighter. The invading thoughts rose like a plague ready to devour any victim in its path, and she couldn't stop them. They pushed and pushed, winning the battle in her mind.

"Stop it!" She cried out in a final effort to win over the memories and feelings. "I don't want you! I don't need you!"

But they came anyway. They were fierce, and she was not prepared.

You'll never heal from this. You'll be all alone. No one will ever understand you.

Eloise covered her ears, trying to drown out the ringing. Her head pounded. All her muscles tightened in defense of this villain coming to rob her and to make her a shell and laugh at what she had become; what her demons had turned her into.

They would laugh and jeer and make fun of her for the rest of her life.

"No," Eloise begged, pushing so hard on her ears that they ached. "Please. No. I don't want this. I don't want any of this!"

You're worthless. Ada's killers took everything away from you. Just look at yourself!

And Eloise looked. She looked hard at her body, tears fogging up her vision. Pale skin with too many dark freckles. Uneven fingernails and calloused knuckles. Her sideways knee that never healed straight. The scar on her face that pulled on the corner of her mouth, showing a sliver of teeth that looked like a chasm.

Her demons sneered, yellow eyes pulsating in the darkness of her mind. *How could anyone love you? They will take one look at those freckles, those hideous, disfiguring scars, and run. They will hate you!*

"They won't. I don't care what you think. I'm stronger than you!"

The demons laughed at her, filthy and dark, dripping with sticky oil. It clung to her body, turning the water into murky darkness, attempting to swallow her whole.

Do you think people will accept you?

"It wasn't my fault," Eloise gasped. She clawed at her hair, trying to dig the thoughts out. They needed to get out in any way possible.

If you hadn't brought her with you, she wouldn't have been murdered!

"Don't say that!"

Murder...Murder. Repeated over and over. Until her ears burned and her scalp stung. She sobbed, trapped in her mind, aching to break free of her eternal torment.

77

And then she retched over the edge of the basin.

Eloise slid out of the sanctuary of the bath, shaking so violently she had no control over herself.

Down she went, bile covering her torso. It stunk.

Worthless piece of nothing.

A heavy sob oozed from Eloise, rocking her body as it crawled out of her mouth.

You are nothing.

Just a shell.

You will never be happy.

Soora entered. She rushed to Eloise and knelt in front of her.

"I can't get up. My body hurts too much."

The doctor shushed Eloise and pulled her into her body. "Let me help you."

Eloise didn't have the mental energy to say no, so she allowed Soora to help her get her legs over the side of the basin.

As if cleaning a newborn, Soora wiped away the stink. She used soft and determined strokes, taking care around Eloise's face.

Eloise did her best to keep her sobs in, but they burst out from her. "I'm drowning, Soora. It's like my whole existence is a series of walls and locked doors and I'm trapped in the maze with the monsters."

"Healing isn't linear. We'll figure this out." Soora rubbed her thumb on Eloise's cheek, wiping a stain from her skin.

Handful after handful of water cascaded down onto Eloise's knees, her shoulders, face. With fluid movements, Soora pulled a stiff Eloise forward. She washed Eloise's hair, splitting apart the fibers to get any caked-on bile. Little by little, it floated away, migrating to the bottom of the tub.

The towel scrubbed off the water from Eloise's body. Soora helped her get dressed, matching Eloise's slow pace. Her limbs were heavy and had their own heartbeat.

Soora took Eloise's head in her hands. "So many people love you. Nothing you do will drive us away. I promise." Then she kissed her forehead.

"Thank you." Eloise's voice came out in a slow drawl, too

exhausted to open her eyes. She rested her head on the pillow and fell into a fitful sleep.

***

Someone knocked on Eloise's door and she rolled. Halfway through, Eloise stopped and hissed as pain shot through her body.

"What do you want?"

"God, you sound horrible," Sibyl said, voice muffled through the closed door. "Am I talking to my best friend, or the ogre she turns into at night?"

"Ha ha. Very funny." Eloise groaned. Her legs threatened to spasm. "Just...get in here."

Sibyl, subdued instead of her usual sunshine self, closed the door. It slammed shut, or at least sounded like it did, and Eloise covered her ears.

"Goddamn it, Leese, could you be louder?"

"Sorry," she grimaced. "Do you feel like you got stampeded or hit by a truck today?"

"Ugh. Not in the mood."

"Okay." Sibyl walked over to Eloise, her feet shuffling on the floor to avoid running into anything in the dim room. She sat down. "Repeat after me."

"Not this again."

"Yes, this again. You know it helps."

Glaring at Sibyl, Eloise finally relented. "Fine."

She smiled. "Repeat after me. I am worthy."

Eloise looked at her hands, unable to form the words, while Sibyl waited patiently. The first few phrases were always so hard. She forced her mouth to form them. "I...am...w...orthy."

"Good. Now, say, what happened doesn't define me."

"What happened...mmm...doesn't define...me."

"What happened was not my fault."

"What happen...ed was not my...fault."

"Getting better. Now. It's okay if all I did today was breathe."

"It's okay if all I did today was breathe." Tears came. She fell into Sibyl, crying softly. "Thank you for helping me."

Sibyl chuckled. "Of course. You're my girl."

"It's just," Eloise wiped at her face, "special."

"Ready for two more?" Sibyl asked, and when Eloise nodded, Sibyl said, "I am safe. I am strong."

"I am safe. I am strong."

I am safe.

I am strong.

Safe.

Strong.

***

Sitting in her room on the floor the next morning, Eloise spun the tip of her kukri in the floor. It had been a birthday gift the year before from Sibyl who had tracked down a cutler selling rare knives.

I miss Seth. Her hands shook, unable to spin the kukri blade, and she let it clatter to the ground. She buried her face in her knees. Closing her eyes, images of Joy looming over her flashed in her head. Eloise jumped to her feet, slammed the tip of the kukri blade into the ground where it stayed standing as she flopped in a frustrated heap on her cot.

Her cat, Bali, had returned from her several days hunting trip and was now happily stalking a black speck. Eloise lifted her head to watch. The hairless cat crouched on the cot, chirping at the large fly circling in front of the windows.

The bug landed low on the glass.

Bali jumped from the cot and shot across the room. But the fly had already taken off.

Her eyes wide, she turned to Eloise.

"What?" A laugh rippled from her throat when Bali hopped onto the bed.

Bali mewed and circled her tail around her rump. Her head darted back and forth watching the bug fly through the air, then the cat kneaded the patchwork blanket, crouched low, her shoulder blades shifting. In an explosion of muscles, Bali leapt into the air and swiped. Her soft landing quickly turned into a low, zig-zagging scramble across the floor.

Eloise jumped to her feet. "You got it!"

With triumph in her bouncing gait, Bali sauntered to Eloise, jumped on the cot, and deposited a black fly the size of a pea in her palm.

Beaming, Eloise lifted her cat into the air. "Bali! The terrifying sky raisin killer. May we all live safe with you on the job."

"You're such a liar."

Eloise jumped, her arms wrapping around Bali in a protective shield. She hadn't heard the door open. An illusion of a man standing in the doorway with a loaded gun flashed in her head. She blinked and realized her best friend stood there instead, but she couldn't stop from scratching her wrist.

"Don't scare me like that, Sibyl!"

Her friend smiled, the deep dimple in her cheek showing off. Sibyl pushed off the doorjamb with her shoulder and made herself comfortable on the cot. She brought her knees up to her chest and tossed a lock of Eloise's red hair behind her shoulder.

"How am I a liar?" Eloise folded her arms.

"You told me you don't like animals."

Eloise scoffed. "Sometimes you have such selective hearing. I said I don't like horses."

"Or cows or bears or rabbits or—" Sibyl lifted one finger with each animal she listed.

"First of all, they stink. Second of all, Bali has no fur to make her smell."

"Well, you stink, too."

Eloise covered her armpits with her hands.

Sibyl's laugh coated the air in honey. "Come on."

"Where are we going?"

"Oh. Don't be such a Nervous Nelly." Sibyl pulled Eloise to her feet. "Live a little! Come have some fun."

"I dunno. I like being in here."

She blew a raspberry. "No more talking."

Dragged against her will but enjoying Sibyl's bright presence, Eloise soon found herself on a concrete patio. The sun glistened off the rain-soaked grass and Compounders loitered about in a large group. Children without shoes darted around and wound through their parents' legs and other bystanders and splashed in the puddles.

"I'm not doing this."

"You're no fun." Sibyl turned to a little boy nearby. "My friend is no fun. She doesn't know how to play."

His eyes widened. "You don't know how to play?"

"I do too!"

"Prove it." Sibyl put her hands on her hips.

The boy parroted her. "Yeah. Prove it."

Groaning quietly, Eloise walked down the steps and stood on the perimeter of the group of kids. Sibyl laughed as she held hands with a little girl who splashed in the water.

"What do I have to do to get you to play with us?" Sibyl twirled in a tight circle, her ballet background surfacing.

Eloise gasped as cold, brown water splashed onto her. A little boy scurried behind Sibyl, water dripping from his fingertips. She wanted to yell at him and stomp off. But his liquid surprise had shocked the hesitation out of her.

"I'm going to get you!" Eloise bent low, cupping the water in her hands.

For a split second, the children froze, then they scattered as Eloise ran at them. She mock-growled and chased the screaming kids, tossing brown water at them. Children scattered and squealed as Eloise and Sibyl chased the tiny humans.

Eloise laughed and shoved Sibyl.

With a squelch, she landed in a puddle. The brown water covered her gray sweater and black hair. For a moment, she stared in shock.

Unable to hold it in, Eloise and the children erupted into laughter. She lost control of her legs and fell to her back, the wet blades of sparse grass stroking her cheek. Laughter had not happened in a long time. She had been so preoccupied with her struggles; she never took the time to enjoy life around her.

As Sibyl stood, they locked eyes.

Thank you. Eloise mouthed and Sibyl nodded, two little ones wrapped around her ankles.

Laughing, Eloise took off after a kid who had slapped a muddy hand on her thigh. For many blissful moments, she forgot about her demons and monsters. She could push back the walls and reveal the carefree person she used to be Before.

Sibyl joined her as she stopped to lean against a tree trunk. She tapped Eloise's arm with the back of her hand, pointed, and said, "Look who it is."

Percie, her curly hair in a beautiful mess around her face, walked past carrying a basket of folded laundry. They made eye contact, Eloise's heart jumping at her striking blue eyes, and Percie gave a shy wave. Eloise continued waving awkwardly once Percie rounded a corner.

"Oh, shut up." Eloise poked her tongue out at Sibyl. She allowed a family of five to walk in front of her. "You are the epitome of a walking cliché. Please go away and stop being my personal parasite."

"Ha! Oh, no you don't. You're stuck with me." Sibyl crossed her arms. "But seriously, you guys were so cute together."

"Yeah. We were. But that was...what...a year ago. She's married now and happy."

"Still, I totally shipped you guys."

To keep her mind off Percie and their time together, Eloise changed the subject. "You came back early from trading with the Rhondian clan. How was it?"

Giving Eloise a sideways glance, Sibyl sighed and said, "Uneventful. We got some good stuff from the clans while we were there. Luke made it bearable though."

Luke Varma, the witty yet coarse heir to the Rhondian clan, kept people at arm's length. Eloise had met him a few times and Sibyl enjoyed messing with him.

"When do you plan on going easy on him?"

"Uh..." Sibyl scoffed. "Never. I can't help but tease him when he gets grumpy. Of course, if my teasing really upset him, I'd stop, but he tries so hard to keep a smile hidden. It's adorable."

Eloise laughed and slipped her arm around Sibyl's, leaning her head against her forearm because Sibyl was too tall for Eloise to reach her shoulder.

Mason walked out of the Compound, glanced around, waved at Eloise, and ran over.

"Been looking for you. I have a class to teach soon, so I can't stay long. You have a visitor."

"I do?" Eloise rarely received visitors. The only people she knew outside of the Compound were Joy, Seth, Smith, Kendal, and...

Bannack stood outside of Eloise's home, which was a one thousand square foot school classroom converted into a studio apartment. Before he noticed her, she watched him as he bounced on the balls of his feet, swinging his arms as he waited. He fiddled with a package wrapped in fabric.

She approached, then leaned in. "Can't resist me, can you?"

The package almost fell to the ground as Bannack fumbled with it in surprise. Eloise realized his bad ear had been facing her, which was why he didn't notice her approaching. It didn't stop her from chuckling.

"Oh...I came to bring you something."

Eloise pointed curiously at the item in Bannack's hand.

He nodded. "It's for you."

She suppressed a chuckle and opened the door to her apartment. "Make yourself at home. Do you want something to drink?" She turned around. Bannack had removed his shoes and was scratching Bali underneath her chin. He smiled, the corner of his eyes crinkling, and Eloise's stomach tingled. "She likes you."

"Yeah?" Bannack looked up. "I remember her. She was Ada's, right?"

"She was." Eloise watched Bali rub her bare face on Bannack and smiled. "Ada had a thing for Indonesia. She loved the temples and the green."

Bannack nodded his head and clicked his tongue, then returned to loving on Bali. The cat pushed against Bannack's hand then looked at Eloise with her bright green eyes, paused, and continued to accept pets.

84

"Traitor."

"Here," Bannack handed Eloise the wrapped package before he scooped Bali up and began whispering to her. The scene was comical. A huge, six-foot-two man flirting with a bald cat. He looked up at Eloise through his eyelashes, smiled, and said, "Happy twenty-first."

Eloise had to remember to shut her mouth. She stared at the present, suddenly unable to open it, and blinked.

How did he remember?

"Why?" She asked.

"Why not?"

"Well, because..." She looked at Bannack, her mind still fumbling over itself trying to understand. To have someone she hadn't seen for a decade remember her birthday made her heart flutter.

Eloise opened the gift to reveal a beautifully carved statuette, a little bigger than her hand, of Ada as a child holding kitten Bali in her arms. Eloise's eyes misted. She had no pictures of Ada, no journal entries, nothing to fuel her mental memory of her sister, and Bannack had captured her essence perfectly. Mischievous eyes stared at Eloise, her signature half grin, bone straight hair, and turned in toes completing the look.

"Oh my God..." A mixture of emotions stung her nose. Love for Ada, gratitude for the precious gift, sadness she could never touch her sister again. Eloise sank into her chair, sniffling and rubbing the tears from her eyes. "Thank you. It's so special. You made this?"

Bannack nodded. "I do a lot of carving. Keeps me sane."

"Well, I love it."

"You're welcome."

She looked at Bannack, aware of a growing warmth in her body, and she cleared her throat. "Do you want a tour of the Compound? I'm not sure how long you plan on visiting, but since you're here..."

He smiled, a small one, but it still made her heart skip.

What is it with that smile of his?

CHAPTER EIGHT
BANNACK

Eloise and Bannack walked past schoolrooms converted into living quarters years ago, unlit torches secured to the walls, and several areas with farming tools. He moved for a group of people to pass, all carrying wicker baskets stocked with various produce and items.

"What are they doing?" He jogged forward. For someone so small, she sure had a brisk walking speed. If he didn't pay attention, she probably would leave him stranded.

"They're carrying wheat kernels to be ground up to make bread and other things. We keep the grain stored in barrels in the kitchens when the wheat can't be harvested. It sucks having to knead for hours, but we all pitch in somehow."

"No wonder your arms are so buff."

Eloise stared sideways at him and her eyes sparkled with mirth. "Remind me to challenge you to an arm-wrestling contest later."

The unmistakable scent of fresh bread wafted from a large common room area with many people gathered around pots of pounding tools. Others pushed rhythmically into containers, their hands covered in sticky, brown dough. They laughed and conversed with one another, pausing to take water from people walking through the crowd. Bannack took a long drink from the boy who offered him some.

He took a moment to glance around the hallway. Remnants of the old high school were apparent in the bathroom sign still on the wall, a peeling pop art mural of a woman crying, and a hallway with many classrooms. In all of his travels, he had never been in a place that felt so comfortable. Everyone worked together like machinery, laughing, talking, and living life in sync. He heard children laugh far away somewhere and it warmed his heart.

Damn. It's gonna be hard to leave.

But he had to. He didn't belong anywhere.

"I've never been so hungry for bread in my entire life," Bannack said and inhaled deeply, his nose filling with the robust scent. It reminded him of home.

Eloise laughed. "Come on. I want to introduce you to Soora. She should be this way."

They continued down the hallway. On one side, the wall fell away to reveal a floor to ceiling window. Green wheat filled a large part of the courtyard and many people, young and old, worked in the stalks, bending over, cutting, binding, and stacking the tares. Other areas teemed with vegetables he hadn't seen since Before. Beets, spinach, carrots, brussels sprouts, and various fruit trees made the entire scene look like something out of a fairy tale. They were farmers and their way of living modest, but to Bannack they lived like kings.

Dumfounded, he turned to Eloise. "Where did you find the seeds?"

"The clans," she said as she smiled. "There are five of them and every few months, their scouts return with tons of stuff from places as far south as California. They bring not only seeds and medicines, but weapons and livestock too. Sibyl takes a group of ten people with her when the scouts return to trade what we've grown for more supplies we may need. It's how I got my knives, too."

She surprised him more and more.

She lives in paradise. Second, she owns knives? How many knives? Does she mean food prep knives or actual kill-you-swiftly knives?

"Does everyone know how to fight here?"

They stood in the center of a sunbeam coming through a tall window. Behind Eloise waited a series of broad stairs, in two groups of three, leading down to a platform with doors on both sides, one leading outside and the other into another room. A man carrying a crate of chicks over his shoulder passed by Eloise and Bannack. The birds peeped nervously.

"Goodness, no," she chuckled. "It's me and about a hundred other people called Sentinels, split into different groups. Someone has to protect this place. We don't need much more because not many people visit looking for trouble. Either that or," a roguish grin spread across Eloise's face, "they're terrified of us."

Eloise bounced down the steps and through a set of open doors. Bannack followed. The room inside was dim, lit by torches and lanterns on tables. To call it a room was an understatement. It was a theater, Bannack realized as his eyes adjusted, with two sections of seats and a large aisle between them. The stage at the front was painted black and the heavy, frayed, velvet curtains were pulled back. The entire place must have been magnificent when in use.

Eloise embraced a woman with a shaved head and sunflower tattoo on her scalp who had been speaking with someone, perhaps an assistant by the looks of the bandages they carried in their arms. The woman smiled and whispered something, concern furrowing her eyebrows. After Eloise responded, the woman nodded, then hugged her again.

"Bannack," Eloise said as she gestured for Bannack to approach. "This is Soora. She's the head doctor and my adoptive mom." Eloise gestured to Bannack. "This is Bannack Owusu. He's staying for a visit."

With Eloise's arm around her waist, Soora extended her hand toward Bannack. "Welcome to the Compound," she said. "I hope you find our community welcoming."

"Thank you, ma'am. I do. It is quite impressive."

Soora smiled. "I appreciate that. We've worked tirelessly these seven years to build a sustainable, safe place for all. How long will you be staying?"

He looked at Eloise then back to Soora, temptation pulling at him. "Not long."

"Well, stay as long as you need. It's good to meet you, Bannack Owusu."

Soora turned and exited the stage, two people trailing her.

"Come on. We need to find Mason."

So many people. He wasn't used to meeting the amount of people Eloise was introducing him to. He felt a bit like a trick pony being carted around to show off and it made him shiver.

"Hey, Eloise?" Bannack asked as she held the door open for him. "Is this going to take long? I have to get back."

"Not long."

Their walk brought them clear across the campus to what Bannack recognized as a football field settled inside a track. The rusted home team bleachers remained intact as people clustered together, sifting through shallow woven baskets, organizing produce, and tossing unwanted plant byproducts. Many other people picked through tall vegetable plants, piling bunches of produce into shallow baskets.

"This is incredible," Bannack said as he took in the well-organized operation.

Smiling, Eloise nudged Bannack's ribs. "Mason's doing. He's turned this whole place into a bit of a farm. Look."

Bannack followed where Eloise pointed and saw a small pasture on the second half of the football field where four horses grazed amidst a flock of chickens. A red necked rooster with long green tail feathers strutted about his ladies, clucking proudly. Three cages on stilts sat against the right side of the pasture and housed rabbits. A little boy in a plaid red jacket held the top of one cage open, feeding vegetable scraps to a grey bunny that looked almost as heavy as him.

"This is incredible."

"You said that already."

Bannack chuckled. "It deserves being repeated."

Tucked away near the forest line close to the horses, was a small group of people lined up. Eloise jogged toward them and Bannack followed, a stocky man with his hands clasped behind his back coming into view.

The stocky man turned at Eloise's call, then smiled.

"Bannack Owusu," Eloise said as Bannack joined them. "Bannack, this is Mason. Head of the Compound."

"Sir." Bannack shook Mason's hand then gave a short nod.

"So, you're the one who helped Eloise." Mason watched Bannack. "Thank you."

Trying to figure out if Mason was suspicious of him or just a gruff man-made Bannack's head ache. His chest had been growing heavier ever since meeting Soora. Now it was turning a bit painful.

"You're welcome, sir."

Without another word, Mason turned back to his class, and Bannack looked at Eloise. He asked, "Did I do something wrong?"

She chuckled. "No. Mason's shy around new people. He'll warm up to you."

"Now," Mason's voice rose above the chatter of the group he was teaching, "who can tell me the quickest way to dispatch or subdue an attacker?"

Intrigued, Bannack watched the group fumble through wrong answers. Some mentioned going for the knees, others the eyes, but Mason shook his head.

"These are super green trainees," Eloise explained. "They're a month into their training and will be added to our Sentinel roster in a couple years. Especially now since Joy's become a problem."

His attention adjusted completely on her. "What is going on?"

Eloise relayed Joy's visit and the details about Mason and Joy's agreement. "We're doing our best to watch her facility and any activity, and nothing's happening yet, but once Seth gets closer to dying, I think we're going to have a big problem."

"I ask again," Mason's voice boomed into the air, "what is the quickest way to dispatch an attacker?"

"Go for the jaw," one trainee called out.

"Okay. And how do you get close enough?"

The trainee grew quiet, thinking. "My dad just goes for it."

Bannack looked at the kid. He stood with his legs shoulder width apart and his chin tilted. Mason stood in front of him, an eyebrow raised.

"You are aware," Mason said, "'just going for it' isn't an appropriate response."

"It's worked pretty well for him, so why not?"

Mason scoffed. "Your dad is a mixed-martial arts master who I've personally fought. I can assure you, he doesn't 'just go for it,' Emille."

The kid, Emille, blinked at Mason, which made Bannack smile. His interest piqued with the turnout of their conversation, and judging by Mason's reactions and body language, Emille was about to be proven wrong on many accounts.

"Sir, with all due respect," Emille walked to the front of the class, "I can go for the jaw or the knees with no problem."

"Really?" Bannack spoke up and everyone looked at him. He closed his mouth, unsure of the attention on him but continued talking despite his concern. "You speak with the confidence of someone highly trained. Are you sure you can subdue an assailant by focusing on the jaw only?"

"I know I can. My dad taught me everything I know." Emille crossed his arms.

"Which is why you are here. In a fighting class." Bannack raised his eyebrow and for the first time, he saw Emille falter in his assurance. He smiled. A flurry of excitement went through his torso. He looked at Mason. "May I?" And Mason nodded. Bannack turned to Emille. "One way to stop an attacker is to use your shoulder and hips to pin them. Attacking without strategy is for amateurs."

Emille blustered at the word 'amateur,' exactly as he expected, then stomped toward Bannack, hands out.

Bannack slapped Emille's wrists out of the way. The boy used his head. Bannack jerked his elbow into Emille's face, grabbed his shoulder, and lifted his arm. Three punches to his ribcage. Emille's grunts fueled a fire Bannack didn't want lit, so he shifted his hips, tripped the kid, and pinned his arm. Bannack held Emille down.

He whispered. "Listen, you don't want to get into close range if you cannot end the fight. I could have easily decorated your face. You did not even touch me while I put you on the ground. Mason is your teacher. Heed his words."

Emille, eyes wide and body frozen, nodded.

"Impressive," Mason said when Bannack joined him and Eloise.

"I'm so glad that wasn't me." Eloise chuckled and eyed Emille as he nursed his ego. "I would've landed at least a few hits on you."

Bannack chuckled. "Sure."

She smiled sideways at him.

"Ever consider joining the Sentinels?" Mason asked Bannack.

Bannack took a half-step back. "Oh...uh...I am not sure if I would fit well."

He didn't even know if he could handle being a Sentinel. If the fight with Emille moments ago made him struggle with going too far, he worried if he'd be able to resist when in a real-life situation.

"I watched you take down Emille in seconds," Mason said. "We could use more people with your skill set."

"I mean no offense, sir, but you know nothing of me or my background."

"That's a valid point," Eloise chimed in.

Mason gave her a sideways stare. "You're correct. I know nothing of you. However, our Compound is open to all and although we've had issues in the past, I am willing to trust you until you prove me wrong."

What is going on with people this week? First Tamra and now Mason. I don't understand this kindness.

"Thank you, sir."

I almost didn't come here at all.

He so desperately wanted to belong. It drove him mad.

"I could stay for a little while. Do you have room?"

Mason's smile widened. "We do. Follow me."

Eloise ran to catch up. "Does this mean you're staying?"

"Most likely."

"I thought you wanted to travel. Do the lone wolf thing."

"I did but since the plan to wipe my memories did not work, I need a backup." Although this was the reason he gave Eloise—and he hoped it was enough for her to stop questioning him further—it wasn't the whole truth. Honestly, being alone had taken its toll. He was lonely, and he hoped—wished beyond belief— that being in the

Compound would ease his misery.

Eloise crossed her arms. "Are you going to keep rubbing that in?"

Leaning closer, Bannack forced his face to be neutral and shrugged. "Only until you apologize."

"Excuse me! It wasn't my choice for you to hel—" Her face scrunched up. "Oh. You're kidding. Jerk."

Bannack chuckled and held the door open for Eloise. "Still just as dense as when we were kids, I see."

"You know what. You can take your pie hole and shut it."

Bannack's laugh echoed through the hallway.

"Here we are." Mason gestured to a room on the first floor.

Bannack walked in. A row of tall windows, one boarded up, sat on the far end of the room. To his right was a pile as high as the ceiling of old, rusted desks with attached chairs, and through them he could see the white of the board. A teacher had once written on it. The only furniture in the room was a loud, creaky bed frame with a mattress, and Bannack sat on it, scanning the side of the room with the door. Graffiti was on the wall and he smiled at the mural of a person in a gas mask.

"We can add more furniture if you'd like," Mason said. "And I'll have someone come in to remove the desks."

"No. I can do that." Bannack rubbed his hand on the mattress. "It's been years since I've had one of these."

"What?" Eloise asked and chuckled. "A room?"

"No," Bannack looked at her. "A bed."

CHAPTER NINE
JOY

Salt spray from the ocean hung in the air as Joy pushed Seth's powerchair along the boardwalk. He could maneuver around on his own, even though it was a struggle some days, but on their daily walks, he liked to lounge back with the sun on his body while his mom showed him around. She tried to enjoy it, the sound of the waves, and the seagulls crying above. It didn't work. It hadn't in a while.

A ping of anger pricked at her eyes. She was angry Seth had asked her to leave Eloise alone, angry her only child was slowly being ripped away from her, and angry she could stop it but that he didn't want her to.

I wish you could understand.

But she pushed herself to enjoy time spent with Seth, even if she had to fake it. She could cry later.

"Mama? Can you bring me...one of those?"

They had stopped at the end of the dock, the waves licking the edge, and she looked down at the rocky beach. On top of the small section of sand was a white sand dollar. She removed her shoes and stepped down. The sand scratched the bottom of her feet as she navigated across the rocks to the treasure. She picked it up. Half fell off into the water.

"It's broken."

"That's...okay. I still like it."

She handed it back to him, smiling. Seth looked at her, large eyes underneath a mass of curly hair. They squinted when he smiled. He lifted his head, scanned the area, then pointed to his right, adjusting the picnic basket on his lap.

"There," he said. "Perfect spot."

Joy lifted her baby boy into her arms. He could walk, clumsily, but in the past week the action took too much out of him so he mostly sat in the chair. Walking the rocky beach was too much of a fall hazard. She sat him down on a log and ruffled his hair.

"Stop," Seth laughed, his grey eyes crinkling again and his mouth opened in a wide smile, batting her hand away. "You're messing...it up."

"Sorry." She smiled and laid out the blanket. "I forgot."

She glanced to his chair, adapted by him to operate via a smaller solar panel, and smiled as she remembered the day she walked in on him tinkering with it. He'd looked up, squinted, his hands greasy, and announced he'd figured out how to attach a scavenged lithium-ion battery to the solar panel to allow for faster speed. To beat Edmund in a race against his old manual chair, he'd said. The memory made her smile.

"It's okay, Mama. I...know you're getting...old."

She laughed as she took the sandwiches he handed her, brought back to earth by his words. "Old? You think I'm old?"

Seth nodded with a sideways smile.

Together, they ate their lunch in silence. Joy thought spending time with Seth would naturally make talking to him easier, but it didn't.

"What do you want to do after this?" she asked.

Seth looked up at the sky. "I think...I'd like to...go home. I'm getting...tired."

"Oh. Sure," Joy croaked.

When they finished eating and packed up, Joy turned the powerchair around and pushed it toward the facility on a bumpy sidewalk. Grass peaked between the cracks. *It's almost time to clean this up again.* She needed the walk clean so she and Seth could use it.

Seth's breathing caught her attention. He was getting worse. A few days ago, he'd stopped eating as much as he used to.

"Mama," Seth took a deep breath. "Don't be...mad at...Eloise. Please. She's only...doing what I...asked."

"I know, baby. It's hard to see you like this."

He reached up and squeezed her hand. The bones and knuckles were prominent and Joy bit back tears. "I'm...okay...with it. Are...you?"

Joy lifted her face to the sky, tears tracing lines down her cheeks. *My sweet, sweet boy. You are a better person than I could ever be.*

Part of her wanted desperately to stop the madness and just be his mom for what little time he had left. But, if she did, she couldn't say she tried everything. Her job, as his mom, was to protect and watch over him.

She couldn't give up.

I can do this.

CHAPTER TEN
BANNACK

His eye had healed just enough to see out of. The fight training he received would be their downfall, and all Bannack had to do was wait like a jaguar in a tree, calculating his attack from above on an unsuspecting impala.

The keys jingled on the other side of the door.

Icy fear flashed through Bannack before he brought his shoulders square and waited.

The fear dissipated and left a deep, bubbling hatred.

Bannack waited for his torturer to enter.

The door opened and Bannack slammed into the man. He cried out in surprise. They crashed into the door. The man clawed at Bannack's hands around his throat.

He squeezed, fueled by a volcanic eruption of rage. His vision blurred at the edges.

Bannack gritted his teeth. He squeezed harder, watching the man's eyes bug out of his head.

A shock of a knee to the gut made Bannack stagger backward. Bruises wrapped around the man's neck. He charged with the stun baton.

Bannack was ready.

One ill-timed swipe was easy to dodge. He caught the stun baton mid-air and wrenched it from the man's hands, then stabbed the tongs into the man's jugular.

He writhed on the floor.

No longer would he suffer at the hands of this horrid human being.

The cries of agony fell on deaf ears.

Eventually, the man lay still.

"No more," Bannack hissed, dropping the baton on the ground. He knelt beside the corpse and whispered into his ear. "I...will not...yield."

Two sharp bangs shocked Bannack out of bed, his arms and legs wildly flailing as he crashed to the floor, the blanket tangling with his limbs. His heart pounded, voracious in its feast of blood.

Unfortunately, the act of sleeping in a bed proved difficult and was most likely a mixture of too many years on the rocky ground and nightmares. He managed them well, or so he thought, by giving as little time between sleep and sunrise as he could, choosing to travel until he dropped out of exhaustion. He tired of living afraid of his own dreams, and so he returned home to find a place to settle down. The first night home and he stumbled straight into Eloise at the lab.

His hand clenched against his chest, Bannack called out. "Who—" Bannack cleared his throat of the shrill pitch, "Who is it?"

"It's me. Eloise. You know, if you want to stay here permanently, you're gonna have to pitch in."

Bannack pulled on the door. Eloise stood before him, her ponytail stuck through the back of an old Seattle Seahawks cap, a thick strand of hair covering up her scar. Golden eyes peered up at him. She wore a yellow tee with the front tucked into the high waist of distressed shorts. Brown streaks of dirt stuck to her cheeks and sweat made the tiny hairs at the nape of her neck stick out at odd angles.

He pulled up short, staring down at the unexpected view. This was a different Eloise than before, and she made his knees weaken for a moment.

Eloise smiled. "Good morning, sleepyhead."

"Morning," Bannack replied, struggling to talk with his heavy tongue. "Thanks for the bed."

Eloise peered past him. "Was the floor more comfy?"

"What?" He turned and saw the pile of blankets on the floor. "Oh. No. I mean, sometimes it is. But the bed was real nice."

"Well, put a shirt on and follow me," Eloise said, flicking her hair off her shoulder. "Today's harvesting day and we need all the manpower we can get."

"Give me a second."

Bannack yanked a shirt over his head and followed Eloise down the hallway, a karambit handle poking out from behind her back. The knife, held in the palm of the hand with an index finger threaded through a ring on the end of the handle, resembled a Velociraptor's claw.

How many other knives does she own?

"What are we harvesting?" he asked.

"Peas, broccoli, brussels sprouts—which are way better than I remember as a kid—potatoes, onions, and some swiss chard. Keep up."

Bannack jogged after her as he struggled to put on his shoes while moving. He didn't even try tying them and left the laces to drag. More than once, Bannack knocked into people passing on the opposite end of the hallway, apologizing several times. His cheeks were still warm when he caught up to Eloise.

"You do not waste time."

Eloise blinked up at him as if his question was strange. "Places to go, things to see. Come on. I'm going to introduce you to Sibyl." She bounced down the two flights of stairs, letting a mother with her three children pass them on the landing. The boy waved at Eloise and she ruffled his hair. Eloise walked toward a group of workers slicing at the bottom of swiss chard stalks but paused abruptly. "Just to warn you, she can be a bit much."

Confused, Bannack followed Eloise to a woman with long black hair in an intricate braid hanging so far over her shoulder, the end tapped her elbow as she worked.

"I'd be careful with that blade," Eloise said. "You might slice the end of your hair off."

The woman, who Bannack assumed was Sibyl, stood and chuckled. The sound was bright and refreshing.

"I am careful, thank you very much."

Sibyl was fairly tall, almost head height with Bannack's six-foot-two frame, and had warm, dark brown eyes. When she smiled, deep dimples appeared. Her eyes drifted to Bannack, and she paused.

"Who's the hunk?" Sibyl leaned close to Eloise, half-whispering.

"Sibyl." Eloise shoved her friend. She turned an apologetic eye to Bannack. "I told you she can be a bit much. She's special."

"Excuse me!"

Bannack chuckled. "Bannack Owusu." He thrust his hand forward, and she took it gracefully.

"Where'd you find him? He's got an excellent grip."

Bannack couldn't help but laugh out loud as Eloise groaned and ran her hand down her face, pulling at her chin. "Seriously, Syb? You're impossible."

"Only on Fridays." Sibyl winked at Bannack and whispered, "She hates it when I embarrass her. Between you and me...I can't help myself. It's too much fun."

Oh, he liked her. A lot.

"Now!" Sibyl clapped him on his shoulder. "Let's get you a job. Do you want to husk the peas or pick the brussels sprouts?"

After an entire afternoon of picking, shucking, and cleaning the produce that would be food for the Compounders, everyone gathered to eat lunch. The cool breeze laced with the humid scent of impending fall blew through the grass as groups of workers settled into their food. Bannack watched, wide eyed, as people scooped steaming, thick potato stew, colored with peas, carrots, and either chicken or rabbit meat. They grabbed some flatbread and settled down in groups, mingling quietly as they used ripped pieces of their bread as a utensil.

"Here."

Bannack accepted a wooden bowl from Eloise. She ladled a serving of the soup, the heavy sloshing driving Bannack mad with desire. As far back as he could remember, he had been living on a steady diet of game, edible weeds, and berries. The quaint lunch with the Compounders was nothing short of a luxury.

"It seems like you're impressed with our Compound," Sibyl said from behind Bannack as she tossed bread and stew into her mouth.

"I am," Bannack replied. "This is something I never dreamed again possible."

Sibyl laughed once. "It's pretty sweet." She took a bite of her food. "I gotta say—and let me know if I'm being nosy—but your eyes are crazy blue."

"Yeah. My mom had a half blue eye, too. It is called Waardenburg Syndrome and affects our hearing, eyes, and skin. I don't have the white in the front of my hair like she did but I'm completely deaf in one ear."

Sibyl's eyes widened. "Woah."

"I can read lips really well. Maame taught me how."

Bannack looked over and watched Eloise laugh with a teenaged boy holding a bucket of water, took a sip from the ladle, and inclined her head to the clouds and sighed.

What would it be like to feel that again? I don't even know how to—

"Hey, Leese!" Sibyl called out and Bannack jumped.

Eloise sat at the foot of a large oak, using her bread to scoop out a mouthful of food. When Sibyl called out, she glanced up, waved, and a thin line of stew dripped down her chin.

Bannack smiled. He remembered her propensity for being h while eating and how one summer, at the neighborhood barbeque, she dripped hot dog condiments and an ice cream cone on her clothes.

"So, how do you know Eloise?"

"We are old childhood friends," Bannack said while walking to the oak. "Our houses were across the street from each other."

Sibyl smiled, and Bannack noticed the mischievous gleam in her eyes. "Best story I've heard all day. How cute! You guys found each other again."

Bannack couldn't help but smile around Sibyl. "You already know that, though, right?"

"I do." Sibyl sat in the grass beside Eloise. "But it's fun to hear you talk about it."

"Talk about what?" Eloise asked as she wiped her chin.

Sibyl crossed her legs and brought her food into her lap. "How you guys met."

Bannack leaned his back against the cool bark of a tree and allowed his sore body to relax. Cicadas buzzed around them.

Eloise nodded. "We were neighbors as kids."

As she crossed her legs, Bannack noticed a brown anklet. "You still wear it?"

Eloise glanced down at the jewelry. "No matter what. Remember? The old string broke, so I got a new one and made it to fit around my ankle."

A ping of nostalgia spread through him. Eloise promised him, when they were ten and eleven after he gave her the bracelet, that she would keep it forever. It hadn't been something he specifically asked for, but she promised him nonetheless. Then somewhere along the way of growing up, the bracelet became an anklet.

"What are the drawings?" Sibyl asked and pointed to the three wooden beads with symbols burned into their surface.

Bannack reached for Eloise's anklet and she responded by lifting her foot out of her sandal. He grasped her leg in his hand. For a moment, he paused and stared at the adinkra engraved beads, caught up in remembering using a wood burning tool to create the small designs.

"This one in the middle is an adinkra symbol for friendship." Bannack explained. "It is called ese ne tekrema, the teeth and the tongue. They may play different roles in the mouth and may come into conflict, but they need to work together."

"And I'm assuming," Sibyl pointed to lettered beads on either side of the adinkra symbol, "those are for Bannack and Eloise."

Eloise nodded. She ran her hand along the beads, peering up at Bannack through her eyelashes. His breath caught and he stared at Eloise, her gaze fierce, matching his beating heart. Suddenly, the act of holding Eloise's ankle felt too intimate and Bannack released her foot, his neck heating. She tucked her foot underneath her in the grass.

After eating in silence, the warm stew seeping into his bones and making his taste buds sing, Eloise sighed. She placed her empty bowl in the grass and rubbed her stomach. "I love Moira's cooking."

"Mmm." Sibyl swallowed a mouthful of food then rotated the spoon in the air several times. "Reason number five thousand and six why having a professional chef is the best thing ever."

"Agreed." Eloise closed her eyes.

Loving the breeze traveling through the cotton tee to his sweaty skin underneath, Bannack laid in the grass. The strands tickled his cheek.

"Did your parents ever cook with you?" He asked.

Eloise spoke up first. "No. Not really. Or, at least, I don't remember."

Bannack sat up. "Never? What about cookies? Brownies? Bread? The meat dish with the wide, long noodles...Lasagna. Not even lasagna?"

When he named each dish, Eloise shook her head while fiddling with her shirt hem. "I don't even know how to cook an egg. And don't look so shocked. Not every mom cooks with their kids."

He realized, when she looked at him, that her shoulders drooped. With a start, Bannack tried to backpedal. "I did not mean offence. I am surprised, is all. Food was huge in my family."

"What did," Sibyl tucked a stray lock of hair behind her ear, "your mom make with you?"

"Maame and I cooked together constantly, which you know." In response, Eloise smiled and nodded. Bannack continued, talking mostly to Sibyl. "At first, I thought it was boring, but I grew to love it. We connected that way. Agya kept recipes from Ghana in a special box he would challenge us to make: goat light soup with fufu, ampesi, jollof rice. Mmm. Just thinking about it makes my mouth water." Bannack paused and smiled. "I miss the way things were."

"Yeah..." Sibyl nodded. "So do I. I remember one time," she laughed, "my dad and mom were spinning pizza dough around the kitchen island and I was in the middle. My dad," she began laughing so hard she struggled to speak, "he lost control and it landed on my head."

The infectious laughter passed to Eloise and Bannack, and they both began laughing. Sibyl leaned forward, her hand against her face, and when she stopped, she wiped the tears from her eyes.

"They're gone now," Sibyl said as she stared at her feet. Her demeanor changed dramatically and Bannack worried her laughing years would turn into true ones. Then she blinked, smiled, and leaned into Eloise who cried out as her food nearly spilled. "But I have Eloise, and that's plenty for me."

He watched her, a bit confused, in the way she shifted from sad to happy but determined not to push further. No one on earth had escaped the trauma of losing people important to them.

As the clouds shifted in the sky, moving the sunlight across the grass, Bannack watched groups of kids pass wicker baskets out among the members of the working Compounders. He sat up, curious.

One boy handed a basket to Eloise. She smiled at him. "Thank you, Finn." While she inspected the basket, contents hidden by a cloth draped over them, Eloise asked, "How is your mom doing with the new baby?"

"Agatha is loud and cries all the time," Finn replied, rubbing his arm. "Mama says she'll stop, but it's been a whole month and she's still doing it."

"Hmm. Let your mom know to visit Soora. She could help." Eloise smiled and poked the young boy's shoulder. "You're a big brother now. How cool is that?"

Finn smiled a bit. "Agatha is kinda cute."

Without another word, Finn ran back to his mom, a lanky brunette with tired eyes and a bundle of wild hair poking out from a sling tied to her back.

When Eloise met his eyes, his heart beat faster. How long had he been staring? To cover up, Bannack said, "You seem at ease here."

"I am," Eloise said. She cleared her throat and stood, hoisting the basket to her hip. "Follow me. I want you to meet someone."

"What's in the basket?"

Eloise moved a cloth from the top and revealed a collection of fresh produce, flat bread, and a metal container covered with a fabric and secured by a piece of twine.

"Stew?"

"Yeah. You noticed the kids passing these out?"

Bannack nodded.

Eloise rotated her body to walk around a man passing by them. "We have many older members of the Compound who aren't mobile. We all take turns bringing them food for the day. This basket is for Alma. She came to the Compound after suffering from a stroke and she struggles to talk. Soora calls it aphasia."

"Why do you need me?"

"To carry the water, Dum-Dum." Eloise nudged Bannack with her elbow. She caught him right under his ribs, where he was the most ticklish—she knew this—and Bannack groaned out a laugh. He jerked from her before she could get him again.

Eloise stopped walking, and Bannack nearly bumped into her. He watched a father bathe his two young children in a large, metal animal trough. A boy and a girl. Bannack's own father used to do the same with him and his sister.

Confused, Bannack drew his eyes to what held Eloise's attention.

A somber group carrying a covered body on a stretcher passed by, not a dry eye among them. They walked slowly, with the men humming a deep song, the melody lost on Bannack. He watched Eloise grip the arm of a middle-aged woman.

"I'm sorry for your loss."

The woman smiled, tears clinging to the edge of her lips. "He spoke often of your kindness. In you, he found a kindred spirit."

When the group had gone, Bannack asked, "You knew him?"

"Yes. William Fitch. I brought him food like I'm doing with Alma. We talked about family we lost and...our trauma. He's—was—quite hilarious. Full of ridiculous, cheesy jokes he owned so well, they never got old."

"Do you need to go? I can take the food."

Eloise smiled, eyes glistening. "No. Funerals here are for immediate family only. I'll pay my respects later."

After a moment, Bannack smiled. "I remember my grandmother was buried in a cheetah. Said she needed all the help she could get to run from my grandfather's...sexual advances." He laughed at Eloise's shock. "Do not worry. She spoke in jest."

"I'm sure she did. But a cheetah, really?"

"Not a real one. In a small part of Ghana, not everywhere, some coffins are built to resemble things like animals, vehicles, or items. A lot of people are still buried traditionally, but my family loved the unique coffins. Once, I had a cousin who told me their dad commissioned a Coke bottle to be made for him when he died."

"Okay. That's just weird."

"For you, maybe. Because your people enjoy boring. Boring in life and in death."

Bannack loved the smile that animated her entire face. It warmed him.

"Hey! We can make intricate coffins, too."

"Perhaps. But has anyone ever been able to say they were buried in a kpakpo shito chili pepper? No. Did not think so."

Eloise laughed into the wind. "What a wonderfully strange tradition."

They walked together in silence for a while, Bannack repeatedly looking to Eloise, still reeling from his rescue of her. So many questions. How did she get the scar on her face? How did her nanites work? Were they so powerful they could prevent her from dying?

"Elle?" Bannack asked, rubbing his hands together. She glanced to him, eyes wide, and their conversation shifted. "What is wrong?"

"That name. I haven't heard it since we were kids. It's...nice to hear it again."

A gentle smile spread across his face. His cheeks warmed. "Then I shall call you Elle more often."

Her face softened. "You had a question."

"Yes..." Bannack paused, unsure he should even ask. "What happened to Ada?"

Eloise played with the edge of her sleeve. "The water table is around the corner. We have to boil all of our water and with the amount of people living here, it's tedious but necessary. There'll be a pitcher for you to grab with cooled water. Once we get it, we can head over to Alma's."

"Good to know. But Elle..." Bannack stepped in front of Eloise, stopping her short. She refused to meet his gaze.

Eloise bit her bottom lip, inhaled, and then glanced up with determined eyes. "I don't want to talk about it."

Silence passed between them. The sun beat down on his back and sweat covered his skin as the wind passed through his cotton tee. He watched Eloise's jaw work, and he knew he had touched a nerve.

"Alright. I apologize for asking too soon. Shall we get the water?"

CHAPTER ELEVEN
ELOISE

The silence made brooding easy.

Why am I so mad that he asked about Ada? This is Bannack. It's not like he's a stranger.

Eloise glanced at him as he walked intentionally to her right so he could hear her better if she spoke. She pushed five foot two with her boots on and the top of her head was barely up to his shoulder. He stepped into the sun as Eloise continued to take strategic glances his way. Soft yet defined jaw, high cheekbones, hair just a bit longer than a buzz cut, and intense blue eyes capable of searing straight through to her core. He walked like a man, broken but determined.

Oh, my god. Eloise's heart quickened. *I need to stop staring.*

Bannack bent and plucked flowers from the ground, bundling them in a bouquet.

"What are you doing?" Eloise cocked her head at him.

After placing three wide blades of grass throughout the bouquet, Bannack peered at Eloise with innocent eyes. "She has no family here. Correct?"

Eloise nodded and stared at the beautiful flowers in Bannack's hands. "I still don't—"

"And," Bannack continued as he crouched to inspect a clump of white daisies, "she most likely is not mobile, so she struggles with keeping a clean home. Right?"

Once again, Eloise nodded. "You really don't have to—"

"Ergo, she might enjoy some wildflowers." Bannack added some lavender bell-shaped flowers he plucked from a field of knee-high grass.

She couldn't help but stare at him. He acted like kindness and forethought was inconsequential.

A decade later and you still think of others.

Eloise gripped the basket against her body as she tapped on a decrepit door, faded grey paint flaking off the surface. Yesterday's basket, void of food and awaiting pickup, sat on the concrete walkway. The door creaked loudly as an old woman in a green, knitted shawl, a slight wobble to her head, and drooping eyelids, opened the door. Her eyes darted to either side, then up at Eloise's smiling face.

"Hello, Alma. I've brought you more food."

Alma turned her eyes up to Bannack. She watched him for a moment, looking to Eloise.

"This is my friend, Bannack. He came to help." Eloise offered her basket.

The old woman had been non-verbal for as long as anyone in the Compound could remember. Her face drooped, and she walked with one leg dragging on the ground. Only one thing could have caused the strange mannerisms. A stroke.

Alma smiled and brought the basket into her small home. It had been a school classroom and much of the scent coming from inside reminded Eloise of old books, and a pile of crocheted and knitted blankets sat in the corner. Alma passed the time making blankets for new babies born to the Compound to be traded for supplies when Sibyl traveled to the Market and for anyone who needed.

The woman reappeared with a small, handmade bracelet. Alma made them herself from the glass and trash on the beach the Compound overlooked.

Eloise smiled, slipping the bracelet, a piece of green sea glass caged in thin silver wire, onto her wrist. "It's beautiful, Alma."

The woman patted Eloise's hand and beckoned them inside. Alma had never invited her inside before. "Oh, no. We couldn't intrude."

Alma's hands shook as she reached up to grab Eloise's arm. "Come."

The simple word surprised Eloise, and she stared then stepped over the threshold.

"You spoke." Eloise flopped into a chair at the round table in the middle of the room. Bannack sat beside her, silent.

"Speak few words," Alma said.

"Has anyone been helping you with your speech?"

Alma rubbed her leg when she sat in the third chair. The creak of the wood filled the small bedroom. "I can't...I can't..." Alma shook her head. She stood slowly, turned, and when she came back around held a piece of thick paper made from plant fibers and a piece of thin charcoal tied to a stick. Her hand moved carefully until she finished writing a word on the paper.

Eloise leaned forward and read it aloud. "Soora? Soora's been helping you."

"Yes." Alma gestured to the side of her head. "Sunflower."

Eloise couldn't resist smiling. "Exactly. Do you like her sunflower tattoo?"

Alma nodded. Her eyes flicked to Bannack, her jaw clenched several times, and then she grabbed his hand that rested in a tight fist on the top of the table. He shuddered.

"Forgive."

For a long time, Bannack said nothing. He sat, shaking like a leaf in an autumn breeze, and worked his mouth. When he spoke, he wheezed the words out.

"How can you after..." Bannack didn't finish his sentence. Instead, he stared at Eloise.

Eloise's heartbeat pounded in her head. She looked at the bouquet lying on the table, contemplating finding them some water.

The entire exchange between Alma and Bannack, plus his reaction, proved he and Alma shared a dark history.

Alma's next words chilled Eloise's bones.

"You. Bad things, yes. But you...walk away. Good for forgiving."

"Why are you forgiving me? I..." Once again, he looked at Eloise, this time with damp eyes. He mouthed words at her that resembled an apology.

Alma reached for Bannack, but he flinched away, gaze stuck on her face. The old woman smiled and lowered her hand to her heart, gesturing to it with a single, gnarled finger.

"Here. Broken. You must pay...correct...no...atone. Yes. You must atone for pain. I hand you mine forgiveness."

Antsy over Alma's cryptic words and unable to stay quiet out of sheer curiosity, Eloise spoke. "Why is she saying she forgives you?" Eloise turned to Alma. "What happened between you two?"

Alma shook her head. "In time. Will share."

"Bannack?"

He wouldn't meet her gaze. Instead, he stared at the bouquet before standing. "I have to go. Enjoy the flowers."

Too stunned to move, Eloise watched the door close behind Bannack and he disappeared.

"Follow."

Alma pushed Eloise from her chair, and she rushed out of the room. Her feet crunched on the gravel path as she ran into the open field near the garden beds. "Bannack!" Eloise yelled, spinning to look for him in the dwindling crowd. The golden light of the sun gave everything a warm glow.

She didn't see Bannack.

Eloise clasped her hands behind her head then looked at the sky. The clouds, lit by the red and orange hues of the sun, moved lazily.

Okay. Think. Where would he go? Is there any place close enough he might run off to? A safe...location...

She knew.

His old house. There's nowhere else on this earth he feels most comfortable.

Her feet propelled her forward and toward the broken bridge that, ten years ago, had been the only way onto the peninsula.

He was going home.

He has to be there.

***

Darkness filled every corner of the house. Cobwebs and vines littered the walls, stairwell, and windows, and blackberry bushes crept in through the gaping holes that used to hold double-paned glass. A thick layer of dust slept on every surface.

Musk from mildew spilled into Eloise's nose. She sniffed, trying to move past the shock of being back in Bannack's old home. What exactly had happened to his mom and sister? Bannack hadn't talked about them willingly, and Eloise hadn't pushed him after finding out he believed he caused their deaths.

As the wind whistled through the house, Eloise remembered the home as it appeared in the past. The discrepancy faded away and life came back. The charcoal carpet spread out through the entire house while paintings, done by Bannack's mom, Gabrielle, covered the walls. As she walked underneath the curved archway, a vision of what the rest of the house used to be formed in her mind. A stunning dining room. Large kitchen. A lived-in living room. Laughter from a young Bannack and Malikah echoed throughout the halls as they ran up and down the stairs, the smell of the iconic chocolate chip cookies spreading through the house. Gabrielle had been famous for her cookies around the neighborhood. During the cooler months, kids would line up like hungry vultures, waiting for their pick of the gooey on the inside, crunchy on the outside chocolate chip cookies.

A bittersweet wave washed over Eloise. This house would no longer have life. Just a skeleton remained.

Glass fractured underneath Eloise's old boot. She paused, dreading the picture hid behind the frame, but she bent over anyway and scooped it up. Using her glove to wiggle the shards from the frame, Eloise revealed the family she had loved as her own.

In the photo, Gabrielle, Kwadwo, Malikah, and Bannack smiled underneath the shade of green trees. Bannack, who looked to be about ten, had his arm wrapped around an eight-year-old Malikah dressed in a red sundress with her wiry brown hair pulled back into a tight braid.

They were so happy. So innocent.

Wiping tears from her face, Eloise placed the frame on a rotting side table, then adjusted her jacket and continued her tour through the house.

A long, anguished cry came from upstairs.

Eloise jumped, her heart pounding, and recognized the scream as Bannack's. Her mind tumbled over itself as she rushed the stairs.

Another scream filled with fury drew her up to the second floor.

"Bannack!"

CHAPTER TWELVE
BANNACK

He heard her call his name from downstairs, yet he didn't care. His parent's study had been raided and no amount of anger or screaming or hate could stop the brick that slammed into his gut. Bannack wanted nothing more than to find those who stole his father's Ghanaian artifacts, his mother's art, and separate their fingers from their hands so they couldn't steal ever again.

How could I have neglected this? If I had been back at all After, I could have prevented this.

The room before him, double doors with shattered glass flung open wide, was in shambles. Spray paint in bright red letters mocked his maame's and agya's work with the local university. Bookshelves behind the desk had been ripped from the walls and were leaning dangerously over the dark cherry wood desk. Bannack remembered seeing his father sitting there, upbeat Ghanaian music filling the study, with a pen clutched between his teeth and a magnifying glass in hand as he poured over old texts. His mother would lean over his shoulder as she pointed at the document, excited. His father would glance up, smile at her, then invite Bannack to sit with them. They spent hours there, Bannack soaking in the stories of his heritage, his father laughing, and eating his mom's cookies.

Now, all remnants of those memories were gone. The raiders not only stole the shield and spear Bannack helped his maame unbox, but they took it one step further and smeared slander and stinging words in paint across the walls and desk. They mocked everything his parents worked for and Bannack was helpless to defend them.

"Bannack? Where are you?"

Eloise's footsteps on the stairs grew quiet shortly before he felt her presence behind him. She said nothing.

Good.

Bannack's body shook. He held no jurisdiction over the words that would come from his mouth.

She touched his shoulder and he pulled away, a quiet growl escaping his throat.

"Who would do something so horrid?" She asked.

Eloise showed more bravery than he as she stepped through the door where frosted glass used to be and into the study. She reached for the spray-painted words.

His stomach lurched.

"Don't." Bannack barked at her and Eloise retracted her hand.

As Eloise walked through the room, occasionally sifting through the strewn contents, Bannack sunk to the floor. His vision spun and blurred, and several tingling waves traveled through him. They had taken every last bit of his family from him. Everything his maame and agya had done together, built, was lost in the world with no way of recovery.

"Bannack?" Eloise asked. She stood close and Bannack lifted his head from between his knees. "I found this. It's not much but..."

She held in her hands the djembe that lived in the south corner of the study. It was a goblet shaped drum, tuned with rope and covered with animal skin. Bannack and his agya had built it during the only trip to Ghana Bannack had accompanied his father on. The instrument his father had learned to play as a boy would come out only on Christmas, and the sharp, happy tone would fill the living room.

He couldn't bring his hands up to touch it. Eloise sat beside him, the djembe between her knees.

"Everything is gone." Bannack swallowed hard.

"We were able to find the drum. That's something, isn't it?"

Anger boiled under his skin. Bannack lurched to his feet and stomped up and down the hallway. He could barely rein in his words.

"No. You do not understand. The kente cloth, the recipe book he gifted my mother, our kigogo game, his papers and books on our people, and the sword and spear. Someone came here and looted all I have left of my family and my people! And I can't even—My maame and agya spent their lives devoted to teaching others our history and they stole it!" Bannack gritted his teeth, air hissing as it exited his mouth when he turned to Eloise's shocked face. "When have you ever had anything taken from you?"

As soon as Eloise narrowed her eyes at him, he knew he'd gone too far but held onto too much anger to fix anything at the moment.

"That's not fair."

With a grunt, Bannack turned from Eloise and down the stairs. He actively ignored all of the items that brought on memories of his family, his sister and mother murdered, and his father taken by sickness, and stood on the back patio. The metal railing still held strong. Bannack clenched his hands around the rough rust and screamed into the forest. He mourned for his family, for the life stripped from him, and cursed the life he was given by the cruelty of fate.

As Bannack leaned over the metal railing, he thought back to coming face to face with the old woman. Alma. He never knew her name before. She was just another empty face. A victim of his own sins.

You must atone for pain. I hand you mine forgiveness.

Those words quickly became daggers to his sour gut. The way she spoke, the issues with aphasia—her way of speech—twisted the knives in more. Eloise believed Alma had a stroke, which was true, but the reason she suffered from one was completely the fault of the weak serum Alma had been subject to in Joy's lab. The lab Bannack had brought her to after stealing her from her bed. He doomed Alma and she forgave him?

"Why?" Bannack yelled to the heavens. Shaking, he slammed his palm into the rusted metal. Then again. And again, until his hands grew as raw as his throat. Tears burned his eyes.

The anger dissipated, and a heavy pain settled in his chest. *All the lives I destroyed are on me. One person forgiving me for what I did to her doesn't change anything.*

Unable to remain in the house, Bannack ran from it. He had to get away from any source of pain.

Eloise, covered in twilight, sat on the mossy rock wall outside, the djembe drum between her legs.

"What are you doing?" Bannack picked up a twig as he sat, snapped it in half and tossed it on the driveway.

"Waiting for you. It's boring in the house." Eloise adjusted her body on the moss-covered wall. "Besides, this moss is way comfier than your couch."

"No." He chuckled. "I meant, what are you doing with the drum?"

"Oh." Eloise shrugged. "I figured you'd want it close."

Her finger tapped against the tight skin, releasing nostalgic notes. It was definitely out of tune, but the noise carried precious memories and he struggled to listen to the music.

"Did I ever tell you what happened to Agya?" Bannack asked and when Eloise shook her head, he said, "He died from the flu—well, sepsis really, but the flu came first."

"That must have been traumatizing. I'm glad you told me." Eloise knit her eyebrows together. "And what about your mom and sister? What happened to them?"

That he couldn't talk about. He rarely even thought about it, choosing to avoid the memory altogether, but hoping he could ignore it had done him no good in the past. Still, he changed the subject. "I should apologize."

Eloise rubbed her palms together and sat in silence as if waiting for his apology.

"What I said back there, about never having anything taken away from you, was not considerate. We all have had things taken from us because of the war." Bannack inhaled, and his chest swelled, then relaxed. "I am sorry. You were trying to help, and I repaid your kindness by yelling."

"Thank you." Her face softened, and she smiled. "Why have you never come back here?"

Bannack looked at the house. "I was going to, but I was scared of what I would find. Then I got busy."

"Hmm," Eloise scooted closer. "And what you found didn't help alleviate the fear."

He shook his head.

"What are you going to do about the house now?"

"Not sure." Bannack said and shrugged. "Leave it as is. Try to work up the courage to visit once in a while."

"You know, we could get some people together to fix it up. Make it kinda like it was."

"Perhaps." He shrugged his shoulders. The offer was tempting, and he realized, as he looked back at the house he grew up in, that he missed it. Would it be so bad to fix it up?

"Well, you have time to think about it."

"How are you doing?" Bannack asked.

"What?" Eloise's voice sounded far off, as if lost in her thoughts.

"With Joy's intentions."

"I'm...doing okay. You know she agreed to leave me alone and be with Seth, right?"

He didn't. He cocked his head. "You seem unsure."

"I'm nervous she'll come back."

"Yeah." Bannack tossed the final stick. "I would be as well."

They sat together in silence with only the beach down the hill as their companion. It lulled back and forth over the rocky sand, water shushing in the night as if it were a mother up late feeding her baby.

"Actually," Eloise said and squared her shoulders. "No. I'm not doing okay. I don't want to sit here and pretend everything is okay when it's not. Being stagnant is awful."

Bannack grunted, unsure how to respond.

Eloise remained quiet for a while, chewed her bottom lip, and kept her head bowed. Their eyes didn't meet as Eloise whispered, "When Ada died...it was horrible and..."

"You lost her," Bannack said. His stomach clenched.

Tears trailed down Eloise's cheek. "I was there...I watched it happen. It's why—" her voice cracked, "Why I struggle with things."

She didn't meet his eyes. He knew what he would find in them if she did; unbearable pain of losing a loved one. The kind of pain that creates a deep emptiness and longing to have them back, even if they are only a shadow.

Bannack knew the pain intimately. He had lived with it for seven years.

For the first time since they'd met, Eloise hugged him and he tensed, petrified by her embrace. Warmth radiated into him and ever so slowly, Bannack enclosed her in his arms.

"I am so sorry, Eloise," Bannack said, stray hairs flicking away from his breath. A crisp scent of fresh air and pine filled his nose, making his head spin. His heart quickened. Her arms were around his waist. He could feel the slight movement of her back muscles and they were strong, defined.

Once Eloise recovered and sat up, she pushed her hair behind her ear.

I should have—Stop! What's wrong with you? Feeling will get you killed. But he wanted to feel. He wanted all the raw emotions Eloise brought up, but that terrified him. A fading calm allowed nausea to fester. He glanced to Eloise, inspecting the djembe drum, and then his hands. He knew what he had done with them, and he clenched them tight.

Feeling will get you killed. Never forget.

***

"Alright, today's a busy day."

Bannack stood in a small group of people, all faced toward a

119

woman in a shawl. Her long blonde hair fell around her shoulders.

A man beside Bannack handed him a paper with a to-do list scrawled on it.

"Whatever jobs are written on the paper are yours to complete by today. Everyone should have different work." She clapped once. "Alright. Get to work, now."

Unsure what to do about people pushing past him and doing his best not to shrivel against the wall, Bannack looked at his paper. Before he could read it, someone bumped into his hands and the paper fluttered to the ground. He bent to pick it up. It wound around the person's legs. Thankfully, they stopped, handed him back the paper, and apologized, then ran off. Bannack's stomach tightened.

He read the paper. "Dust bookshelves in the library. Clean out horse stalls. Fix fence on north end of the field. Deliver eggs to kitchen."

Simple enough.

He made his way to the library. The entrance was pushed to the back of a large alcove with stairs to the right. Books lined shelves, some even crossing overhead. Old and faded rugs, tasseled or woven with intricate patterns, covered the floor in a sea of regal whimsy. The shelves sagged, their paint peeling or mismatched.

As Bannack glanced around, no lanterns or torches touched the walls, like they did throughout the rest of the Compound, and the library relied solely on the natural light that filtered through large windows.

He closed his mouth. "Excuse me," Bannack said as he caught the attention of a Compounder. "Where are the cleaning supplies?"

She glanced up at him and pointed to a metal shelving unit behind an old desk. "Look there first."

Bannack thanked her and looked for something to dust with. He found a rag and an old feather duster so covered with dirt, it left a small pile behind when he grabbed it.

He returned to the woman. "Apologies, but," Bannack held up the duster, "is there another one?"

"No," she frowned, "it's all we have. In storage, we have some cleaned feathers we stuff blankets and pillows with. There should be a bag of longer feathers there you can use, too."

"Okay. Thank you."

Exhaling, Bannack walked to the storage.

Feathers...Feathers...

Nothing was labeled. Bannack scratched his head. His first day on the job and already he was running into a snag.

"Ugh. This is going excellent."

Bags were everywhere. He opted to feeling all twenty bags. By the fifteenth, he found one he could squish easily like a down pillow, and he opened it to find...short feathers.

More searching finally yielded results, and he gathered a large handful of them. He grabbed a piece of string hanging on the wall, then tied the feathers together.

There.

The new duster wasn't pretty, but it had to do. Bannack rushed back to the library, already an hour into his day, and wiped the dust from the shelves.

For the rest of the day, Bannack worked on his tasks, each one breeding additional tasks to get the original one finished. He took a short break to eat with the Compounders, giving them a wide berth and wishing either Eloise or Sibyl, the only two people he knew so far, were eating with him. He struggled with the ambient noise inside and the energy Bannack possessed earlier waned. By dinner time, he retreated to his room, opting to find his food in the forest.

He relaxed, his body deflating, as he found a meal comfortable to him. Huckleberries were in season. He picked those first, standing by the bush for several minutes, crunching on the tart berries, and enjoying the clean scent of the trickling brook in the air. It wasn't so stale or filled with noise. He found cattails and some seaweed in the bay below the Compound, then sat on the rocky beach, eating his dinner. Relieved to find peace.

The moon covered the world in a silvery light by the time Bannack closed his door. He grabbed the blanket and pillow, filled with the feathers he had searched for that morning, and settled on the floor.

What was I thinking, agreeing to stay at the Compound? I'm going to go crazy if I have to spend the rest of my life around humans.

Maybe I'll get used to it?

The last question lingered in his mind until he fell asleep.

***

The days blended together. He spent much of his time working and although he became proficient and able to do more tasks as time passed, the ambient noise and growing to do lists got to him.

He awoke in a daze, still exhausted from the day prior, worked, ate alone in the forest, worked more, then went to bed. Dinner became a luxury and didn't happen often. He struggled to eat.

Bannack sat on his bed, trying not to move to avoid the squeaking, with his head in his hands.

I just need to breathe, recoup, and figure out what I'm going to do.

He didn't want to leave. Despite drowning in socialization, Bannack desperately wanted living at the Compound to work out because the alternative was a life alone. He'd be able to visit, sure, but the bliss the Compound offered was too tempting to pass up and his life whenever he left would pale in comparison.

"Okay," Bannack scrubbed his head, struggling to breathe. "Alright. What did Maame say? Write it down. Yeah. Paper...paper..."

Bannack raided the old desks. No paper. Inside an old storage chest, Bannack found a small collection of items. Soap, first aid supplies, extra blanket, change of clothes, and Bannack's akrafena were together, and he had to move everything from the bottoms to find the paper and charcoal. He sat at his bed and wrote a to-do list, recording the requirements to complete each task. He needed to prepare for more tasks. During the past few weeks, he had figured out how much time the tasks would take and then figured out how often they rotated back onto his schedule. He recorded the approximate time needed to perform his jobs, then he listed how often he'd had each one, and realized he did a lot more cleaning than anything else. Good. It gave him something to expect.

***

Over the next week, Bannack put his list to use. He checked each box, waking in the early morning to practice fighting. If Joy were to come back, as Eloise suspected, he needed to keep his skill razor sharp.

For a few days, the process worked. Then the overwhelm crept up, he fell into a rut again, and he was back to square one.

What am I missing?

Bannack needed out. He needed to spend his time in the forest, the quiet, and avoid humans. He tried to stay, but the constant need for recharge and time away from the hustle and bustle wore him down.

One morning, after Bannack's workout, he sat outside on a rock, watching the birds peck at the ground. Footsteps grew louder, and Bannack turned.

Mason smiled at him. "How are things going for you here?"

"It's..." Bannack shrugged, "unexpected."

"Mmm. I thought so."

"Sir?"

"I've been watching you and your adjustment. I want to offer you an alternative."

Bannack furrowed his eyebrows.

"Are you still interested in becoming a Sentinel?"

The offer, when originally spoken of, made Bannack hesitate, but now that he had learned the depth of difficulty in adjusting from being alone to being around people, becoming a Sentinel charmed him.

"What does a Sentinel do?"

"Patrolling, hunting, protection of the Compound. You keep

watch over the Compounders here. Once you are assigned into a group, you spend your time with them for a month before I switch you out with other members. Some groups are strictly patrol, while others strictly hunt. If your skill is the same as when you took down Emille, I'd most likely start you off in my east group. They're out hunting now, so I'll introduce you later. What do you think?"

It sounded like heaven. Few people, little talking, and only the forest around them.

"When do I start?"

"Right now." Mason clapped Bannack on the back then turned, rifled through his desk, and handed a red strip of fabric to Bannack. "Welcome to the team. All Sentinels, while on duty, are required to wear this." He waited for Bannack to tie the cloth to his arm then opened the door. "Come with me and I'll introduce you to a group about to head out on a hunt. I'd like you to go with them."

Relief flooded him, and he sighed. *Finally, some peace and quiet.*

Bannack walked with Mason around the south side of the building and up a wooden trail to a clearing. Several individual groups between five and ten people gathered there, either sparring, packing gear, or caring for their weapons. As Mason passed them toward a group of five against the tree line, each person greeted Mason with a tap to their forehead.

As Bannack and Mason approached, Bannack got a better look at the group he assumed he was being paired with. They were sharing a meal, three of them crammed onto one log, and the last two members were sitting together, one laying on the ground. Bannack recognized Eloise immediately. She kept her head in the other woman's lap, oblivious to Mason and Bannack's approach. The women were chatting and smiling, while the woman with a shaved head twirled a lock of Eloise's dark red hair in her fingers. Eloise turned her head away, and he saw a flush of color.

Mason cleared his throat.

Eloise noticed Bannack and Mason then and sat up. The other woman looked at Bannack, then whispered something in Eloise's ear, and she lowered her eyelashes, smiling gently.

What shocked him the most was his stomach clenched. He wanted to be the one swirling Eloise's hair and whispering things into her ear to make her smile. Who did this other woman think she was?

"Bannack." Eloise pushed her hair high on her head, revealing her neck. Bannack swallowed, and his jealousy fluttered away.

"He's your new member."

She blinked several times. "What?"

Ignoring her, Mason called to the other Sentinels. "Hey, guys. I brought you a new friend."

The three on the log jumped to their feet and stood around Eloise. One began chewing his nail. The tallest of the group and dressed in a leather jerkin, two leather vambraces, and a green kilt, looked at Bannack with bright eyes.

"I'll leave you to it," Mason said and walked away.

"Hey," the tall man smiled. "I'm Mal. That's Abe, Finch, Eloise—"

"We've met," Eloise said, and looked at Bannack. Her eyes bored into him, dark and narrow, and he took a step toward her. Her gaze pulled him in. She didn't back away, only watched him.

"Great! And this guy is Nails."

"Dude!" The man chewing on his fingers rubbed them on his thighs. "Why is this a thing? My name's Blake, you idiots."

The group all looked at each other and smiled. Bannack shook Abe's hand. He was a stout man with wild curly hair, patches of pale skin on his arms and face, a pierced nose, and he wore a cape lined with fur at the shoulders.

Finch, heavily tattooed on her arms, adjusted the crossbow slung to her back and extended her only hand, the other gone at the elbow. "Welcome," she said.

"Where we going?" Abe asked.

"Up north," Eloise said, and she picked her knives up from a stump, loading them individually onto her body. He counted seven. She put her hands on her hips. "The deer population there is getting a bit out of control because too many predators are being killed by humans, so we've been given permission to hunt there." She turned to Bannack. "Do you have something to hunt with?"

"I...uh...have my akrafena in my room."

Blake called over his shoulder. "A sword won't do you much good against deer, newbie."

"Leave the guy alone, Blake," Finch said and shoved him. He fake-stumbled, gaining a few cackles from the other Sentinels, and rubbed his arm.

"Ow. You're so mean to me."

"Whatever."

"There's a supply of weapons over there," Eloise pointed to the left side of the clearing at some racks of bows, crossbows, and knives. "Grab whatever you like and meet us at the horses."

CHAPTER THIRTEEN
ELOISE

"Just pretend to be my date." Mal knelt, his hands clasped together in a pleading gesture, and stared up at Abe.

"No way, vato!" Abe knocked Mal's hands out of the way. "I ain't pretending to like you so you can get him to notice you."

Mal groaned, loud and dramatic. "You're the most boring person. Finch?"

"Uh-uh. Nope." She shook her head. "You're on your own with this one."

They had been traveling for much of the day, taking turns riding the two horses they brought with them, unable to give each Sentinel a horse because of the small number of them at the Compound. The two mares waited, tied by a tree and tended to by Nails, while the rest of the group sat along the riverbank drinking from their water canteens.

Eloise looked at Bannack.

I can't believe Mason threw him on me.

Mason's expression, with the sly smile, irritated her more than Bannack being in their group. She recognized that look.

He knew exactly what he was doing, putting him in my group.
He can go eat rocks, for all I care.

She still loved him, even when he failed miserably at playing matchmaker.

While she filled up her canteen, Eloise asked, "What are you doing here?"

Bannack looked at her, his bright blue eyes making her skin tingle wonderfully. "I'm a Sentinel. What did you think I was doing?" He leaned in, the warm, earthy tones of lavender and leather filling her nose. "Picking daisies?"

She narrowed her eyes at him. "Never mind. Just ..." Eloise wiggled her hand in the air, "stay over there. The Sentinels are my thing. Go find something else to occupy your time. Knitting, maybe."

He smiled.

Why does he have to do that?

The smile made her heart thump faster, and it stayed on his face so long that she had to look away to hide the reddening of her cheeks.

"I'm quite good at that. My mom taught me. I can make you and Bali matching hats."

She made a face and stuck her chin out. "I still don't like it. You're invading. Go away."

"What's there to be defensive about when it was Mason's idea?"

"Well, Mason's nosey and put us together purely for his own entertainment. Plus, you're a suck up."

The laughter that came out of Bannack ruffled her feathers and sent a wave of butterflies through her stomach at the same time. She didn't know whether to blush or glare at him.

"What's so funny?"

"You," Bannack looked at her and leaned his body against a tree trunk, cocked his knee up, and put his other arm on top of it. "You seem threatened by my presence here and it is making you flustered."

Don't let him get to you.

Eloise grabbed her bag and began rifling through it.

"What are you doing?" Bannack asked.

With her head in the bag, Eloise replied, "I'm looking for the opinion I asked you for. It must be in here somewhere. Oh wait..." She looked at him, "It's not here."

Bannack's face blanked, then he smiled. "Fair enough."

"You guys ready?" Finch walked over to them, her boots crunching the rocks. She touched Eloise's hand. "We're heading out again. Bannack? Do you ride?"

He shook his head.

"Hmm. That's a problem. We'll have to figure something out, then, once you get tired."

***

Hours later, Eloise rode the bay mare. She poked her tongue into her cheek, glared, and inhaled a long breath.

"The only reason you're on my horse, not Abe's, is because mine can carry the weight and I'm smaller than him, so we fit. This is not because I felt bad for you."

From behind her, his chest pressed against her back and legs hanging, Bannack spoke over her shoulder. "I got tired."

"You could have waited."

"The hill was steep."

"One hour. That's it."

"My ass got cold, and the horse is quite warm."

Eloise clenched her teeth. "Just...stop talking."

Bannack's laugh rippled against her back.

Nails trotted over on the second mare. "We're heading into the city to make camp. If you go under the double overpass, through the tunnel, we'll be in the old theater with the red carpet inside the glass doors."

"Got it," Eloise waved at him. "We'll do a quick patrol and then join you."

Abe trotted off and down the hill.

"Hey, Eloise," Bannack's voice puffed air past her ear, "what's up with you and Finch?"

The name of her fellow Sentinel brought a smile to her lips. "What do you mean?"

"It kinda looked like you guys were flirting."

"Yeah," Eloise shrugged and turned her head. "I like her face and her tattoos. She's really smart, too." When Bannack said nothing, she added, "You know I'm bi, right?"

"Oh," he said. "I didn't. I mean, I saw hints here and there, but was not sure. Have you had many other women partners?"

"A few. I like guys more than girls though."

"Hmm...cool."

"Why are you all of a sudden interested in the people I associate with?" His strange question confused and frustrated her. It wasn't any of his business.

Bannack stumbled through several 'oh's,' 'well's,' and 'uh's,' before explaining himself. "It is not my place to pry, and I'm sorry for my mistake, but the truth is rather embarrassing."

"One that you're going to share with me, I hope?" Eloise asked. Too many times she'd been disappointed by partners keeping things from her that made them uncomfortable and she hated it. If she could trust him, she needed to have open dialogue. Without it, she would struggle with worrying what he wasn't telling her, and especially because they would be working together.

"I may have been a tad jealous."

A laugh almost escaped as his answer was so unexpected. "You were jealous?"

"Yes. And I can feel you trying not to laugh. We *are* on a horse. Touching."

"Oh, stop," Eloise smiled beside herself, glad he couldn't see. "I'm not laughing at you. It was unexpected, is all. Why were you jealous?"

"I do not quite know. The experience was unexpected for me, as well. Perhaps it is because...I may like you. Or not. Jury is still out on that one."

Unfortunately, Eloise couldn't convince her mind to move on from his revelation. Also, unfortunately, she didn't want it to. His words lifted her heart, against her direct wishes, and wouldn't come down.

What the hell's wrong with you? You're acting like a giddy, love-sick woman and it's not allowed.

"Well," Eloise swallowed, "keep me updated."

"I shall let you know the minute I figure it out."

Eloise stopped the mare at the top of the hill and peered down into the valley. The wide road allowed for eight lanes of traffic, and the cars were spread out, rusted, broken, and growing plant life. Skyscrapers reached for the heavens like souls clawing at Death's ankles, their glass broken by brambles, moss, and grass. The overpasses grew vines like hair.

Deer carcasses of varying decomposition littered the road, some growing maggots and attracting flies. A murder of crows flew away from their meal.

"Where are all the people?" Bannack asked.

She turned her head, his warm breath puffing against her neck. She shuddered, and said, "The locals live about five miles from here. I've never met them, but they aren't a people I want to meet. Word is, from the scouts, they are hard, brutal, and attack anyone who comes close. The only reason they've allowed us to hunt here is the deer are overpopulated."

The day turned cold while they walked through the city, pushing vines out of their way and patrolling the area. A derailed train, the engine and three of its cars pouring over the edge, lay still and forgotten on tracks high above the road.

A long screech shocked the air. The mare stopped, her ears forward and nostrils flared. Eloise searched for the source, unable to see but still able to hear the awful noise. Something was dying a slow, miserable death.

"Hey, Eloise," Bannack's tone revealed he too was nervous. "Are you sure there's nothing here with us?"

She whispered back, "Up until now, I was positive."

"And now?"

"Eh...forty percent sure."

"Better make that zero percent."

The mare took a few steps back and tensed underneath Eloise's thighs.

Deer bolted past, bounding and scrambling, and the mare reared. Bannack held onto Eloise so tight she worried he would crush her bones, but she stayed on and gained control of the horse even though the mare pawed the ground, bounced on her hooves, and tossed her head.

"Woah, girl," Eloise stroked her neck, her stomach and heart in her throat, and panted. "Easy. We're okay now."

A low growl sounded above her. She turned, pulling the horse around, and looked straight into the yellow eyes of a tawny lioness. Three more appeared.

"Eloise—"

"I know. I see them. I'm not blind."

The lionesses crouched low, one jumping off of a truck bed, and advanced. The mare tensed, ears back, then roared, and took off. Eloise tried to pull her around, to stop her, but once she began running, Eloise knew they were toast if they stopped. The mare shot through the city, chased by the lionesses who ran after her.

Eloise pulled the horse down alleys and side streets, desperate to find a building that a rampaging horse could fit into without stopping.

"We need to get inside."

"I'm looking!" The only thing she could hear above the wind and Bannack's voice was her loud, heavy breathing. Her throat burned from the cold she gulped down.

A lioness Eloise hadn't seen jumped in front of them. The mare reared. Eloise gasped as her feet left the stirrups. She fell on top of Bannack, eliciting a sharp grunt from him. The mare took off, chased by two of the lionesses.

Pulled violently to her feet by one arm, Eloise took off running with Bannack. They couldn't outrun them. Their only chance was to hide in the nearest building.

"I'll shoot, you run." Bannack notched an arrow.

"Don't tell me what to do!" She flicked one of her throwing knives. It pierced the skull of a lioness with stripes and she fell.

"Come on!" Bannack grabbed her arm and ran into a building only a few yards away.

We're going to die.

Eloise's stomach ached. She could hear the heavy padded gallop of the lions after them. It was only a matter of seconds before—

Bannack cried out and Eloise, still attached to him, landed on her knee. She opened her mouth in a silent scream as pain crashed up her thigh. She spun, drew her kukri and an arrow from Bannack's quiver. For a split second, she watched in horror as the big cat pulled her paw away from Bannack to strike again, blood in the tawny fur. Eloise stabbed the lone lioness's eyes, screaming so loud her voice cracked. The cat, smaller than the others, withdrew, roared, and writhed on the ground.

She pulled on Bannack, unable to get him inside with merely her strength. "Get up!"

Groaning and stumbling, Bannack cradled his arm and they walked into an old mall. As they trudged through the swamp that used to be a floor, Bannack dripping blood into the water, Eloise searched for a place to hide. Anywhere. Escalators stood solemnly in the center of the concourse. Three wide hallways branched away, and above them, a balcony ran along the outside perimeter with overpasses connecting it. The glass ceiling no longer existed and vines hung down from the hole.

Eloise released Bannack. Adrenaline coursed through her body and made her tremble. She turned on him. "What's your problem?"

Pushing off from the wall he was leaning against, Bannack blinked at her. "Come again?"

"Don't tell me how to fight. I know what to do."

He scoffed. "You are a Sentinel. If you did not know how to fight, you would not even be one. I was trying to escape with our lives."

"By telling me what to do." Eloise held her frustration and anger barely below the surface. It pushed on her, begging to be let out. Her hands shook.

"No," Bannack said and groaned, grabbing at his shoulder. "By attempting to work as a team."

She walked over to him and clenched her fists, yelling, "A team I never asked you to be on!"

"Is that what this is about?" He kicked the water and it sprayed all over. "You are angry at me for joining the Sentinels?"

"Yes, I'm angry at you for joining the Sentinels. It's my thing!"

"Sentinel duty is for everyone."

"Not you." Eloise's voice cracked. She poked her finger at him, jamming his chest. Quick as a whip, he grabbed her wrist, which pulled a gasp from her lips. Her jaw tightened, and she looked up at him. "You're not allowed."

"Why?" He asked, whispering. "And never touch me when you're angry. I didn't give you permission."

Bannack leaned in close and released her wrist. Being near him allowed her to absorb his energy, and she realized it was chaotic, a boiling pool of fury and anger, kept together by a deceptively quiet tone. That energy burned through her with a thrilling burst.

She tilted her chin. "Because I don't want you on the team."

"Why?"

"Because you infuriate me."

"Why?"

His whispers made her shiver. "What are you doing, asking why over and over?" Eloise pulled away. "Aren't my answers good enough for you?"

"No. They are not. It is obvious your anger is directed at me and I deserve to know why so we can work together efficiently. I ask again. Why?"

The dam broke. Her grief, anger, and fear poured out of her mouth in a giant wave and she lost control of her body, collapsing waist deep into the water and weeds. "Because! Because you're a reminder that I lost everything, okay?" She gestured wide, tears burning as they fell. "What Joy did took everything from me! The minute you waltzed into my life, you won't stop helping. I don't want your goddamn help, Bannack! None of it! I can't even look at you without seeing what I lost: my sister, my parents, Seth." Eloise pointed at Bannack and her next words made him jump. "And you! I lost everyone, and it's because of that woman. I can't ever get it back!" Words turned to anger, and she growled, her face contorted. "So, yes, I don't want you here. I want you to go away."

She stood in the middle of the swamp, wet up to her knees, and shook. Eloise's teeth chattered. Her bones creaked.

"I am not leaving," Bannack said as he exhaled. "Your pain is real. It is valid. You cannot push me away because of it nor can you hold it in and hide it. If progress is to be made, if we must work together, we need to understand each other. I cannot work with someone who wishes for me to go away. We will both die."

Eloise exhaled, all strength to fight any longer gone, and fell onto a metal bench. She put her forehead in her hands. "Can we just...agree to move past this? You need help and my head hurts from the yelling."

"Sure." Bannack nodded.

They found a utility room. Bannack stood in the center, trying to remove his shirt, but hissed and groaned with every movement while Eloise searched through boxes on the shelves. She slammed them shut or tossed them through the air when they yielded no results, items clattering to the floor. Her head pounded.

Come on! Next time I'm giving everyone a pack of first-aid. What was I thinking having one person carry it all?

She looked at Bannack, watched him struggle with his shirt, then jerked her attention back to her frantic hunt for first aid supplies. Bannack panted behind her.

"Yes!" Eloise's hands found a box of rolled gauze and another of plastic wound closures. She turned around, both boxes in her arms, and let out a small squeak. Bannack stood by the door, body tilted and torso bare. He had removed his shirt. The sunset created an orange and yellow halo around the outside edges of his body, his shoulders, and arms.

"Did ya find it?"

"I..." Eloise gulped. "I did."

"Well? Whatcha waiting fer? Help me. I can't do it myself."

He's so grumpy. Sounds a bit like Kendal.

Eloise smiled a little. She knew full well the danger they were still in, but it was a side she'd never seen before. Ever. As kids, he always cried when he got hurt. Not if he scraped his knee or bumped his head, but if he saw blood, he was crying. As an adult, and probably because of the history she knew little of, Bannack reacted differently.

"Turn around."

He spun, placed his hand high on the doorjamb, and leaned forward, exposing claw marks down his shoulder blade to his ribs. They were deep, but none looked damaging.

"You're lucky the lion was young. Any of the bigger ones and you'd be toast."

"Lucky me." He growled, and she could hear him rolling his eyes.

Eloise placed the box of wound closures on a nearby shelf and dismantled them, using the three steps labeled clearly to guide her, and pulled the wounds closed. She used the entire box. Fluttering, color coded tabs covered the floor. She dug into the next box, wrapping Bannack's shoulder, and ducked underneath his arm to get a better angle.

He looked at her, face sweating.

He's so tall.

Eloise barely reached his chin. Getting her arm around his shoulder forced her to stand on her tiptoes until he compensated for her and knelt. Heat radiated off him. She made the mistake of looking at him. His jaw flexed, and his chest expanded, deep and wide to hide the pain, she knew, but it still made her stomach flutter. Thoughts swirled around her head like a cyclone, none of them touching ground and all of them wonderful.

"Finished," Eloise said, her eyes widening when she turned her back on him and realized her voice had cracked.

Ohmygod.

"Thanks."

She nodded her acknowledgement.

"Hey, uh, can you help me?" He chuckled. "I can't get it on."

Eloise turned around. He held his shirt out for her, an apologetic wrinkle to his forehead. Her knees nearly failed.

"Uh...sure, but," she motioned to the blood, "you probably want a new one."

"Yeah."

"We are in a mall."

"Yeah."

They stood apart from each other. Pigeons fluttered through the air. An invisible rope, attached to her heart and connected to him, pulled. She took a step. She looked at the ice he possessed for eyes, the tiny wrinkle in his forehead. Another step. Her hand extended. She wanted to touch his and the prominent veins, calloused palms, and she wondered if he would allow her to feel the stubble of his chin beneath her fingers.

She took the shirt from him. "Wanna look for one together?"

As they walked, searching for a clothing shop with clothes still in it, they ran across rabbits, frogs, snakes, and foxes living within the mall. The scent was musky and sometimes potent. Grass, moss, vines, and random assortments of fast-growing weeds infested some stores, but others lacked the vegetation that ran rampant. The mall looked like a place between worlds; the one where Fade had never attacked and the one where they did.

"There has to be a zoo close by," Bannack said, almost to himself. "It's the only explanation for the lions."

"And what's with their stripes?" Eloise pushed away a fallen rod and began rifling through a clothing rack with only a few items. "Lions don't have stripes."

"Interbreeding?" Bannack kicked a ceiling tile. "If the zoo had lions and tigers, they could have gotten out and bred together."

"What other animals are out there, then?"

Chattering and hooting came from the hallway and Bannack and Eloise poked their heads out of the shop to watch a group of black monkey's swing across the ceiling then disappear around the corner.

"Guess that answers that." Eloise looked at Bannack.

He handed her a maroon button-up shirt, gave her an apologetic smile, and stood still for her. She clambered, rather unattractively, onto a nearby shelving unit that once held folded clothes and helped pull the shirt over his shoulder. He grunted but didn't show any other signs of discomfort.

"What I'm wondering is why did the locals give us permission to hunt here? They had to have known about the lions, so what's the deal?"

He finished with the buttons and walked to the next shop, half the sign still visible but covered with grime. "Hey, look at this."

Paper littered the floor. Eloise grabbed the one Bannack held and read it out loud. "President Raquel Santos has corrupted our way of life and must face the consequences."

Her chest tightened, and she looked at Bannack who was reading another paper.

He read it. "We are Fade. We unite against our enemy. Join us and witness a new age." He paused, his lips tight. "Isn't that what created," Bannack gestured, "all of this? They kidnapped the President and forced her and her people to give up the launch codes."

"Yeah. I think you're right." Eloise looked at the propaganda, the President shown as a terrifying beast eating citizens. She crumpled the paper up and dropped it. "I don't really remember all of it from history class as a kid but I do remember Fade turned the people against the government. Hawaii doesn't even exist anymore because of what they did."

She remembered the coverage of the bombs vaguely since she'd only seen it once. For weeks, her family watched footage of bombs, tsunamis, and fires. And then the electricity collapsed. The economy never recovered from the devastation.

"What did your family do?" Eloise asked.

He rubbed the back of his neck. "I remember them trying to take us to my grandparent's but we got stuck in traffic. People attacked our car and we had to escape. My mom got hurt, though. Someone hit her in the head. She wasn't completely the same afterward, always afraid and hiding us away in weird places."

Eloise put her hand to her mouth. Imagining Gabrielle, a proud, confident woman turned into a fearful one was almost too much to bear and it made her stomach queasy.

"I did not think she'd be there. Why was she there?" Bannack scrubbed his head. He turned around and walked away.

"Bannack?" Eloise walked out. She stood behind him. "What happened to your mom?"

He kept his back to her, leaning against a wall with his hand and he half turned to her. Eloise walked around to get a better view of his face, but he turned away and whispered, "I don't want to talk about it."

"Alright. That's fair."

Bannack yanked her arm and she fell backward into him.

Anger shot through her. "Excuse me! I—"

His hand covered her mouth and before she could wrench it away, a hatchet, the handle wrapped in leather, crashed through the glass wall Eloise had been standing in front of. Her anger dissipated.

Bannack whispered. "You need to be more aware of your surroundings. You almost got your head chopped off."

Eloise narrowed her eyes at him and scrambled behind a leaning shelf. Voices came from her left and she watched as a young woman in a tawny fur cloak picked up the hatchet and secured it in her belt. The rest of the group showed up, three men and four women all in the same color cloaks, and blocked the doorway.

Her mouth soured as she watched them from her hiding spot.

Beside her, Bannack made a noise. He clenched his teeth and notched an arrow to his bow.

"Don't—"

He did anyway. Hissing, Bannack stood, planted his feet, and drew the bowstring back but jerked halfway through and grunted. Blood seeped through another shirt.

Eloise unsheathed her kukri. *Ugh. Why? He just had to go and ruin my hard work.*

Sudden, distressed screaming made Eloise freeze. Her back stiffened and her knuckles grew white as she gripped the hilt of her kukri. The screams were from a young man, his voice bitterly angry, who had come out from behind the wall.

"It's your fault! She's dead because of you!"

CHAPTER FOURTEEN
BANNACK

The knife blade gleamed. Bannack sucked in a shaking breath and took a half-step away, the kid's voice filled with so much hate and anguish it shocked him. Knuckles white as he gripped the bow, Bannack's back throbbed.

Damn.

Warmth spread on his back and he knew the lacerations opened. He held the bow but never fired which took all his mental strength. He would do good. Killing an obviously tortured man would destroy any progress he made.

The man lunged. A primal scream leapt from his throat. Eloise stepped in the way. He slammed into her, kicking and screaming profanities with a wild fury directed at Bannack.

Eloise shoved him away. "Who are you?"

Bannack noticed the minor shaking of her hands and her red-rimmed eyes. His knees weakened.

The man spoke first, his grief rampant. "I'm Cassius and you're traveling with a monster!"

Cassius yelled and lunged again. Preparing for the worst and refusing to lay a finger on Cassius, Bannack shrunk against the clothing rack and closed his eyes.

Nothing happened.

He opened his eyes.

With the tip of her kukri at his throat, Eloise kept Cassius at arm's length. "Cross me and I will pin your heart against the wall behind you."

Cassius's eyes fluttered, but he sniffed and lifted his head proudly.

Eloise stepped forward, her knife arm bending and shoulders pulling together. "Back...off!"

He followed her command. Eloise sheathed her blade.

Bannack remembered to shut his gaping mouth before Eloise turned to look at him. Her eyes were an inferno of chocolate brown and deep olive green flecked with sunlight.

She wiped her hands on her thighs. "Now, wh—"

Four people stepped from the shadows, yelling and demanding. They carried a mixture of primitive weapons. Eloise stepped beside Bannack, her breathing slow and coupled with a quiet growl that reminded Bannack of a suspicious cougar.

When they continued advancing, Eloise released her three throwing knives. Six more men came out of hiding. His shoulder throbbed as he threw his attackers over his head, quickly learning to never do it again, or knocked them into the trees and rocks. Each action he used sparingly as more plastic closing strips snapped and his wounds re-opened.

Both Eloise and Bannack backed further into the store, driven to the landing of a large staircase. His kick sent a man tumbling down the steps.

Someone touched his back and in a jolt of surprise, Bannack whirled around, ready to fight off another attacker. Eloise jumped away. Her lip bled. He watched her mouth move but heard nothing.

"What? My damn ear—"

Eloise yanked Bannack toward her, stepped sideways, and swung a board through the air. It hit a woman rushing toward them and she collapsed.

"You're welcome," Eloise said into his good ear. "I need a lift."

Bannack hooked his fingers underneath Eloise's boot and heaved upward as she pushed off with her leg. Her body launched through the air. Above them was a display platform and a man with a crossbow, caught off guard, lifted his weapon to shoot her. Before he could get a shot off, Eloise used her board again and clocked him upside his head. The man stumbled, dropping his crossbow, then straightened his body, growling.

In the time it took Bannack to pick up the crossbow, find a bolt in the bushes and notch it, the archer was forcing Eloise further toward the edge of the platform. She slipped a couple times and Bannack's heart leapt. Frantic, his hands trembled as he notched the bow and ran up the stairs.

Bannack pulled the string into the latch.

The man froze.

He felt nothing. Heard nothing. Only the release of the bolt and the violent, heavy clunk of the latch.

The bolt pierced the man's chest; he stumbled back and fell from the platform.

Eloise's face contorted and she ran at Bannack. She grabbed the crossbow, but he held on and that inflamed her even more.

"Do you want to prove you're a monster?"

"He was going to hurt you."

"Everyone here is trying to hurt us, you idiot!" She pulled on the crossbow again and screamed. "You killed him!"

Anger lashed out like a cobra striking. Bannack wrenched the crossbow from Eloise's grip. She stumbled. "And I will kill for as long as I need to be safe! You don't get to judge me! What I do to protect everyone is my business and mine alone. So what if I'm a monster? You certainly believe it!"

The fear in her eyes as Bannack roared would stay with him for a long time. Her arms went slack. He'd never seen her afraid of him and he knew, immediately, that he'd gone too far.

"Eloise...I..."

"Just shut the hell up." Then she gasped and said, "I need your shoulder. Kneel." Eloise took the crossbow and rested it on Bannack's shoulder, the weight of it digging into his skin, and fired. It jarred him a bit, made him wince, but Bannack got a good look at her form and the way she cocked her head to use her sight. He couldn't help it; his heart fluttered. Sticks and dirt wound through her hair. She gritted her teeth and the blood from the healed cut on her mouth cracked.

Someone grunted behind him and Bannack turned to see a woman cradling her thigh, the bolt protruding from her flesh.

Eloise gave him a cold, emotionless stare and shoved the weapon into his chest. She ran toward the final attacker.

Where's Cassius?

Cold metal touched his throat. Bannack froze.

"Stop!"

The screaming in his good ear made him wince, and the blade pressed closer to his jugular. Realizing defeat, he forced his body to calm.

Bannack's eyes reached Eloise. She licked her bloodied lip and shoved against her captors. They pinned her on her knees, her hands trapped underneath their boots. With each quick exhale, Eloise's cheeks puffed. She glared.

Through gritted teeth, Eloise said, "I need my hands back. Your feet will make excellent door stops for my apartment, boots and all."

Growling at her comment, the men stepped harder on her hands. Eloise squealed and jerked in response.

Bannack's anger erupted out of him but had nowhere to go. Cold steel from the knife scratched his throat as he spoke. "It's me you want!"

Cassius leaned forward. "That's true," he motioned at Eloise with an open palm, "but she was in the way."

"Then release her. Your business is with me."

"She deserves to know! You sent people to their grave."

Bannack gritted his teeth and balled his fists, nails digging into the flesh of his palm.

"Not going to talk? Fine." The knife pressed further into his neck.

His heart pumped against his chest. He tensed and blurted, "Yes! I did! I kidnapped innocent people and gave them to Dr. Pierce to do as she wished."

The blade released from his throat and Bannack sank to his knees. His shoulders slumped, and he stared at a young sword fern peeking through the ground.

"We're going to punish you for what you did," Cassius said, kneeling in front of Bannack. "You'll finally understand the pain."

"Keep your hands off him!" Eloise's rage made Bannack flinch.

"How are your actions any different from what she did to you?"

A slap reverberated through the forest. Eloise cried out. This fueled a rage in Bannack and he lunged at the person who slapped her, grabbed his throat, and slammed him into the ground. Before he could attack, a rope snagged Bannack's raised arm, yanking him back and down. His shoulder cracked into a hidden rock. The pain blasted through his body and he cried out, holding his shoulder as he crouched.

"Bind your tongue!" The venom in Cassius' voice was blood curdling.

Eloise shook her head. "I'm pretty damn close to cutting yours out."

The sliding of a knife out of its sheath caught Bannack's attention. Cassius held Eloise's kukri horizontally to her throat.

What is it with this guy and throats?

Bannack knew when to admit defeat. He forced his body to relax. With the kukri against her tender skin, he'd kill her if he tried to protect her.

"Eloise..." Bannack warned. Her eyes darted to him and she clenched her jaw.

The rope was still around Bannack's wrist and when he pulled at it, his shoulder throbbed. He sucked in a breath.

"What's your plan, Cassius?" Eloise asked. A rectangular bruise formed on her cheek. "What you're doing is barbaric."

"Is it though?" Cassius laughed. "Look at you. You're seething like a wild animal. It's rather comical." His face changed from amusement to raw hatred. "I want you to pay for everything!"

I've seen that rage before. This is not going to end well.

He looked at Eloise, giving her a warning glance, as Cassius marched them down the path.

***

Animal and human skulls, paired with an assortment of masks with teeth, extra eyes, fur, and black painted handprints, hung on spikes. Red paint on signs depicted violent wars. Crudely formed weapons hung from trees wrapped with leather or animal body parts hanging from the handles. The village was the site of an abandoned campsite, fortified by tall, pointed logs. Cabins, covered with wood, tarps, and moss, sat on either side of a wide main roadway framed by lanterns. There were two plots of immature crops at the entrance.

He knew this village. When Eloise spoke of the locals and them being vicious and brutal, he didn't connect it to the same place he had stayed with his family years ago as they escaped the danger from the war. The wards to warn people away must have been put in after he left.

Where's Kendal? He looked for her but didn't see her.

Cassius led Eloise and Bannack toward a single hut at the end of the wide pathway. Villagers passing stopped to stare. Many murmured angrily to each other. Some ducked into their homes, afraid.

I won't give in to the shame.

I won't give into the shame.

The hate and surprise singed the hair on the back of Bannack's neck. They didn't have to speak; one look told him he was not welcome.

Kendal stormed from her cabin, her locs flowing freely as she struggled to button the rest of her shirt up. "What's going on?"

"Out of the way, Kendal."

"No." She planted her feet, took a crossbow from one of her guards, and trained it on Cassius. "Let them go. Now!"

"You know what he did. Why are you defending him?"

"He and the woman with him are my guests now. You have no right to do anything without my consent. Now. I'm going to say it one more time or I shoot you. Let them go."

Villagers gathered behind Cassius. They were silent, making Bannack's blood run cold.

Kendal lowered her weapon. "What you're threatening is no better than what Joy did to you. The entire point of this village is to give people a place of refuge and solidarity."

"And you're going to allow him inside?" Cassius scoffed, then waved in the air to tell his man to release Bannack. "The same person who killed my sister is the reason so many are crippled. Without him, there'd be no village!"

"Even without him, there'd still be a village, only someone else would have taken his place. Yes. He caused pain but look at him."

All eyes moved to Bannack. He squared his shoulders, trying to cover up the shaking, but couldn't stop the quivering of his lip or the rising fear in his gut.

"I've known Bannack Owusu for years and he has proven himself to be worthy of my friendship."

"Don't hurt him!" A girl burst through the crowd and straight into Bannack. He grunted as he tried to stay on his feet.

"Nora!"

The last thing he expected was to see Nora and, at first, he kept his hands off her, but when she looked up at him, teary-eyed, he caved and hugged her tight.

Nora glared at Cassius. "He saved my life!"

Hushed whispers spread through the crowd. Cassius took a stumbling half-step back as he scanned the villagers then looked at Nora.

"He's a bad man."

"No, he's not!" Nora shoved Cassius. "He's my friend!"

She was crying now, angry tears trickling down her cheeks. Her round, brown eyes glared at Cassius and then looked at the crowd.

"Why are you being like this?" Nora asked. She walked back to Bannack, who was on his knees and stunned into paralysis, and stood protectively in front of him. "You're the bad people if you're going to hurt him. I know he feels sorry, so you should all just leave him alone!"

He shouldn't be worth the protection of Nora or Eloise or Kendal, not with what he did to the villagers, but they believed he was worth saving and that was enough to encourage Bannack to do more.

Standing to his full height, his hand around Nora's shoulder, Bannack called out to the entire village. "I have allowed others to speak for me, to defend me. While I am grateful for their love and loyalty, I must speak." He smiled down at Nora, took a deep breath, and spoke. "What I did to you is unforgivable. I do not expect you to forgive me but recently Kendal has helped me to realize something important. There are few times in a person's life where we are defined by our actions. What we do in that moment shapes our future. I did not quite understand what she meant until now." Bannack turned around. "Joy is a scourge on this land. She has destroyed countless lives and lied over and over again. If you want the scientist to be stopped, you must let us go."

More angry whispers spread through the crowd, and Bannack scanned each of their faces. He watched the anger and hatred calm on most, while some still stood with clenched fists. The tension in the air was claustrophobic.

Someone panted in the crowd. Bannack turned around and his eyes went straight to Cassius who sneered, his nostrils flaring, while his breathing made his chest rise and expand dramatically.

"No!" Cassius screamed. "Don't you want revenge for all the damage he's done? Just look at yourselves! Lepers in a world of people who want nothing to do with us."

Bannack stood statue still. His feet wouldn't move as he looked through the crowd of villagers, many deformed in their faces and extremities. They limped, held their arms at odd angles, and when they spoke, half of their face didn't react as if they suffered a stroke. Many glared at him. Some spit on the ground.

"Disperse." Kendal called. "Now! I will not have his blood spilt today."

Tension lurked in the air as Kendal stared down her people until they stomped off, mumbling angrily. One or two smacked into Bannack and he stumbled backward, avoiding their furious stares.

They wouldn't hurt him with Kendal around but he knew he was hated. It stung.

Cassius huffed like a wounded animal, trying to convince the others to join him again. But no one listened.

Eloise walked over and stood beside Bannack, then smiled. "You've lost, Cassius."

The enraged gleam in his eye put Bannack on edge. Cassius reached behind his back and pulled a gun from the waist of his jeans. Nora rushed to her parents who pulled her away. Eloise squeaked and backed up. Bannack outstretched his hand in a placating gesture. His vision blurred at the edges, leg muscles tightened, and he blanched.

"Please," Bannack said with a gasp. "Stop this."

"Cassius." Kendal slunk toward him. "Put my gun down."

"No!" Cassius screamed and pointed the barrel straight at

Bannack's head. "He killed my sister. I want him to suffer."

Bannack's insides coiled tight. Out of the corner of his eye, he saw Jerome sneak through the forest's edge in a wide circle.

His attention flicked back to Cassius.

I cannot jump him. He is too far away, and I cannot tell if he is even a good shot. If he is not, he could accidentally shoot someone else. Eloise or Kendal or Nora. Bannack's heart raced. *My best bet is to distract him and hope Jerome can sneak up on Cassius enough to subdue him.*

Step by step, Bannack crept closer to Cassius, talking in low tones. The gun remained in his hands. Sweat beads appeared on Cassius' forehead and then his eyes locked on Eloise.

"Or maybe I'll just kill her."

The gun lifted.

Bannack lunged at Eloise, his body connecting with her midsection at the same time a loud pop hurt his ear. They hit the ground and he scrambled to his knees, searching Eloise's body for blood. He only heard his heartbeat.

Please. Please, please.

Cursing made Bannack turn. Cassius's face made friends with the dirt, a brown cloud surrounding him while Jerome lashed his hands then wrenched him to his feet.

"You're all gutless!" Cassius fought Jerome. "You won't do what has to be done!"

Bannack looked back at Eloise as she sat up and said, "I'm okay." She wiped his face and showed him her wet fingertips. "Tears."

He touched his face and sure enough tears were on his cheek. *When did I...?*

Kendal, gun in her hand, sighed. "We'll keep him detained. I apologize for this."

On the ground, Bannack panted. His vision swirled and tilted.

Get it together. Feeling will get you killed.

The emotions came anyway. Tremors ran through him as he curled into a ball, shivering.

She almost died. Shot and killed. Because of me.

Because of me.

He couldn't stop the tremors as he pressed his forehead to the ground. Images of the gun, Eloise's face filled with terror, and the revelation of his past flashed through his mind. The memories crumpled his body like a piece of paper discarded in the waste bin.

Bannack shuddered.

I did not want her to find out yet. Not like this. Not forced out of me.

Pain in his back made him tense. He opened his mouth, nothing coming from it, and reached around to his shoulder.

More pain.

Only then did he remember he still needed stitches. The past hour he had been so full of adrenaline and anxiety, his body had masked the pain. Now it came full force, nearly doubling him over again.

A hand touched his back. "Once again, Blue Eyes, you are bleeding on my doorstep with your stray." She held out her hand for him. He slowly stood. "Let's fix you up, yeah?"

***

Kendal finished her sutures within half an hour. She sighed and put the needle and horsehair thread in the bowl. "Please take care of yourself. I do not want to start sewing scars back together because you have no more space left to fill."

"Yes, ma'am."

She walked away, grumbling.

Eloise sat at the foot of the bed and he ignored her as he dressed. The stitches stung.

"Can we talk about the mall?"

"There's nothing to say."

Eloise released an exasperated sigh. "Yes, there is, and you know it. I'm not going to tiptoe around you like you seem to expect me to do. It's infuriating sometimes. And Bannack..." She touched his knee, which made him shiver. He turned to her as she continued. "You killed a man in cold blood. You're lucky he wasn't connected to the village."

"That is what you're worried about?" He laughed and pushed her hand away. "I told you I was one of Joy's agents and you're more concerned with a dead man?"

No emotion touched her face as she looked at him. "I'm surprised you aren't."

"Look," he sighed and rubbed his face. "I was trained to kill, to force my emotions out of my mind, and do what needed to be done to get my reward. It was selfish of me and cruel of the man who trained me. Joy let the abuse happen. She wanted it to happen. I did not have the luxury of safety. Kill or be killed. That is it." A slight growl rolled off his tongue. "So, forgive me if I don't behave the way you want."

"It's not about what I want." Eloise glared at him. "It's about who you can become. You are terrifying and it's taking all of my willpower to sit here and not be afraid of you. I still do, because I believe you are capable of great kindness."

He looked at his hands. His jaw worked, and he sniffed.

She's right. I can't expect her fear of me to drive her away, but how can I not expect it when I have known nothing else?

Eloise continued. "Pull yourself together. We aren't given this life to destroy ourselves out of self-pity or hatred." She stood in front of him. When he refused to look at Eloise, she kept on talking. "This life is to better who we are, to take our mistakes of the past and move past them, not let them fester in an open wound. If you keep talking like the way you are, she's won. You are giving her power over you still. Don't give her the satisfaction. You say you didn't honor your family in death and maybe that's true...years ago but honor them now. Honor them by picking yourself up and loving yourself enough to do better. Be better! Start now. It—it can be a new beginning. You're not the only one to have experienced trauma."

Eloise's last words brought his gaze to her face. She watched him, calm. He chewed on her words for a moment, blinking through the angry and frustrated tears that blurred his vision. Then he dropped his head.

"I know," Bannack whispered.

"Then allow me in. Let me help you. If you do, maybe I can help you realize you are worthy of love."

How can that be possible?

He bore the weight of lost souls, maimed innocents. He couldn't atone for what he had done, despite what Alma and Tamra had said.

And yet, he desperately wanted to be loved again. To be accepted and appreciated was as lost to him as Atlantis was to modern civilization, but he wanted it. His mind screamed for it.

He eyed Eloise for a long while, chewing on his lip as salted tears leaked into his mouth. She held her soft gaze and in it sat acceptance and respect, given to him not because he earned it—he knew perfectly well he hadn't—but because she was Eloise and through her hard exterior was still the little girl who had shared her cookie with him when no one else wanted to be near him. The one who offered to punch a kid making fun of his name. The one who lectured him when he made fun of his sister. She always believed in him. And now? He didn't deserve any of her belief, but still, she gave it. Without hesitation. Without question. It was as if he had been floundering in a bottomless lake and Eloise had just thrown him a lifeline.

I need to be strong. For her. For me.

"Hey, Elle," Bannack said as he rubbed his hands together to get them to stop shaking. She glanced at him. "Lately, I have been an idiot. You are supportive and strong and here I am being a weak ass—" he paused, glanced sideways at Eloise, then cleared his throat. "Sorry. What I am trying to say is I have to change. Be and do better. Earn that respect, you know?"

"Good." Eloise punched him lightly. She winked. "Cause I'm getting tired of making you feel good about yourself."

Then she left him alone. A few minutes later, the door opened and Eloise walked in with two steaming bowls. "Hungry?"

She put his on the bedside table, and he peered into it. Carrots, some kind of reddish meat, white beans, and celery in a clear, glistening broth.

"What is it?"

"Ham and bean soup, I think. Doesn't matter," Eloise licked the corner of her mouth and made a noise. "Mmm. Because it's really good."

He took a bite with the hand-carved spoon. The briny broth was hot, smooth like velvet, and warmed him as it traveled to his stomach. The meat's robust, smoky flavor melted in his mouth with each bite. He sighed. Lost in his enjoyment of the food, Bannack jumped when Eloise sighed loudly.

"It seems we argue any moment we are together," Bannack said.

She watched him with the same intense gaze he had come to enjoy. It showed a fire, a passion, hidden underneath the calm. "Seems so."

"Then we have a problem. I do not wish to argue. It makes me...angry." He scratched the back of his head. "That is an emotion I must keep in check."

"Why are you telling me this?"

"Because," he put his bowl on the side table, "I intend to change that. Perhaps a truce? We no longer argue. I can keep my anger in check. And you will have a friend you do not need to be afraid of."

Her eyes narrowed a bit, but she nodded. "That's fair."

Eloise stacked Bannack's bowl onto hers. He got out of bed, his back stinging, then grabbed her arm to stop her. "Are you upset about my past?"

She said nothing for a bit, most likely only a few seconds but for Bannack it lasted hours. Silence while waiting with a rushing in his ears turned the nervous beating of his heart torturous.

Bannack shrank. He tensed, preparing.

"No," she finally said.

Eyes wide, Bannack stumbled back and slumped onto his bed. He shook. "No? Why?"

CHAPTER FIFTEEN
ELOISE

"Why were you in the facility?" She shot back, answering his shock with her own question.

Do I really want to know?

Eloise's head pounded with her heartbeat. She looked at Bannack. His head hung and shoulders slumped.

That can't be the face of a man who doesn't regret what he did. No way.

"Okay." Bannack held up his hands. He took a deep breath, closed his eyes, and when he opened them, they glistened. His voice was barely a whisper as he said, "After my father died, my sister, mom, and I traveled back over The Narrows and ran into Kendal. We were exhausted. She gave us a place to stay in her village. While there, I heard terrified whispers about a woman—Joy—who could wipe memories. When Maame and Malikah were killed, I remembered the whispers and searched for her. When I found her, I begged her to wipe my memories. She agreed. In return, I would give her six years of service."

The temperature dropped ten degrees. Eloise stumbled into a

standing position, grabbing onto the bedpost to hold herself steady.

"I will forever be ashamed of what I did. She sent me to collect people for her..." Bannack swallowed "...experiments. After five years, she asked me to kidnap Nora. She was twelve."

No...

Sweat rose into her neck and around her armpits and the world spun. Her body pulsed, thumping and pounding her insides with a meat tenderizer.

"I could not do it," Bannack said. He wrung his hands and wouldn't remove his eyes from his feet. "One more year until Joy would wipe my memories and I chose instead to save Nora. I helped her family escape to Canada."

"And now you're back. Why?"

He scrubbed his arm. "I wanted a blank slate. Us being in the same facility at the same time was mere coincidence.

"I know what I did. I can never atone for it, and I will walk away right now if you ask me to."

Emotions swirled in her head faster than she could focus on them. Anger over his past with Joy, concern he would let his shame overwhelm him, and despondence the war had changed them so much. Everything bunched together in a muddy mess. Eloise fought with her composure, shaking if she stood or sat, and unable to look at Bannack. The small glances she managed were of a man tormented. He wrung his hands, shrunk into the bed he was sitting on, giving the illusion he was suddenly small, then covered his face.

Eloise paused, eyeing Bannack.

He's tormented by this.

She had to admit she felt sorry for him. His past was dark, and she understood the fear and nightmares too well.

He remained small.

If I had the chance to forget Ada, I don't think I would take it. So why did he?

"Why did you want to forget your family?"

When Bannack spoke, it was through hitching breath. "It is not that I want to forget them, but how they died. My inaction is the reason they are dead."

How awful.

A thought sparked in Eloise's head. "What were you going to do once Joy wiped your memories? You would be ignorant of everything important and knowing Joy, she could have taken advantage."

Bannack furrowed his eyebrows, and his shoulders drooped. "I...I did not think of that."

Sounds like the old Bannack. That version never thought things through completely, either.

She approached Bannack and put out her hand. "Your past is dark and you're going to have to continue facing it head on to see some real change, but I do believe you regret what you did. I also understand you did it because of trauma and, like me, you are working every day to overcome it. What do you say we leave the past here and start with a new beginning?"

"Thank you," Bannack said, his voice tiny and shaking. "Your words mean a lot."

Kendal walked in followed by Mal, Abe, and Finch. Mal was the first to embrace Eloise. "We can't leave you alone ever, can we? Thank goodness you're alright. Mason would have my hide if you weren't."

Eloise laughed. "How'd you guys find this place?"

"Jerome found 'em," Kendal said. "They were poking around the village wall looking for you so he brought them here."

Finch, sporting a black eye, sat on a nearby chair, leaned back, and put her ankle over her knee. "Clocked me upside the head. What's the deal with all the scary stuff?"

Kendal answered, "I created the rumor that we are brutal and will attack on sight to protect the people here. They don't need trouble. Most of the time," Kendal looked pointedly at Abe, Nails, and Finch, "it works."

Eloise stifled a snort. Those three, no matter where they went, found trouble, and recent events proved their tendency was rubbing off on her, or maybe—she glanced at Bannack—it was someone else's. Either way, Mason placed her with the three Sentinels to keep them in line. Not join in on their trouble making. She rolled her eyes and sat down.

"Where's the horse?" Eloise asked.

Abe inclined his head. "Outside. Where's yours?"

"Gone," Eloise said. "Chased off by the pride of lions. You didn't happen to see her when you came looking for us, did you?"

"No. Mason's gonna be pissed." Nails inspected his fingers.

Eloise groaned and leaned forward, her hands covering her face. She lost the horse. "What are we going to do? The Compound can't afford to lose any of their animals."

Abe patted her once on the back and smiled. "We'll manage. Trading season is in a couple months and we can gather enough resources to trade for another horse."

"Well," Finch stood, "I will be long gone when that conversation happens."

"Ha! No, you won't," Eloise said and leaned toward her. "If one of us has to go down, we all are."

Finch raised her eyebrow and sighed. "Well, we gotta get out of here so Mason can yell at us."

Eloise laughed and put her forehead on Finch's shoulder.

***

Their return trip from hunting proved to be more productive than the first. A herd of deer outside the city limits grazed in the tall grass and after Bannack killed one, Eloise and Finch lashed it to the horse's back. They later collected some quail and rabbits a few hours from the Compound.

Mason waited for them at the stables. "Where's Ruby?"

"We..." Eloise rubbed her fingertips together and stood aside so Abe could lead the other horse into her stall, "lost her. I'm sorry, Mason."

She had expected frustration. Not concern. "Tell me what happened."

Eloise relayed the news but kept her and Bannack's conversation secret. Mason listened while Abe and Mal attended the horse and Finch and Bannack cleaned and shined the tack and unloaded the hunting cargo.

"I wish we hadn't lost her. She was our best horse."

"I know," Eloise said and hung her head.

Mason put his hand on her shoulder and when Eloise looked up, he smiled and said, "But I'm so glad everyone came back in one piece. Get some rest." A smile brightened his face. "Tomorrow's your day off."

Relief ran through her, and she sighed. She turned to the crew. "I'll water and feed the horses."

"Hey, guys!" Sibyl walked down the concrete incline with her usual bouncing gait. Abe, Mal, Bannack, and Finch all waved at her as they walked home. She watched each of them pass, her eyes flicking to Bannack's bandages underneath his shirt collar, and raised her eyebrow at Eloise. "Something happened. Didn't it?"

"Lions attacked us. We lost Ruby. No! Wait. Don't cry, please. I hate it when you do that."

Sibyl was always happy, so when she wasn't, it made Eloise nervous.

"I'll be okay." Sibyl wiped at her eyes, sniffed, then put her arms out. "I just need a hug."

Eloise chuckled and wrapped her arms around Sibyl. When they broke apart, Sibyl smiled mischievously.

"Come on." Sibyl pulled Eloise toward the horse stable.

"Where are we going?"

"We need to share our boy woes with Beau. He's an excellent listener."

"He makes me nervous."

"Hush up. He's the perfect person to share things with."

"He's not a person!"

Sibyl had leeched herself onto Eloise years ago. No matter how hard she tried, Sibyl refused to go away. Ignoring her made things worse. Trying to scare her off by being rude didn't work either.

Eloise adored her.

She liked Sibyl's company. She was loud and obnoxious but had a kind heart, was incredibly loyal, and thought about others more often than Eloise did. Sibyl also had an uncanny ability to pop in when Eloise needed her most.

She allowed Sibyl to pull her along. They passed through the open gate of the chain-link fence that led to the football field. Grass grew in place of the Astroturf, ripped up long ago, and now the area grew food for the five horses—now four—housed in the building underneath the home team bleachers.

It was the perfect place. The five classrooms were large enough to keep a horse. The upstairs rooms could hold any tack and supplies they needed.

Beau was Sibyl's favorite, most likely because he was sweet on her. The other three horses were black, chestnut and grullo, but Beau was a beautiful buckskin tobiano Gypsy Cob. His mane covered his eyes and flowed with every shake of his thick neck.

He terrified Eloise. Beau was smaller than the other horses, standing a bit taller than pony height, but was higher strung and had a solid build. Since his arrival to the Compound as a colt, Eloise had seen Beau send several people to the medical ward before being gelded.

One thing was for sure. No one could make Beau do anything he did not want to do, yet with Sibyl's persistence, he had grown leaps and bounds. She could get him to do anything. He was like a puppy with her and she soaked it all in. If Beau was being an idiot, they called Sibyl to help.

"So, Beau," Sibyl crooned to him as she brushed his black and white mane. "I heard my friend spent a lot of quality time with an adorable man."

Eloise rolled her eyes. "Now you're feeding him lies? He's a horse!"

Sibyl gasped, and Beau puffed in response, his mane shaking out. She covered his ears. "You take that back!" Sibyl rubbed his ears between her fingers. "I'm so sorry, Beau. She just doesn't understand us. You and me. Forever."

"He is a freakin' hor—never mind." Eloise made a lazy throwing motion with her hand. She would much rather collect water for the horses instead of watching Sibyl gush over a smelly animal.

She found the trough sitting in the shade of an awning against the tree line. Buckets hung on rusty nails hammered into the doorjamb. The glass from the top half of the door was missing, and the horses peaked out, eager for their turn with the water.

Eloise spent several minutes carrying buckets to each horse. She enjoyed it; the not-getting-inside-with-them part.

She gave a scratch to one horse on her forelock and poured the bucket of water for the mare.

Finally, the last horse. He was getting up in years and had become quite grumpy. Impatient, he began banging his large black hoof against the wall.

Bang, bang, bang.

"Hold on! I'm coming!"

Bang, bang, bang.

"Will you just hold on a minute?" Eloise rushed back to the trough and plunged the bucket deep into the water.

Bang, bang...*bang*...*bang*...

The world around her blurred at the edges. Eloise shook her head. Her heart pounded against her chest.

The bucket hit the ground, and water spilled onto the asphalt.

Bang...bang...bang.

"You stupid horse! Quit banging your leg on the wall!"

Her sudden screaming brought Sibyl out of the stall. "Are you all right?"

Eloise covered her ears, the *bang, bang, bang* rattling around in her head, tormenting her. The scent of blood filled her nose.

The man cut Eloise.

Ada's body hit the floor.

Every inhale and exhale sent an inferno throughout her body. Eloise's feet tangled when she ran, and she tumbled to the ground, landing in the puddle made from the water bucket.

"Eloise?"

"Don't touch me!"

The minute her words came out, Eloise regretted them.

Sibyl stepped back, her eyes full of concern.

"I...the banging...I..."

Eloise stood, unable to look at Sibyl, and stumbled away as quickly as she could.

I have to get away. I have to get away!

More banging.

More blood. This time, hers.

More gunshots.

She collapsed against the wall inside the Compound. Her chest heaved so heavily, her ribs hurt.

I have to get away! I need to move. Why won't my legs work?

A sob rolled out of her throat as she pulled herself up on the wall.

Bang, bang, BANG.

The door.

The darkness.

Warm hands on her.

A cloud.

No. A bed.

Why was there a bed?

Where am I?

***

The next day blurred, her day off plans ruined, but she didn't care. Everything hurt.

When Bannack came to visit, she was sitting up in bed stroking Bali. He knocked and entered. Day old stubble kissed the lines of his jaw and his warm masculine energy consumed the room, bringing with it the familiar scent of lavender with an added treat of earthen air. He'd been outside, proven by the dirty smudges on his shirt and ripped jeans. Her eyes shifted to his hands. Calloused from manual labor with wide knuckles and lines of subtle veins. They were strong,

161

powerful, and made Eloise's breath hitch.

Ohmygod.

His hands? Really, Eloise.

He shouldn't have looked so beautiful, but he did.

"And you didn't even wash up," Eloise said, mirth heavy in her tone.

Bannack smiled. If Eloise was standing, she would have fallen over. As he approached, he said, "And miss a chance to get you dirty?"

Eloise stopped stroking Bali, stared at him, and pushed down a snigger. Her face heated, and she put her hand on her hip. "Well...I mean...getting dirty could mean so many things."

"Huh?" Bannack mumbled under his breath. "What did I say?" He looked at her then and cocked his head. "Why are you reddening?"

"You just said—" Eloise lost her battle over keeping her composure and cackled. Bannack stood in the middle of the room, his arms hanging limp at his side, and blinked slowly as she laughed for a good while.

When she stopped, she wiped her eyes so she could see him. "You have no idea how sexual that sounded just now. And your face..." she chuckled, "your face is so...so confused."

"Wha...?" More confusion. He looked at his feet, then back at her. "I meant to give you a hug. I don't—"

Realization spread across his face and he pulled his head into his shirt like a turtle. Muffled words flew from behind his hands. "Oh my God," he said. Bannack peaked out from his shirt collar, only his eyes visible, and lowered his eyebrows. "No laughing. Why are you laughing again?"

They were both smiling now, Eloise on the verge of sputtering. "You can..." she wheezed, then cleared her throat, "you can give me a hug. I don't mind."

"Oh, good." Bannack stood and walked over.

A small spread of black peach fuzz covered his chin and when he leaned in close, his scent evolved into an entire lifeline, and she became intoxicated by the fragrance. It engulfed her in a gentle caress that should have been impossible for a man of his stature. This embrace was different than when they were riding Ruby. It was different than all the other times they were close. His one touch, a simple hug, spun her head. She lifted her arms around him. His skin flickered, and the muscles moved, strong and masculine. She knew he felt something because he inhaled through his nose. The sound was faint. She almost missed it. But it lit her stomach on fire.

What...is happening?

When he straightened, she scanned his face, looking for any sign of his realization. She knew it was there. His dark skin hid it well.

Bannack scurried for the door.

"Wait."

He paused, his back still turned.

"You're not going to sit down and talk?" Eloise asked.

He turned around with twinkling eyes.

God. He's so beautiful.

Bannack pulled up a chair. One corner of his mouth lifted higher than the other in a half smile, showing a small part of his teeth.

"What is it?" she asked.

"I am remembering the last time I saw you," he said and leaned on his elbows, his hands hanging limp at the wrist.

Intrigued, Eloise cocked her head. "I don't remember."

"It was summer. About...six months Before. You stood on my back porch in the doorway teasing me for how I made my sandwich." He smiled and glanced sideways at her, his blue eyes twinkling. "You were brutal."

"Was that the peanut butter and jelly sandwich?"

Bannack nodded.

"Yes! I remember now. You put butter on it."

"And you never let me live it down."

"No. Because it's weird. Everyone knows you're supposed to use the curved side of the butter knife. And who puts butter on their PB and J?"

"I do, thank you very much, because who wants ripped bread?"

163

"Your bread rips when you put peanut butter on it?"

"Yours does not?"

Eloise shook her head.

"Huh. Maybe I was doing it wrong..."

"Uh, yeah. That's the whole point of our conversation. You make sandwiches weird."

Bannack tilted his head back and laughed. "Well, at least I do not dig worms out of the dirt, lick them off, and put them back in for more dirt."

"I was what? Five? It doesn't count."

He tapped his chest with his finger. "If I get flack for my peanut butter and jelly sandwiches," then he jabbed his finger at Eloise, "you get flack for your secret worm licking."

"You know what?" She paused, unable to think of anything to say.

Bannack, his eyes narrowed and lips curled in a shy smile, flicked his nonexistent hair and leaned back against his chair. She scoffed then folded her arms, watching him smile. Her heart jumped.

She looked at her chest.

Listen you, if I have to get a beating from you every time he smiles, looks at me, or breathes, I might just have to tear you out and throw you away.

***

Eloise laid in the grass, her eyes closed, listened to the birds and enjoyed the sunlight warming her face and body.

Bannack was right. This is kinda nice.

"Yo!"

Eloise's ears perked up to the sound of Sibyl's call and turned.

"You're such a slacker," Sibyl said as she got close. "It's your turn to get the herbs and plants for Soora's tinctures and you're out here lying in the grass. Here's the list."

"Nah," Eloise said, pushed the list away, and grabbed the wicker basket from Sibyl. "I think I got it."

164

"Really? Come on," Sibyl motioned with her fingers, "tell me what Soora needs."

She sighed. "Seaweed, broadleaf plantain, lichen, sphagnum moss, horsetail, cattail, and..." Eloise paused, and Sibyl raised her eyebrow. "Shut up! Okay. Yes. I need the list."

Sibyl laughed and pulled a piece of thick, handmade paper from her pocket.

"I'll be back."

Sibyl nodded. "See ya."

***

Cold water wrapped around Eloise's bare legs and sent a shiver through her body. If she wasn't careful, the water flowing down from the snow-capped mountain on the horizon would numb her bare feet—she had left her boots on the shore—faster than she could collect the cattails. Mud squelched between her toes. A family of ducks quacked in alarm, then fluttered their wings to escape Eloise's presence as she waded through the grass and water.

Children's chatter danced through the air. Eloise, tying a piece of rope around the cattail stalks, grabbed her boots, tied them together, and hefted both shoes and bundle over her shoulder. She walked toward the noise, laughter occasionally rising up then fading behind the sound of running water and splashing.

The bushes rustled gently as Eloise pushed them out of her way and she watched kids of varying ages, gathered along the riverbed, splashing in the water and digging in the sand. Their parents either sat on blankets, patches of smooth rock and grass, or played. A laugh caught Eloise's attention. Her eyes flickered further up the riverbank. Kids surrounded Bannack.

Eloise watched him. His smile. The way his shoulders moved as he walked. The slight swagger to his hips. Jeans rolled up to his knees. Tattoos along his arm. He held his hands out, cupped, for the kids to grab something from his palms.

Tucking her body behind a mangled oak tree, Eloise watched as a flock of ducks gathered around Bannack and the kids, some flapping their wings as they waited for what the children and Bannack held in their hands.

"One, two, three, throw!" Bannack whooped, tossing a handful of what appeared to be seeds onto the surface of the water.

The kids squealed. Bannack laughed, an unrestrained and bright noise.

Their eyes locked.

She tried to hide, and for a moment she thought she had succeeded, but when she peered around the tree to look for Bannack, he was leaning against the tree trunk inches from her. Eloise squeaked, falling backward and panting as her heart pounded in her chest. He shoved his hands in the pockets of his rolled-up jeans, a sideways smirk pulling at the corner of his deep-set, crystalline eyes. Once she recovered, a subtle warmth tugged at her chest.

"How long were you spying?" He asked.

"Spying?" Eloise sputtered. "I'm offended."

His eyes glistened. "Uh-huh."

"You're good with the kids." Eloise inclined her head toward the crowd of children at the riverbank.

Bannack followed her line of sight. "Ah..." He shrugged. "I enjoy the ducks as much as they do."

They watched each other. He stood with his shoulders square, proud, and with a slight lean to his body. He took a step, foot resting on the grassy embankment Eloise stood on. Her cheeks reddened and then her ears. Because why not? If her emotions continued to betray her, wearing a box over her head would be an appropriate solution.

"Your lying is substandard," Bannack whispered with a growl.

Eloise's body shuddered when Bannack's fingers brushed her own, looking at her through an awning of black eyelashes. An invisible string pulled gently on her chest, coaxing her closer, touching his hand. She inhaled through her nose, acutely aware of his stare on her lips. She smiled. "You're close."

"Am I?"

Swallowing, Eloise nodded.

His breathing increased, and Eloise, unwilling to resist, leaned in. Breath puffed across the surface of her skin. Her muscles hummed.

Children screamed, and they separated.

Ohmygod. Her face heated. *We almost...*

She stole a glance his way—he was still looking at the kids—and smiled, touching her mouth.

CHAPTER SIXTEEN
BANNACK

He sat up, sweating, and told himself it was the fault of the morning sun on his blanket.

Eloise filled his dreams during the night. Her hair had spread out from her head in vibrant tendrils, covering the grass she laid in. She motioned to him, her voice low and seductive. He dreamed he had laid down next to her, felt her ivory skin underneath his fingers, and kissed her neck. The imagery was so vivid, so alluring, he spent most of the night awake.

Yes. The reason he was sweating was because of the sun. Most definitely. For sure. Probably. Maybe.

Bannack groaned, walked to the water basin on a side table, and splashed his face. A view of Eloise's collar bone flashed in his head.

"Come on," Bannack growled as he gripped the edges of the side table. "Clear your mind. No feelings. I can't..."

It's no use.

More flashes of Eloise. They mocked him, haunted him, and he wanted them gone and to stay all at the same time.

Would allowing myself to feel this be so bad?

168

It didn't help that he had touched her hand at the river and leaned in close to her. That had to stop. Completely.

He let the thoughts swirl and sway in his head, images and desires forming a vibrant dance. At first, he avoided showing emotion over it, but as he entertained the feelings, a smile grew on his lips. She utterly captivated him.

Despite trying to feel nothing, he felt everything.

Someone knocked on his door. Bannack gasped, fumbling with the water bowl as it sloshed and tipped before he managed to wrangle it to submission.

"Yeah?" He called out.

"It's Mason. Be at the sparring yard in five."

"Sure, boss."

He turned to the mirror hanging on the wall above the washbasin and put his index finger on it. "Listen," he said. "If she's there, you are going to feel nothing while you're with her and this will all pass quickly."

This is going to go the exact opposite of what I want, isn't it?

He looked at the water in the basin, then grabbed a shirt from the new dresser he brought to his room a few days ago. It didn't slide open well, but it did a decent enough job. With the shirt around his upper arms, Bannack turned to look at his back in the mirror. Four long scars, running diagonally from his shoulder to his spine, were purpled but fading. He'd never sustained scars so severe before. Soora had removed the stitches a week ago. Bannack reached around and touched the longest and deepest raised mark.

He scooped some ointment up with his fingers that Soora had given him to encourage better healing, massaged it into his skin, then lifted his shirt over his head. The scars pulled but didn't hurt.

Bannack walked to the sparring yard, resolve in his mind and determination in his step. He had a plan. And he would stick to it.

The plan dissipated once he turned the corner. Eloise stood in the hallway, leaning against the doorjamb into Mason and Soora's room, her ankle crossed over the other and her arm propped over her head. Her olive jacket hung off one shoulder.

I should run. Yeah. Get away from—

She turned. Her upturned eyes drew him in, locking his feet into place. Through them, Bannack saw her soul. It was wild, on fire, and nothing stood a chance against the inferno. Including Bannack.

If he wasn't careful, she'd burn him.

The only thing to do now was mask the hurricane inside his own mind.

"Good morning," Bannack said, smiling at her.

She stretched. "Good morning. I hear you're hitting the sparring yard soon."

"I am."

"Cool." She gave a smile. "I'm heading there myself. Just stopped to say hi."

Brilliant. This is going so well.

She leaned into the room and waved goodbye to Soora and Mason, then looked at Bannack. They locked eyes for a moment.

"Do you want to walk together?" She asked.

All he could do was nod.

Eloise watched him for a moment, a faint smile twitching at the corner of her mouth. She leaned in and he stepped back. Eloise masked his movement, stepping forward until his back was against the wall. He stared down at her, his heart loud in his head.

Eloise chuckled. "Come on, Bo."

They took the long hallway and after a few minutes of walking, Bannack and Eloise stepped into the sunlight. When his eyes adjusted, he saw people hanging out in the area, some eating breakfast, others playing games.

Eloise pointed. "Sparring section's this way."

Old traffic cones marked off an area on the far end of the yard where a pile of sticks and various blunt weapons waited. A heavy bag hung on a metal frame. As they approached the blocked off area, Bannack pushed the heavy bag. Its chain chinked together gently.

"Ready?" Eloise asked.

Sticks clacked together, and Bannack turned around to see a thick piece of wood flying toward him. He jerked out of the way, heart racing, and snatched it out of the air.

Wind rushed against him. She disappeared underneath his arm. Next thing he knew, her boot slammed into his backside and he stumbled. The ground rushed out from underneath his feet. He caught his footing, then unleashed several forward attacks to push Eloise back. He needed the upper hand. And fast. Or Eloise was going to best him in a simple fight.

As Bannack brought his stick up, jarring vibrations shaking his shoulders, Eloise danced around him like a cat. Her movements were controlled. Fluid.

"Come on, Bo. Don't go easy on me. Fight me!"

He *was* going easy on her. Truth be told, fighting her at his best terrified him, not because he would hurt her—she had proven she could hold her own—but because of too many bad memories.

Eloise crouched in front of him, her gently defined muscles flexed to support her position on the ground. "I want you to fight me. I can tell you're holding back. Come on!"

Her yell resembled more of a battle cry and in one leap, she pushed off a concrete block sitting against the chain-link fence and brought her stick down toward him. The collision of wood-on-wood rattled Bannack's teeth. She smelled of sweat. His heels made tiny mounds in the dirt.

"Is it because I'm a girl?" Eloise whispered through gritted teeth and a smirk.

"No!" In one heave, Bannack shoved her off him. He ran his stick along the chain-link fence, making a rattling sound, and took a defensive stance.

On the next attack, Bannack faked an uppercut, then swiped with his legs. Eloise hit the ground, coughing. Sweat made the edge of her hair wet. Her chest expanded and contracted. She chuckled. "Sweet move. Now watch this!"

Eloise rushed him again. He picked out a tell—her elbow moved a second before the rest of her arm—and with that information, he dodged the incoming punch, faked his own, grabbed her shoulder, and slammed her body into the ground.

"What were you going to show me again?" Bannack asked, laughter at the edge of his words.

Eloise narrowed her eyes.

Something exhilarating awoke in him. He thought it was adrenaline at first. He was almost...having fun. He smiled. Then a chuckle rippled gently through his body.

Underneath him, Eloise smirked.

Her feet dug into his stomach and he hit the ground. Hard. Shock that Eloise had the leg strength to lift him into the air made his hair stand on end.

Bannack's lungs crackled when they expanded finally. Eloise appeared over him, her braid swinging as she brought her stick down. He rolled. Sound waves from the sparring stick made his ears ring.

"How in the world?" Bannack gulped precious air to fill his angry lungs.

"Mason's a good teacher," came Eloise's rasp. She stood straight, stretched out her back, and rolled her neck. "Why? You tired yet?"

He chuckled, shaking out his arms. "You wish."

Bannack surged forward.

Eloise danced away.

Gritting his teeth, Bannack attacked with an overhead arch. Eloise brought her arm up to defend but reacted slower than before and he clipped her face. But she kept attacking. Bannack's arms threatened to fail. An ill-timed swing gave Eloise the advantage, and she ducked under his arm. His spine absorbed a sharp blow. A pained groan clawed out of his throat. Then she touched his Adam's apple with the end of her stick.

"Gotcha."

Huffing, Bannack grabbed her stick and twisted. Eloise gasped and stumbled into the chain-link fence, pinned.

His entire body burned from the countless bruises he would wake up to the next morning.

She should have counterattacked.

Eloise remained still against the fence. When she placed her hand on his chest, the gentle warmth and dampness of her skin bloomed across his torso. The scent of salty sweat and fresh air tumbled off her body, reminding Bannack of the ocean. He leaned in dangerously close. She should have pushed him away. She didn't.

Bannack whispered, "No. I got you."

Those words, tossed from his mouth before he could stop them, froze Eloise in her tracks and she released a quiet shaking gasp. The pressure of the stick Eloise kept against Bannack's chest eased, allowing him more room to draw closer to her. Their noses almost touched, and electricity hummed in the space between their bodies.

They assessed each other. Eloise's breaths made her upper torso push against his own. Her hand drifted to his waist, and she kept it there. The smallest amount of pressure almost made him collapse and the air surrounding them cracked with an energy foreign to Bannack.

Eloise swiped the tip of her nose against his own. A shudder ran through him, from his back to his shoulders, and it was all he could do from falling over in a massive heap.

"Bannack," she whispered. A shiver moved through her. "I like fighting with you."

He thought for a moment, his eyes flicking to her lips, and smirked. "So do I."

"I need you to tell me something."

Her breath exploded across his face as he inclined his head down to her. The most powerful urge to kiss the line of her scar seared his lips, and if he didn't kiss her soon, he would burn. He wanted to kiss all of her, love all of her.

Bannack licked his lips. "Yes?"

"Do I have any chance with you?"

Oh, my God...

After a quiet groan, Bannack said, "I thought you were taken." When she furrowed her brow, he clarified. "Finch."

"Well, she's great and all, but I don't like sharing. If I went with her, I'd have to."

Spontaneous combustion wasn't possible, but he came

dangerously close to debunking the myth. He tilted his head to the sky. When he brought his head down to look at Eloise, she was smiling at him with her head tilted. He shuddered. Her hand touched his hip and chest, and her palm burned a hole into him, making him take deep, shaking breaths.

"You are the most beautiful human being I have ever met. I..." He stared at her lips. As if to tease him, she parted them.

"Bo," she whispered, and he responded with a quiet grunt. She continued, "We have an audience."

All his willpower went into looking where she gestured with her head and he noticed the crowd, Sibyl at the front, smirking.

"We should probably go," Eloise said. Her voice was heavy.

"But I like it here." When he leaned in, he wrapped his arms around her waist.

Eloise put her hands on the back of his neck, cleared her throat, and the previous sultry tone to her words left. "Me too, but they're waiting."

Pouting, Bannack relented and stepped back. Eloise slid her hand into his, making a wave of gooseflesh rise on his arm, and she smiled. Together they walked past the crowd.

"Don't you dare," Eloise said as she pointed at Sibyl who threw her hands in the air.

"What?" Sibyl asked, faking shock. "I didn't say anything!"

Eloise smiled, and Bannack watched, fascinated by her face. She looked up and nudged him, saying, "Wanna run away with me?"

The words warmed him, and he squeezed her hand. "Let's go."

They spent the rest of the day together, most of it at the river.

While Eloise gathered food for their dinner, Bannack meandered through the open forest glade, looking for the perfect piece of wood to carve. His maame had taught him. She spent much of his childhood combing the beach for the perfect piece of driftwood. As she carved, her tongue poking out the side of her mouth, Bannack would sit on her lap, on the table, or in a chair next to her and watch her hands move and create effortlessly. When he asked her to teach him, never did he expect woodcarving would become a way to stay close to her. To remember her.

Eloise bumped into him, and he smiled down at her. The way her gold eyes, so light they almost were golden, blazed through his skin was enough to make him shiver deep in his bones, and his eyes shifted to her face.

God, you're beautiful.

He took inventory of his emotions. Beating heart in his chest and neck. Heated face. An electrical buzz between them as she stood in her warrior's stance.

I've had other crushes. Other women. So why her? Why is she different?

It couldn't be one thing. It wasn't just her strength, or her skill with a knife, or their shared past. His attraction truly blossomed because of her wit, strength, and kindness. He...wanted to share things with her.

"Oi, Spaceman." Eloise grabbed his hand.

She kissed his palm.

Good God. She was going to kill him. He'd have a heart attack right there on the sand.

The way her lips brushed his callouses, feather-light, threatened to bring him to his knees, reduce him to a shuddering mess, and by God, he'd thank her for it.

They settled onto the grass at the riverbank, admiring the setting sun's rich yellow, red, purple, and orange. Eloise nestled against his chest and he rested his forearm on his bent knee.

Eloise crossed her legs. "I'm curious...Morning person or night owl?"

"What?" Her hair tickled his nose, and when he hung his arm over her shoulder, he couldn't help but smile. He pressed his lips to the back of her head.

"Are you a morning person or a night owl?" She clarified. "This is important information."

Bannack chuckled. "As a kid, I was a night owl, but I am getting old and like my sleep."

"Ha!" Eloise snorted. "You're old? Please."

"Okay, smartass, now it is my turn," Bannack inhaled as he thought. "Mmm. Got it. Why are your eyes gold? They were hazel when we were kids but now, they are not."

"The nanites."

That took Bannack off guard, but he stayed quiet.

"When the nanites fused to my organs, something in them changed my eye color. I don't really know why but I've never tried to find out because I kinda like people's reaction but also it doesn't hurt me. Just some weird quirk, I guess."

"Now you have metal organs."

Eloise gave a far-off smile. "Yeah."

Crickets chirped as darkness grew around them. The space between his socks and hem of his pants chilled when cool air ran across his body and he was grateful for Eloise's body heat.

"As a child," Eloise snuggled deeper into his chest, "what did you want to be when you grew up?"

"My dad."

Eloise turned to stare at Bannack for several seconds, surprised. She shouldn't have been, though. Kwadwo Owusu was a quiet man, preferring to remain in his study, prepping lectures for his students at the local university. When he spoke, it was calm, careful, and slow, like the ebb and flow of the ocean waves. He rarely smiled with his mouth, preferring to do so with his body and actions. Kwadwo, called Kojo by Bannack's mom, was a peaceful presence and made everyone feel at home whenever they visited.

I miss you so much.

"Why your dad?"

Although it stung a bit to open up about his dad, which he hadn't done since his father's passing years ago, what struck him as pleasantly odd was opening up to Eloise made the pain less severe.

"He came here from Ghana with nothing. The amount of hard work he must have put into just getting that far is incredible, but then he went even further and became a professor of Ghanaian history, then later my Maame joined him and they became a team. Separate from Maame, he was known for his papers and progress in

176

the field. People came to him. They revered him. He became the world's best historian. He and Maame gave me and Malikah an incredible life because of his perseverance. Yes. I want to be just like him. Fearless, strong but quiet, and kind." When he stopped talking, Bannack noticed Eloise smiling at him. "What?"

She smiled and leaned forward. "It's nice to hear you open up."

A sad chuckle escaped through Bannack's nose. "It has been a long time since I talked about him but you," he spread his arms around Eloise's waist, drawing her close, and warmth radiated off her, "make it easier to talk about him."

CHAPTER SEVENTEEN
JOY

"Dr. Pierce!" A guard rushed out from the facility. "Seth had a seizure minutes ago. We did our best to help, but—"

Joy bolted into the building, the glass door shattering as it collided with the wall. Banging footsteps echoed in the stairwell and as Joy reached the first landing, she heard her name.

"Mama!"

Her stomach clenched.

I can't take many more of these.

Four. Four seizures since she agreed to leave Eloise alone

What if they get worse?

He was in his room, a few of her employees around him. One guard approached. "We've managed to stop the bleeding."

"What?"

They parted for her. Seth held a bloody cloth against his face, more heaped in a basket by his bed. Her mind separated from her body.

Seth tossed the fabric into the basket and grabbed a fresh one. "I promise...I'm okay now."

"You had a seizure. You're bleeding."

"Mama, please..."

She shook her head and sat on his bed. "I'm worried about you."

"I'm fine."

"Baby, it's my job."

Seth scrunched up his face and turned away. "Stop."

She put her hand on his leg. "You'd prefer I didn't worry?"

"No. I...you always worry. I'm dying...Mama and I want things...to be happy, but when stuff like...this happens, you get a...wrinkle in your forehead and...I'm all of a sudden a helpless little child who...needs to be babied. Then you get...in a funk. I don't...like it."

Joy's heart dropped to the floor. She desperately wanted to fix things, losing sleep over trying to figure out how to still save him, but nothing worked. Nothing could stop his disease. She'd tried.

"I'm sorry." Joy gave him a hug, pressing her mouth into his shoulder. "I'm trying."

Seth nodded.

"What do you need me to do?" She asked.

He thought for a bit, then a small smile crossed his lips. "Take a sick day with me?"

The bed sheets rustled as Joy hooked her arm around his. "What do you want to do first?"

***

"You called me, ma'am?" Adam, one of her most skilled men, stood at attention in the hallway. He had only six months left before he could return to his family. It wasn't pleasant, the manipulation and lying, but she did it anyway for Seth.

Joy turned around after releasing the handle on the lab door where she had been testing yet another small batch of failed nanites. She threw them away. "Yes." Her lower back was sore from standing so long. "Walk with me."

He obliged and followed Joy to her office. "What's on your mind, ma'am?"

"My son. He's not going to like what I'm about to do."

"I'm not sure I follow." His dark eyes narrowed.

Joy turned the corner. Another one of her employees, Kira, presented her with papers documenting Seth's recent incident and Joy signed it. She looked at Adam and explained Mason and Joy's agreement. "So, you see, if I remove Mason from the picture, Eloise will be unguarded."

"She has plenty of others to protect her. Including one of our own."

She gritted her teeth. "Bannack Owusu is not one of ours. He defected a long time ago and, as far as I'm concerned, is in the way." Joy looked at Adam, his eyes round and body angled away from her. She rolled her eyes and said, "Don't give me that look. You know what the job requires."

They entered the dark office together. Joy grabbed the torch off the wall and lit the other torches. She placed it back on its mount.

"What are you going to do when the Sentinels learn about your secret agreement with the Compound leader? They'll come after you and we don't have the numbers to survive an attack like that."

She sighed and sank into her chair. "I know." Seth was going to die if they didn't do something, and even though she loved him more than life, she *had* to do everything in her power to protect him. He was her only child, one she had fought so hard to keep during the pregnancy, and he was still being taken from her.

The thought pressed on her neck, making each swallow ache. Warm tears formed. "We need to make sure Eloise is with Mason before you inject him. She'll put up a fight, so bring a second person with you to subdue her. Then bring her to me. The Sentinels may attack, but by the time they've gathered, we'll have her blood. They'll be too late."

"Ma'am—"

"Go to the lab. There's a small freezer there powered by the solar panels. In it is a vial."

"Ma'am." Adam stepped close, his face grim. She knew he hated doing errands for her and she'd never asked him to do something so inhumane before, but she knew if he didn't do what she asked, he would not only lose all chances to get his family back, but she would lose Seth as well. "I'd like to take Liam."

Excitement boiled in her stomach. "Get in contact with him and send him my way. Tell him he has three days." She grabbed a stack of papers, then paused. "Oh, if anyone gets in your way...kill them."

"Ma'am." Adam nodded.

After he left, Joy deflated.

What am I going to do once Adam and the other mercenaries leave? They'll finish their term and realize I can't turn their families back.

She massaged her temples and looked at a photo she kept on the wall of the original Project Nemosyne team. Merrick and Amanda were next to Joy, Merrick's arm around one of the senior scientists, Henry Marchant.

What was your secret? What did you do to them when you built them? Why can't I make them like they were?

She turned away and wiped her nose.

CHAPTER EIGHTEEN
BANNACK

Screams awoke him. Bannack launched from his bed in the darkness. Sweat covered his skin in a thin layer, and he prepared for an attack.

It didn't come. The screams continued.

At first, his brain didn't register where they were coming from or from who, but as the fog of sleep lifted, he recognized her voice.

Eloise.

He shot upstairs to her room and pushed past Mason and Soora.

Eloise writhed on the bed. Her skin glistened with sweat, and as she shifted, he could see a wet shadow on the mattress where she had lain. Her hair stuck to her skin in long tendrils.

Soora wrapped her arms around her torso and leaned against the wall, watching Eloise with pain in her eyes. "We've tried everything to wake her up."

Each scream from Eloise wrung his stomach in a suffocating knot. She needed help.

He flinched as some part of her body smacked against a hard surface. Unable to stand by and watch any longer, Bannack rushed to her side, pushing away the side table she hit her head on. It screeched across the floor then clattered backward.

He spoke to Eloise, trying to remember the long-ago memories of what his Agya did to help his Maame. "Hold onto me. Come back."

Bannack kept his voice low and consistent. Then he squeezed methodically on her arms, running his hands up and down her skin. Her muscles calmed underneath his touch.

Eloise surged upward.

She fell into his body and shook, gasping and grappling at Bannack's neck. Sobs forced her body to jerk with each inhale. He held her, solid and steady, giving reassuring pressure to her torso, trying to imitate the effect of being wrapped in a weighted blanket.

"You are safe. I have you."

He sat on the edge of the cot, holding her as she cried into him. His heart broke for her. He understood the pain and the nightmares so severe, you wake in a cold sweat, confused and hurting. Bannack waited until her body relaxed and she pulled away from him, drying her eyes. He hooked his finger around a strand of hair stuck to the corner of her mouth and pulled it free.

She gave him a sad smile, then glanced up at Mason and Soora. Her voice hoarse, she asked, "How long were you standing there?"

Soora knelt in front of Eloise. "Several minutes. How are you feeling?"

"Like I just got a load of bricks dumped on my head."

Soora smiled, kissed Eloise's forehead, and said, "I love you. We're going to go to bed, okay, but we're here when you need us."

Then she and Mason left.

Eloise turned to Bannack. "Thank you."

"You are welcome. Do...do you wanna talk 'bout it?" Bannack asked.

Her eyes glistened. Her hair cascaded to the end of her ribs, a waterfall of dark fire. Eloise glanced down at her hands, stopped rubbing her thumb, and tucked her fingers underneath her thighs.

"Not really."

Bannack nodded. "Okay."

As he stood, Eloise grabbed his arm. The touch ricocheted a

single blast of electricity through his body and down to his toes, emptying his mind in one sweep. Bannack stared down at her slender fingers with chewed nails.

"Have you ever been so terrified of something, it haunts you, even in your dreams?" she asked.

Bannack nodded. The accuracy of her question stabbed at his gut.

"...Seth was there," Eloise stared at her feet, "and I've never dreamed of him before."

Bannack sat beside her and the bed creaked gently under his weight. "What did he say?"

She bit her lip, but he noticed the quiver of her chin. "He was dead. He...Joy killed him and then she blamed me for it."

"Sometimes our brains play horrible tricks on us." He wrapped his arms around her and kissed her temple. "Thankfully, it was a dream."

Her frustration exploded from her. "I know it was a dream! That's not what's bothering me." She turned to him, tears in her eyes. "What if this is really what I think of myself?"

He stayed quiet.

Eloise sighed angrily. "Are you going to say something, or do you just like looking at me like a deer in the headlights?"

"I dunno what to say. What would you like me to say?"

"That I can get over all the nightmares and flashbacks and triggers. That it wasn't a dream and I'm just being crazy."

"You are not crazy." Bannack shifted. "Healing from trauma is not like those flat roads down there. It is like white water rapids; sometimes you know what you are doing and sometimes you have to hold on for dear life. You can get through this. It will get better."

"When? How? I have so much *guilt* boiling inside me."

The mention of guilt jerked forward the memory of his family's deaths. He worked his jaw, staring at his bare feet. A strong knot formed in his chest and he tilted his head back to blink them away. He said, "Guilt is a strong force and can consume you easily, but you cannot let it."

184

She nodded slowly, her eyes down at her hands again. "Bannack," Eloise laid down on the cot and closed her eyes. "I miss life Before."

He watched her scoot deeper underneath the blankets, snuggling her head into the pillow.

I wish we had found each other sooner. Perhaps we could have protected each other.

As Bannack stood, she mumbled. "Stay here for a moment. Please. I need to know you're close. Drag the loveseat over."

He did what she asked, and the legs screeched against the linoleum. As he settled beside her, she laid her hand on the surface of the cushion.

Eloise mumbled. "I'm going to hold on to you."

A new knot formed in his stomach. This one spreading warmth and peace.

Bannack let his hand rest near Eloise's face.

You are everything.

He wondered how to admit he was falling in love with her. To himself. To Eloise. Succumbing to his feelings and allowing them to awaken was not a matter of if, but a matter of when, and he was already there. Wall after wall stood as a defense against his emotions. But that didn't matter. Not with Eloise. She broke down every wall with a light flick as if they were nothing and the most ironic thing was...she had no idea. Her breaking of his walls was effortless. Flawless. She was unlike any woman he had ever encountered, and she captivated his heart before he realized it was possible.

***

Bannack rubbed his eyes. His neck throbbed.

Eloise slept with her arms hanging over the top edge of the cot, surrounded by a sea of hair. Her blanket laid discarded on the floor and as he bent to fold it, he noticed goosebumps covering her ivory skin. He instead covered her body with the warm fabric and smiled as she quietly groaned in response.

As he folded his blanket, Eloise stirred. "Bannack?"

He turned. "Good morning. Did you sleep okay?"

She blinked, brushed her hair away from her face, then said, "Better after you came."

Eloise wore an off the shoulder graphic tee, the image long since faded, and a single silver ring on her right thumb. The golden light of the morning touched her freckles.

He smiled and kissed her forehead. "Good."

Eloise grabbed a pile of clothes and slipped behind a changing screen, her belt, jeans, and jacket flopping over the top. "What's your plan for the day?"

"I will figure something out..."

His voice trailed off. Eloise flipped her hair out of her jacket, walked across the room, boots untied, to reveal a small arsenal of lethal blades. A closed balisong, a silver blade with handles that counter-rotated around the tang. A karambit, a blade that resembled a velociraptor claw. Three ten-inch metal throwing knives. The last one in the lineup, and the knife he had seen when he first met Eloise, was her kukri blade. Eloise slung it to her thigh, then began loading the others onto her body.

As if she could sense he was staring, Eloise said without turning around, "One for each year I've been without my sister." She slipped her boot knife between her ankle and the leather of her vintage-style combat boots. "Sibyl calls me a walking pincushion. Which is accurate."

When her nonchalant mention of the reason she kept knives registered in his brain, he blinked at her. She didn't seem bothered by it, although he knew quite a bit of loss, and wasn't convinced Ada's death didn't hurt, at least a little bit. He decided to wait for her to open up more, if she chose.

"I..."

She slapped him on the shoulder. "Shut your mouth."

He chuckled, the heat from her hand leaving an imprint on his body.

She's something else.

CHAPTER NINETEEN
ELOISE

Eloise sighed and dried her wet hair.

I so needed that shower.

Digging a cow out of the mud in the lagoon was the last thing she wanted to do for the day, and she had been the unfortunate person who had to get into the mud and tie the rope around the cow's horns. She was wet, cold, and irritated by the time she finished the task.

I hate cows. They stink, they're huge, she almost broke my foot and—

Eloise stopped. Bannack waited by her door, chewing on his lip and bouncing his leg. Excitement jumped to life in her chest and she called out to him. When he didn't answer, she moved into his line of sight so he could see her and looked closely at his bouncing leg and flexing hands.

"Are you okay?" She asked.

"I need to talk to you about something. I want to be honest with you," he finally said, "but I'm not sure how you're going to react."

"Alright..." Eloise invited him inside and, in unison, they sat on the bed. She tried to comfort Bannack by placing her hand on his bouncing knee, but he quickly stood, paced, and shook his hands out several times.

"I am sorry. I—I am really nervous."

"Whatever it is, I'll do my best to help."

"See," Bannack wagged his finger at her, still pacing in a tight line, "that is the problem. I am nervous—and honestly terrified—you will not."

"What?" Eloise blinked. "I thought we were going to work on trusting each other."

"We are," Bannack said. Then realization turned his eyes wide and his mouth opened. "Oh no! That came out wrong. I do trust you." He knelt at her feet and grabbed her hands. His palms were warm. Sweaty. "There is no one else I trust as much as you, but—and I am trying not to mess things up again—what I need to tell you has been bothering me ever since you showed me around the Compound. I knew then my life was on a different course than I thought, and what I had wanted for so long was no longer what I wanted. Does that make sense?"

"Yeah." Eloise's heart throbbed in her temples. She ignored it and grabbed Bannack's hand. "Bo. What is this all about?"

"It is..." His breath shook as it came from his mouth. "It is about Maame's and Malikah's deaths."

Eloise leaned back. Her eyes widened. Freely, Bannack had told her about his father's death from sepsis, a symptom of an untreated, severe case of the flu, but never Malikah or his mom. He'd actually avoided the topic all together.

"They were not supposed to be in the store. We were hungry, and it was my job to get the food. But I was late. When I was passing an abandoned store, I heard gunshots. Instead of running to help like my parents had taught me—'whenever there is trouble, always be the one to help' they would say—I ran instead. The screaming was so loud, and the popping guns made things worse. I was terrified of it all. Of what it meant.

"I got back to the house we were staying in," Bannack continued, "but they were gone. So, I waited, hoping they went out somewhere. The worst part about that is I didn't leave for days. I was so damn convinced they would eventually return that I waited days—days, Elle!—until I realized something was wrong. I found them but—"

Bannack crumpled to the ground.

Unsure what to do with a six-foot-two man on the floor in front of her, Eloise froze. This was not a side of him she recognized. This side of him came from a place of great anguish. With a start, Eloise realized...

This is the Bannack that was torn down, stomped on, ridiculed, banished, and abused.

"They were in there! They took Maame and Malikah from me."

His words, the way he said them, put Eloise's chest into a vice grip. She still couldn't move, petrified with uncertainty, and watching hurt, but she tried.

Ice-blue eyes rimmed in red looked up at Eloise. "I want the ones responsible dead. I want to torture them. Rip off their fingernails, gouge out their eyes. They took my entire life from me and for what?" Bannack screamed the next words. "For what! For a little bit of fun? A night on the post-apocalyptic town? Shits and giggles? What right do they have to rip my Mama and baby sister from me? Shot them right in the back of the head with Maame holding Malikah to her chest! All this hate and anger festering and swirling inside me and I cannot get rid of it!"

A dam broke inside Eloise. With the ability to move, finally, she gathered Bannack into her arms and held his trembling body. She cried with him, held his head against her shoulder, slipped her arms around his back.

"I'm so sorry. So, so sorry."

Bannack, shuddering, snuggled into Eloise's shoulder. He whispered, "I could not live with the knowledge that I did nothing. They are dead because of my inaction. It did not take long for me to go to Joy. I groveled at her feet to get her to take away my memories. I figured," a shuddering breath from Bannack shook Eloise's cheek, "if I had no memories, I'd be able to live in peace. When she promised to take them after I served her for five years, I agreed."

"Why?" Eloise's heart dropped.

"Because living without my memories was worth the wait. She had one of her goons teach me to fight. My training wasn't like yours. It was brutal and abusive. Eventually, I killed him. And you wanna know what? It left me relieved."

Just when the boulder in Eloise's stomach was fading, Bannack threw a curveball. Now she saw another side of him, one that used the rage and hatred created when his family was murdered and channel it into something useful. A machine.

"Fighting came easy. All I had to do was to envision *them* and I could do anything. Feel nothing. My inferno had somewhere to go instead of burning through my soul." Bannack peered at Eloise. "Are you doing okay?"

Stiff, Eloise nodded. "I think so. It's a lot to take in. Is...there more?"

"Yeah. If you're up to it." Bannack watched her, his wet eyes flicking across her face. "We do not have to keep talking about this."

Eloise smiled, albeit a weak one, to encourage him to continue. "I am. It's important to you. I," she put her hand on his cheek and watched his lashes flutter, "want to hear. No matter how hard it is to get out."

Somewhere, far off, children giggled. They moved outside to a mossy bench near a tree. Scattered light bounced off the patchwork grass underneath the pine tree the two of them sat under. Roots peaked out from underneath the ground. Carefully, Bannack lowered his head into Eloise's lap.

"She promised me she would take the memories away," Bannack continued. "It was too painful...to live with the guilt and rage. I was neck deep in helping her. First, she told me I needed to bring someone to her. A—a deserter from her facility who was selling her formula. I believed her. Then it was another, and another. Until I was so far into her treasonous dealings that I could not hope for redemption."

"Oh, no." Eloise closed her eyes. When they first met, Bannack had revealed he worked for Joy and what he did, but hearing the details carried a heavy weight. As she looked at Bannack, his head in her lap, she bent down and placed her forehead on his cheek. His skin was soft. Piney floral notes of lavender swirled in the air.

"I did it all. Many died. Finally, she asked me to kidnap Nora. I refused. Dug the tracker out." Bannack rolled up his sleeve to show Eloise the thick scar on the inside of his forearm. "By the time Joy realized I had taken Nora and her family, we were already too far for her to get to us. Lived in Canada for a bit and then I came back. Now, you know everything."

He turned his head to look at her. The exhaustion she carried when he finished his story wasn't out of relief but out of emotional weight.

Life hasn't been kind to either of us.

"I'm glad you told me," Eloise said when Bannack sat up. "It's...a lot to take in." One thing bugged her, though. She couldn't shake the question, so she asked, "Where did your family die?"

"A store right off the old highway. The one tucked behind Cushman Trail."

Blood rushed from her face. She put the pieces together. Eloise knew Ada's and Bannack's family's deaths were not similar by coincidence.

"What is wrong?"

"Newman's? Is the store you're talking about called Newman's?" She couldn't breathe. Her heart was going to explode from her chest. Unable to sit still, Eloise stumbled to her feet, walked a few feet away, and wrapped her arms around her stomach, trying to keep the nausea from producing bile.

"I...yes. But how did you—"

She spun around. Her eyes red with warm tears trickling down her cheeks.

"We were there."

Bannack furrowed his eyebrows as he stood. "You—"

"We were there," Eloise repeated. She shook. "Remember how I said Ada was killed in front of me in a store? That was Newman's."

Bannack took a step back. He kicked a rock with a grunt. It hit the concrete wall, and he crouched low, his back to Eloise, then put his head in his hands. "Why didn't I do anything?"

"You didn't know." She knelt beside Bannack.

"I could have done something, though." Bannack's whisper rasped out of him so quietly she had to lean in to hear him. Then she saw his face. Contorted. Tears trickled down his cheeks. His chin quivered.

"Hey, hey," Eloise said and reached out for his face.

Gasping, Bannack pulled away.

She kept her hands on her knees. "I know you feel responsible for what happened to us, but it wasn't your fault. Those men chose to hurt all those people. You were scared."

"It...it is eating away at me, Elle." His breath hitched. "I am suffocating. I keep going back to that day, wishing I did something. Ran inside. Fought them. Anything."

Her stomach hurt, and she wanted to touch him, hold him. "Don't let this eat at your soul. Don't give up on belonging, joy, and love. You're vulnerable. It means you're human."

The way he looked at her, with his forehead wrinkled, tears on his face, and shoulders shaking made Eloise want to groan, his pain affecting her too. It clawed off of him, terrified and anguished, and into her bones. She wasn't a stranger to shame. She knew how debilitating it could be, but where she had people to nurture her and take care of her in times of vulnerability, Bannack didn't. He had been beaten until he forgot who he was and only recently tried building himself back.

"You are an incredible human." Eloise said. Bannack looked at her as if she possessed a third eye, but she continued, slowly inching her way closer to him. "You're still here. That's an incredible feat. The night we met, you put aside what you wanted to help me. And yes, I know what I said. Do you realize how incredible that is? You saved me. Even when you didn't want to. I know," Eloise reached for Bannack and he didn't flinch away, "your family is watching you and they're so proud of you for persevering. It couldn't have been easy."

His body seemed to crumple into her hand, and he shuddered. "No."

Leaning in, Eloise whispered, "You're here and you matter."

An audible groan of relief flooded from Bannack. He became limp under her touch.

"I'm not leaving. Even if it takes a lifetime of healing, I'm never going to leave you and you'll never have to experience loneliness or judgement ever again."

A shaking sob rolled out of Bannack.

CHAPTER TWENTY
LIAM

The Sentinels were easy enough to get through and they never even saw him sneak through their lines. Chuckling to himself, hidden by the thick, leaf-laden branches, Liam marveled at the ease of it all.

Pitiful, Mason. Truly pitiful.

He looked to the sky. Dark clouds blocked out most of the sun.

All he had to do now was wait for Mason to leave the Compound, then he could strike when least expected in one last beautiful job. A job so perfect, he could retire from. His magnum opus.

If it wasn't for that idiot Mason taking his sweet time, I'd have done the job already and be home sipping tea.

Liam gritted his teeth, his mouth watering as he thought about the bachelor button petals mixed in with the black tea leaves from his garden, and watched Mason from his perch in the large oak tree. The Compound leader sat at his desk, one hand supporting his head and the other writing on a piece of paper.

A woman approached and leaned against Mason's back. He paused, smiled, put his palm against her arm.

So, you finally married her, huh?

Before Liam left the Compound after their disagreement on how the Compound should be run—Mason wanting a more pacifistic approach—Soora and Mason had been dating for several years.

His attention, bored watching Mason, shifted to locating Adam in the bushes. The assignment required finesse and planning; he had the knowledge needed to get Mason and Eloise, but Adam did not. He was clunky and bulky whereas Liam was thin and nimble, able to dance away and dodge easily when the situation called for it. The one thing he loathed about being with Joy was patience. She made him wait for far too many things.

It's what brought the downfall of Liam's and Mason's relationship.

"I will not subject the people who come and live at the Compound to war again! They need a sanctuary, not a military operation."

"You haven't changed, have you?" Liam balled his fists.

Soora, Mason's fiancé, came to his rescue. "He's right, Liam. They're worn out and tired from the fighting."

Liam turned to her and contorted his face. "Oh, please. You're so predictable to run to his aid the moment he needs it. I would never have asked you to do such things if you'd just stayed with me instead of being swept off your feet by this bastard."

Soora blinked at him and he knew he had been cruel, but he couldn't take back his words.

A fist crashed into Liam's nose, breaking it. His eyes watered and stung, and he tumbled backward over the desk, hitting his head on the linoleum. When his eyes focused, Mason stood over him, knuckles red and seething.

"How dare you," he growled. "Get out. I never want to see you again."

Liam stood, blood dripping from his nose. His head pounded. "You need me, Mason. No one is going to protect the Compound if you kick me out."

"I will protect them."

"You?" Liam laughed and wiped blood from his lips. "You

always were a dreamer. Even when Fade attacked the twenty-seventh battalion, you insisted they would be okay despite their base being blown up! Then you ran in there and risked everyone just for a couple of kids!"

"Those kids were alive, and I'll be damned if I don't save every single life worth saving. I'll die trying if I have to!" Mason advanced, and Liam glared at him as he said, "I will do everything in my power to protect people who come to live here by giving them peace. God knows we need it. Now, get out of my Compound or I'll break something else."

Ego destroyed, Liam's self-preservation kicked in and he left, vowing to prove Mason wrong, no matter what it took.

The memory made Liam's nose hurt.

Liam settled in. He trained his eyes to the back door.

Any minute now. He adjusted the pack on his lap. *And I can stop being so bloody bored.*

***

Mason emerged from the Compound and Liam, whose backside had been in pain for hours, sat up with a grunt. He leaned forward in the tree while raindrops landed on his head, shoulders, and back.

"There you are," he said and smiled when Eloise appeared, too. "Mason, you predictable git."

Liam caught Adam's attention, gestured with his hands, and climbed down from the tree. He followed them from a distance. Long ago, when he and Mason were stationed in the fifty-fifth battalion, Liam had learned how to walk silently and he'd used it to his advantage. Spying became his specialty.

He could hear them talking in hushed tones.

"How is the farmer's cow doing?" Mason asked.

"Fine. He cleaned her off and she's perfectly healthy. A little scratch on her knee, but that's it. Meanwhile," Eloise lifted her shirt to her nose and made a face, "I smell like cow."

Mason laughed. "Tell me about the meetings with the committee. Is Francine still giving you a hard time?"

"She's come around. We should be able to start digging for the underground refrigeration spaces soon. It's going to be so nice to have cold things again."

Alright. That's enough talking. Liam nodded to Adam. *Time to wipe some memories.*

CHAPTER TWENTY-ONE
ELOISE

"There's nothing like a cold glass of wine," Mason said.

Eloise flicked her hood on to protect her head from the rain and watched Mason react to the memory of cold wine, something Eloise couldn't empathize with because she'd never had cold wine before. She smiled.

He looked over Eloise's shoulder, and his eyes widened. He stepped forward. "Liam," Mason said with a growl. "I told you I would break something else if I ever saw you back here."

Eloise turned around. Liam, a tall and skinny man, sauntered toward them with his chin tilted down. She noticed his limp.

"So, you steal my girl, kick me out, and start your empire. Did I miss anything? Oh! That's right. You broke my fucking nose in the process." He ran toward them. "I liked it the way it was before!"

Mason lifted his arms and braced his body for the attack. Liam crashed into him, using his legs as a propeller to land two hits. Mason grunted, twisted his body, and slammed Liam into a nearby tree.

"After all these years, you've still got it."

Like before, when Cassius attacked Bannack, Eloise stepped in the way despite Mason's warning cry. She glared, doing her best to hide the fear ransacking her body. She'd never seen Mason attacked, except during training exercises. The experience jarred her.

"Stop this," Eloise said, her kukri outstretched and a reverse grip on the karambit. "I don't know who you are or what you want with Mason, but I won't let you hurt him. Leave now!"

Liam's angry laugh made her blink and he looked at Mason. "She's feisty. You should really listen to Daddy."

Mason made a defeated noise as Eloise turned back to Liam, the fire of anger exploding through her. "Excuse me?"

She leapt forward, slashing with her karambit to follow through with her elbow. Something solid hit her ankles. She gasped, landed on the ground, and watched Liam advance. She faked a slash with her kukri, but he hit it from her hand, spun it in the air, and grabbed onto it.

Mason crashed into Liam, allowing Eloise to scramble to her feet.

Someone grabbed her from behind. She squirmed in surprise and her attacker squeezed, her lungs unable to expand. Somehow, in her frantic fight to break free and breathe, she caught footing on a boulder. Eloise pushed off it. The person holding her lost balance for a moment and she took her chance. Eloise searched behind her for the back of a neck, adjusted her weight forward, and fell. The man flipped over her head into the mud. Thunder made music in the sky. He rolled away before she could knock him out.

A foot flew into her vision and she had no time to even gasp before it got her in the face. The treads scraped along her skin, taking a chunk out of the bridge of her nose. She cried out, holding her face, and bent over.

"Run!"

Lightning flashed.

Mason slammed his elbow into Liam's sternum, knocking him back, and rushed the man who attacked Eloise. He picked up her discarded kukri on the way and stabbed him in the neck. Blood splattered across Mason's face.

He yanked the blade out, turned, and panted. A needle stuck out from his stomach.

Eloise's pupils dilated. She pointed at it. "Mason…"

"Oops," Liam sneered. He hadn't even tried to stop Mason when he ran over to the second man and now, they knew why.

Mason looked down and pulled the empty syringe out. "What…" he stumbled and blinked, then shook his head. "What did you do to me?"

He fell onto his knees, his head rolling.

"Mason!" Eloise grabbed onto him, his body heavy against her, and she turned to Liam. "What did you do?"

"He got what was coming to him." Liam sneered again.

The syringe was small, about the size of her hand including the needle. Eloise tossed it away.

"Mason, hey," Eloise patted his face and tried to push him to a sitting position. "Hey. You gotta stay awake."

"I'm okay. I think." His eyebrows knitted together. "Just help me up."

She did, but he struggled to keep his balance, so he leaned against her.

"He's not attacking," Eloise whispered as she glared sideways at Liam. He stood some distance from them, a crazy gleam in his eye. "What should we do?"

"I-I don't…know. Something's…" Mason groaned and grabbed his head, "something's wrong."

"Hey, Daddy's girl!" Liam paced, and another lightning strike lit up the sky. "What are you going to choose? Daddy or a chance to avenge him?"

"Can I engage?" Anger boiled inside her again, and she gritted her teeth. "He attacked you."

"I know." With much effort, Mason stood to his full height. He wobbled but stood on his own. "I'm okay for now." He smiled at her. "Go get him."

Eloise launched forward, a growl turning into a yell, and attacked. She undercut, swiped with her legs, and slashed with her knives, trying her best to get the better of Liam. Each attack he deflected easily. Mud flew. More lightning, this time too close. Liam pinned her to the ground by her throat. She jammed her knee into his ribs, making him grunt, then she gouged at his eyes.

Liam screamed and stepped away.

Gasping, Eloise stood. Her chest burned and her eyes watered.

He rubbed his eyes. "That hurt. My job isn't finished, though, and you killed my assistant."

"What are you talking about?"

"One word, bird. Joy."

Eloise's arms went slack. She stared at Liam. "Of course, she sent you. I should have known with the syringe and the attack aimed at Mason. She wants him out of the way. But that means..." She gasped and turned to Mason. He didn't look off, but she knew something was happening.

Maybe the serum doesn't work right away?

"I'm going to kill her!" Eloise's fury drove her to charge Liam.

Mason yelled.

The rock in Liam's hand flashed across her vision.

CHAPTER TWENTY-TWO
BANNACK

He stood by the steps, flowers in his hand, waiting for Eloise. Alma helped him pick them out. He had been visiting her often, enjoying their simple conversations as they made blankets and clothing for Compound members. Her lack of speaking left Bannack relieved and recharged after each interaction.

An icy breeze paired with thunder and lightning meant they'd have to do their date indoors, but he didn't mind. When a second flash followed almost immediately by thunder, Bannack flinched. A child screamed.

She's going to be drenched, isn't she?

Mason came out of the forest first, and Bannack jogged over.

*Wait...*Bannack slowed, noticing the limp in Mason's gait and blood on his body.

"Eloise?" He asked, fearing the truth.

Mason blinked. "Who?"

Bannack backed up and fell, his heart torn out of his chest. He couldn't form words. The signs were all there: dilated eyes, uncontrollable shaking, balance issues, and memory loss. All the signs confirmed the serum ran through Mason's veins. Eloise wasn't with him. A stab of fear hit him when he saw the blood.

Joy did this.

"Do you remember Soora?"

"Sure do." The sideways smile on Mason's face was new. "We made love all night. Ah." He locked his hands behind his head and looked at the sky. "She's the most beautiful woman I've ever met. You know, I'm going to marry her one day. Just watch me."

Bannack looked sideways at Mason. He nearly threw up several times as he helped Mason the rest of the way to the Compound.

"Woah," Mason said when he stumbled and nearly took Bannack down with him. "Exactly how much did I drink last night, Private?" He squinted at Bannack. "Wait...who are you exactly?"

He thinks he's back in the military. The serum is acting faster than I remember. This is bad.

"Corporal Owusu, sir." Bannack shoved the door of the Compound open. "Just got in last night."

"Ah, well, welcome to the fifty-fifth but I gotta warn you. It's a shit show. Rumor is, Fade's planning an attack and we're charged with stopping them."

How close was Mason to the war?

"Soora!" Bannack cried out, his back aching. "Soora! Get out here, now!"

She appeared, a flurry of dark hair and white from her doctor coat, and the minute she saw Mason, she gasped and rushed to him. Before she could touch her husband, Bannack stopped her cold with a shake of his head.

Confused, Soora looked at Mason. "Bring him inside."

Once they situated Mason on a bed and Bannack had dried the rain off his face and neck, Soora pulled Bannack aside. "What's going on?" She asked and folded her arms. "Why does he look high and drunk?"

He didn't want to lie. She would find out eventually. Bannack pushed past the trembling hands and inhaled. He said, "The symptoms match Joy's serum."

Soora blanched. She grabbed the doorknob. "Do...do you know what happened?"

He shook his head. "Eloise is also missing."

"Something changed on Joy's end." Soora swayed then sat. "She would never have attacked like this if something hadn't changed."

Tears welled in her eyes, and she looked at Mason. He knew the serum and its effects, and for Joy to wipe Mason's memories could only mean one thing: She wanted Eloise. An overwhelming surge of fury hit him.

"Hey, Mookie," Mason reached for Soora and she walked over. He smiled slowly and ran a soft hand across her cheek. In a low voice, he whispered. "Have I ever told you that your mind is incredible?"

She smiled and lowered her eyes. "Many times. Now, sit there and wait for me. I have to talk to Bannack, but I'll be back to run a physical, okay?"

"Oh. Agreed. Physicals are very important."

She chuckled under her breath and walked back over to Bannack. "He's acting like a young man again. I'm not sure what the serum will do to him or how you even know of the symptoms it causes, but you have to get Eloise back. Make sure she's safe. The weather is going to be a problem, though, so I want you to stay low, find shelter as soon as you can, and stay away from the forest if you can avoid it. It's dangerous, but we can't risk Joy getting to Eloise or she'll die."

Bannack nodded. "It'll be easier if I have a second pair of eyes. Who's the best tracker here?"

***

After following Mason's trail, finding the location of the fight was easy. A dead man marked the spot.

Bannack bent over him. He had a wide stab wound in his throat and blood turned the ground crimson around him. He was still warm.

He must be the source of the blood on Mason.

It made him feel a bit better, but he wouldn't stop worrying until he could confirm his assumption. He found Eloise's karambit and kukri discarded in different areas of the forest. He picked them up and put them in the pack he wore to hold basic medical supplies, food, and rope. His sword waited at his hip.

"Here," Sibyl pointed to a spot where a scuffle occurred. Smashed grass, pieces of ground dug up by boots. "Eloise landed there really hard. You can see the impression of her head."

Bannack's chest heated. The fool had thrown her. He ran his fingers around the indentation Sibyl pointed to.

Another body indentation was several feet from Eloise's. Bannack walked over and crouched, staying away so he wouldn't ruin the tracks.

"He ran over here." Sibyl joined Bannack. "Then picked her up. He's got a bad right leg. See the limp?" Sibyl crouched beside him and pointed at a small but long mound of gravel. "It's minor, but there. You can tell by the two-inch long disturbance of the dirt his toe made when he dragged it. That'll work to our advantage. You know why?"

Never having seen the man, Bannack shook his head. "It slows him down?"

"Exactly."

Bannack ran some grass through his fingers. The textures ranged from thick and coarse to wispy and thin. He followed the trail the man left with his eyes, and it led past the end field and up to the gate.

"This gravel...it's disturbed. You see? Here."

"Yeah, I see." Bannack crouched and lightly traced the impression of the footsteps and the tracks left behind by Eloise's attacker's limp. "He pushed the gravel with his toe again. Only this time, with the extra weight, it is more pronounced."

"Yeah."

"Unless this kwasia—eh, fool, I mean—has a good amount of endurance, he's going to need to stop. We will get him there."

The rain pelted Bannack's body. Sibyl made noise of agreement and glanced up at the dark sky. "We have to hurry. I don't know about you but," she glared at the trail left by the man who attacked Mason and Eloise, "I have a craving for scumbag."

CHAPTER TWENTY-THREE
ELOISE

"Run!"

Ada shoved Eloise so hard, her armful of nonperishable food scattered. The popping of guns echoed through the store. People screamed.

One man appeared around the corner, eyes flashing with malice. Eloise froze. He lifted his arm and brought a machete down across her face. She screamed, her skin ripped apart by the blade, and fell to the ground. Blood dripped into her eyes, burning them. Ada screamed, and Eloise spun.

"Ada!"

Eloise shoved through the crowd, desperate to reach her sister. Ada let out an unholy screech. Eloise's blood froze. A man, his gun clenched in his free hand, held onto Ada's throat.

He lifted.

Ada's legs flailed.

"No!"

Three pistol bullets ripped through Ada's torso. She bucked backward, still held by the throat, then her arms went slack, and *her head flopped.*

Bile rose in Eloise's gut, mere feet from her sister.

She wasn't in time.

They dropped Ada.

Rain fell on her cheeks and her eyes fluttered open. The ropes on Eloise's wrists dug into her skin. She flailed as much as she could until Liam's burning slap against her rain-soaked cheek shocked her vision out of focus. Eloise stumbled, her knees squelching into the soft ground. It ran down her shins when Liam yanked her to her feet.

Mason.

Tears filled her eyes and rage replaced grief. "You bastard!"

"What did you say?" Liam turned on her. His lips quivered and revealed his teeth.

She stood her ground. "I know you heard me. You did something to Mason, and I'm going to kill you."

"That's right," the man growled. "I hurt him. But you're tied up. Far as I can tell, you're helpless."

"I still have my head." Without giving him time to process her words, Eloise slammed her head into his face. He reeled backward, hand on his mouth, then wrapped the rope around his palm and yanked. Eloise's shoulder smashed against a moss-covered boulder, pain shooting throughout her body. She wheezed as her captor grabbed her shirt collar. Breath snaked across her skin.

"You will come nicely or Joy's going to wonder why I came back empty-handed."

Eloise glared, the rain dripping down both their faces. She fought again. He slapped her, and her body lurched sideways.

"Get up," Liam said. "And don't do anything stupid."

Blood from her top lip entered her mouth. Rain soaked through her clothing as she walked, always aware of the man behind her. The crying wind imitated Ada's screams.

Eloise blinked through the rain. She smelled Ada's blood. Her vision flipped, and her stomach tightened. The world around her blurred.

She did her best to ignore the voice carrying on the wind she knew only existed in her head, but that didn't make it any less difficult to deal with. Augmented by her memories, the coarse ropes became like barbed wire on her skin, and she could hear Ada's screams and the gunshots, smell the rancid breath of the man with Ada's blood on his hands. Ada died point blank. Executioner style, in the middle of the dessert aisle of the abandoned store. They had been in the wrong place at the wrong time, and it cost Ada her life.

The forest opened up to a clearing. Liam stopped shoving her. Eloise stood still, swaying as the wind pushed at her sore body. The rain cooled her skin, and she watched Liam stalk over to a shack. He knocked. The door opened.

If she didn't do something, her life would be over the minute he delivered her to Joy. But what could she do?

He searched me. What can I–

Then she remembered.

My boot knife. He didn't take that one.

She dug into the top of her boot, grunting to get her fingers around the hilt, and sat with her knees spread so she could hold the blade with her boots.

Eloise glanced at Liam. Good. He's still distracted.

The ropes around her wrists fell away once she cut through them. She ran. Liam's screams followed her, but the soul-shaking thunder and bright lightning drowned them out. It wasn't smart to be out during a lightning storm, and it sure as hell wasn't smart to run into the forest, but she figured the trees offered a better alternative than the open beach.

Liam slammed into Eloise. Her boot knife tumbled away when she fell, gasping for the air escaping her lungs. She punched Liam, making her knuckles ache. He dug his knee into her sternum. She grappled at it, coughing and wheezing.

"Joy warned me you would be a handful." Liam leaned in close and his breath warmed her cheek. He smelled of meat. "I'm going to enjoy giving you back to her."

The knee to her chest prevented her from speaking. It dug into her bones, making them sting and burn, and all she could do was pray his weight wouldn't crush her ribs.

She felt around for something, anything, to attack Liam with so she could get to her knife.

"Yo, ass pastry!"

The crack of a board against a body came immediately before Liam's knee left her sternum. She gulped air into her lungs, snatched her boot knife from the grass, and ran. As she looked behind her, she saw a man in a cloak disappear into the forest. Liam stirred on the ground.

"Get back here!"

She squealed and began zigzagging through the forest, lightning flashing around her, thunder shaking the ground.

Liam caught up to her when she reached a concrete structure. Most of it had crumbled, but a single wall remained. Liam slammed her so hard against it, she was sure the skin on her forehead split open. He let go, and she crumpled, crying.

"Why can't you accept your fate?"

"Because," Eloise wiped her face, "I'm not weak!"

Liam picked her up.

He had neglected to relieve her of her knife and when he set her on her feet, she drove the knife up into his ribs. His eyes flashed wide open, and he grunted.

"Wh..." Liam's words gurgled from his mouth.

Eloise twisted the blade, metal grinding against bone, and Liam slumped against her, pinning her to the wall.

As she moved to push him off, lightning struck, traveled through the metal rebar inside the wall, and into Eloise's body. A thousand bees stung her at the same time. Her body locked. The knife in Liam burned her hand, and she couldn't let go, powerless to move.

Then the lightning left.

Her palm sizzling, Eloise convulsed, gasped, and fell to the ground.

Darkness swarmed.

Water ran down her cheeks.

Then nothing.

CHAPTER TWENTY-FOUR
BANNACK

"Elle!"

Panic pounded into Bannack's chest and he thought his bones would crush under the power. He struggled to breathe.

He followed the trail, right behind Sibyl, to a concrete wall amid rubble. Two people lay in a heap. Bannack saw red hair spread across the ground and his lungs tightened.

"No..."

They had found her.

Singed human flesh sat heavy in the air.

"No." Bannack pulled her away from the concrete wall and looked her over. Clothes were a mess, smoking, singed, and completely shredded. He removed his coat and wrapped it around Eloise, unable to cover her completely, then he looked for injuries. Fractured lines tattooed onto her body in a lightning pattern, snaked down her neck and spread across her chest. Her hand clenched a bloody knife. As he pried her fingers open, small pieces of her skin peeled away.

He heaved into the grass.

He checked for a pulse. Nothing. Grief threatened to overwhelm him, but he pushed it aside and began chest compressions.

Sibyl cried out and fell to her knees. "Please tell me she'll be okay."

He ignored Sibyl and locked his elbows to push in rhythm. "Come on. Come on. Breathe!"

Seconds ticked on.

Her body convulsed, then she vomited. With her eyes closed, Eloise leaned into him, gasping, and Bannack intertwined his fingers with her hair, now coarse with rainwater and sand. He held her close, releasing the pressure in his chest with a heavy sigh.

"Can you walk?" He asked when his tears calmed.

Eloise's head rolled back. Her open eyes were slits as she looked at the dead man on the ground, and when she spoke, her voice didn't sound like her. It was coarse. Sickly. Weak. "...Did I kill him?"

"Yeah." Bannack clutched Eloise to his chest, aching so bad he struggled to stand. "You did good."

"We need to get out of the storm!" Sibyl yelled over the howling wind and thundering rain. Pine needles and branches flailed in the air.

Despite her weakened state, Eloise managed a smile. "I'm now one in seven hundred thousand people to get struck by lightning." She winced and held her hand. "Someone make me a plaque."

Sibyl stepped beside Bannack. "How are we gonna find a shelter in this? I can't even see in front of my face."

Bannack shook his head, lifting the severely lethargic Eloise. She groaned as they wandered blindly, her head bobbing in rhythm with Bannack's gait, and she soon developed a hacking cough.

He turned to Sibyl. "We—"

Out of the corner of his eye, when lightning flashed, Bannack noticed the figure of a hooded man standing amid the bushes. The small hairs on his body rose.

"I see you!" Bannack screamed into the storm. For several moments, nothing happened. Lightning flashed again and then he really saw the figure, tall and hooded with a growling, waist tall, black and white dog standing next to him. Rain dripped from the rim of the man's dark cloak and he gripped a bow notched with an arrow.

"Please," Sibyl pushed past Bannack. "We aren't safe out here. Help us?"

"Sibyl..." Bannack whispered.

She turned to him, rain dripping from her eyebrows and water flying off her lips as she said, "Do you see any other options?"

Mud squelched underneath Sibyl's boots as she took a few more steps closer to the person in the grove. "We can pay you well. Back at our home, we have fresh produce and a few livestock we can give you for your troubles."

"I don't need your bribes," a voice barked from underneath the hood.

Sibyl gasped. "Luke Varma!" She folded her arms and glowered at him. "You scared us, you asshole!"

Eloise groaned and squinted into the darkness. "I know your voice."

"What?" Sibyl asked and stepped in front of her. "You know Luke?"

"I..." Eloise grimaced, "I didn't know it was him, but he hit Liam over the head to help me get away."

"I called called him an ass pastry."

As Bannack looked at him, he saw a smile grow on Luke's face.

"Ooh," Sibyl said under her breath. "I need to remember that one."

Luke gave a command to his dog in an unfamiliar language, then removed his hood to reveal a younger man, his lips tight, with shoulder length black hair. In the dark of the night, it was difficult to see his eyes. Bannack's stomach knotted up. Sibyl seemed to know Luke well enough, but without being able to read his face, Bannack didn't know if he could trust the man. Eloise's life was too precious.

"Have a plan?" Bannack asked, speaking under his breath while he eyed Luke. The rain made him shiver. Sibyl shook, too. They all needed warmth.

Sibyl nodded. "Of course. We go with him. He can be trusted, even if he is beyond annoying."

Luke huffed through his short beard. "You guys look like shit." Luke lifted his hood and adjusted a rope onto his shoulder, a mass of something attached to it. "Mom would murder me if I didn't help family. So, you should follow me."

"Family?"

"Yeah." Luke nodded in Eloise's direction. "Eloise's adoptive parent is my aunt."

Bannack blinked, surprised by the connection.

Luke stalked off.

Bannack caught up to Sibyl as they followed him through the brush. "You know each other well, then?"

"I wouldn't say well, but yes. I've traded with his father many times, but mostly he keeps himself scarce. You know Luke's basically royalty, right? His mom's the Rhondian clan leader."

"No." Bannack watched Luke's back. Unshaven, tattered cloak, primitive hunting weapons. Nothing about him signaled his status.

"He doesn't flaunt it, but he is. Between you and me," Sibyl's voice quieted, "I don't think he even wants it."

"Hmm." Bannack contemplated the information for a moment. "A royal who doesn't want to be royal. When have we heard that one?"

Sibyl's eyes brightened. "I know, right? It's like a living, breathing fantasy trope."

Eloise moaned, falling into another coughing fit.

***

Inside a grove of hanging branches sat a cabin. The roof, covered by moss, curved low on one side and leaned so much that Luke had to slam his shoulder against the door to get it to open.

The dog burst through nearly knocking Bannack over in his rush.

Luke lifted the bundle he had been carrying since they ran into him. Rabbits. He attached them to a hook screwed into a support beam in the corner.

Sibyl stopped at the cabin entrance. "Oh," she blurted, her hand on her mouth. "Don't tell me you're going to skin them in here!"

Luke glanced sideways at her and flicked the sheath of his blade across the room. "I remember you've skinned a deer with no problems."

"Those poor bunnies." A slight smile made Sibyl's lips twitch, her eyes twinkle, and Bannack realized she was joking.

"What would you have me eat instead, Sibyl? Dandelion leaves? Or maybe," Luke wiggled the knife in the air, "I'll hop around the forest dressed in a bunny fur coat, sprinkling rabbit meat everywhere like a flower girl at a wedding and hope the air fills my belly."

"You're so morbid," Sibyl snorted. "It's disgusting."

They bantered playfully in the background as Bannack laid Eloise on an open cot covered in animal furs. Her wet hair flopped over the edge.

Eloise's teeth clattered, and she groaned out a single word. "Fire."

He wiped her hair from her eyes. "Your clothes are destroyed, Eloise. I need to remove them."

She nodded, her eyes closed.

Several thick blankets dropped beside him and his eyes followed Sibyl as she handed him a knife and began piling dry wood together.

"Why have the nanites not done anything yet?" Bannack aimed his question at Sibyl, doing his best to keep Eloise covered while cutting the rags from her body.

Her injuries were still raw. In the few times he witnessed the nanites healing properties, he had observed rapid healing. There should at least be new skin growing around the edges, but he saw no signs of healing.

"I have seen them work faster than this before."

Sibyl shrugged. "As far as I know, Joy's the only person to have achieved working nanites of this precision. There could be a number of reasons why they aren't working faster. Maybe they don't like water? I have no idea."

"Luke," Bannack asked, "where do you keep your first aid and clothes?"

Without a word, Luke pointed at a chest underneath the only window and as Bannack rummaged through the chest Luke directed him to, he heard sobbing. He turned.

Eloise was sitting up and staring at her hand. "It's not working. And it hurts!"

The scream yanked on Bannack, and he launched to his feet involuntarily. He snagged the bandages in his rush to her side and knelt down in front of her. The contortion of her face frightened him.

"My hand..." She gripped her wrist and shook so violently, Bannack thought for a moment she was seizing. "It's numb and it burns. And where's pieces of my skin?"

"Shh..." Bannack lifted her face to his, trying to remain calm as terror raged inside unchecked. "Sibyl's going to get some ointment from the chest and we're going to fix you up. We'll wrap this, and it'll start healing in no time."

Eloise sobbed while Sibyl prepared the poultice. Bannack knew nothing of how to care for burns, and even though the nanites should speed up the healing process, he still wanted to avoid the risk of infection. She sobbed, her face contorting with each flinch as Sibyl spread the antiseptic blend on her palm and then wrapped it. Her eyes were heavy, puffy, and her breaths entered her body in wet hitches.

"Mason." Eloise pulled her injured hand in. She looked at Bannack with hope he feared he could not give. "Did you see him? Is he okay?"

"I..."

"What? What's wrong?"

"I am not sure how to—"

"Oh, God!" She squeaked. "He's dead, isn't he?"

"No! No. I promise he's alive. Soora's taking care of him." At his words, Eloise sighed. Bannack continued. "But he is...not the same."

"What do you mean?"

His body crumbled under her gaze, and Bannack looked away

from her.

This is it. This is the moment my past, my mistakes, catch up to me. I have to tell her, but if I do, it'll be the end of everything for me.

Forcing himself to look, Bannack stared straight into Eloise's beautiful eyes, and opened his mouth to blurt the words he knew would destroy him. But he loved her too much to—

Love? He...loved her?

The realization pounded into him and nearly knocked him over. Bannack looked at Eloise, really looked, and saw her dark red hair cascading around her face in muddy tendrils, eyes puffed, cracked scars across her chest and neck, and a bandaged hand. Despite all her injuries, her lips were soft, her eyes intense in their complexity, and her mind remained sharp. She was the most exhilarating, addictive woman, and he couldn't stop the desires and feelings crashing into him. Perhaps it marked his demise, but he couldn't not feel while around her. She emanated too much of it.

Don't feel. They will get you killed. No feelings. You can do this. You can...No. I can't. I have to feel. I want desperately to feel.

"What do you mean, Bannack?" She clutched the blanket to her as she stood, looming over him.

"It's the serum. Joy's. The symptoms: memory loss, confusion, inability to balance. All of them point to the same serum Joy used to keep people in line."

There they were. The words that would incriminate him and seal his fate. He would lose the woman he just realized he loved. If he wanted to live up to the adinkra tattooed on his arm, he needed to admit it.

But the anger, hurt, and yelling never came.

Eloise's face contorted, and she inhaled as if to blow out some candles. The words that whispered from her mouth were not complex in their design, but the way she spoke them chilled Bannack to the bone. He almost shrunk away from her. "I'm going to peel the bitch's skin off her skull, bit by bit, and then leave it hanging."

"Joy is going to know you killed one of her men. I am unsure exactly what she will do, because I have never known her to get her hands dirty, but if she attacked Mason, then she is desperate. And desperate people do things they may not have otherwise."

"Let her come. Tomorrow morning, we'll leave here and go back to the Compound. We're going to gather as many people to fight as we can, and then Joy will realize how wrong she was to hurt my family."

While he admired her fight and raw anger, he attempted to reel her in. "And Mason? Do not forget he has lost his memory. We need answers and we will not find them in a fight with Joy."

Eloise fluttered her eyelashes, and her lips drew together. "Are you suggesting we do nothing?"

"No." God, her words terrified him. "I am not suggesting we do nothing. What I am suggesting is we breathe, take a step back, and assess what is most important. Prioritize."

"Fine." She rolled her eyes, and the anger dialed back. "Answers first."

***

Eloise quietly slept with Luke's dog Boatswain, as he was called, snuggled beside her.

Sibyl walked out of the cabin. The rain had stopped. Bannack stayed inside for a moment, then slipped out the door. He found Sibyl, a blanket wrapped around her, inside a lean-to greenhouse built up against the cabin, an extra handmade chair empty beside her. He sat with his knees awkwardly lifted higher than his hips.

"You are tall." Bannack grunted. "How come you sit in this thing and look so comfortable?"

She didn't respond, only stared at the ground.

"Are you okay?"

"Mmm. Not really." Sibyl pulled the blanket closer to her body. "I thought she was going to die. She's the only family I have, and if I lose her, I'll have no one." Sibyl sniffed. "I can't live alone again."

"Well, I got loads of experience with that."

Sibyl chuckled, and she looked at him. "I'm sure you do. What was your experience like? Sunshine and rainbows, I bet."

Bannack almost missed her wink. He smiled, trying to answer Sibyl without dimming the already dark mood settling around her, so he tilted his head sideways a bit and smiled as he nodded, hoping his expression would make her feel better. "Sunshine for days. I could pro'lly blind someone with how much sunshine I experienced."

Sibyl laughed, leaning back as she did so. "You are one awkward dude. No wonder Eloise likes you."

The chair creaked loudly and collapsed in a heap of wood, Sibyl landing on top. She screeched in surprise. Bannack jumped to his feet, but she waved him off, laughing. Between gasping breaths and wiping her tears, Sibyl said, "Remind me never to let Luke build any of my furniture."

The shock wearing off, Bannack laughed with Sibyl. He helped her up, and she dusted off her backside.

"I may be awkward," Bannack said, closing the door of the greenhouse behind him, "but I'm really good with my hands."

Sibyl stopped mid wipe and snorted.

"I...that is not...we have not..." Bannack stumbled through his words, face heating to dangerous levels. Through hands covering his face, Bannack whispered, "That is not what I meant."

"Relax. I wasn't thinking that way." She winked, laughed again. "You did it all on your own."

Desperate to change the subject, Bannack asked, "Do you have family close? I did not see them at the Compound."

"I don't." She hugged her body. "We've been separated since I was a kid. I'm not sure if they're alive or dead."

He knew the pain of losing loved ones and he softened his face. "Do you miss them?"

A shadow passed over Sibyl's face and she stared at her feet, clicking her worn hiking boots together. The grass folded under the movement, then sprung straight again.

"Sometimes. When big things happen, I wish they were with me. I want them to be alive, but I haven't looked for a long time. I still have the scar from when the building fell on me. See."

On the outside of her forearm was a white, L shaped scar raised against her tan skin.

"A building?" Bannack's mouth dropped open a bit. He'd never known anyone who survived a building collapse.

"Yeah. It was an earthquake from the bombs exploding a few cities over. I remember playing with some other kids after hula recital in the hallways – my parents were closer to the door – and so when it fell, I couldn't get out in time. I never saw them again." Sibyl stared at the ground. "When I woke up, I had a broken arm but was able to claw my way out."

"Did anyone help you?" Bannack asked, his eyes wide, and leaned forward.

"Well," Sibyl tucked a piece of black hair behind her ear. "A family found me wandering in the forest. The dad reset my arm and they watched after me until I healed, then I left, wandered for a bit, until, a few years ago, I found the Compound and decided to stay. I know my parents are out there. Somewhere. I did look for them, but after several years, I stopped looking."

"Losing your family could not have been easy."

"You lost people too, right?"

"Yes." His heart twinged a bit. "Both my parents and my sister."

"I wish I had a sister." Sibyl looked down. "That would've been cool."

"It was. But I miss her a lot." Bannack pulled Malikah's locket out from underneath his shirt collar. Since getting it back the night he rescued Eloise, he never took the locket off. "This is hers."

Sibyl touched the jewelry. "It's beautiful." Then she looked up at Bannack. "Us orphans gotta stick together."

Bannack laughed and nodded.

"Welp," Sibyl pulled her blanket around her shoulders. "Better go check on Eloise."

She yanked open the door of the cabin.

"Sir!" A frantic voice made Bannack pause with his hand on the doorknob and turn to a young boy, no more than ten, running toward him covered in soot. He stopped, bent over to recover, then straightened. "It's my mother's barn. Struck by lightning. Help us."

"Come in," Bannack said.

Minutes passed from the time the boy, named Pete, relayed his tale of he and his single mother fighting to free the animals from the flames that engulfed the barn, hence the reason for the soot. They lived close by, a little over two miles, and Pete had exhausted himself to gasps in his sprint for the closest help. Both Luke and Sibyl pulled on coats, grabbed some cloth and rope for the animals still in danger.

"Back soon," Luke had said to his dog before giving his jowls a good ruffle. "G-guard the books."

It was an odd comment to leave a dog, Bannack reflected, and wondered if it were in jest. Luke did have many books. A shelf filled with them lined the far-left wall. It framed the fireplace mantle and the sweet, musky scent of the old books reminded him of the hole-in-the-wall bookstore that used to be in his hometown.

As he spread his fingers over the handmade shelves, he read the titles of the books. Worn and ripped classics like *The Three Musketeers* and *The Count of Monte Cristo* filled a shelf. Then came rippled fantasies, burned edges of romances, and stained spines of science fiction.

"I feel so lost," Eloise said. She watched him with a dangerous tempest of sadness. Her eyes blazed into him. "I hate Joy for what she did to us and I hate her even more for hurting Mason and breaking their agreement. I should have expected it. Then I ran off during a lightning storm..." She shook her head. "That makes me angry most of all."

Bannack was no stranger to helplessness. It was a pain on the same level as a bull goring a matador.

"You did what you knew best." Bannack watched her chew on her bottom lip. He moved closer to her. "You are not completely helpless, though."

"What?"

"You fought for Mason. You killed with that knife." He pointed to the boot knife, clean from blood, sitting on the table. "I understand feeling helpless, weak and powerless, but you are not. In this moment, perhaps you feel that way and that is okay, so embrace it. Then rise up and fight against it."

Eloise smiled, tears dripping off her lips, then she looked at her hands. "Why did you save me back at the lab?"

"I guess...I wanted an excuse. To be mad. To get back at Joy, even though I did not know it then. But mostly it was my mom."

"Your mom?"

"Well...her voice. She always told me my whole life, we do not leave those we love behind, and I always despised it. In the moment when I realized it was you, I wanted to leave and turn my back. I wanted to run as I had before. Then her voice turned on, and I couldn't deny her."

She didn't speak for a few moments. "Because you are capable of great kindness. I won't say I told you so, but..."

They shared a laugh, his with a note of sadness. He desperately missed his mom. She would offer advice, wrap her arms around him, and give him a place to belong. Bannack glanced down at Eloise's fingers peeking out from the blankets. He touched her pinky in a silent request to hold her hand and Eloise wound her fingers with his.

Without realizing, he had found his belonging and his mom still had every single part in it. With Eloise. He could feel Maame smile.

Eloise sighed. She leaned against his arm. "I can't keep going like this forever. One of these days, she's going to win. Whether she succeeds or not...I'm still broken."

"Eloise," Bannack turned, "I care not if you are broken."

She blinked. "Why?"

Her frustration was intoxicating. Her eyes glinted with a brilliance and zest for life, and a subtle vein appeared on her neck when she became angry.

"Because," the hand he placed on her cheek made her eyelashes flutter, "I need you to understand I ain't leavin'. I am gonna hold on to you with everything I have."

Glistening eyes peered up at him. After a few moments, Eloise said, "Thank you for helping me, but it may not have been enough. I feel like there is a massive hole in my body I can never fill because nothing good will come out of this entire, messed up situation. Either Seth will die, or I will. I can't see another way around it."

"There must be a way," Bannack whispered.

She looked at her hands.

The downward angled perspective showed off Eloise's high cheekbones, something Bannack had never truly noticed until then, and he inspected them for a few moments. Deep golden freckles covered the surface of her skin, some distorted by the curve of her facial structure. Her lashes were long, dark, and wet.

You're stunning.

It's what he wanted to say but lacked the courage to do so. His feelings still felt so new and raw, he didn't know what to do with them yet.

Tears created wet lines down Eloise's cheeks when she glanced up. A quiet gasp stuck in his throat. The woman's eyes shone bright, mostly from her crying, and they were brilliant. Bright and golden.

Bannack leaned forward and wiped away Eloise's tears.

"Do you know of the Japanese tradition of Kintsugi?" Bannack asked. Eloise shook her head. "When a ceramic plate or bowl is broken, they make it whole with beautiful ribbons of gold between the pieces. They recognize the beauty of shattered things. You may be broken, as you say, but if you allow yourself to heal, your soul will glisten so brightly, it will rival the sun."

Moments like this, with her, are eternal.

CHAPTER TWENTY-FIVE
ELOISE

A twinkling glass wind chime rotated outside the window, and she watched the blue and yellow colors dance across the floor in front of her. She reached up and pressed the place where Bannack's hand used to be. His gentle caress lit her skin on fire. His quiet and intense whisper slid across her body, turning every bit of it to mush. The image of his face so close to her own, shining blue eyes making her nerves crackle and splinter, was enough for Eloise to melt where she sat. She felt like the negative side of a magnet, and he the positive, pulled by a force out of their control and one they could not sever.

Sitting near Bannack, alone, heightened her awareness of him. His every deep breath, the shifting of his weight from one leg to the other, and the click of his tongue. She remembered he always clicked whenever he wasn't sure what to do. She turned to him.

"I should...really go wash this." Eloise lifted a handful of her hair. Her scalp itched from the dried mud to be tolerable anymore.

She stood, holding her bandaged hand to her chest. It throbbed in time with her heartbeat and she kept it as still as she could or else it would explode with pain.

It's been half a day and the nanites still haven't healed me.

Bannack stepped forward. She held her good hand up, coming in contact with his chest.

"No." Eloise swallowed and jerked her hand away. "I'm fully capable of doing it by myself, thank you very much. You just sit over there and...give the dog a rub. Something."

His frustration emerged in a sigh, and Bannack sat.

Eloise shuffled through Luke's chests and shelves. She rifled through blankets, clothes, and bottles of various liquids. She grumbled to herself in the loft area where Luke slept.

"You've seen that man's luscious locks, right? Where the heck does he keep the soap?"

Stifling a laugh, Bannack called up to Eloise. "He does not keep soap."

Bannack held up a bottle of rum.

"You're kidding..."

Bannack shook his head.

"No wonder he's so sweet."

Eloise took the bottle from Bannack, quickly scrunched her nose to tease, and snatched a holey towel from a shelf. She knelt in front of a metal trough filled with fresh water and threw her hair over her head.

She didn't get far before the muscle spasm built in her back. At first, Eloise managed it well. Then her back clenched, along with the back of her thighs and her shoulders. Her arms weakened, struggling to get past the first step of pouring the water over her hair.

Eloise dropped her hands. "Dammit."

Bannack glided to her side with amazing speed. "Hey." His hand wrapped around her cheek, his lower two fingers resting on her neck.

Eyes full of tears, Eloise turned to him. "I can't even wash my own hair."

"Your body needs time to heal."

She shoved his hand away then stood, coughing. "Stop trying to make me feel better, Bo."

Bannack's hand appeared on her hip. "Wait. Let me do it."

"Do what?"

"Wash your hair."

She scooted away. "I-I think I can still do it. I just need some more time."

"Okay."

Eloise leaned over the water again, clenching her teeth so hard they ached when her weakened body spasmed. A groan rolled out of her as pain tightened her muscles and her hands shot out to steady her body.

"I can help. Please."

Bannack was beside her. His warmth radiated through her body, and he hooked a long arm around her waist, anchoring her. His chest rose and fell, waiting for her response. She looked over her shoulder and followed the line of his collarbone down to his hands, knowing that if she agreed, those hands would be on her in a way she was not prepared for. She desperately wanted them on her. Even if it was just her head.

"Okay."

Grabbing a worn stool for Eloise to sit on, Bannack leaned her back and supported her with his thigh. He filled a metal cup with water and poured it over her scalp. She gasped quietly as he began massaging the dirt from her hair, his touch coercing goosebumps to her arms and shoulders.

She watched him in wonder as he leaned forward, supporting the stool with his narrow hip. The muscles in his forearm contracted and relaxed with every stroke through Eloise's hair. As he grabbed the rum, his cheek brushed Eloise's nose. He smelled of the leather from his jacket and the unexpected sweetened herbal scent of lavender. She closed her eyes. When he ran his fingers through her hair, releasing some stubborn tangles, her muscles grew heavy and pliable underneath his fingertips.

"Is the pressure okay?"

All Eloise could do was mumble incoherently.

Bannack wrapped his hand around the back of her neck and

lifted her to a seated position. They stayed there, Eloise with her fingers on his stomach and he with her neck in his hands. Vulnerable. Panting. She watched him, the electricity of the moment in the air. He leaned in, his eyes locked on her neck, and came dangerously close to kissing the tender skin. She carefully inhaled as if balancing on a tightrope and if she made one wrong move, inhaled too heavily, she would fall into the abyss.

Do it. Kiss me. Please.

Then his head lifted, following the line of her neck to her chin and then her face. Desire sat within his ocean eyes, a vast and bright sea crashing and breaking against the rocks, poised for destruction as well as calm.

His attention flicked to her hair, attempting to smooth out the last few pieces with his fingers, and the moment broke. Water dripped down her long strands, soaking the front part of her shirt.

Bannack swore and reached for the towel. Eloise caught his wrist.

"It'll dry."

With their faces close again, Eloise drank in his entire existence. Drowned in it.

"You can't be so close," whispered Eloise, breathless.

"I can back away if you like."

Eloise shook her head. "It's not that. I like when you are close."

Something devilish flashed in his eyes and he leaned forward, talking in a hushed growl. "How about this?"

"Closer."

"This?"

Fire burned within her. It ignited her soul. Bannack held her neck in his hands, cradling it as if a newborn babe. He dragged his lips from her neck to her chin, leaving a trail of gentle kisses along her scar's ridges, forcing a noise from deep within her. Every kiss from him was calculated, gentle. Reverent.

When his hands wrapped around her waist, lifting her body to his, the raw power in his arms made her gasp, breathless. Bannack settled beside her. His kisses threatened to melt her into oblivion.

"Elle..." his whisper was torture. "If you'll have me, I'm going to make up for all the years we lost. The ones we should have laughed, cried, and kissed through. I want to make up for all of it."

She grabbed his face before he could pull away. His stubble scratched against her palm. Then she kissed him. Those full, soft lips made her heart sing, and she knew, fully and completely, she never wanted to let him go, worried he may float away. The way he consumed her with his arms, sunk his fingers into her hair, and worshipped her with his gaze, was now as familiar to her as breathing.

"A long time ago," she said as she fought to catch her breath, "I promised myself and the universe to listen when the time came to chase. I hoped there would be a sign or something that told me to run forward and never look back. Then you crashed into my life. I was expecting someone, but not you. Never you. All of a sudden, right there in front of me, was my answer."

Bannack's eyes flashed with surprise and excitement. He touched her lips with his thumb and kissed her. "God, I love you." He put his forehead on hers.

They sat together, running their hands lazily over each other's arms and legs. When he stood to poke the fire with the poker, she noticed the black tattoos down the back of his arm.

"What do your tattoos mean?" she asked, and her feet found his. As if on reflex, he wound his ankles with hers.

"My adinkra are how I strive to live my life. And how I want to be remembered in death."

"They're beautiful."

Bannack touched the tattoos from top down. "This one is sankofa, sometimes shown as a bird twisting its head to pluck an egg from its back." His symbol was a heart with swirls on the bottom and top. "It translates to "return and get it" and means we must learn from the past." He continued to announce the names of the tattoos and their meaning. "Aya is a fern because it is a hardy plant. It can grow in the most unlikely of places and symbolizes endurance. Akofena, with the two crossing akrafena blades, is a symbol of courage, heroism, and valor. Dwennimmen, the touching ram's horns, means even the strong must be humble. And Nea Onnim means the continued quest for knowledge and lifelong education. These are how I choose to live my life...or at least attempt to. I'm afraid, in the past few years, I have not done very well."

"You've been doing your best." Eloise snuggled in close.

"Eloise..." A spring in the bed thunked when he rotated to face her. "Can you tell me about your scar?"

Eloise's hand went to her face. "I'm not sure you want to hear. About any of it. I don't know if I'm ready to say."

"You do not have to tell me now."

"Okay." Eloise took a deep breath, surprised the memory was harder to think about than she anticipated. "Ada and I were gathering some treats for our girl's night. We had those a lot. Keep in mind, this was after our parents died, so Mason was a bit more lenient with what we did together, hoping space would help us heal. We went to Newman's. Two men carrying guns killed everyone in there...including Ada. They did this." She pointed to the facial scar. "The nanites saved me, but I don't know why they left a scar instead of healing all the way. I think maybe the injury was too severe."

For a long while, Bannack kept quiet, chewing on the inside of his lip. "Why do you help Seth?"

"He asked me to," Eloise replied. Her hands twisted together. Her composure threatened to break. "And I'm the only one who can. When my parents destroyed Joy's facility, the rest of the serum perished, except for mine. If anyone can do anything about his disease, it's me. Before agreeing to help Joy, I made sure Seth wanted my help. He did."

"You have placed a great weight on your shoulders. You do not have to bear it alone."

Tears fell down her face. An emotional weight she didn't realize had been sitting on her chest, lifted from her heart like an air-powered rocket shooting into the sky. She squeezed his wrists, her head low, and wept. Then his thumbs were on her cheeks, wiping away the waterfall from her eyes. As her shoulders shook, he pulled her close and held on, patiently waiting.

And, just like Bannack predicted, he filled in the cracks with gold.

***

An hour later, Luke, covered in soot, shoved through the door of the cabin. Boatswain jumped at his master's feet in greeting. A wide smile Luke attempted to hide flashed across his face as the dog used his enormous tongue to lick something from his fingers. Water dripped off him.

"I found this...rat-t thing." He pulled off his pack, lifted the top flap, and a feline face, pink-skinned with large black spots and green eyes, poked her head out of the hole. She blinked. Dirt covered her entire body.

Eloise gasped and gathered Bali up. "Where did you find her?"

"In the w-forest." Luke pulled down his cloak to reveal several long, thick, and blood-tinged scratches down the entire length of his neck. "She fell from the sky like some possessed, knife-wielding sugar glider and landed on my shoulders." A smile crept onto Luke's lips. "She's devastatingly ugly. Perhaps we should eat-t her."

Rolling her eyes, Eloise placed Bali on a bookshelf. "You're hilarious."

A cool breeze rushed through the open door and curled around Eloise's arms and neck as Sibyl entered, also covered in soot.

"That was the hardest thing I have ever done." Sibyl sucked on a cut by her thumb. "Cows are so much bigger than I imagined."

"Sibyl!" Eloise laughed. "You work with horses."

She gave Eloise an incredulous look, blinking several times. "Uh...so? Horses are graceful and majestic. Cows are bumbling and awkward."

"I happen to like cows," Bannack added.

"They stink."

Luke snorted. "All animals smell. Just depends on what smell you are willing t-to put up with." At that, he groaned loudly and stretched. "I'm sleeping in the barn. There's room here for you

232

three."

He snapped his fingers and Boatswain was at his feet.

"I'm going to go to bed, too." Sibyl yawned. "I'll wash up tomorrow when we get to the Compound."

***

The sunset had long disappeared, yet Eloise remained awake, staring into the night sky through the window in the loft. She fiddled with the end of her hair. Sibyl slept beside her.

A quick peek over the banister revealed where Bannack slept. A blanket curled around his legs with an orange glow from the dying fire cast across his torso.

As Eloise watched, her nose in line with the banister railing, Bannack groaned. His hand moved on top of his stomach, and he inhaled sharply. Eloise thought she heard mumbled words but couldn't quite make them out.

Occasional twitches and quiet words quickly became jerking movements and yelling.

Sibyl moaned, then rolled over. "What's going on?"

"I don't—"

"Elle!"

At Eloise's name, Sibyl jerked fully awake and Eloise jumped to her feet, gesturing for Sibyl to go back to bed. She stumbled down the stairs, then knelt at his side, placing her hand on his soaked skin.

"Bannack. Wake up. It's not real."

She shook his shoulders and grabbed his hand, placing it, open palmed, on her face.

He cried out again, wrenching from her grip to turn on his side. For a moment, he stilled. Then jerked into a sitting position, his back stiff. Eloise gasped and fell on her hind end.

Bannack's chest heaved. His eyes glazed over. The anger swirling inside them frightened Eloise.

"Bo..." she whispered.

With an angry grunt, he whipped his body toward her voice.

Eloise swallowed hard and dodged a lazy swipe of his fist.

"I cannot find her! I lost her!" Bannack's trembling voice broke Eloise's heart asunder. Her eyes moistened, and she inched closer.

"Who? Who have you lost?"

"Get away! Do not hurt her! Eloise! You cannot go. You will die. Please help me find her. I will do anything."

Nothing made sense. He jumped from word to word in a confused panic. Then he shook his hands, at first, and soon his entire body followed suit. His teeth chattered. Eloise furrowed her brow in confusion. "I have learned my lesson and I will not defy you again. Let me out! You cannot leave me here!"

He muttered, terrified, in his native language, Twi. His words stuck together as he spat them from his mouth.

Bannack's typical composure shattered. In front of her sat a broken man, yet in spite of the darkness of his past, he had become kind and gentle.

How is that possible?

"Bannack...wake up. You need to wake up!" Eloise grabbed his fumbling hands and placed them on her chest. "Do you feel me? Do you feel my heart? I am real! Your demons aren't! Wake up!"

Keeping his hand on her fluttering heart, she slapped him. He gasped, flinched away and blinked, his dull eyes returning to their vibrant hue within seconds. Bannack fell into her, shuddering. Eloise grunted underneath his weight and wrapped her arms around him.

"Thank you. Thank you. I am so sorry. Thank you."

"You're welcome. We'll get through this together," she said.

To feel his strength falter and shake from fear like a mouse confused Eloise. Bannack had braved a lightning storm to make sure she was safe. He played with children simply because he wanted to. She knew he had a warrior's heart. And yet, he refused to think he possessed one. Why?

Soon, his shaking calmed, and he released his near crushing grip on her midsection. She inhaled.

"Sorry," Bannack apologized again, his head hanging low.

Normally, he would have his shoulders back and head high.

Eloise reached up and wiped away the tears on his cheeks. "Never apologize for your nightmares."

"They will not go away. I have tried so hard, Elle, but they always come back. Most nights, I do not sleep. I train and try to meditate or breathe. When I miss a single day, they return."

She smoothed out his shirt collar as she listened. "I understand." Eloise wiped her thumb across his cheek and smiled. "We need to stay strong if we are to defeat our demons."

He nodded and yawned. Eloise gave him one last affectionate touch and then stood.

"Eloise?"

She turned at the bottom of the stairs, her long hair falling over one shoulder.

"Will you stay with me? I am afraid to sleep."

She clenched the railing. If she laid next to him, her mind would overflow with his scent, his warmth, his touch. She should say no, give the responsible answer. But then...he looked so sad. Bannack sat on the cot with his head ducked low, his hands over the back of his head. His usual might had been stifled. She couldn't, in good conscience, deny him comfort when he needed it most.

"If you need me to."

The cot was really meant for one person, so Bannack made a bed on the floor for them both out of a few pieces of animal fur while she plaited her long hair into a side braid and secured it with a thin strip of leather. As he lifted a blanket, Eloise slid underneath, taking care not to touch him, even through the barrier of blankets. Her body would surely burst into flames like a phoenix if she made contact with him.

Eloise's skin crackled as he settled under his own blanket.

Bannack fell asleep fast, nuzzled against her back like a young puppy. His slow breaths tickled the small hairs at the nape of her neck, and he wrapped his arm around her upper torso and pulled her in close.

With a heave of her body, Eloise twisted around to face Bannack.

He inhaled deep, a slight smile on his face. His angular features had grown soft and his skin warm from sleep and she locked the contours of his face, his nose, eyes, and lips in her memory to retrieve in case of an emergency.

She fell asleep, finally, with tears under her cheeks and her hand resting on Bannack's neck.

***

After a breakfast of rabbit, eggs, and cattails, everyone busied themselves with leaving. Luke packed a small bag of items for his aunt, Soora. Bannack helped Eloise secure her bandages.

"I should have healed by now."

Bannack gave her a halted look when she hissed and jerked away.

"I'm sorry, Elle. I do not mean to hurt you. We can search for answers when we return to the Compound, okay?"

The pain still radiated up her arm, but she managed a brief nod.

"So," Sibyl tightened the drawstring on her bag and gave Bali an affectionate scratch, who purred. "Are we all ready?"

"Let-t's go." Luke attached a bundle of rope, using a carabiner, to the outside of his pack and slung it over his shoulders.

Eloise blinked at him, confused, then smiled. "You're coming?"

"Joy harmed my family. Now I'm pissed."

"That's fair," Eloise said.

Bannack bumped Luke. "Welcome to the team."

CHAPTER TWENTY-SIX
ELOISE

"They're back!" A guard's words cut through the air and two more, tailed by Soora, ran down the hill toward Eloise, Bannack, Sibyl, and Luke.

"Lukesha." Soora sighed when they embraced.

"Hello, Chachee." Luke's expression softened when he looked at his aunt. The change was so drastic and different, Eloise's brain stopped working. Luke's eyes sparkled. "Are you...good?"

Soora nodded, solemn, and gathered Luke into her arms. He smiled, his large mass hiding Soora's body completely.

"Luke helped us," Eloise said when she recovered from the shock. She looked at her hand. There was no hiding the injury from Soora who could sniff out one like a bloodhound.

Soora caressed Eloise's face and glanced briefly down at the bandages on her hand. "Tell me everything as we walk."

Sibyl informed Soora of the lightning strike, Eloise's condition, and the issues with healing. Concern flashed in Soora's eyes, but she said little other than telling Eloise to visit her later.

"What about Mason?" Eloise asked, eager to check in on him.

Based on what Bannack said earlier, and the small flinch Soora gave, she knew to steel her mind against what she may encounter in meeting him.

"He's alive, which is the most important thing, but Eloise," Soora stopped walking and turned, "he's different. Not the same."

Those words made Eloise freeze. What would she find when she confronted Mason? She'd seen the people at the village. Would he be disfigured? Unable to speak?

All of her worries spoke at once, their voices a loud crescendo in her head.

"Hey." Bannack smiled down at her and bumped his elbow against her arm. "I'll be with you if you need me."

"Thanks." Eloise smiled back at him. "But you saw him after the nanites took effect. Was he...de-deform—did he look okay to you?"

Bannack thought for a moment. "He wasn't walking well, but that's a common side effect. Listen. I am not one hundred percent sure what we will find, but we need answers, remember?"

"Yeah. Okay." She followed Bannack with her arms wrapped around her body.

Before they arrived at Mason's office, Soora paused. "You need to know something else." Her eyes lowered as if she were thinking, opened her mouth, closed it, then sighed. "Joy's acting strange."

"How strange?" A thought occurred to Eloise, her stomach tumbling. "She hasn't been here, has she?"

"No. Our patrols have been reporting odd behavior at the facility. Yelling from inside, nervous whispers. No guards are in the courtyard and have been instead seen wandering the forest as if looking for something."

"And you know nothing else?"

Soora shook her head. "What I've told you is what I know."

Her mind reeling over the possibilities for Joy's sudden increase in movement, Eloise followed Soora into Mason's office and stopped short.

A man sat at the desk, head bent over papers strewn across the top, clean shaven with a scar across his chin but with the same build and salt and pepper hair as Mason. He mumbled to himself.

When Soora rapped on the door frame, he glanced up, paused, then slid his eyes up her body, an expression of longing flashing in his eyes. Eloise blinked rapidly. He looked like Mason, but he wasn't. Not completely. And he definitely didn't act like Mason who commanded a room by simply entering it, who held his body like a seasoned veteran, straight and poised. This version of Mason had a youthful charm and no problems admiring his wife in front of people as if she were Aphrodite.

"We have guests."

He smiled. "Come in, please."

Everyone entered except Eloise. She stood just inside the room, staring at Mason. He was lucid and sane, able to function perfectly, but something felt off.

Soora touched Eloise's arm. "I know it's strange seeing him like this, but we've been closely monitoring him and aside from the years he lost, he's healthy."

"Years?" The words weighed down her mouth.

"Yes. Around twenty years are gone."

"So...he won't remember me?"

"No."

Eloise swayed. *He won't recognize me?*

"Have you noticed any symptoms other than memory loss?"

"None so far. I do need to talk to you about something. There—"

Mason groaned, his hands clenched around his head. Soora rushed to his side. The groaning grew louder, and Eloise couldn't move as she stared at Soora struggling to keep him in his seat. He banged on the table, swaying his head from side to side. Sweat formed on his neck.

Eloise's eyes lost focus. Her skin crawled.

Soora yelled something at Bannack, her terror hung in the air like a plague, heavy and soul-crushing.

The man she considered her own father, who had taught her how to fight and lead, was panting and growling like an enraged animal with his foot caught in a trap. In his struggle, he unknowingly shoved

Soora, who crashed into the window behind her. Mason turned, stumbling, and fell at her feet. He shuddered.

Soora, tears in her eyes and chest heaving, flicked her gaze to Eloise. She rushed over and knelt.

"I don't know what to do." Eloise didn't dare touch him.

"Help...me," Mason growled.

"How? With what?" Her voice had a high-pitched desperation. "What do I do?"

A hand on Eloise's shoulder made her jump. Bannack's voice spoke by her ear. "You must let it pass. This is a symptom of the nanites."

Worry morphed into anger. Eloise stood. "You expect me to sit back and let this happen? Are the headaches, or whatever this is, going to kill him?"

"No one has died yet from an injection."

Eloise rolled her eyes. "Oh, good. Great. That's one worry off the list. What I want to know is this..." Eloise stepped in close to Bannack and he stared down at her. "Are you going to help me kill her?"

"We need—"

"I forgot. You need your precious answers. Well, here's an answer. I'm going to kill Joy for doing this to him!"

"We do need answers," Soora said. She was kneeling next to Mason, his shaking body leaning against her chest as she held him. "I know where you can find them."

Mason opened his eyes and looked at Eloise. The same eyes he used to smile at her were now devoid of any recognition.

She took a step back.

"What's your name?"

When Eloise looked at Bannack, angry tears pouring down her face, he shook his head at her. He knew what she would do, even before she realized, and Eloise stared at him. Her entire body ached with tension.

"Level head, Elle."

Eloise's hands shook and she clenched them. "When have I ever lost my head?"

"Elle—"

"No! No." She backed away, panting. "She promised to keep her word. I gave her everything!" Her scream filled the room as she waved her arms and pounded her chest with a finger. "I kept my end of the bargain! Then when things get hard for her, she ruins my life? Bullshit! Other people may be afraid of her, other people may let her get away with a slap on the wrist, but I sure as hell won't. If you won't help me, then I'll do it myself."

Shaking and unsteady on her feet, Eloise opened the door. It slammed shut. Her body jerked forward and she looked at a tanned hand, then to Luke. She glared. Luke dropped his arm.

"Have you heard? We're the good guys. Killing people makes us no better than Joy." He stepped forward, looming over her. "Walk out the door, fine, I won't stop you."

"I'm nothing like her." Eloise gritted her teeth. "And stop trying to intimidate me. It doesn't work."

With a curt nod, as if satisfied she wouldn't go anywhere, Luke rolled up his sleeves and stepped away.

"What are we going to do about Joy?" Sibyl asked. "It's only a matter of time before her mercenaries meet up with our people and I don't want to think about how bad that could be. Also, why is she acting strange?"

Mason adjusted in his chair and leaned forward, and his index finger curled under his nose. The action was something Eloise had seen countless times before. She looked away. "We prepare," Mason said. "You say I'm the leader of this place. Well, I want the...uh..."

"Sentinels," Soora offered.

"Yes! I want the Sentinels to double up on patrols in the area. Anyone who isn't a known member of the Compound must be brought through here."

Eloise blinked. "That's a lot of people."

"Is that a problem?"

His eyes were hard. The affection he normally looked at her with was gone and in its place sat the stiff unwavering stare of a man who hadn't seen his country fracture and break, hadn't buried his children and first wife, hadn't become a leader of a successful commune and raised Eloise to adulthood. As he stared at her, Eloise felt cold and alone. Joy ripped Mason from her and she couldn't imagine a worse consequence, aside from his death, for ignoring her son.

She looked down. "No."

"Mason," Soora put her hand on his shoulder, "try to speak gently. She's your daughter."

He looked at Eloise, inspected her, and nodded. "You're right. Although I don't remember you, I trust my wife. If anyone has a better idea, I would like to be informed."

The room erupted into conversation and they spent the next hour planning and plotting how best to handle Joy if she showed up. Luke and Sibyl agreed to be Sentinels temporarily until Joy's terror ended. Bannack worked with Mason to split the Sentinels into groups based on their skills to maximize their efficiency. Eloise went with Soora so she could look at her hand.

In the infirmary, Eloise sat on a bed and waited for Soora to come back with fresh bandages. She looked at her wrapped hand. Feeling still hadn't returned to it.

I don't feel different, but something isn't right. The nanites should've healed me.

"Alright." Soora entered the room, a bundle of salves and bandages in a basket she carried. "Let me see your hand."

She hissed and turned away as Soora unwrapped the bandages. The air stung. She clenched her jaw.

"I'll try to be careful, but," Soora leaned in, "your hand is badly injured."

"I know." Eloise sniffed.

"I won't peel the dead skin, but there's quite a bit of it. I believe you may have third-degree burns." She paused and turned Eloise's hand. "Were you holding anything when the lightning struck you?"

"My boot knife."

Soora made a noise and opened a bottle of her salve. It was

opaque and had a slight golden tone to it, as if it were oil based, but it came off her fingers like a gel. "This is an aloe vera based ointment and should help soothe your skin. It contains some curly dock to help prevent infection. I worry your nanites were affected by the lightning somehow."

Eloise put her free hand on her face. "I don't know what to do about it. Why aren't they working? If I get sick, that's it for me, isn't it?"

"Many people without spleens live happy and healthy lives. It's not a death sentence if yours is missing, but I do worry about infection with this hand injury, so I want you to re-wrap this twice a day and apply new salve. I'll send you home with some."

Her nanites not working had been bothering her for a while and she knew, deep down, something had happened to them. It made her stomach churn. "Could the lightning have fried them?"

"I don't know," Soora finished wrapping, "but we'll find some answers. Since we don't have immune boosting medicine, I want you to be extremely careful. Stay apart from others. Wash your hands every hour, more when you eat or touch things. Getting sick could be fatal."

"What about the Sentinel duty?"

Soora paused for a moment as she placed her items back into the basket. "Once a week should be okay. But no more." She put her hand on Eloise's cheek. "You're too precious to lose."

***

Branches slid against Eloise's face and arms as Luke, Sibyl, Bannack, and she walked through the forest. They were on their last round of patrols for the day and Eloise bounced on her heels, happy to be free of her cage. She had spent too long cooped up in her room. Bannack visited often, talking with her while she sat on her bed and him standing by the door. It sucked. Being so deprived from human contact, especially Bannack, put her in a headspace she buzzed with excitement to be free of.

"Finally!" Eloise kicked at the grass, dandelion puffs flying into the air. Bannack laughed and pulled her into him. He felt so good, his body pressed against hers, and his hand wrapped around her back.

"I'm glad you're happy." He nuzzled into her neck and gave her a kiss. He tasted of the raspberries he'd been snacking on. "I missed you."

She chuckled, tossing her head back. The wind whipped at her hair. "I missed you, too." She kissed him. "You taste so good."

Without warning, Luke pulled on Boatswain and took a sharp turn down a grassy embankment behind some tall, round bushes, and Sibyl and Bannack, Eloise still attached to him, followed. Eloise gasped, her blood accelerating through her body. She fell from Bannack's arms feet first, slipped in the soft dirt, and landed on her back.

When Eloise gathered her wits, she could hear several voices coming from her left. She tilted her head, listening to the quiet footsteps not yet attached to people. Then they appeared, five in total, armed with knives, a crossbow, and clubs. Eloise's eyes widened.

"Who are they?" Sibyl whispered into Eloise's ear.

Eloise shrugged.

"I told you we should have ended Graham when he walked past us carrying the rolled-up rug," a skeletal man said in hushed tones. "I told you it looked suspicious. And now boss lady has us busting our butt trying to find them!"

Eloise looked at Sibyl, her eyes wide.

What's going on?

"Well, we can't fix it now." The only woman in the group who held a crossbow, knocked Skeleton Man upside the head. "Our best bet is to hunt them down and stop anyone who gets in the way."

Eloise covered her mouth and used her free hand to grip Bannack's shirt, balling it up in her fist.

We're going to be okay. She chanted, shaking, as she placed her face on top of her hands, the grass tickling her nose. *They can't see us. The bushes will hide us.*

"Where is Edmund, anyway?" A burly man with a club resting on his shoulder glanced around.

Skeleton Man barked at the other two. "Taking a piss. Here he comes."

Eloise couldn't see the man named Edmund, but she could hear him. Heavy footsteps followed by panting brought images of an overweight man struggling up the hill, but when he came into view, he was a giant of a man, musclebound, and clenched a coarse rope in one hand and a saber in the other. On the end of the rope was a mastiff. He dropped his chestnut head to the ground and sniffed the surrounding area, turning in circles.

"They ain't up here," said Skeleton Man to Edmund who grunted out his dissatisfaction. "We better double check the house. Might be hidin' out in there."

"Shit," Luke growled and buried his face in his hands.

The group with the mastiff moved on, wading through the grass along the trail. Fortunately, they didn't take the same path Bannack, Eloise, and Luke took out of the forest and instead made their way, the mastiff's nose glued to the ground, down the hill.

Once out of sight, Eloise counted. *One one-thousand. Two one-thousand. Three one-thousand.*

Boatswain lurched to his feet, shaking his shaggy coat free of the broken sticks and dirt lodged in his fur, and Luke plucked a bramble off his forehead, ruffled his hair, then cooed, "You're such a g-good boy for staying quiet."

Boatswain panted.

Eloise stared down the road in front of her, a rollercoaster of sparse, overgrown grass swaying in the wind, and she noticed, barely visible past a line of dense forest, an abandoned gated community.

"We can avoid them if we go that way."

She looked at Sibyl, Bannack, and Luke, a silent conversation passing between them, and they all nodded.

Luke said, "There might be supplies or or weapons there, t-too."

Sibyl made a noise. "They're not looking for us. Why do you want weapons?"

"If they think we're in their way, they're going to try to kill us. Weren't you listening?"

"Duh. But you can be less of a jerk about it."

Luke groaned. "Sibyl! I'm not-t-t capable of being nice so much. I've hit my quota for the day."

"Who said anything about being nice, dumb quat? You should be kind. Nice is easy. Being kind is the hard part."

"Dumb quat-t?" Luke stared at her with his head cocked.

"I don't know." Sibyl tossed her hands in the air and walked toward the abandoned neighborhood. "It sounded better in my head."

As they approached the community, they stepped over the gate which lay on the ground, mangled like a crumpled piece of paper in a heap through the closest manufactured home. Something big had smashed the gate.

They wound through the abandoned houses, taking in the apocalyptic scene of the ghostly neighborhood. Of the homes that weren't burnt, crumpled by fallen trees, or covered in moss, the rest stood in eerie silence, forgotten souls waiting in line to be delivered to their fate. It was a graveyard. But instead of bones, it was row upon row of ruined, decrepit houses.

Eloise shuddered and hugged her body tight.

***

Sibyl, Eloise, and Bannack stood in the kitchen, searching through the cupboards for anything they could use and waiting for Luke to join them.

"They could find us?" Luke adjusted Boatswain's rope leash in his hand as he entered the living room. "How are we going to prove we're not in their way?"

"We could talk to them." Eloise opened a cupboard door and a rat carcass stared back at her. She balked and closed the door. "I don't know who they're looking for. It could be anyone. But we have to get back to the Compound soon, so we can't afford any hiccups."

"Okay," Sibyl said. "Then we avoid the people with the dog and focus on getting back to the Compound in one piece."

The sound of crashing glass gave Eloise barely enough time to turn before the bolt of a crossbow sunk deep into the cupboard door she held onto. The force swung it wide, wrenching it from her hand, and cracking it against the wall. Eloise gasped and stepped backward. Her foot touched nothing. Doing the most painful splits of her life, Eloise fell to the laminate floor. Her body partially fell through rotting drywall, the inside of her thigh near her crotch crackled and burned, and she remained there for a moment, trying to figure out how to move.

Bannack's hands were on Eloise, helping her stand.

"Move!" Luke yelled.

Another bolt sunk deep into the fridge, an awful metal crunch followed by the freezer crumbling around the entry wound, made Eloise and Bannack duck then scramble.

Eloise slammed her boot into the screen of the low window in the dining nook then slid through. The mastiff let out a deep bark. It fought against its leash, tied to the metal railing of a house. Her feet hit the top of an air-conditioning unit. She slunk around the corner, placed her back against the siding, and whispered, "Now what?"

But when she turned, Bannack, Sibyl, and Luke were missing. Her pupils dilated as tingling waves rolled underneath her skin. How could she lose them?

They must not have followed me out of the window. But I could have sworn—

Voices coming from the front of the house caught Eloise's attention and she stood slowly. Her body ached and hand burned. She panicked when she heard the exchange Bannack and Sibyl were having with the people they hid from earlier.

"We're looking for a man named Graham, and a teen named Seth. They've gone missing."

Seth's gone missing?

"Let-t us through!"

"So, you can take him right back to his prison?" Bannack. "Like hell!"

Clanging of metal, yelling, and the unmistakable sound of fists on human flesh filled the air. She peered around the corner, still reeling about Seth going missing, as Skeleton Man tumbled across the gravel, Luke hot on his heels. His cloak fluttered with his movements. He swung a metal garbage can lid. It landed mere inches from Skeleton Man.

The mastiff barked.

An ear-splitting sound of trash cans being overturned made Eloise jump, and her heart slammed against her chest. Bannack lay sprawled on the ground for a moment. Edmund loomed over him. In an effort to halt his forward progression, club in hand, Sibyl jumped on top of Edmund's shoulders. Bannack scrambled to his feet.

Before Eloise could move to help, a bolt from the woman's crossbow glanced off the asphalt several feet in front of Eloise, then clattered out of sight. Eloise ran, sending gravel flying as she took refuge behind a fallen tree. Her breath forced itself from her lungs.

Breathe. Just breathe.

Eloise lurched to her feet. She ran, tripping as she did so, to help her friends.

A body slammed into her shoulder. She tumbled sideways, crashing through an old door. She slammed into the half wall separating the entry from the living room. Her hand stung as she moved it. A laceration on her upper arm bled into her shirt. Eloise covered it with her hand.

Great.

Glancing up gave her barely enough time to roll away before Edmund charged her with his saber raised. She squealed, her eyes dilating in fear and ran through the living room. Out of nowhere, Edmund slammed into her again. This time her feet left the ground. She sailed over the bar stools and crashed, back first, onto the top of the kitchen island. The wind flew from her lungs. Eloise half screamed, half grunted. When the back of her head hit the kitchen sink attached to the island, her entire body shuddered. She tipped over. Her ankles slammed into the metal gas stove top and she folded as she fell the rest of the way. Everything hurt.

Hands clamped around her throat.

Barely able to make out Edmund through her blurred vision, Eloise's feet left the floor which swayed unnaturally. She tasted bile and the metallic tinge of blood.

"You and your friends gave us a damn headache, you have." Edmund hissed at her and Eloise vaguely thought that he sounded British, but she struggled to form anything else coherent.

Her throat burned. Her back collided with the fridge.

Claw at him! Get to his eyes!

Eloise willed her mind to clear. Despite the red nail marks in Edmund's hands and arms, he continued to hold on to her throat, pushing her further against the fridge and tightening his large hands around her neck. Panicked, once again, Eloise thrashed, kicking at him with everything she had.

He laughed. "You're cute."

"P...plea–lease." Eloise croaked out. Words were sandpaper in her throat. "Let me go."

"Do as she asks."

At some point, Luke had equipped the crossbow and stood with the bolt trained on Edmund who chuckled.

"You're just a kid. Think you can fight me and a dog?"

The fierce, terrifying growl of the mastiff came from the door Eloise had crashed through and Luke stepped sideways, his eyes wide.

"Then I'll just have to shoot his mast-ter." Luke swallowed and raised the crossbow again.

"Ha!" Edmund squeezed Eloise's throat. "I have your girl."

"False." Luke smiled. "Not mine."

Edmund whistled.

The mastiff leapt at Luke. Expecting the attack, Luke fired.

The bolt lanced Edmund's cheek, but the injury was enough to make his head jerk sideways and his grip release Eloise's throat.

She stumbled away, wheezing. Her throat burned, and she could feel the red handprint around her neck.

Jaws clamped down on Luke's elbow, and he cried out. He fell, the crossbow forgotten on the floor, and fought with the large dog, pulling on ears and arching against the animal's body.

Eloise half-crawled toward Luke.

Edmund's laugh, mocking and deep, abruptly stopped when, as Eloise turned, Bannack pulled a kitchen knife out of the man's neck. Her stomach rolled. Blood pooled down Edmund's barrel chest and he sat against the cabinet door, twitching, trying to speak but unable to. Then his head tilted, and he stilled.

Ignoring Eloise, Bannack stalked toward Luke, blood dripping from the metal tip of the blade. She saw his face and her blood froze. He was on auto-pilot, eyes blank yet dark, as if he were a cold, metallic machine. Murder flashed in his eyes.

Sibyl appeared at Eloise's side and pulled her close. The warmth of the hug released some tension and Eloise began hyperventilating. Without speaking, Sibyl coached her through breathing, pushing her hands away so she couldn't scratch at the inside of her wrists.

"Don't hurt-t the dog!" Luke, still trapped, held his hand out for a moment then screamed and grappled with the animal again.

Bannack advanced.

Luke tried again. "Stop! He's—Ach!—He's only doing as he's commanded!" Luke arched his back when the dog shook his head. "His legs. Damn it! G-g-grab his fucking legs!"

Eloise rushed past Bannack, which seemed to wake him up, took hold of the mastiff's feet. She gave one giant heave sideways. The dog's body hit the floor, knocked off balance, and released Luke.

The dog whined and padded over to his owner, cautiously licking his cheek. With one droopy-eyed look at Bannack, Eloise, and Luke, he turned and laid down by his master.

Luke hissed when he rolled up his sleeve to inspect where the dog had bitten him. He had bruising, but no broken skin. "I'm fine. If the dog really wanted to hurt-t me, he would have." Luke pushed his sleeve down. "I'll be sore for a day or so."

"Are we going to even talk about Seth?" Eloise's brain fumbled over itself, trying to figure out why and how Seth escaped.

Luke tended to his arm and mumbled angry words underneath his breath. Sibyl sat on the porch, her head in her hands, and Bannack leaned against the siding, his arms crossed and foot flat against the wall. No one spoke. Eloise didn't blame them. They had just been attacked for no reason except that they were in the way.

Sibyl finally spoke. "Seth could be anywhere right now."

"Not without help," Luke said and winced. "From what we heard, someone named Graham helped him. T-take that and and add it to Joy sending her goons out to find him, we can assume he he succeeded in disappearing."

"Then we have to trust him," Sibyl said. "He's seventeen. That's old enough to be smart about running away, especially that we know someone is with him. Until we know more, we have to assume he doesn't need us. And, Mason is still a mystery."

As much as she hated it, she knew Sibyl was right. Seth wasn't a priority. She had to stay focused on their true goal: getting answers for how to deal with Mason. They hadn't made much headway, but they knew that in the couple weeks since his memory wipe, he hadn't degraded, and his headaches had slowed down.

"Fine," Eloise rubbed her neck. "We'll deal with our injuries and head back to the Compound. Hopefully, Finch's crew makes better headway than we did."

"Hey," Luke spread his good arm and smiled, "we at least discovered Seth is defying his mom. Very exciting."

CHAPTER TWENTY-SEVEN
JOY

The metal chair flew out of Joy's office, the horrid clang and crash barely audible through her pounding anger.

Joy stood behind her desk, shaking hands splayed across the top, and her shoulders shook. Hot, furious tears fell down her face, getting stuck on her chin before they dropped. She glanced at her employees, fifteen of them, standing at attention and sweating.

"How," she whispered to Amy, the only person willing to speak, "have you not found him yet?"

"Apologies, ma'am. We're doing our best."

Anger made Joy lose control again. "Your best isn't good enough! My son is missing and you've spent weeks looking for him! He's in a wheelchair. Either you're all incompetent, or someone is lying."

Amy jumped when Joy slammed her hand on the desk. "I'm sorry. He must be—"

"Stop!" Joy glared at Amy. She could barely speak now, her breath heaving. "I want you all looking for him." Joy straightened as a thought burst into her mind, then inhaled. "Whoever brings me my son and Graham's head, I will end their service to me and reinstate their families' memories."

"Excuse me?" Amy blinked at Joy. Excited mumbles rose from the group.

"You heard me. Go!"

The group scuttled away and disappeared.

Joy inhaled, still shaking, and looked at the framed photo of Seth as a six-month-old baby. His nose was scrunched up and eyes sparkled as he held a tiny pumpkin. People walked in the background, blurred out of focus. She had taken the photo at a pumpkin patch Before and as a single mom who spent much of her time in the office trying to discover a cure for Alzheimer's disease, the day trip to the local pumpkin patch was priceless. It was her favorite memory of him.

I'm going to find you.

Graham had kidnapped Seth and her heart ached to think what was happening to her son if she wasn't there to make sure he stayed safe. Avoided getting sick. His body had grown too weak to endure much of the outside world.

She screamed and punched the wall.

He's going to kill Seth faster than the disease! I knew I shouldn't have let Graham near my son, or Eloise. She probably put the idea into his head in the first place.

"Damn it."

She'd been careless.

Trusted too much.

Because of that, Seth was gone.

Nothing remained except Joy, the cold walls, and soulless machines.

CHAPTER TWENTY-EIGHT
BANNACK

The rain soaked him to his bones as he rushed inside, holding the door for the other Sentinels in his squad.

"Man!" A Sentinel named Isaac flicked water from his hands. "Too much rain for me."

"I'm soaked!" Another Sentinel, Lance, scrubbed his hair, making droplets of water fly all over the people close to him while they all voiced their upset. He chuckled. "Sorry guys."

The four of them gathered in the alcove just inside the door, shaking off the water and drying their bodies with the towels waiting on a rack.

Marcas finished first and tossed his towel into a basket. "Drinks on me, boys?"

Bannack didn't respond as Isaac and Lance ran off with Marcas. Why should he celebrate when Mason was struggling? It felt...disrespectful. He fiddled with the towel, carefully drying off his arms and neck as he stared at his feet.

We're no closer to figuring out how to help Mason, Seth is still missing, and it's only a matter of time before Eloise gets sick.

"There you are."

Soora's voice made him look up. "Hey, Soora," Bannack said, and the towel made a muffled thump when he tossed it in the basket.

"How's the weather treating you?"

"Have you seen outside?"

Soora smiled. "Don't like the rain, huh?"

He opened his mouth to respond and then noticed a slight change in her posture. She sighed, her shoulders drooped, and a small wrinkle appeared between her eyebrows, so small he almost missed it. "Is everything okay? Mason has..."

"No. No. He's perfectly fine." Soora glanced away. "I'm concerned about Eloise."

His heartbeat pounded against his chest and he stepped forward, eyes wide. "She's sick, isn't she?"

"Came in two nights ago. Shortly after you left."

A bitter ache latched onto Bannack's throat. "And no one came to get me?"

"You were gone. I had no way to contact you, you know that."

"Yes." Bannack sighed. "Can you take me to her?"

The walk to Eloise's room made his chest ache with every step, and by the time he stood on her doorstep, he barely contained his fear. His hands shook. Eloise laid in the bed, sweating, her eyes closed. People bustled around her carrying fresh water and towels. Something brushed across his leg. Bali mewed up at him. Bannack picked her up and held her to his chest as he watched the activity of the room and memories flooded into his mind of his dad lying on a bed, sweating and breathing heavily, unable to understand anything around him. The memories crowded his head, all vying for attention, until they gave him a headache. He set the cat down, groaned, and turned his head, trying to escape the thoughts. He'd seen death before. Why did it have to be exactly as his father had looked days before his death?

If she's taken from me, I'm not sure I'll survive.

Come on, Bannack. Stop worrying. The nanites are probably just tired.

"B...Bannack?" Her voice, weak and frail, petrified him. He stared at her. Golden eyes looked back, bloodshot and dull, then her arm lifted, hand hanging as if she didn't have the strength to finish the motion.

He stepped back, tears in his eyes, and he croaked out words. "I am sorry. I..."

Bannack ran. He should have gone to her, held her, wiped the sweat from her face and arms like his mother had done with his father. That was the honorable thing to do. She needed him.

But he was too much of a coward to face the inevitable stench of death or bear witness to Eloise's last breath.

***

Bannack stalked along the riverbank. Angry, terrified tears gathered along his lower eyelids. He launched another flat rock at the clear water and it skipped three times before succumbing to the shallow river.

This is some cruel joke.

She is being taken from me the same way as my father.

"Hasn't my suffering satisfied you enough?" He screamed into the forest, rage surrounding his words and consuming. His entire body shook. With a grunt, Bannack launched a speckled rock into the river.

Why do I have to love her so much?

Bannack feared the question might never be answered. He loved her. Adored her.

And she was dying.

It made him simmer.

The path of the river Bannack walked beside led him out of the fading evening sun and under the cover of trees. He tipped his head back. Between the earth and sky stretched branches filled with needles and leaves, and they swayed in the light breeze. The oasis of green and earthen fertility was suddenly foreign, as if he were walking through an alien planet. And Bannack wanted to stay forever.

This was the earth Before.

He needed a good polar dip. The events of the next day threatened to haunt him forever.

Stepping up to the river, the water lapping at the grassy bank, Bannack removed his shoes, shirt, and pants, leaving only his undergarments. He crouched, letting the frigid water slide through his fingers. Then he placed one foot in the water, cold shocking up his spine and out through his fingertips. Another foot. Same reaction.

If she dies...

He shook his head and willed the thought away.

Bannack inhaled rapid, sharp breaths, calming his pumping heart. The water rose up his back and the algae covered rocks beneath the water slimed up his arms.

He lay there, slowly bringing his breathing under control, and stared at the sky once more. It was grey. The clouds drug through their domain, leaving a trail of more clouds behind them.

I do not want to return.

I am afraid of what I will find.

I do not want to be alone again.

Crisp water coursed over his body, pushing at his feet, and moving him centimeter by centimeter up river. Bannack closed his eyes, the rocking motion calming his mind, helping him to think clearly.

"Maame." Bannack's voice came out in a way that was not his own; it was coarse and heavy, weighing his throat and heart down with a force he had known only once. His words came out in Twi, crying to the heavens. "I need you here. I am lost, and I do not know what to do. Please, Maame."

More than anything, he needed her. He needed her to sweep him into her arms and hug him tight, whispering with her smooth, warm voice while she caressed his head as she had done when his father died.

She appeared in front of him, an apparition of his own making, and held out her hands. His knees buckled.

"I cannot do this without you. I need you, Maame."

"My sweet, darling boy," she crooned, her invisible arms around his shoulders. "You must return to her, my brave one. She needs you."

"It hurts too much."

"I know. I know."

He looked at her, barely visible as she faded. His mother placed her palm on his cheek and he envisioned the touch that never came, the memory etched in his brain. Retrieving it burned like a hot poker. His mom's caress was warm, motherly, and everything he missed about her. She hadn't been perfect, but he always knew she loved him unconditionally.

Then she was gone.

And he was alone

Bannack screamed. The water sprayed across the river when Bannack slammed his fists into it. He covered his face and huffed over and over.

He had to return. If these were his last days with Eloise, he needed to spend them with her and perform the same caring rituals for her as his mother demonstrated years ago. He needed to whisper to her, to help her feel safe and validated that she, although terrified, was going to be okay.

But he hated it.

Hated that he cared. Loved. Hated he knew better. Hated he would watch her die. Hated himself for being so unwilling to be beside his woman as she took her last breath.

Bannack sat up, the water dripping off his skin.

I am going to be there for her.

Even if she takes a part of my soul.

Even if it means I die as well.

***

Bannack entered the dark Compound. He padded to the

bathroom, slid a towel off the rack, and finished drying his body. The toilets were missing, removed because of the lack of running water.

He picked up his shirt, a dark, muddy splotch on the front. Letting out a quiet growl, Bannack bundled it up and opted to carry it with him upstairs. He changed in his room, slipping on sweatpants and a sweatshirt.

Then he made his way to Eloise's room. Soora sat by the door, her head back and arms crossed over her stomach.

"Hi," Bannack said and sat next to her.

Her eyes were bloodshot. "What time is it?"

"Late."

"That's right. Habit from Before."

"Sure. How is she?"

"Weak. Tired. But she's doing better. No fever. Able to go on short walks." Soora rubbed her eyes. "My shift is almost over."

"I can take it from here."

"Thank you," Soora said and smiled. "Check on her soon. I left some fresh water for her."

Bannack nodded. When the doctor left, he opened the door.

Moonlight draped over her body as she lay asleep on the bed. Eloise kept her hands tucked underneath her chin. Her long hair spread out over her face, a section falling across her forehead and over the edge of the mattress. Eloise took his breath away.

Bannack grabbed the bowl of water, knelt by Eloise's head, and squeezed liquid from the washcloth, the trickling ear-piercing in the quiet. With a shaking hand, he washed the sweat off Eloise, moving in slow, meticulous strokes, struggling to remember how his mom had done it.

"Soft strokes, Akoma," she used to say. "As if the wind were kissing his skin."

As if the wind were kissing her skin.

He took extra care in the grooves of her scar to make sure perspiration didn't sit too long and then moved onto her shoulders and arms. Although the room was dark, aside from the moonlight, he could feel her muscles. They were tight and defined. Bannack remembered back to the day of their time in the sparring yard and how she had almost gotten the better of him because he had doubted her strength. He bit back tears.

These memories...they're either going to be precious or they'll destroy me. Probably both.

When he finished, Bannack set the bowl back on the dresser and pulled the end of the blanket over her feet. He glanced back at her face. Her open eyes bore into him like they always did. She possessed a habit of looking deep into his soul and pulling out the remnants of good. Nothing in his life felt more real. Or more beautiful.

"Your toes looked cold."

She ignored his comment. "I waited up for you."

"I see you did. Why?" A twinge of guilt attacked his gut.

Eloise groaned and stretched. "Because I needed to make sure you didn't run off."

"Akoma," Bannack whispered, tucking a silken strand of red hair back behind her head. "I will always return to you." Her expression was difficult to gauge in the poor lighting, but Bannack thought he glimpsed a small smile when he asked, "Can I lay with you tonight?"

"Yes."

Without another word, Bannack leaned toward Eloise. Her eyes fluttered close, and as he climbed into the bed beside her, he slid one arm underneath her neck and the other he placed on the curve of her waist. Even though she was wet from sweating, would shiver when she breathed, and made Bannack's throat clench so tight he could barely speak, her touch sent his heart soaring. She was everything. Eloise's warm softness of sleep sunk into his skin. She snuggled against him.

"I like you," she said sleepily, and Bannack barely heard her. "But just a little bit."

Eloise drew lazy circles on his chest and she kissed his neck, lingering after each painfully slow caress. Bannack's entire body quivered at every touch, every kiss, and he felt himself slipping, lost.

He grasped her face in his hands and tilted it. "I love you."

"I know."

"I am yours. Forever. You need to know that."

"I do."

Bannack slid his fingers up her neck, behind her ears, and into her hair. He wound his fingers in the strands and placed gentle pressure on her scalp, silently asking to kiss her. Probably for the last time. Tears leaked from his eyes.

"I was taught to hide away my feelings," he whispered. "They'd only get me killed. For years it worked. But you...everything I do when I am with you is feel. I have been holding myself together with nothing but flimsy wire and nails. Hurting. Terrified to fall apart. Now, I fall apart every day and you pick my pieces back up, cherish each one of them, and make me whole. I am damned to Hell for wanting you, yet here I am, giving you my heart."

"Bo?" Eloise asked and passed her hand over his face to wipe the tears. "I want you to love me."

A stab of bittersweet excitement hit his stomach and he couldn't stop the deep whisper from exiting his mouth. "But, you're sick."

"Shh." Her fingers on his lips made him melt underneath her. "I can't die never knowing what you felt like and I want you to know what it was like to have me."

"Are you sure?" Oh, he wanted this, more than he had ever realized until now.

She nodded. "I'm sure."

The air snapped and crackled, and Bannack inhaled sharply as their kiss deepened, wanting and asking for more. Then he felt her tears. The salty liquid entered his mouth as he began kissing them away. Sadness spread like a wildfire through his body. He became helpless to stop it as it overwhelmed everything in its wake. The fire blazed, consuming, relentless. Its heat burned and licked at his terrified heels.

Then Eloise's touch came like the rain, pushing away the fire and bringing calm. It banished the terror and guilt from his body, replacing it with hope and warmth like the first starts of the morning sun.

"Take whatever you want, Akoma. Take all of me, but

261

please...stay with me. Stay."

No matter how many years followed in his life, he would never forget the silk of her hair, the scent of pine mixed with crisp morning air that clung to her, the physical scars that told the story of a woman who had overcome, and the way her body fit perfectly inside his like a missing puzzle piece.

He would remember her forever, and that stung more than he had ever known.

CHAPTER TWENTY-NINE
BANNACK

Carrying the records of crop yields from the season, Bannack walked to Mason and Soora's room to go over the documents with them and plan for the next year. The door was open, so he stepped into the doorway and paused.

Mason leaned against the desk, smiling sideways at Soora who stood a foot or so apart from him. She looked like she had just finished laughing.

"I think I'm still feeling under the weather," Mason said, grabbing at Soora who squeaked and jumped away. "I may need another physical."

"I will give nothing of the sort!" Soora squeaked a second time when Mason pinched her backside, smiling wide as if she were barely holding in a laugh. "You're not cognizant. And, besides, we have a visitor coming any minute. Keep control of yourself."

"I'm perfectly sane, Mookie. Now, come here. I want to repeat what I did last night."

Bannack whirled around, face hot, and hid behind the wall.

Well...this is awkward. I'll just wait.

Soora released a gasping laugh. "Stop this! You are the most ill-mannered, mischievous man I've ever met. If you don't stop right now, I'm going to have to restrain you."

"I'm counting on it."

"Stop it," Soora chuckled through her words. "I mean it, Mason. Poor Bannack is hiding because of you. I expect you to be civilized."

Bannack peaked around the wall and looked at them both.

Pouting, Mason mumbled underneath his breath. "You're no fun."

Soora gave him a dark warning glare and he stiffened. Then she motioned for Bannack to enter. "I'm so sorry. He's like a young pup again, and I don't have the endurance." She reddened when she realized what she had said and whirled around to Mason. "Do you see what you've done to me? I can't have a normal conversation anymore."

A wolfish grin spread across his face.

Desperate to change the subject, Bannack walked around to the other side of the desk, sat in the chair, and spread the documents out on the table. "The crops have done well since we combined compost tea and horse manure. See this," he pointed to a new page, "that's our yield."

"Twenty-five percent increase is excellent!" Soora clapped her hands together and leaned over the papers. "And look at this, Mason." She put two documents side by side. "We have enough revenue and supplies to begin the underground fridge system in only a couple weeks!"

Even though Mason smiled, Bannack noticed his eyes never engaged. Soora had taken much of the responsibilities, passing out whatever she could, but Mason had to learn about the policies and inner workings he had put in place all over again. Bannack knew he was exhausted.

"I'm so proud of you, Mookie." Mason gave her a kiss. "I know how much this project means to you and to see it all come together, with you so excited, makes me happy."

Soora beamed. "Thank you."

"Sir!" Abe rushed into the room, panting.

"Yes?" Mason and Soora said together, then shared an amused smile.

Abe bent over, his hands on his knees, and put up one finger. "Hold on. Give me...a minute." He panted for several seconds, then straightened. "I gotta do those stairs more often. Phew! We have a man named Graham waiting for you downstairs. Sounds urgent."

"Graham?" Soora asked as she approached Abe. "You sure."

"Unless I got my abuelita's ears."

She turned around. "Bannack and Mason, I need you with me. You're going to want to hear this."

***

They walked around the back of the building where a lanky, blond-haired man in a muddied traveling cloak waited with his back to them. He turned around as they approached. Bannack paused, watching the man closely to determine if his body language gave off hints he was dangerous, but when Soora hugged him, Bannack relaxed. Before the blond man lowered his arm, he saw a still-healing, thick, short scar on the inside of his forearm.

"You're one of Joy's," Bannack stepped forward, his shoulders square and hands clenched, "aren't you?"

"Was being the key word." The white man gave a concerned glance to Soora who nodded. "I see you dug yours out as well."

"Why did you?"

"I couldn't have her tracking me. What's your reason?"

Bannack narrowed his eyes, still on edge. "Couldn't let her find the little girl."

To his surprise, Graham laughed. "That was you?" He made a whistling noise. "Joy was pissed for months about what you did!"

"I'm glad you find this amusing. Why are you here?"

He glanced at Soora again before talking. "You're right, I was aligned with Joy, but that's not my true role."

"Graham," Soora said as she motioned to him, "is one of the

265

original founders of the Compound. Graham, this is Bannack Owusu, Eloise's partner."

"What?" Bannack took a couple steps back and his breath caught in his throat. He stared at Graham, then rubbed the scar where his tracker used to be. "Does Eloise know who you are?"

He shook his head. "No. When Mason, Soora, and I founded the Compound, I did much of the diplomatic work. Planning how things will operate, finding people willing to come live at the Compound, working out a monetary system, and getting the fields set up for harvesting. I also began leading the scouting parties. She only saw me a handful of times, and I had a beard then, so I doubt she'd recognize me." Graham folded his arms and leaned against the concrete wall. "To keep a close eye on her and Joy, and maybe a little bit of revenge for what she did to my family, I agreed to serve her. That was...eight years ago, now. Since I was a new recruit, Joy kept a close eye on me. For a few years, she made sure I stayed in the facility. You were gone so often searching for people, it wasn't hard to keep away."

"Wow." Bannack shuffled his feet. "Why have you come here, then?"

Graham sighed and sat down on a concrete bench, then leaned forward. "As soon as I learned of Mason's injection, I knew he'd want me to find answers. I searched for a while. It wasn't until Seth found an entrance to—"

"Seth?" Bannack and Soora jumped at the mention of Joy's son.

Soora spoke first. "What are you doing with her son? You were only meant to gather intel, not kidnap a teenaged boy."

"We barely escaped one of Joy's search parties because of you!" Bannack growled as he stepped forward.

Realizing his blunder, Graham put his hands up. "Hold on. Let me explain. He wanted to come, and I tried to stop him."

"He's in a damn wheelchair," Bannack said. "You don't have to do much to make him stay where he is."

"Believe me," Graham gave a nervous chuckle, "if Seth doesn't want to stay put, he won't. So, he threatened to reveal my secret identity to his mom unless I helped him sneak out, said he was tired of being trapped and wanted to stand up to his mom. I took him with me." Graham shrugged.

"Ugh." Bannack rubbed his forehead with two fingers. "Okay. Seth found an entrance?"

"It was a gate, vines in front of it, that opened up to a cave. When we walked past, trying to find a place to hide, he could feel the cold draft coming from it. We followed the path, and it led us through the cave system. On the other side was a small valley and a farmhouse. We didn't know anyone lived there at first, but we later met the family that occupied it. We chatted, and in our conversation about finding a solution to our Joy problem, he mentioned that he knows of something that will flip the tables in our favor." Graham paused, blinked, and looked at Soora. "Where is Eloise, by the way?"

"She's sick," Bannack said.

Graham rubbed his face and looked at the ground. "I wish I had gotten here sooner. Henry's a good guy. He worked with Eloise's parents back in the day and knows about the nanites and how they work. He mentioned Eloise is the key, but he wouldn't expand on it. I do know that he asked for Eloise specifically, so if you want to learn more about how to defeat Joy, she has to go."

Bannack grumbled. Moving her might make things worse, but then a thought occurred to him and he looked at Graham. "You talk of Seth as if he's still alive."

"Yeah. He is. The kid's strong."

"I don't understand."

Graham smiled. "I do love a good surprise. You'll see when you get there."

Bannack looked at Soora. "What do you think?"

"You have to take this chance. I trust Graham's information and if he says it's good, then it's good. I'll pack some extra supplies for Eloise, but I'd listen to Graham. You have to go if you want her to get better."

Nodding, Bannack eyed Graham. Instinct told him to distrust the man in front of him, but he seemed genuine, so Bannack extended his hand.

Graham shook it, and Bannack said, "Thank you for your efforts. I need a map." He turned to Soora. "Tell Sibyl and Luke to be ready for traveling. We leave in a few hours."

***

The map Graham had drawn led them straight to the secret entrance. It took longer than expected to get there because they had to navigate the forest while pulling Eloise on a small cart. By the time they reached the cave, all of them were sweaty and tired.

After taking a brief break to make sure Eloise was comfortable, Bannack lifted her into his arms because the cart didn't do well on the rocky floor of the cave.

She laid her head on his chest. "How much further?"

"We're almost there. It's just on the other side of this passage."

Since Eloise had gotten sick, she alternated between sleeping for days and having energy to do basic tasks. Her body had grown small, different from the power she used to have, and it made Bannack's heart sick.

Henry better have something good.

Sunlight blinded Bannack as they walked out of the darkness. Graham had been correct in classifying where Henry lived as a valley. Tall cliffs surrounded them, littered with sparse trees or dense forest.

"Henry's house should be just beyond this hill," Bannack said.

Bushes rustled behind Bannack. The hair lifted on his arm, sensitive to the light breeze rolling through the gnarled trees and he reached for his sword, shoulders tight.

A little girl with braided pigtails, welding goggles strapped to her forehead, and a double-barrel shotgun pointed straight at them stepped from the bushes. The girl couldn't have been more than nine. Her wide eyes darted through the group, chest heaving and hands trembling.

Eloise whimpered beside Bannack and crushed his fingers in her grip. Her strength surprised him. For a moment, Bannack considered pulling away to ease the pain, but then he saw her face. Her typically fair skin had turned ashen, as if her body was preparing to faint, and she stared forward, eyes glossy. She didn't move; short, gasping breaths made her chest heave in jerking movements.

Bannack glanced at the little girl again, trying to figure out what had Eloise so terrified. The entire group stood together in a tense moment, but Eloise's rigid body and Bannack's numb hand hinted at something far more serious.

"Hey," Bannack whispered to Eloise, nudging her with his elbow. "What's going on?"

"Th-the...it-it's her...that thi-thing."

"What thing?" Bannack, his eyebrows knitted together, blinked at the little girl. A tremor passed through Eloise and the ripples of the movement crossed into Bannack's arm. She shuddered twice more and tried to shrink into Bannack's body. He asked, "The gun?"

Eloise nodded. Her hands, knuckles white, clutched at her chest. "I-I can't breathe."

"What are you doing here?" The girl asked, her face scrunched in anger and a hint of fear. She pointed the gun at each person. When it scanned past Eloise, she stiffened against Bannack again. He wrapped his arm around her and applied pressure, hoping he could alleviate some of Eloise's fear.

"We're here to see Henry," Bannack said, holding out his free arm in the hope the girl would lower her gun. He had no way of knowing if her weapon was loaded. Guns were so rare because finding or making bullets proved to be difficult and she most likely had it for shock factor. If fired, the gun would launch her backward and he didn't want to take the chance.

"Do you know who he is?" Sibyl said. She had crouched low in the tall grass just as the little girl appeared, but now stood. "We won't hurt you."

The girl squinted at Sibyl. "Those weapons make me think you're lying."

"We'll put...put them away," Luke said and sat down.

Both Bannack and Sibyl set their weapons in the grass, and the little girl relaxed.

But Eloise didn't. She shrunk. The scent of pine, of her, wafted from the top of her hair as the wind moved through it and Bannack's mind drifted. He wished he could take her somewhere away from her triggers and the danger that shadowed them. He lowered his head to the top of hers, pine scent becoming more pungent, and inhaled.

The girl stepped forward, lowering the gun. Her pigtails swung just above her shoulders as she pointed at Sibyl. "You're her!"

"Excuse me?" Sibyl asked.

"The one in all of the drawings!" No one moved, and the girl grumbled impatiently. "Come on. I'll show you...My name's Alice, by the way."

Eloise wouldn't move. Even while the rest of the group disappeared from sight, Eloise remained frozen.

Bannack called out to Sibyl and Luke following Alice. "We'll catch up with you guys."

Luke waved his hand in the air without turning around.

Bannack turned to Eloise. "Alright. What's going on?"

"The gun." Eloise croaked and her grip around Bannack's waist tightened.

He knew. The day Ada died. For her to react so adversely to the gun in Alice's hand, the day had to have traumatized her so severely; she froze like a deer in the headlights at the mere sight of one.

"Because you saw it?"

Eloise's face rubbed against his neck, buried against his skin, when she shook her head. Her hair cascaded down her back in a deep red waterfall. "Because she pointed it at me." Eloise looked up at him. "At all of us. I thought-thought she would use it."

"We must follow them."

Eloise sniffed, then nodded.

She pushed away from him, moving her hair from her eyes, and tripped over a rock. Bannack watched her fall on her knees, unable to catch her in time, and the sob she let out tightened his chest.

Bannack didn't think. Only acted. He stepped behind her and picked her up from the grass, hearing her gasp under her breath.

"Breathe deep, Elle."

Eloise pushed gently on Bannack's chest and he released her.

"I'm fine." She walked away.

"You are not," Bannack called after a beat. "You can see the demons. Your chest hurts. Like an anvil is sitting on top of it. Your mouth is dry."

"Go away."

He knew she didn't mean her words. They were from a place of pain, the gun triggering more than just memories, and she became hostile. It was the nature of what she struggled with. "Please, Elle," He held out his hand. "Let me help."

Eloise stepped away. She shook her head. A combination of fear and anger spread across her face.

Bannack jogged to stand in front of Eloise. "They cannot hurt you anymore. The men who..." He wanted to finish his sentence, but he saw the cringe of Eloise's shoulders and dared not finish. "Do you understand?"

She turned her tear-stained face toward Bannack. "Yes, they can! Every time I close my eyes, every night, I see them. They are everywhere. Haunting me!" Eloise stepped back. "The nightmares...you can't make them go away!"

He hurt for her. All the pain she carried on her shoulders. It had to ache.

He took a step forward, his arm reaching. "But I can help. Please, Elle, I want to understand."

Eloise's body tensed. "You can't fix me, Bannack. I'm broken. I've always been broken—and don't look at me like that!" Eloise cried, tears falling onto her chest.

"Listen to me," Bannack said. He relaxed his face, reached for her hand but paused, closing it into a fist, and dropped it back at his side. "How long are you gonna let it eat at you until you pull out those knives and fight back?"

"I—you—" Eloise fumbled through her words, eyes glistening

with tears, and huffed at him.

Bannack covered her trembling body with his arms. She cried into him. Shaking and weeping, tears soaking through to his skin, warm and full of long-hidden emotion.

"Oh, Eloise," Bannack whispered and kissed the top of her head. "What I would not give to take this all upon myself. We are going to fight this. I promise, no matter what happens or what you do, you will never loose me."

Chirping of birds in the spring weather came from all around them, and they both stood underneath the old, gnarled boughs of the apple trees that creaked in the wind. The sweet yet crisp scent of tree-ripened apples hung in the air. The sun drifted across their bodies.

Eloise's cries grew quieter. Then she sighed.

As he held her, Bannack sensed the release spread through her entire body like a gentle wave. It began at her shoulders. Her arms around his midsection relaxed. Yet, he held on to her.

"Thank you, Bo," Eloise said against his chest.

"Akoma." Bannack clasped her cheeks in his hands. Eloise's lips parted ever so slightly, igniting a fire inside his core. "I love you." He brushed her face, cradling it in his hands. "Every single imperfect blemish, demons and scars be damned. I cannot promise if there will be a tomorrow or five minutes from now, but I vow to you. All of who I am belongs to you, my akoma mu tɔfe. My sweetheart."

He surveyed her eyes, searching for an answer. Eternities passed in her calm expression until she attempted to speak with her mouth. But no words came. The pounding of his heart was too loud.

Her lips found his, so fierce and smooth. Then her arms were around his neck.

He knew, at that moment, he would never leave her or give her reason to doubt. He would hold onto her for eternity.

His woman.

His goddamn dangerous woman.

CHAPTER THIRTY
ELOISE

The house Eloise and Bannack walked into was well-maintained and decorated. Vibrant house plants were nestled in a few corners of the home and set upon several surfaces, the décor was mostly handmade, dishware was stacked in a metal dish drainer next to a sink of water, and the furniture, despite having a few nicks, tears, and stains, were all in decent condition.

In the center of the living room, looking as if he had become one with the creaking rocking chair, sat a tall, tan, middle-aged man with a shawl draped around his shoulders and streaks of grey in his long braid. Tribal tattoos peaked out from his rolled-up sleeve on his right arm. Sibyl knelt in front of him, her upper body in his lap, weeping.

As Eloise walked further into the room, hesitant and confused, she saw a woman, raven haired and stocky, standing at the stairs with both hands over her mouth. Tears poured down her cheeks.

"My girl," the man said, and his voice wavered. "My darling little girl. You've finally come back to us."

"Daddy." Sibyl nuzzled her face into his chest then peered over his shoulder and stood, holding her hands out to the woman at the back of the room. "Mom."

Sibyl's mom made a shaking noise of relief and rushed to her daughter. They sunk to the floor, Sibyl's mom brushing the hair from her face. "Is...is it really you?"

"Yeah," Sibyl said and laughed.

Eloise couldn't help but smile. Her body coiled tight from excitement and joy. For as long as she knew Sibyl, she had mourned the loss of her parents and now that she had them back unexpectedly, Eloise struggled to keep her own eyes dry watching the reunion.

Bannack cleared his throat and Sibyl's dad turned. His eyes were colorless and clouded.

Blind? Sibyl never told me.

Alice didn't skip a beat in offering introductions. "Daddy. These are the other two people I was telling you about. One is a tall man named Bannack, and the other is a short, skinny woman named Eloise. He has ice blue eyes, like how yours used to be, and likes to carry a sword at his right hip. She has red hair—but not red like a carrot. Red like..."

"Copper," Eloise helped.

"Welcome to our home. My name is Henry Marchant. Charlotte is with Sibyl, and you've already met my daughter, Alice. Please, sit down." When the man spoke, his voice was calm, intelligent, as if he had seen a thousand lifetimes, and youthful.

"You're Sibyl's family?" Eloise asked.

Henry became emotional again. "Yes."

Until then, Eloise's gaze had been transfixed upon Henry's face, but she broke from him and glanced to Sibyl. Tears lined her brown eyes. She held a leather-covered wooden box her mom must have given her.

"How? I mean, she thought you guys were dead."

Charlotte sniffed. "We looked for years, even after Alice's birth. It broke our hearts to stop looking for you, but Henry's eyesight loss forced us to slow down. We settled here, at this little farmhouse, hoping we were close enough for you to find your way home."

"I can't believe it," Eloise said, sitting on the love seat next to Bannack.

"Neither can I." Sibyl hugged her sister. "It's like this is all a dream."

"What is in the box?" Bannack asked.

"Me," Sibyl smiled.

Intrigued, Eloise leaned forward. Sibyl knelt at the coffee table and the box made a gentle, wooden clunk as she set it down. She lifted the lid. Paper upon paper of different sizes, textures, and colors expanded higher than the rim of the box like a child's pop-up book. "These are my mom's drawings of me."

Charlotte grabbed the top paper, a charcoal drawing of a little girl in a sundress dancing in a field, her black, double braided hair bouncing around her shoulders. "We used a lot of these to post on trees, hoping people would see them, but once we had no word, I collected as many as I could and put them in this box. Others I drew so I wouldn't forget you."

Sibyl stood and hugged each of her family members. "I accepted you were dead a long time ago, but I never dreamed you would be here, waiting for me." She looked at Eloise. "I even have a kid sister!"

Eloise chuckled. "I'm so happy for you!" She turned to the blind man. "Henry, I don't mean to sound intrusive, but how—"

"How did I become blind?" Henry offered.

"Yes."

"It happened when I got sick. We have no ability to visit a doctor nowadays, but I'm fairly certain I contracted glaucoma. There's a history of it in my family." Henry tilted his head as if he were listening for something far off. "Don't be afraid to ask questions, Eloise. I don't mind."

"Well, then," Luke rubbed his neck, "we have many."

Eloise chimed in. "Starting with how do you know my parents? Why do you know so much about the nanites? What information do you have that's so important? And where's Seth?"

"I was a scientist on Joy's team. They—she, your parents, and the other scientists—worked for years on the Nemosyne project. It was in its tenth year by the time I joined them. We were so young and bright eyed. I believe your parents were dating then."

Eloise smiled at the idea of her mom and dad living a normal life.

"We worked side by side for years, trying to perfect Nemosyne. Once we felt it was ready, we applied for FDA approval through drug trials. But it never got that far. Nemosyne always had something wrong with it. Seth got sick shortly after the third denied application. At that point, Joy went off the deep end."

Henry shifted in his chair and cleared his throat, eyes glistening. Talking about the past seemed to affect him more than Eloise realized. "Your parents were extremely intelligent, and they suspected something would go wrong. In secret, they created another Nemosyne and used their DNA to craft it. I wouldn't fully understand how that decision would change everything until years later.

"When you were in the accident and your condition worsened, your parents first went to Joy, but she refused to help. Desperate, they came to me. I helped them steal a vial of serum to inject you with it, which was their idea—"

"Wait, wait," Eloise held out her hand. "You were the one who gave me the serum?" At Henry's nod, her hands lifted to her scalp and she ran her fingers slowly through her hair as she exhaled. Anger built in her stomach, making it queasy. "That lying—Joy told me she did it."

"Well, she lied."

"Yeah. I get that now." She chewed on her lip, scratching at her wrists until Bannack stopped her with a touch. "You can continue."

"The drug was extremely experimental, and we didn't know if it would work, but recent testing had given us a strong possibility the nanites would successfully attach to a host *if* they were immuno-compromised. You see, they were programmed to always be healing the human body. In a healthy subject, they would die because they had nothing to do."

"That's why," Eloise looked at her palms, "I'm able to keep them in my body and Seth isn't? I'm immuno-compromised."

Henry nodded. "Partly. He's still an odd case. We used your parent's nanites to inject you and because you are their daughter, they recognized both sets of DNA within you, making themselves at home in your body. This never would have been achieved had we used the original nanites. As for Seth, without examining him, I would hypothesize the nanites do heal him, but since they have nothing more to do, they die, and because his disease is degenerative, his body goes right back to breaking down. Again, this is completely speculation, so take it with a grain of salt."

"So, there's nothing that can be done for him?"

Henry put up a hand. "Not quite. Once you recovered, we knew Joy would catch wind and attempt to simulate your circumstance, so Amanda, Merrick, and I planned to destroy every last thing we all worked to build. Not only to save you but, hopefully, countless other lives." He hung his head. "Their death and our failure to prevent that outcome has haunted me ever since."

"Hold up," Sibyl adjusted in her seat. "Then what's Joy been using to brainwash everyone? The facility was destroyed."

"It was. Amanda and Merrick had me remove fifteen vials of their serum and replace it with the originals in the fridge, knowing Joy would try to recover them and they wouldn't work as expected. Apparently, she did, because Graham has informed us that people have lost their memories. I'm not completely sure, but I think Joy may have found a way to continue her work, except Amanda and Marrick aren't around to share their DNA, so she's doomed for failure. Only you remain. The key."

"Me?" Eloise leaned back, her head spinning.

"Yes. You are their daughter and without your blood, your DNA, she cannot create a true serum. It will wipe memories as it has been doing. However, from what I remember of the nanites your parents created, if you use your blood mixed with the nanites, Joy's off-brand ones will be targeted and removed, allowing Amanda and Merrick's nanites to renew the memories of the patient, and, possibly, allow Seth's body to heal. The best way I can describe it is similar to white blood cells—Eloise's nanites—bonding to viruses—

277

Joy's nanites—to eradicate them."

"So..." Luke scratched his head, his face scrunched, and sighed. "You're saying that...that Eloise's blood plus the nanites can heal the people with memory loss and reverse Seth's disease, but not the serum minus Eloise's blood?"

"Yes."

Luke exhaled, and his cheeks puffed. "Alright. People can't donate their blood to just anyone, though. She'd have to be a..." Luke glanced at the ceiling for a moment. "...universal donor."

"I am," Eloise said. As a child, upon learning her blood type during her hospital stay after the car accident, she thought it was a bit of a super power to be able to give her blood to anyone she wanted.

Quiet fell throughout the house. Eloise sat with her hands under her thighs, staring at her feet, while she tried to understand everything Henry had shared. Her parents making a new serum. Her blood, not just the nanites, being the key.

It was a burden.

"What about Seth?"

Henry and Charlotte smiled in unison.

"Hi, Eloise."

Her heart leapt into her throat and she nearly choked on it when she heard Seth's voice. It was different. Deeper. Stronger. She turned, slow, and looked straight at him. He was sitting in a pink living room chair, smiling.

"S-Seth? You're..."

"Alive? Yeah, I am. The Marchant's have been...taking care of me. They're pretty great."

"Tell me everything."

After Eloise rushed over, she got a better look at him. He had more color to his skin, and she realized he was slightly darker than before, probably from a combination of being outside and his natural skin tone. Seth looked stronger, too. His chest had widened, his arms and legs thickened. Not by much, but any change from his skeletal body was huge.

"It's been about a month since...I left. Graham overheard...my mom talking about hurting...Mason and he came to talk to me, to...ask me what I wanted to do." Seth looked at his hands and forced them to relax. "I decided to leave. Graham...left to find answers but he told me that when he...came back, I should be ready. No one knows about...this place. I'm safe here. Charlotte has...been helping me outside and with exercises and look what I can do!"

Seth stood on unwavering legs and Eloise, crouched on the balls of her feet, toppled over. Seth laughed.

"Pretty cool, right?"

"Uh...yeah. It is." Eloise couldn't stop the smile from spreading across her face. She hugged him, and he felt good. Strong.

"This means I'm getting...better! I stopped believing it could...happen, but now I can actually...do things like I used to!"

Seeing him well and excited brought tears to her eyes but still put her on edge. As their conversation died out, Seth, with Charlotte's help, walked over to the dining table with a partially complete puzzle. Alice joined him.

Eloise watched them enjoy each other's company, excited to have him alive, terrified when her sickness would force them to switch places. No longer would it be Seth's death by disease, but hers. No one could seem to figure out what she suffered from. Guesses, sure, but not even Soora, a highly skilled doctor at the nation's top medical hospital Before, could figure it out. Some days she was fine, others she was bedridden and sweating, her entire body in pain. The running hypothesis was the nanites were malfunctioning because of the lightning strike. They would keep her alive but also slowly kill her.

She stood, walked outside and sat on the swing suspended from the porch roof. A few minutes later, the door swung open and closed.

Bannack sat next to her. "You're worried about Seth."

"I'm worried about everything. I feel like we're on borrowed time with my sickness and Seth's disease. Eventually, it could be a year from now, it could be tomorrow, but someone is going to find us and snitch to Joy."

"Seth is stronger than he used to be."

She looked at Bannack as tears formed. "I know and I'm mad at myself for not being able to enjoy it. He's not a skeleton anymore. I'm glad, but I have this pit in my stomach that won't go away. I need answers! Not knowing is eating me up."

"How about this: we go back inside, and we'll talk to everyone, get their input, and come up with a plan. Sound good?"

With much effort, Eloise nodded. "Something is better than nothing."

Back at the house, Eloise sat with Sibyl, Luke, Bannack, Henry, and Charlotte. Seth had moved away from the puzzle table and was in the far room, silently reading a book. Alice was upstairs.

"I want to talk to you," Eloise said and looked to the room Seth occupied then bit her lip, "because I'm concerned about Seth."

"But he's been doing amazing." Sibyl's brow wrinkled. "Why are you concerned?"

"I'm worried because he's getting better. When I started working with Joy, he was really sick. So sick that he suffered from seizures and couldn't talk very well."

Charlotte chimed in. "Those are becoming less frequent in the past week. His strength *has* increased, not decreased. I can feel it when I work with his legs. And he's gaining muscle faster than any human should."

"So," Luke put his fingers to his lips, paused, then splayed them on the table in front of him, "he's not going to die, and he has super healing abilities?"

"It would seem so," Charlotte said.

Luke still wasn't convinced. "Not-t possible."

Eloise watched the floor, thinking. *The only thing that could heal him this fast are the nanites. But they don't work. So, it can't be them, can it?*

"Or his nanites have awoken."

Everyone looked to Henry. He couldn't see the reactions people gave him, but Eloise knew he could hear it in the silence because he smiled with one side of his mouth.

"I can't confirm this hypothesis unless I run some tests but the only explanation it seems we have is the nanites Eloise gave him, combined with the exercises Charlotte has been doing, fresh air, and diet, have all contributed to the awakening of the nanites."

"What's happening to me?"

Eloise turned to the sound of Seth's voice. He was sitting forward on the chair, a thick novel on his lap, and his eyebrows close together. She knew he worried. So much change was happening to his body no one could prepare for, but she knew she loved him enough to help him find out.

Anything was a step up from emaciation, and to experience his body going from skeletal to looking like an actual teenager with muscles in only a short while had to put a strain on his mental state.

It was Henry who spoke first. "We aren't sure, but we have to go back to the facility to find out. Run some tests."

"I don't want to go back...home." Seth balked. "I don't want to...see my mom ever...again. She's so mad right now."

"We understand, honey," Charlotte said. "If we're going to find out what's going on with your body, and fix it for good, we want to run some tests to get answers. Is that okay with you?"

Please say yes. She needed to know, especially if he could finally live a normal life. She wanted it so badly for him.

"I don't know," Seth said after a few moments. "Can I think about it?"

"Not too long," Henry said. "We need a decision soon."

Seth nodded and looked down. "Okay."

Charlotte fidgeted in her seat and then stood and looked to Bannack, Eloise, Sibyl, and Luke. "We have some empty bedrooms upstairs. You're more than welcome to stay the night. I'll set out some old clothes, and Alice can boil some water to draw up a bath, if anyone needs one."

Taking his gnarled stick in one hand, Henry stood gracefully and tapped his way to the kitchen. "If anyone is hungry, we have leftover bread Alice made herself, some eggs you're more than welcome to gather—I heard the hens out back lay clucking about an hour ago—

and some goat milk waiting in the brook that runs beside the house. Help yourself. If you need me to start a fire, let me know."

"Honey," Charlotte rolled her eyes. "You haven't started a fire in years."

Henry ignored his wife. "I may be blind, but I'm not incapable of getting soot on my hands. Alice will show you where the eggs and milk are. I need to talk to a man about a horse."

"A man about a horse?" Eloise whispered to Sibyl who shrugged.

Luke piped up. "He's going to the bathroom."

"Where are you going?" Eloise asked.

Luke, standing between the living room and kitchen, shrugged a pointed thumb over his shoulder. "Well, first I'm g-going to get some of the milk Henry talked about. Then I'm using the warm bath water—I can g-get that myself—and then drink the cold milk while soaking my sore body. Would you like to know what...what I'm going to do with my rear end later on, too?"

Alice giggled, and Sibyl scrunched up her nose.

Eloise chuckled silently. "Ew. No thanks."

From beside Eloise, Bannack raised his hand and laughed. "I would."

Luke turned red and walked away.

***

The next morning, Bannack and Luke walked in the door as Eloise slid the apple pie into the brick oven just off the porch. Seth was sitting on a stool at the counter inside with his entire head in the large mixing bowl, lapping up the last little bit of pie filling, and jumped at Boatswain's excited barking. Sibyl, her mom, and sister were out caring for the animals.

"Look!" Seth held the bowl out. "We made...pie!"

"Awesome, dude." Bannack waved at Seth and smiled. His kindness made a vast difference for Seth's mood, who had been happy all day after having a long, late-night conversation with Bannack.

Eloise wiped her fingers on the towel, chuckling, and turned around. Her hand shook, and she clenched it, worrying the sweat on her brow was not from the oven but another bout of her illness. She couldn't let Seth see. The decision to leave Henry's needed to be completely his own and not dictated by anything or anyone else. Eloise flexed her hands and put on a smile. "Hey, guys."

Luke plopped on the couch. His grunt was almost a yelp and his feet jerked into the air as Boatswain leapt onto his stomach.

Seth laughed, then lowered his gaze. He'd been doing it a lot. "Do you think...I should go...back? She's probably...lonely."

"Don't you dare." Sibyl walked in from outside, carrying a basket of lettuce, swiss chard, and collard greens. "Don't let your mom, or anyone else, choose for you."

Behind her came Charlotte with a tied and defeathered chicken carcass and Alice, feathers in her hair, holding two glass jars of milk. They each took their turns placing the food on the counter and when Sibyl released her French braids from the bandana she was wearing to keep them off her neck, she looked Seth dead in the eyes.

"You are not responsible for Joy's choices. Whatever is going on is because of her, not you. This is your decision. Don't let your mom's voice guilt trip you into doing anything for her you don't want to." Sibyl waited until Seth nodded his agreement and then patted the carcass, her words trailing off into sing-song. "Now, I need help with this chicken and no one seems to be willing..."

Seth's eyes lit up. "Can I help with dinner? I've never seen a dead chicken before."

Everyone laughed. Sibyl brought the carcass over to him and showed him how to stuff the cavity with rosemary, thyme, and apple slices. Eloise watched, a smile stuck on her face. The room swayed. Her hand flew to the armrest of the couch.

Don't faint. Don't faint.

The sensation faded as fast as it had come, but she knew what it meant.

Damn it.

Panting and keeping the sound as quiet as possible, Eloise caught the concerned eye of Bannack. She shook her head to tell him to stop worrying, and he nodded as if he agreed.

After working for several minutes to prepare the chicken for the smoker, Seth dried his hands on a towel, and went with Charlotte to begin his exercises. She massaged his legs, helping the tight muscles to relax and started moving his legs, coaching Seth on how to breathe through any uncomfortable sensations.

"If anything hurts too much," she said in a low voice, "let me know, okay?"

Seth nodded.

They continued for an hour, having built up his endurance from the ten minutes he could do originally before becoming too tired. When they finished their training, Seth grabbed a towel to dab at the sweat on his forehead, and scanned the room, chewing on his lip. His eyes paused on Eloise.

"I have an announcement," he said, and put the towel on the counter. "I...think I'm ready to go back. I want to know what's...happening to me."

"Are you sure?" Eloise asked.

"Yeah," Seth straightened his shoulders. "When can we leave?"

"After dinner, if you want," Eloise said. She turned to everyone and they all nodded or voiced their agreement. She looked back at Seth and braved a smile. She couldn't see him very well, as if a fog had covered her eyes. "I need to try the Seth Special."

CHAPTER THIRTY-ONE
BANNACK

The facility was empty, yet an odd feeling lingered in the halls, almost as if they were whispering: 'Turn around. Go back.' The lanterns in the naturally dark hallways were completely cold. This put Bannack on edge. When Eloise grabbed his hand, he jerked away from her, terror making bumps on his skin raise. A rapid wave traveled from his arm to the top of his head.

"Are you okay?" she asked. "You're dripping sweat."

"So are you." She truly was, and he worried. She'd been fine since they had arrived at Henry's. Sickness was due to rear its ugly head. "I'd feel better if we had to fight our way in. We shouldn't have come here. It's too easy and I hear people in here, Elle. Whispers and movement. But I see nothing."

Light from the torch blinded Bannack when Sibyl came close. "In here, guys."

The room he entered had a single, large window in it, which allowed for a flooding of light, and had a metallic and moonshine scent to it. Someone had recently sanitized the room.

Charlotte and Sibyl helped Seth to the empty bed. While they prepped the needle and vial to collect his blood for testing, Bannack stood close to the door, listening for footsteps.

"Hey," Eloise said and leaned against the wall. A thick layer of sweat dripped down her scar and Bannack's stomach clenched. Her next words were heavy, as if she struggled to breathe. "Still uneasy?"

"I wish they would hurry." Bannack watched Charlotte remove the butterfly needle from Seth's arm, and Sibyl handed him a cloth to hold on the puncture wound. Luke turned around, saw Eloise and Bannack, then walked over.

"Do you guys feel as helpless as I do?" He asked.

Bannack stayed quiet, still jittery from his suspicion that something waited for them. He stared at the floor, arms crossed, and chewed on the inside of his lips, then jumped at the loud grinding of metal chair legs on the linoleum floor when Charlotte sat down. Henry talked her through using the microscope and locating the nanites.

After a few moments, Henry walked over, and whispered, "Is Eloise close by?"

"No," Bannack said and glanced at her a few paces away with Sibyl.

"Good. Because Eloise's nanites are dead."

Bannack had to hold onto the wall for support. "What are you saying?"

Henry bowed his head. "If she gets sick, even a cold, her nanites won't protect her. She will be at extreme risk of infection or death with any injury or illness. Without her nanites…"

Flashes of his dad's death from a flu that turned into sepsis flooded his mind. Seizures. Bleeding. The cold, dead eyes Bannack had to close. His worst fear for Eloise would come true sooner than he thought.

To distract his mind from imagining Eloise's death and stop the stinging of his nose, Bannack asked, "And Seth?"

Henry rubbed his face once. "They won't heal him because they don't recognize his DNA, but they won't kill him either. His healing is stagnant. There's only so much they can do in their deformed state. Bannack," Henry touched his arm but Bannack flinched away, "there's no more serum that we know of."

"Does he know?"

Henry didn't react right away. He just stared, his eyes gentle and brow pulled together, making Bannack nauseous. He finally nodded. "Seth knows. He's—"

A shuddering noise caught Bannack's attention, and he turned to see Eloise slump against the wall. He ran to her. "Hey." He shook her. "Stay on your feet."

Eloise blinked and looked up at him. "Sorry...I'm not—"

She lost consciousness. Bannack gathered her up in his arms, her appendages and head swinging, then called for Luke. "Help me!"

Luke rushed forward.

"There's a room not far from here," Bannack looked at Eloise, his eyes watering, "that has some basic medical supplies. There might be something there."

"What's wrong with her?"

Bannack jerked his head to Seth, the boy's eyes round. "A few weeks back, she was struck by lightning and we think she may have lost her nanites. She got sick and her body can't fight it. I will bring her back in one piece."

"Let's at least test her blood," Henry said, "so we can find out how the nanites are doing."

"Alright."

With Eloise shaking in his arms, Bannack waited for Sibyl to draw a vial of her blood, then rushed from the room. Bannack barreled down the hallway, Luke following, desperate to find medicine to help her.

"Hang on, Elle. Just hang on." His throat burned.

"Bo..."

Light appeared at the end of the hallway. Luke and Bannack skidded to a halt. They whirled around.

Joy stood in front of a group of ten or so of her employees. All of them held crossbows, clubs, and swords.

Bannack spun around to run but four men moved in the way.

They were trapped.

"Put me down," Eloise demanded.

"But—"

Her hand on his cheek stopped him short, and he did as she asked. Anger from being trapped and the threat on Eloise's life built in his body until he sucked sharp air in through his teeth. Eloise's cheek was so soft. Snarling, Bannack unsheathed his sword and sliced through the air, aiming for Joy. His arms vibrated as he connected with another blade. Before he could recover, the defender smashed his fist into Bannack's ribs. He cried out and fell.

"Tie up the boys." Joy's eyes narrowed. "I want Eloise alive."

Idiot! You knew something was wrong, and you did nothing.

"No!" Bannack's head cracked into the wall and his vision blurred. All he could hear was Eloise's screams, driving him to stand and ignore the massive headache. Again, a fist collided with his face. Off balance and fading into unconsciousness, Bannack slumped against the wall, then slid to the floor.

He couldn't see.

His muscles wouldn't move, no matter how hard he pushed them.

Warmth trailed from his lip, nose, and his bum ear.

Silence.

CHAPTER THIRTY-TWO
ELOISE

Eloise gasped, held back by Joy's fist around her hair, and watched in terror as Bannack and Luke, beaten until limp and bleeding, were left on the ground. Anger surged through her. Her lungs lacked the air needed to yell, nor did she have strength in her body, and it would be pointless, so she grew silent to calculate her escape.

Men and women walked on all sides of them as Joy led the way down the hallway. A man pulled Eloise along, her scalp stinging. She tried to shout, but her voice came out in a rasp instead. "Do we have to keep doing this?"

"Yes. We do." Joy stopped walking and gritted her teeth. "My son is dying, if he isn't already dead. It's too late for him...and you."

She's going to kill me.

Fear gripping her lungs, Eloise pulled her silver-handled butterfly knife from her pocket. With one swift motion, she sliced through the radial artery of the man holding her. He screamed and fell, but not before he sprayed her with blood. The red liquid spread across the floor, and Joy's employees scattered away from the dying man.

Clothing bloodied, Eloise crouched on the ground and watched Joy's composure break.

"Contain her!" Joy screamed, eyeing Eloise's knife.

"What?" Eloise asked, and she chuckled. The chuckle turned to a cough that clawed at her throat and she lost her balance. On the ground, Eloise groaned, pain ricocheting against her bones as she said, "Afraid of a paper cut?"

They came at her. Eloise sacrificed her throwing knives into the heads of three people. Her muscles burned. The boot knife stopped a man in his tracks, his eye impaled. A fist swung at her. She ducked and slashed her claw-shaped karambit through the woman's vest, shoving her away with an unbalanced flat-footed kick.

Eloise fell on the ground, crying out. All she saw was red, the ground ebbed and flowed like ocean waves. Her entire body was on fire. When she coughed, crimson sprayed from her mouth. The hallway reeked of body odor and blood. Like when Edmund died, Eloise's stomach began pushing her last meal up her esophagus and Eloise spit.

A man ran at her, this one too large for her to fight off. Eloise backpedaled along the frigid floor until her back hit the icy wall, her hair lifting at the nape of her neck, and she gasped. The man loomed over her. He stared with apologetic eyes before grabbing her arm, which made her reflexively dropped the remaining knife. It clattered onto the floor.

He kept squeezing. Eloise's cry built from a low growl into a whimpering scream as the bone bent. Tears sprung from her eyes. The man jerked his wrist. Her arm snapped, and she screamed again, this time from the hot, searing pain the exposed bone caused. It had a pink color to it and her blood ran down her arm. Only then did the man release her.

"You're so majestic when you fight, darling," Joy crooned. "Like a wolf. I would love to watch you beat up my men all day, but I must insist you stop, or I will kill Bannack and your friend."

Five dead bodies lay in front of Eloise. The pain from her fractured arm restricted her from speaking, so Eloise cried and whimpered on the floor.

Joy's face contorted, and she screamed, "Test me again and watch me prove to you I will do as I say! Now," she cleared her throat, "I want to show you my favorite view."

Arms pulled Eloise forward. Every step jarring until her body took pity on her and blocked the pain receptors. Her head became a dense fog of nothing. Blood trickled from her mouth.

When they reached the balcony, a large area overlooking the ocean, the man released Eloise and stepped away. Joy stood in front of her, frigid air whipping at her pants.

"There," Joy said, then pointed at the horizon. "If you look out there, sometimes a pod of orcas will pass by."

"I don't...care." Eloise crumpled to the ground. Her jaw loosened, and tears blocked out her vision. She knew Seth would be okay. Joy was distracted enough with her that when Henry finished his analysis, it would confirm the nanites had awoken. Somehow, though, Eloise had to get rid of Joy or she would continue her tirade until she found Seth. Unfortunately, in her moment of pain and confusion, Eloise struggled to think.

I don't have my knives. My arm's broken. If Joy doesn't kill me right now, I'm going to die because my nanites don't work.

Footsteps pounded on the roof above Eloise and she looked up to see a body swing down onto the balcony.

Bannack.

He landed with a thump, then dragged the tip of his sword across the ground, the sound an ear-splitting screech. If Eloise had use of her arm, she would have covered her ears. Instead, she just winced as her teeth and bones rattled together.

Then he slid his arm around her and held on as he crouched. He extended his sword. Threatening. Daring them to come close. Eloise cried out when he moved her.

"You hurt my woman," he whispered. "No one...hurts my woman."

Eloise looked up at him, and she knew why the entire room had quieted. His eyes were dark and narrow, his glare holding the people around him hostage, and the power in the way he held onto her, protected her, was thrilling. He sneered. The entire expression was terrifying and promised, without a doubt, he would spill blood.

No one moved. Bannack's reputation at the facility, even after years, was still intact, proven in the way Joy's remaining five employees looked at him in complete terror.

"I'm so...tired, Bo. I can't fight anymore. I can't. I can't." Eloise buried her face in Bannack's chest, her broken arm limp and blasting through her body. Blood dripped from the bone protruding out of her skin. She whimpered.

"Akoma." Bannack set Eloise down, caressed her cheek, and the last she saw of his face before he swung his sword in a giant arc, was pure hatred and tears. He drew his lips up to reveal his teeth, which made his eyes shrink to slits, and he let out a bellowing battle cry.

Two people, cut down by the akrafena, thrashed on the floor as blood left their bodies from their throats. Blood covered his chest, face, and arms until it coated his clothes. Bannack Owusu, the man Joy had trained and the man he spent years rejecting, finally came exploding out of him. He held nothing back.

A hand snagged Eloise's hair and pulled. The pain from her arm rendered her helpless, and she cried out, fear clenching around her chest. Joy had slunk around Bannack's onslaught, and she held half of Eloise's body over the edge of the balcony. She screamed. The wind whipped her hair about her face, closing off the world, and it howled into her ears. She panted, deep ripples of fear making escape impossible.

When her hair blew away from her eyes, she caught sight of Bannack held on his stomach, his face in the ground and his arms spread out to the side.

"Ban—" The rest of his name disappeared in to the salty air when Joy pushed her further until she balanced precariously on her backside.

She cried. "Please, don't."

"First, you failed to save my son. Then you ran away, leaving him helpless and dying so you could get rid of the one thing that could save his life. Since I don't," Joy's voice faltered in her hatred, "see you with him, he's probably dead. You took my son away from me!"

"I didn't." Eloise shook her head and used her good arm to hold on to Joy's jacket. "He wanted to go. I never made him do anything. Let me go. Please!"

"You are useless to me!"

Bannack screamed over the howling wind and Eloise cried harder, hot tears covering her cheeks. She was losing her grip and soon she'd plummet to her death.

When Bannack tried to escape, breaking the nose of one woman to free his arm, he was attacked. Desperate, Bannack clawed at their faces, screaming until he was hoarse.

This is the last I'll see of him.

That realization hurt more than her broken arm. She was going to die after months of trying to run from it. Death was coming for her and she couldn't stop it. At first, he would mourn her, the pain would be terrible in the early months or years, crushing even, but then he'd adjust. He'd learn how to live with the grief. Eventually, he would rebuild his life, but he'd never forget her. No. He'd never forget, and he'd never be the same. She wouldn't want him to be. She'd stay with him as long as she could, holding him but never touching, snuggling close but never smelling him, speaking words he'd never hear, and maybe, just maybe, he would recognize her presence and find comfort.

A voice rose above the howling wind. "Mama! Stop!"

Joy let out a shaking gasp. Her eyes widened, she released Eloise safely on the ground, and turned.

Seth, holding onto the door jamb for support with Sibyl, Charlotte, and Henry behind him, glared at Joy. "What's wrong with you?" His lips quivered.

Joy scrambled away a few feet, and watched her son as if he were a phantom. "Y...you're stan—standing." She stared, barely able to breathe, and Seth smiled. "How?"

"Practice. Also, Henry checked and co...nfirmed. Charlotte's exercises gave my body the...blood flow it needed to wake the nanites

293

and start...working." Seth let his smile fall as he turned to his mom. "Because of Eloise, I can walk. You did nothing...except keep me trapped. I never got to make...friends. You never taught me how to bake pie or took me...to see animals. I never got to pet a goat. Eloise...gave me all of that. Not you. I want you to look at her." Joy didn't move but flinched when Seth screamed. "Look at her! She's dying!"

When Joy rushed to her son, Eloise crumpled onto the floor. She held her numb arm and laid in the fetal position, snot wetting under her nose and lips, and her body convulsing with sobs. Bannack's familiar arms wrapped around her and pulled her into his lap. He folded his body around her.

Eloise blinked back her tears as she watched a blurred Seth. He looked at his mom. "You hurt her," he said. "Why?"

"I thought you died. I—"

"What's wrong with...you?" He asked again, this time yelling. "You spent all this time trying to save me...but you hurt everyone to do it. That's so messed up and I ha...te you for it."

Joy blinked several times, and although she tried to speak, she only fumbled over her words. "You—I—you we're dying. I...I had to do something."

His voice quieted. "Why couldn't you just be...my mom?" Tears flew off his lips. "Instead, you turned...into a monster." Seth looked away. "Your heart is hard, like metal."

Joy stumbled and fell, shaking. "Seth, please, I did what I had to do to save you."

"And look where that...got you. Alone." From behind his back, Seth pulled out a needled syringe, lavender colored liquid inside, and spoke in a dark, accusatory tone. "I found this in your...desk."

Joy gasped and stood. She reached for it, but Seth pulled it away.

"It's from before, isn't it? Before the expl...osion that killed Eloise's parents?" Seth asked. Joy nodded, and Seth glared with hurt and anger in his eyes. "I can't believe you. You had this all...along and you still insisted on using her...nanites!"

"I'm so sorry, Seth, I knew Eloise's nanites worked, which is why

I used her. "I only had one of those." Joy pointed to the syringe. "If I used it on you...If you died because it wasn't tested correctly, I—"

"I was dying anyway!"

"I was trying to keep you safe." Desperate—so much in fact that the sting of sympathy hit Eloise's gut—Joy reached for her son, but he flinched away. She dropped her hands. "I understand you'll never forgive me for what I've done, no matter how I justify it. What I did was wrong."

"It was worse than...wrong. It was evil."

Seth's last word made Joy flinch, but she recovered quickly and nodded. "I deserve that. But," she looked at the nanite syringe, "I can go away forever. The nanites, if you inject me with them, will wipe my memories completely because there's nothing for them to heal and they'll turn on my mind. You can sleep better knowing I never knew you."

In the silence of the balcony, while Joy's few employees, Sibyl, Henry, Charlotte, Luke, Bannack, and Eloise watched, tension grew. Seth's arrival was unpredictable, his ability to stand shocking, and now one more unknown hung in the air. Eloise watched Seth, his anger toward his mom palpable and Joy's desperation to keep her son bordering on tragic. They waited for his decision.

"You're right," Seth said.

He walked toward Joy and she closed her eyes, ready to accept her fate. Clenched in his fist was the syringe, his knuckles white.

Then he pivoted away from her and, on wobbling legs, stood in front of Eloise. Her throat constricted.

"Seth," she said as she stared into his eyes. They were hard and determined, the look of a boy who had grown ten years in only a few moments. She could see the fracturing of his heart, the hurt and pain. "What are you doing?"

"No..." Joy's voice carried on the wind.

"I'm saving you." He looked down at the syringe in his hand. "Please?"

Without saying a word, Eloise lifted her good arm. Bannack rolled up her sleeve and Seth drove the needle home.

A strange sensation grew from the injection site. Her veins became ice, almost painful, as the nanites rushed through her body. She grappled for Bannack, suddenly afraid. Real blood warmed the ice the nanites caused. They recognized her and coursed through her body. Physical relief consumed her. It made her skin crawl and grow goosebumps, and she shuddered. The fever left, taking chills and weakness with it. Eloise looked at her arm, expecting it to heal, but nothing happened.

"I think we have to set it before they will start healing," Bannack said with an apologetic look.

Eloise closed her eyes. "Not now." The idea terrified her, and she made a disapproving noise. "It's numb, anyway."

"Wh—what? Why?" Joy asked. Her mouth hung open, and she looked from Eloise to Seth, who completely ignored her.

Eloise glared at Joy. "Because you don't deserve it."

"But I did everything to save him." Joy stood up but struggled to gain her balance. Her voice grew louder. "Wouldn't you have moved heaven and earth to have your sister back? To save her from death?"

Through gritted teeth, Eloise growled out her words, finding the strength that hadn't been in her before. "Don't you dare talk about my sister! Her death should have never happened. It destroyed me."

"But you are stronger for it."

Eloise laughed in disbelief. Joy had absolutely no understanding of trauma; how it burrowed itself into the victim like a tick and sucked a person dry. Eloise couldn't stop her body from shaking. "I am not stronger because of my sister's death. I am destroyed. Annihilated. My mind is at war because of those men's actions. None of what I witnessed has changed me for the better." Eloise paused, her breath hitching and painful as she exhaled. "I decide my fate. I am strong in spite of my trauma. And I will never give it, or you, the satisfaction of being responsible for making me who I am today. Stronger? What an idiotic idea."

Right then, Joy seemed to give up completely. Her shoulders fell, her head drooped, she put her head in her hands. The scientist melted away and left only the mother. "What am I going to do now?

The only thing I've ever wanted for you is to live. I realize all I had to do was love you more and because of me," Joy hiccupped as she continued to crumble in on herself, "you lost so much. I spent your entire childhood chasing after something you never even wanted. If I'd only asked..." Joy's shoulders began shaking. "I'm so sorry. So, so sorry."

Seth knelt down in front of his mom, hugged her for a long time, then walked away. He never looked back or flinched, like Eloise did, when Joy screamed, unearthly and heart-shattering. Joy's employees followed and one of them locked the door behind them. She would be contained. Whether or not she jumped off the balcony was her choice.

"What now?" Luke asked when they were all outside.

"I, for one," Sibyl raised her finger, "am going to go release my emotional tension through crying. Who's with me?"

Everyone laughed. Eloise inhaled and exhaled, the action cleansing. "I just want to go home." Then she turned to Seth. "Wanna meet Mason and Soora?"

Seth's face lit up. "I'd like that."

EPILOGUE

Cool, autumn wind caressed her face as she stood in front of the Compound. She watched the workers mull about, barking commands to each other as they cleared debris to begin the underground refrigeration system. The air blew through her damp hair, carrying the biting scent of impending Fall. Leaves clung to the branches, a bright bouquet, albeit sparse, of yellow, red, and orange.

Eloise absent-mindedly scrubbed her choppy, short, and wet hair, smiling. The sacrifice of hair to the river had been symbolic, a releasing of an insecurity caused by her scar. She kept her hair long for years, using it to hide the imperfection on her face. No more. The entire world could see it. The best part was the air against her neck.

Life at the Compound was over for her, and even though she still lived close, she and Bannack had begun their own happiness, away from the pain of Joy's looming shadow. They were living their way. Safe. Free.

Seth was enjoying his own freedoms, as well, and Eloise smiled as she remembered his parting gift, a crown of daisies, before leaving to travel. He promised to send letters once in a while to inform her about his changing condition after Eloise donated her blood, nanites included, what life was like being independent, and if he still struggled with his asthma and balance, leftover symptoms of his disease.

Bannack had made him a new cane before he left out of beautiful dark wood so he could walk.

Kendal's report on Joy came a few days later. The scientist travelled into the forest, lost and confused. When Cassius caught sight of her, Kendal hadn't stopped him from charging after Joy. In returning to her cabin and discovering the gun – a single bullet loaded into it – missing, she heard a shot go off. Cassius had returned with the gun, blood on his hands and tears in his eyes. Joy wasn't heard from again.

Gravel crunched as Eloise turned away from the building. She paused, her eyes watering in response to the relentless wind, and stared at a small cabin, built with love by Mason, Bannack, Luke, and several others. It sat against the forest line, inviting her in from the heat.

For months after their fight at Joy's facility, she and Henry worked together to help Joy's victims. They restored their memories, using Eloise's blood mixed with the nanites, beginning with Mason. It was hard work and Eloise struggled to keep up some days, but soon the last victim left the Compound.

She smiled when she opened the front door. This was her new home, and she adored every surface. From the bald cat lying on the bed, to the man carving the last remaining holes in his djembe drum, deer hide top and ropes on the table beside him. She loved the way his hands moved with delicate precision, thoroughly invested in the project.

Her eyes flicked to the akrafena hung on the wall above their bed. Sunlight touched the metal, making it gleam. He no longer needed the proud sword, so he kept it where he could remember his family always.

"What do you think?"

Bannack jumped, his tools clattering to the floor. She laughed at his surprise.

He stood and ran her short hair through his fingers. "It looks like you cut it with a knife."

Eloise punched him in the chest. He chuckled, warm and deep, and feigned injury.

"You have wounded me, my angel." Bannack laid on the ground, his knees bent and held his chest, blubbering. "I may die. Do not forget me."

She gave in to his childish jesting and knelt at his feet. "What can I do to save you?"

He opened one of his closed eyes and peered at her, whispering, "You are not dramatic enough."

"Shut up. You're supposed to be dying."

In response, he moaned again. "A kiss, from thy fair lips, will wake me from the deep sleep. Quick, Elle! I am slipping."

She gave him a peck on the cheek.

The groaning was real this time. "Completely unacceptable. You must kiss like this."

His hands wrapped around her face and pulled her into him. He kissed her. His warm breath cascaded around her skin, heating her cheeks and nose. A little noise escaped from the back of her throat and she leaned in, straddling his body with her arms.

"Akoma," Bannack whispered, smiling as he nuzzled into her neck.

They stood, and he stumbled back, then collided into the small table. Wildflowers and water toppled from the overturned vase which made Bali yowl and scramble away.

"Oh, no!" Bannack half-whispered, his voice husky from the kiss.

"No, Bo. It's okay. No—Ow! You dork."

Eloise tried to stop him from picking up the flowers while at the same time he leaned forward and stepped right on her toes.

"Here. Let me fix that for you."

Grunting, Bannack lifted Eloise from the floor. His movements were choppy and slow, as if he struggled to get good footing, and Eloise laughed. She jostled in his arms and her shoulder blades hit the wall. A frustrated groan came from Bannack, and Eloise laughed harder.

"Am I too heavy for you?"

"Stop it," Bannack smiled down at Eloise, his blue eyes sparkling with play. "I am old."

"You are not, liar!" Eloise's laugh radiated the room.

Bannack kissed her arm wrapped around his neck, then much more gracefully than before, carried Eloise to the bed and nestled in beside her.

They laid there, watching the clouds pass over their cabin through the skylight, and pointing out the shapes they saw there.

"How are we going to have a normal life after what happened?" Eloise asked. She snuggled her body into his and released a deep sigh.

"Mmm." Bannack pressed his lips to her head. "How do you mean?"

"Before, we were fighting for our lives. Now..." Eloise wrapped her fingers around Bannack's dark forearm. "It all feels so...normal. I'm not sure if I know how to do normal."

"One day at a time, akoma mu tɔfe. Some days will be hard, but others will be glorious and it will all be worth it."

THE END

ACKNOWLEDGEMENTS

This book has been the ride of a lifetime for me. It all began when I was in high school, rapidly typing a half-baked story onto an outdated Word program on the old computer. Back then, Eloise was Sophie and Bannack had an older step-sister who rode horses. I spent ten years on that story, trying to figure out how a character (Eloise) could be so dang difficult to nail.

It wasn't until I scrapped that old manuscript three years ago – called The Dovetail Effect – that I finally learned why I was having a hard time with Eloise: she suffers from PTSD. That shot me down a rabbit hole of wonder and I learned so much about mental health, trauma, and what healing looks like. What began as a high-school romance evolved into a beautiful commentary on mental health, trauma, and toxic masculinity. I've always been a huge supporter of the idea that the characters of a novel dictate how their story is told, and because of that, I was able to witness something beautiful unfold.

No novel is without the people behind it. First, I'd like to thank my wonderful husband, who is my biggest cheerleader. He has taken everything in stride. All the nights where he's gone to bed alone as I finished up a chapter. Conversations as I employed his help in getting my character out of a sticky situation. Listening to my book excerpts. Ever since I shared that early draft of high school aged Eloise and Bannack before we were engaged, he's been there, pushing me forward and cheering me on. Thank you for being there for me.

Second, I'd like to thank all the amazing beta and sensitivity readers who shared their wisdom, criticism, and excitement. This book is amazing because of you!

Third, I cannot forget Riley (editor) or Danielle (cover artist). You both helped my book become what it is today and were so patient as I fumbled through trying to give voice to my vision and erasing all those spaces between all those ellipses. Both of you did such an incredible job and now I have a shiny book to show everyone! I'm beyond grateful.

ABOUT THE AUTHOR

Liahona West spent her entire teenage years glued to a book. Whether it was escaping the dreaded high school lunch room or hiding under the covers at 2:00 AM, ruining her eyes, to finish "one more chapter" five times in a row, Liahona never went without literature. Now a mother and fueled by her unwillingness to sleep, she is bringing her characters to life and fulfilling a lifelong dream of becoming a published author.

When Liahona isn't writing in every location possible, she is chasing her three boys, breaking up fights, and eating their leftovers in their home in the Pacific Northwest.

Metallic Heart is her debut novel.

CPSIA information can be obtained
at www.ICGtesting.com
Printed in the USA
LVHW020537210721
693211LV00010B/314